THE HOUSE IN

MISTRES

Elizabeth Elgin is the ... *the Sweet Promises*, *Whisper on the Wind*, *I'll Bring You Buttercups* and *Daisychain Summer*. She served in the WRNS during the Second World War and met her husband on board a submarine depot ship. A keen gardener, she has two daughters and five grandsons and lives in a village in the Vale of York.

FREE BOOK HAPPY READING
This Book is NOT For Resale
Donations of Books/Mags/Comics
In ANY Condition Are Welcome!
Please Return Me & ThankYou!

By the same author

WHISTLE IN THE DARK
THE MANCHESTER AFFAIR
SHADOW OF DARK WATER
THE ROSE HEDGE
ALL THE SWEET PROMISES
WHISPER ON THE WIND
I'LL BRING YOU BUTTERCUPS
DAISYCHAIN SUMMER

Writing as Kate Kirby

FOOTSTEPS OF A STUART
ECHO OF A STUART
SCAPEGOAT FOR A STUART

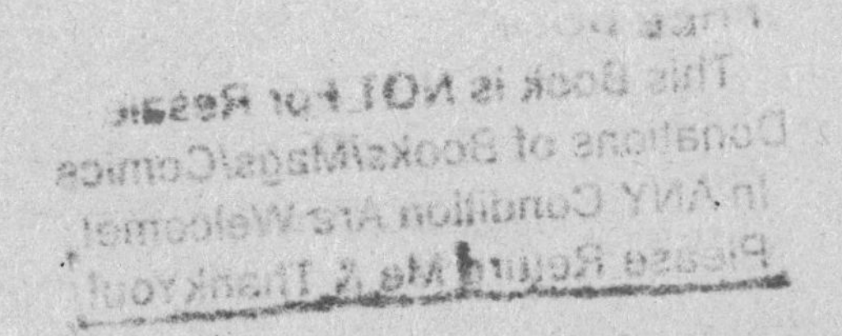

ELIZABETH ELGIN

The House in Abercromby Square

Mistress of Luke's Folly

HarperCollins*Publishers*

HarperCollins*Publishers*
77–85 Fulham Palace Road,
Hammersmith, London W6 8JB

This one-volume paperback edition 1995
1 3 5 7 9 8 6 4 2

The House in Abercromby Square first published
by Robert Hale & Company 1976
Mistress of Luke's Folly first published
by Robert Hale & Company 1981

ISBN 0 00 649617 2

Set in Linotron Sabon
at The Spartan Press Ltd,
Lymington, Hants

Printed in Great Britain by
HarperCollinsManufacturing Glasgow

Contents

The House in Abercromby Square

One

'But Patrick, *dearest* Patrick,' Arabella Harrington's small pale forefinger intimately traced the hairline of the man in whose arms she stood, 'why must you go to Liverpool? It is a nasty, dirty place – you have said so yourself. Why must you get a sudden urge to visit your aunt and completely upset Papa's holiday arrangements?'

'Because, my love,' Patrick Norris sighed, 'there are things I must do before we are married and,' he added almost as an afterthought, 'I have not seen Aunt Hetty for nearly three years.'

'But why *now*?' The soft mouth arranged itself into a childish pout. 'Since I have known you, you have scarcely mentioned your family in Liverpool and now, when we are all ready to travel to Harrogate, you announce you are going elsewhere. Papa is not a little put out!'

Patrick smiled into the small face upturned to his. Even now, he could hardly believe his good fortune in being accepted as Robert Harrington's future son-in-law. He had no wish to upset the wealthy Harley Street physician who employed him, nor for that matter, to cause one moment of annoyance to Arabella.

Gently he kissed the tip of her pert, dainty nose. She had, he thought, with her white skin and eyes blue as periwinkles, the fragility of a china shepherdess and when she tilted her head, her pale yellow ringlets bobbed about her ears in a way he found endearingly irresistible.

'I am sorry, Bella, if I have upset your plans but it is important that I visit my aunt. I will join you in Harrogate within three days at the most – surely you will not die of a broken heart in so short a time?' he teased.

'I will try not to, Patrick.'

She gave him a small smile, 'Though I will miss you on the journey. I had looked forward to your company. I have never travelled by railroad before. It would have been comforting to have you with me.'

'But you will have your father to take care of you, dearest, and the railroads are safe as houses.'

'I know, but . . .'

Arabella released herself from his arms, whisking her frilled muslin skirts to show a flurry of lace petticoat and a disturbing glimpse of pretty ankle. She stood by the broad window, her back to him, ' . . . but since we are to be married, I would have thought that my wishes came before all else.'

'They do, my love, and they always will, you know that. It is merely that my aunt must be told about our marriage. It is common courtesy – surely you will allow me that?'

'But you have already written to her about it and she did not allow *us* the courtesy of a reply!' came back the tart retort.

Patrick sighed. Motherless since babyhood, Arabella, the only child of a doting father, had been outrageously spoiled and though blessed with a usually sunny nature, there were times when she could be wilful as a small child when her wishes were flouted. When they were married thought Patrick with a flush of unease, he must take a firm hand with Bella's little moods.

It seemed strange that he found it impossible to confess to the woman who was to be his wife that Aunt Hetty had not sent her blessing because, quite simply, Aunt Hetty had never learned to read or write.

He felt a small prick of annoyance that he could not confide the fact to Arabella. Aunt Hester Norris had been mother and father to him. He loved her dearly and he would admit her shortcomings to no one. Nor could he bring himself to admit to Arabella that there were things he now felt he should be told; things about himself and his past.

Many times before, when he was a young medical apprentice, he had tried to broach the matter but Aunt Hetty, with her usual adroitness had sidestepped his efforts. Now, with his marriage to Arabella Harrington soon to take place, Patrick felt the time had come to take a firm stand. The *Private Matter* must be brought into the open. And besides, he reasoned, if things were as he supposed it would be all to his advantage in this new society to which he would soon belong; a society into which, if he were truthful, he had tenaciously fought to enter.

Patrick had small vague memories of his past but they amounted to nothing more than fleeting remembrances of large, lofty rooms; of an elegant staircase and rows of bells on circular, bobbing springs.

But one thing was certain in his mind. Not all Arabella's pouting or pleading and, most probably, even her pretty tears, would prevent him from visiting Aunt Hetty at Liverpool.

And there was Adam, too. Suddenly Patrick had felt a longing to see his friend and talk over old times with him. He wanted to know how Adam was making out in the life he had chosen and exactly what Adam's last letter had meant to imply.

Deliberately Patrick shut down his thoughts and walked towards Arabella's indignant little back. Gently he placed his arms around her tiny waist, pulling her close to him, whispering softly into her sweet-smelling hair.

'Darling Bella, we must not quarrel. Tell me how much you love me.'

But Miss Arabella Harrington was now firmly astride her high-horse and deftly removed his hands.

'Patrick, you must not hold me so intimately when we are alone,' she chided. 'It is not seemly and besides, one of the servants might come in.'

Patrick cupped the indignant face in his hands.

'I don't care about the servants.'

'Well I do!' Angrily she brushed past him, 'and so should *you*, Patrick!'

There were bright spots of colour now in her soft cheeks and her blue eyes flashed dangerously. Soon, thought Patrick, there will be tears and that he must avoid at all costs. Bella was being unreasonable but he cared for her and he did not like to see her cry, not even when her tears were slightly suspect.

'Arabella, my dear, if you command me not to go to Liverpool then I shall not go. But can you, sweet creature that you are, deny two days of my company to an old lady who has not seen me in years? Can you do this?' he rushed on as an uncertain sniff told him she was weakening, 'when soon you will have me all to yourself for the rest of our lives?'

He paused, his eyes pleading, hoping his cajoling had made its mark. Then suddenly she was in his arms telling him she was being selfish and that it was only because she loved him so dearly that she hated to be parted from him.

'Forgive your Bella,' she pleaded, so earnestly that he promptly kissed her, partly from affection and partly from relief.

'Come, darling,' he coaxed. 'It is a lovely evening. Get your bonnet and cape and we will take a turn in the park. Remember, I will be leaving very early in the morning. Let us hold hands where there are no servants to interrupt us and I will tell you again how dear you are to me.'

Eagerly she agreed, for as much as she was able, Arabella loved him.

Patrick stood by the ornate glass panel of the booking-office and took two sovereigns from his purse.

'A single fare to Liverpool – first class.'

'Change at Manchester, sir.'

Respectfully the ticket clerk nodded his head.

Despite the early hour, Euston Square station was busy and noisy. It would not be long, thought Patrick, before the railroads had quite outstripped road travel. A journey by steam-train was more comfortable and reliable than by coach-and-four and it was quicker by far with no overnight stops at inns or hostels. Why, he reasoned, given a good driver they would be in Liverpool by night-fall.

A small hunchbacked porter picked up his bags.

'The Manchester train, sir?'

The man, Patrick realized with not a little pleasure, had taken it for granted that his services would be required. But then, he was fast becoming aware of the fact that a gentleman must never carry his own baggage. And not only in his new prosperity was Patrick beginning to dress like a gentleman, he was also becoming to feel like one. In his checked trousers, his topcoat with its matching checked edging, a fine tall hat and hand-sewn gloves, he was well satisfied that he looked the part.

He sniffed the smell of sulphur and grease that mingled with coal-smoke and listened to the hiss of escaping steam, a faint excitement stirring inside him. He still felt a sense of adventure when he entered a railway station. He could understand Arabella's apprehension at the thought of such a journey. Soon she and her father would be leaving for Harrogate but since Doctor Harrington was of the opinion that to travel such a distance would be too much for Arabella's constitution, he had decided to stay overnight in Leeds and make the remainder of the journey by coach. The drive over the moors to Harrogate in the clear air he considered, would be extremely beneficial, provided they were well wrapped up.

Patrick indicated the centre door of the three-compartment gentlemen's carriage. The London and North-Western Railway Company looked well after their passengers, he thought. The seats were soft and well-sprung and the floor was covered with fine quality carpeting. At the windows, plush curtains ensured privacy should the traveller wish it.

He watched as his bags and tall tin hat-box were placed on the seat beside him, then, handing the man a penny, he pulled up the window as a precaution against smoke and smuts and a possible invasion of fellow-travellers.

By mid-day, Patrick had tired of watching people and houses and fields slipping past the windows. At first, the sight of green fields and cow-pastures and thickly-wooded slopes had filled him with pleasure. It was so different, he thought, from the crowded, roistering town he was travelling towards at a steady thirty miles each hour. Liverpool was, as the dour-faced Doctor Duncan had so often stressed, the dirtiest, most unhealthy town in the whole of Europe. And Doctor Duncan, whose lectures he and Adam had attended at the Medical Institution in their student days, was an authority on dirt. It had seemed to the young pupils that the worthy Scotsman was obsessed by the squalor of Liverpool's meaner streets, of the airless courts of small houses and the need for a decent supply of fresh water and properly laid sewers. They had joked about his preoccupation with and perpetual grumbling about the matter but they had known, inexperienced as they were, that every word he preached was nothing short of the truth.

Patrick sighed and opened his hat-box. It was packed with food, socks, clean handkerchiefs and the large, thick muffler Aunt Hetty once knitted. Soon, of course, he would be able to afford more than one top-hat but at the moment the tall black box with its patterns of gold-leaf scrolls was more a symbol of his new-found status than the receptacle for which it was intended.

Gratefully he unwound the white starched napkin from a half-bottle of wine and placed it across his knees. Doctor Harrington's cook, he decided as he unpacked the parcel of chicken legs, was the treasure of a woman for she had thoughtfully provided peaches and apples for his dessert. He was glad that after their marriage, he and Arabella would continue to live in the large house in Harley Street, assured still of every attention to their comfort.

He wondered what smell of cooking would greet his nostrils tonight when he opened the door of Aunt Hetty's little house. Would it be one of her famous stews, a stockpot of broth, or good, nourishing cow-heels? He had come a long way since his cow-heel days, Patrick thought with a downward quirk of his mouth. Now, he ate at Robert Harrington's elegant table, gracefully laid with crisp white linen, silver, and bowls of flowers. And no meal was considered acceptable unless it was accompanied by at least two wines. He had quickly adapted himself to such luxury but then, it had not been all that difficult a task. He had intended right from the start that it should be so. From the beginning of his apprenticeship, Patrick Norris knew exactly where he was going. Liverpool was of no use to him, he long ago decided. When his apprenticeship was over and his examinations taken, he vowed that no less a place than London should have the benefit of his undoubted talent and that nothing and no one should be allowed to stand in his unswerving path.

'But, Patrick,' Adam had protested, 'do you feel nothing for these poor people? Doesn't your conscience upset you when you talk of leaving Liverpool?'

'It does not!' Patrick had grimly retorted. 'I have slaved for five years, Adam, and come the day when I face the Board in London and pass my examiners, this town has seen the last of Patrick Norris, I promise you!'

'I cannot believe that you mean it,' Adam's gentle face showed concern. 'They are your people. Don't you owe them something? Don't you want to help them? Heaven knows,' Adam's blue eyes were troubled, 'they are not able to help themselves.'

Patrick had laughed.

'There is a saying that heaven aids him who aids himself. Well, Adam, I have been giving heaven a gentle shove for years, now!'

'Then I am sorry, Patrick.'

The soft voice held no anger.

'Why should *you* be sorry, Adam Carmichael? What

do you know of life save what you've seen in those stinking wards? You were born to position and wealth. You've never tipped your cap to your betters or had your backside kicked by them. What do you know?' he demanded, angrily. 'When have you ever tasted poverty?'

But Adam had only smiled.

'Perhaps, Patrick,' he said sadly, 'I would have been a better person if I had.'

Patrick shook away his thoughts and reached for a peach.

It had all been talk, he supposed. True, Adam Carmichael had stayed in Liverpool but his address was a good one. Abercromby Square in which he now lived was populated by merchants and shipowners. Its houses were tall and grand with well-kept gardens in the centre of the square. He remembered it from his childhood. Those who lived there owned their own carriages and many drove out with a footman in attendance.

Whatever Adam's intentions had been in their student days, he had certainly picked himself a good address from which to practise, Patrick decided.

Still, he thought as he lowered the window and threw out the remains of his luncheon and the empty wine bottle, it would be good to see Adam again. He remembered the pale, gentle face with its shock of fair curls tumbling about it as though it were only yesterday they had shaken hands and parted. For all that, he had been a little surprised when, not so long ago, he had read Adam's last letter.

There is so much work here, Patrick. I need you . . .

Patrick shrugged his shoulders. It was a pity, he thought, but *he* didn't need Adam. No matter how busy a practice Adam might have built up, it could not offer one small part, Patrick decided, of the benefits in store for him in London.

It all started, he supposed, the day he and Adam had taken the steam-train to London. They had completed their Liverpool apprenticeships; dutifully attended the lectures demanded of them; done more than their fair stint of work in infirmary wards and now all that remained was the final hurdle – the grand gentlemen of the Board of Examiners.

Luck had been with Patrick that day, for Arabella's father had been a member of that board made up of surgeons, apothecaries and physicians; one of the elite who sat in their solemnity and decided whether finally a student might be accepted as a licentiate of the Society of Apothecaries and call himself a doctor, at last. On that day, Doctor Robert Harrington, on the look-out for an assistant, invited Patrick to join his London practice.

And so he had come to Harley Street, that broad thoroughfare of grand houses and favoured by doctors, originally, because of its close proximity to the railway stations along the Euston Road that brought in patients from the provinces.

From that day on, he had taken to Harley Street as though he had been born to it and he had never looked back. Soon, on his marriage to his employer's only child, he would be made a partner. One day he would be a rich man and a man of property when Arabella came into her birthright.

Return to Liverpool? Return to those mean streets when he had spent half of his life getting away from them? Give up the promise of wealth because Adam needed him?

'Ha!'

He let out a small, derisive laugh.

Sorry, Adam, old friend, whispered his conscience, *it will be good to see you again, but . . .*

Besides, thought Patrick, it wasn't as though he was making this journey solely to talk over old times with Adam. Far from it. The reason for his visit was a firm intention to wrest from Aunt Hetty the truth of his parentage. It was plain that Hester Norris was in no way related to him other than perhaps by the ties of love they felt for each other. Patrick was, he was sure, of nobler birth than anything Aunt Hetty could have bestowed upon him. He had been certain of it for a very long time. Aunt Hetty was an ordinary working woman; she had no private means or any other income that he knew of. Some person of substance must, he was sure, have made her some allowance.

But his aunt could be tight-lipped as a stone statue when it suited her purpose and it suited her to become vague or forgetful whenever Patrick had tried to broach what he had come to regard as the *Private Matter*. Now, with his marriage into the upper-middle class imminent, the truth about the *Private Matter* must be made known to him. A man had the right to know about his parentage, if only for the sake of his wife and children.

Of course, being a love-child would not exactly be acceptable in the polite society that surrounded Doctor Harrington, but being the love-child, perhaps, of the daughter of a family of substance would be a little more decent. His mother – his *real* mother, that was – had been a lady born, he was sure of it and a lady of means into the bargain for who else could have paid for his education? It had been an expensive business he knew and utterly beyond the means of Aunt Hetty Norris.

Norris. It was the only name he had ever known but it couldn't be his real name. Would he perhaps, when the truth became known, take his mother's name? It might well be to his advantage, the more so if it were a well-known name. Patrick Johnstone, perhaps? One of the Liverpool Johnstones, the shipowners, don't you know?

Had Aunt Hetty been his nurse in that vaguely-remembered house with the sweeping staircase and the rooms so tall that they seemed to a small boy to reach right up to God?

Would his family, once they had been acquainted with the success he had become, be willing to acknowledge him as one of themselves? They must at least be a benevolent family for he could never remember being hungry or going barefoot as a small boy; he had never worked or sold matches in the streets; had never heard the rent-collector hammering on the door. His real family were good people at heart and what was more, he had good blood in his veins. Now he must be told whose it was. It mattered a great deal to him. Aunt Hetty must be silent no longer.

Irritably, Patrick stared out of the window. The green fields had given way now to scattered knots of houses; small, greystone dwellings so reminiscent of the north country. Soon the sprawling mills would dominate the landscape, their chimneys spewing foul black smoke, their shuttles clacking out prosperity for some fortunate owner. Soon, he would be in Manchester where the new machines had ousted the craftsmen spinners and weavers and brought more poverty to the poor and more riches to the rich. The mill-owners cared little that their money sprung from grass roots set in misery and muck.

But that was the order of things, reasoned Patrick now unashamedly attached to middle-class thinking.

He stretched his legs luxuriously. They had made good time to Manchester for it was still only late afternoon. Soon he would change trains for Liverpool. He was impatient, now, to be there, for the sooner he arrived, the sooner he could do what he had set out to do and then be gone.

The sun was setting, sinking it seemed into the summer-calm waters of the river Mersey when the train clanked and shuddered into the glass-domed vastness of Liverpool's Lime Street station. Almost at once, mingling with the railway smell, Patrick caught the stench of the closely-populated streets. It was so instantly familiar that for a moment he could scarcely believe he had ever left them. With a feeling that was almost distaste, he deposited his baggage at the luggage office. He intended to walk to Aunt Hetty's house for a horse and cab drawing up at the small cottage in Lace Street would attract too much attention, he decided. It was only a few minutes walk and he was not as yet so well-endowed that he could afford to waste what he had on unnecessary expenditure.

He crossed the road, resisting the cries of small ragged boys who touted for the cab drivers, closing his ears to the mongrel accent that was part Lancashire and part Welsh and Irish.

'Give us a ha'penny for a hot tattie, sir?'

Patrick looked down at the small pinched face of the dirty child who trotted beside him.

'Only a ha'penny for a hot supper, me lord?'

A ha'penny for a tattie, was it? Patrick knew full well that the ha'penny and all the other coins the street-waif begged would be handed over to a shiftless father and end up in the ale-house before nightfall. But he fished in his pocket for a small coin and threw it on the pavement.

'Be off with you!' he jerked, ashamed almost of his stupidity. Then he quickened his steps lest before long the word went round that there was an open-handed toff in the vicinity and he became surrounded by hordes of child-beggars.

He turned sharply from Fontenoy Street, trying not to see the choked gutters, the barefoot mothers and children and women who stood brazenly, offering their bodies for the price of a loaf of bread or a slug of gin. He was glad when he reached the little court at the end of Lace Street.

It shocked him that it looked even smaller and meaner than ever he remembered it. At one end the stand-tap that provided water for the little huddle of houses was surrounded by women, patiently waiting with jugs and buckets until it dripped and splashed into life for a brief half-hour before it was again turned off for the night. And at the other end of the court the stench of the open midden told him he was home again.

Had it always smelled so foul? he wondered. Had the gracious London street in which he now lived dimmed the memory of his early years? Only one thing had not changed and his heart lifted a little at the sight of Hetty Norris's small house as it stood out clean and shining amidst the squalor.

The door-stone was newly scoured and the uneven flags outside swilled clean. The windows sparkled brightly, softly illuminated by the light of a single candle.

Gently Patrick lifted the door-latch and stepped into the small bare room. No fire burned in the grate but from the back of the house came the familiar smell of the clothes-boiler and the pungent odour of primrose soap.

Dear Aunt Hetty. Patrick's heart throbbed with long-forgotten love. She was still doing her washing for charity, as she called it.

'Hullo?' he called in a voice that was rough with emotion.

Then she was standing there, her grey wispy hair hanging in damp strands about her face, her body looking smaller and frailer than he had ever remembered, with a look of such unspeakable joy in her tired eyes that for a moment Patrick felt a wave of shame he had never thought possible.

For a moment he stood still, his eyes taking in her fragility and the defiant tilt of her head. Then he stepped forward and gathered her into his arms, lifting her towards him, holding her close.

'Aunt Hetty,' he breathed.

Two

For a little while Patrick held her to him, surprised that she felt so light in his arms, so very fragile. It was, he thought, like lifting a small child.

'Dear Aunt Hetty,' he whispered. 'Oh, but it's been so long . . .'

'Impudent boy! Put me down this instant! Have you forgotten how a lady should be treated since you went away?'

But there was kindness in her eyes and love and laughter and Patrick felt her warm tears on his cheek as they held each other close.

'Let me look at you.'

She held him at arm's length and gazed into his face.

'My, but aren't you just the fine gentleman? Aren't you the handsome one?'

Her eyes took in his crinkly black hair, cut now in the fashionably longer London style; hair that had caused him many a fight in his childhood, she remembered fondly when local lads had yelled,

'Curly! Curly! Hair like a girlie!'

And his newly-grown black moustache – how it suited him. What a fine young man he had become. It had all been worth it, she thought proudly.

'You'll be hungry, boy,' she said in her usual practical way. 'Are you getting enough to eat? They do say that

London women haven't the same way with the cooking as we have up here.'

Patrick thought of the skill of Robert Harrington's cook and the remains of the plenteous luncheon he had thrown from the carriage window.

'I do tolerably well, Aunt; tolerably well, thank you.'

'Then you shall sit down and have a meal and tell me how long you plan to stay.'

She gave a small, excited laugh. 'Oh, we have so much talking to do. There is so much I want to know.'

'But you got my letters, Aunt?'

'I did, boy. I did. And the Reverend read them all to me. But you must tell me more about your little sweetheart, Patrick. Does she cook well, and mend and sew?'

Patrick thought about Arabella. It would be useless to try to explain to Aunt Hetty that in fashionable London society young ladies were expected to lead inactive lives; to look pale and decorative and to faint at the dropping of a lace-edged handkerchief.

Cook? He doubted if Arabella had ever filled a kettle of water in the whole of her nineteen years.

'Miss Harrington will make me a good wife, Aunt,' he returned gravely.

'And does she go regular to church and say her prayers at night?'

'She does, Aunt.'

That at least was the truth.

Hetty Norris busied herself with laying the table. The cloth was patched but snowy white and heavily starched. She set out a knife and fork and mug and laid a plate of brawn before him.

'And the Queen, Patrick? Have you seen dear Queen Victoria?'

'Indeed I have. She is an extremely gracious lady. She

often rides in her carriage in the park near Harley Street. I have had the privilege of raising my hat as she drove past.'

'*Ahhhh!*'

For a moment, such news silenced even Miss Hetty's excited tongue.

Patrick looked with distaste at the homely pig's-head brawn but at least, he thought, it wasn't cow-heel!

Suddenly he wasn't hungry but he broke a piece of bread and on finding there was no butter on the table, started reluctantly to eat.

'Are you not joining me, Aunt Hetty?'

'No, Patrick. No, I'm not hungry and besides, when you get older you'll find a body needs less food inside it.'

Patrick sliced into the meat on his plate, letting it slip down his throat without tasting it.

Aunt Hetty pulled up a chair.

'I'll join you in a mug of tea, though,' she said, settling down to hear his news.

'I fear I shall not be able to stay, Aunt.'

Best he should make his point before the old woman had time to make up the bed in the little top room.

'Not stay, boy?'

Hetty Norris's face registered disbelief and disappointment.

'I am due in Harrogate to meet my employer in two days' time and I have promised to call on Adam Carmichael.'

'Ah, Adam.'

A look of tenderness crossed the tired face.

'He is a good man, Patrick. He has called to see me several times since you left. We talk about you a lot and about the old days.'

'Is he doing well?'

Patrick was glad that further protests about his too-early departure seemed to have been successfully side-tracked.

'Adam tells me very little about his practice in his letters.'

'He works very hard. People trust him. He is a good doctor and he is a gentleman, too.'

'He was *born* a gentleman,' Patrick retorted, roughly. Then, without raising his head from his plate he said, 'I have something to ask you, Aunt Hetty. I want you to give me a truthful answer.'

'Yes, boy?'

A guarded look crept into the faded blue eyes.

'What is my real name, Aunt? I think I should be told, now.'

He asked the question abruptly as if he hoped the sudden approach would find the old woman unprepared, but she raised her head and looked him steadily in the eyes.

'It is Patrick Norris,' she said, evenly, 'the name you have had for twenty-six years. If there is another, it slips my memory, for the moment.'

'*If* there is another? There must be another, unless I am *your* son!'

He flushed guiltily. He had not meant to be so direct.

'That was a foolish thing to say, Patrick,' was the only reply she gave.

'I am sorry, Aunt, but with my marriage approaching I feel I should be told more about myself. I have a right to know.'

'No man has a right to *anything*, boy. You are Patrick Norris and you have been loved and wanted since I first set eyes on you. That is all you need to know. Some day, perhaps . . .'

The voice trailed off into a weary silence and Patrick knew he had been thwarted again. But this time he was determined he would not give in so easily.

'It is likely I will stay the night at Adam's house,' he replied, 'but I will see you before I leave.'

He lifted her hand and held it to his cheek.

'Aunt Hetty, won't you tell me?'

He made one last despairing appeal.

'I will see you tomorrow,' she said quietly and sadly as she walked ahead of him to the door.

Slowly the horse strained up the steep incline of the street most ineptly named Mount Pleasant, weariness echoing in each hollow step. Like himself, thought Patrick, the horse and driver had probably been up since early dawn. It would be pleasant to be received warmly into the comfort of Adam's home. He was surprised that he should feel so dispirited and spent.

'Which number, sir?' called the cab driver.

'Thirteen, if you please.'

'That'll be Doctor Adam's place. Folks around these parts call it *The Haven*.'

Patrick did not reply. He was not now in the habit of engaging in conversations with cab drivers unless it suited his purpose. But it suited him quickly enough as they turned slowly into Abercromby Square.

'What on earth . . .?' he jerked.

Gone was the air of prosperous respectability. Many of the houses appeared to be empty or badly neglected and a great many more seemed to be bulging with a surfeit of occupants.

'Well might you remark, sir. Bit of a mess, ain't it? But they can get ten or a dozen into one of them big rooms. It's pretty plain you've not visited these parts for some time.'

The sight of the once-proud houses shocked Patrick into silence.

'It's the in-comers you see, squire. Landing by the boatload, poor creatures.'

Patrick knew about the Irish immigrants, forced from their own country by the hunger that followed the repeated failure of their potato crops; knew too that Liverpool was the first step in their bid to reach the promised land that was America and the new life and new freedom they hoped to find there.

'But they don't live *here*, in Abercromby Square?'

'Not so's you'd notice, sir, but they're crowding out the lodging-houses and even bedding down in old warehouses. Local folks is getting out and since the gentlemen from these fine houses have taken themselves off, it's natural that others should move in.'

He shrugged.

'It's bad for trade, an' all. The gentry have moved out, up to Everton Heights and West Derby and such-like better places. Can't blame 'em, either, only it's a pity . . .'

He shook his head like a mournful old dog.

'But why?'

The lodging-houses and tenements and warehouses were to be found along the waterfront, Patrick reasoned. Surely they need not have concerned those people who had lived in comparative isolation in Abercromby Square?

'Well, sir, there's the water shortage for one thing. Not enough to go round now, with all the extra folks come in from Ireland and there's the troubles they brings with 'em!'

'Troubles?'

'Aye,' the man nodded his head sagely. 'Like the thieving and the street-women. They've got no money and stands to reason they got to eat. And there's the fevers and Lord-knows what else. They do say as there's more cholera by the tobacco warehouses. I has to be very careful who I picks up, these days!'

Patrick wanted to hear no more. Quite suddenly he wanted to place the distance of many miles between himself and Liverpool.

Without a thought he handed a florin to the driver and only vaguely heard the surprised, 'Coo! God bless yer, squire!' as he slowly walked up the steps of the house that was numbered thirteen.

Its door was thrown wide open. Beside it a highly-polished brass plate bore the name *Adam Carmichael L.S.A.*

Patrick's feet echoed loudly on the uncovered, spotlessly-clean floor, vibrating to the ornately moulded ceiling that had obviously not felt the ministrations of a decorator's brush in years.

On the walls, faded red silk covering reminded of an earlier prosperity and an elegant, uncarpeted staircase curved upwards to a large bare window on the half-landing.

Patrick blinked his eyes with disbelief. What would he think now, that man who once must have lived here in splendour if he were suddenly to return? What could have happened? Patrick demanded silently of himself. The comfort he had imagined to find in the home of a man who lived in Abercromby Square was nowhere to be seen. That some kind of surgery was in progress was obvious he decided, glancing at the huddle of miserably-dressed people who sat without a murmur of complaint in the bare lofty hall.

Bemused, he sat down to wait at the end of one of the well-scrubbed benches. Glancing at the quietly-waiting patients his professional eye quickly diagnosed a goitre, a well-pregnant woman suffering from malnutrition, two cases of rickets, a woman who obviously had contracted . . . Good Lord! Adam didn't allow *those* creatures in his surgery – and a man with a heart condition.

How different from the pampered, bored matrons on whom he lavished his attentions in the comfortable Harley Street rooms.

Few of *his* patients were sick; not really sick. Their ailments, he had to admit, were often imaginary or currently fashionable. There was little wrong with most of them that a Gregory powder or a loosening of too-tight stays would not have cured in half an hour! And a good day's work spent over a wash-tub and rubbing-board would set the majority of them up for life, he thought wryly.

But they settled their large accounts promptly and without question and that, Patrick told himself as he had done so many times before, was all that mattered.

He was beginning to collect the muddle of his thoughts now. The realization that Adam had such poor patients was beginning to register.

But surely, Patrick reasoned as the pregnant woman rose clumsily to her feet and knocked almost apologetically on the surgery door, Adam must have other patients. The poor who waited so patiently on the hard benches were obviously a prop to Adam's conscience; they must surely be his 'charity' as was Aunt Hetty's perpetually bubbling wash-boiler.

He was glad when the last of them had left and a familiar voice called, 'Next, please.'

With a little smile Patrick rose to his feet, straightened his coat and gave a tweak to his cravat. Then slowly, a pulse of anticipation beating in his throat, he walked towards the door.

For a moment the face before him registered disbelief then broke into a wide, slow smile of pleasure.

'Patrick! Patrick, my dear old friend, you are here. I knew you would come!'

Adam Carmichael held out his hands, his face betraying his emotions and they stood, hands clasped, laughing with delight.

Then Patrick felt a small shock of fear for he noticed the droop of his friend's shoulders, the tired eyes and a face too thin and colourless.

'Well, doctor?'

The words sounded inept and trite but they were all Patrick could find to say. 'I think I have come in the nick of time to diagnose a severe case of over-working and to prescribe,' he said with mock severity, 'a two-week holiday in the Welsh mountains.'

Adam smiled, a yearning look fleeting across his face.

'I wish it could be possible. Sometimes, I think, I would like nothing better but I cannot leave *The Haven*.'

He stopped as a spasm of coughing shook his thin body. Then he smiled apologetically.

'But sit down, Patrick, and I will tell Sarah you have come.'

'Sarah?'

Had Adam taken a wife, then? And if he had, had she taken leave of her senses in allowing him to work so hard when it was so obvious that . . .

He shuddered inwardly and tried to shut out his thoughts but despite his long sabbatical in the Harley

Street practice, Patrick's skills had not left him. He did not like the sound of Adam's cough nor the startling decline in his appearance.

Adam smiled.

'Sarah Rigby,' he supplied. 'I don't know what we would do without her. She is a fine woman, Patrick.'

'She works at this place?'

'She *is* this place, Patrick. She drives herself without mercy.'

'As she drives you, it seems.'

'No, friend. Sarah scolds me often and says as you say that I must take a rest in the fresh air but . . .'

His voice trailed off as the rasping coughing once more caused Patrick to crease his forehead into a frown of concern.

'You are right, Adam. She says it often!'

Patrick turned to where a tall, slim young woman stood in the open doorway, a tray bearing brown mugs of steaming liquid in her hands.

'She says it so often that sometimes she tires of the sound of her own voice!'

'Ma'am.'

Patrick jumped to his feet, inclining his head in her direction.

The woman walked into the room.

'Dicky-Sam told me you had come. I have brought you a drink,' she said, handing hot cocoa to Patrick with hardly a glance in his direction. 'Molly has some meat and bread,' she said gently to Adam. 'The *Bounty* arrived this morning and there is food in the pantry again.'

'God bless the *Bounty* and the angel who sends it,' smiled Adam, 'but thank you, no. This drink will do nicely.'

He rose to his feet.

'Sarah, my dear, this is Patrick Norris. I said he would come. I knew he wouldn't fail us.'

Uneasily, Patrick remained silent, offering his hand to the tired-faced Sarah. She was, he thought, a mixture of contradictions. Her long homespun dress and white apron belied her proud bearing and the look of condescension she tossed in his direction. She wore the stamp of breeding and the garb of a servant. Her fire-red hair was scraped back from her face and tied without ceremony with a black ribbon, small wisps of it escaping to hang damply on her flushed face. She briefly offered her hand before turning once more to Adam, her blue-grey eyes tender with concern.

'Are you sure you will not eat? A little of Molly's broth, perhaps?'

'Thank you, Sarah, but no,' Adam smiled. 'I will wash my hands and put on my old jacket. Then we will take our drinks into the back parlour and talk and talk.'

He turned in the doorway and smiled again his slow gentle smile of pleasure. Then the two people in the room waited until his footsteps could be heard wearily negotiating the stairs.

'Well?' Sarah demanded, abruptly.

Patrick gazed into the strong face, gentled a little by the fine, high cheek-bones. He shrugged his shoulders.

'Doctor Carmichael is working too hard and he is not well,' he admitted.

'*Working too hard? Not well?* He is exhausted and he is sick and if you are half the doctor he says you are, sir, then you should know it!'

Patrick flushed angrily.

'I know it, ma'am.'

'Then what are you going to do about it?'

Patrick took a deep, steadying breath.

'Might I first ask, madam, who you are?' he begged the question, pointedly.

'I am Sarah Rigby and I work at *The Haven*. That is all you need to know, doctor.'

'You are employed here as a servant?'

'There are no employers and no servants in this house. We are poor and we work for the poor. We are all equal, here.'

'We?'

'Adam and Molly O'Keefe and Dicky-Sam and me.'

She gave an impatient shrug.

'But that is beside the point. Adam is coughing his lungs away!'

'Yes,' Patrick acknowledged gravely, trying hard to retain his composure, 'but that, Miss Rigby, is surely no concern of yours.'

'When one of us is sick, it is the concern of all of us,' she flung back.

Patrick shifted uneasily.

'Might I know exactly *what* your position is in this house and how you came here?' he hedged.

'You may not,' Sarah Rigby answered, flatly. 'It is sufficient to say that since society in its stupidity will not allow a woman to become a doctor, I am doing what I consider to be the next most useful thing!'

'A *woman* doctor!'

Patrick did not try to conceal the horror in his voice. 'Madam, you are . . .'

He broke off abruptly as a heavy thud was followed by a small, stifled moan.

There was a moment of frozen silence then Sarah flung her body across the room and wrenched open the door.

'Adam!'

In an instant she was on her knees beside the inert form that was huddled pathetically at the foot of the staircase.

'He's collapsed. Help me lift him,' she ordered.

Obediently Patrick placed his hands beneath Adam's slight shoulders. Without ceremony, Sarah took his feet.

'Upstairs,' she jerked, brusquely.

Carefully Patrick edged his way in the direction of Sarah's nodding head.

'The room on the right,' she panted.

Gently they laid Adam on the small bed.

'Help me get him undressed.' Already Sarah had removed Adam's cravat and unfastened the buttons of his shirt.

'*Help me!*' she demanded again as Patrick stood bemused by her flagrant disregard for convention.

Carefully they eased off the threadbare clothes.

'Here!' Sarah flung a nightshirt at Patrick. 'For God's sake, *doctor* . . .'

With heavy sarcasm she accentuated the last word, stinging Patrick into action.

'Open the window wide,' he rapped, 'this room is airless!'

Automatically his fingers searched for the pulse at Adam's wrist.

Slowly, as they stood over him rubbing his hands, the pale eyelids flickered then opened.

'Patrick?'

'Yes, Adam? I am here.'

'I'm sorry. I stumbled on the stairs.'

'You collapsed,' Sarah whispered fiercely. 'You're a fool, Adam Carmichael!'

Patrick held up his hand.

'Easy now, Adam.'

He settled the limp body more comfortably on the pillows.

'You'll be all right, now. But Miss Rigby is right, you know. You need a rest – a *long* rest.'

Meaningfully, his eyes met Adam's.

'I know, Patrick. I've known it for some time – that's why I asked you to come. I need you and my poor people need you, too. There is so much to be done and so little time . . .'

His voice whispered into silence.

'But, Adam,' Patrick felt an uneasy flush burning in his cheeks. 'I cannot . . .'

'Patrick, I *beg* of you?'

Desperately a thin, anxious hand grasped his.

'Stay for just a little while. For the sake of old times, help us?'

Patrick could not bring himself to meet the trusting eyes. He looked across the bed to where Sarah stood unmoving, asking silently for her understanding and support. He saw that the soft blue that had shaded her eyes was gone. Now they flashed a challenge of anger and contempt, grey and cold as storm-tossed waves on the river.

So this, they mocked, *is the brilliant Doctor Norris, the man who has forsaken his own and exchanged his talents for an easy living? This is the friend who will not fail us!*

Patrick caught at his breath, fighting to control the feelings that writhed inside him; feelings of shame and uncertainty, of anger and pity.

He stood, unspeaking, whipped by the scorn in Sarah Rigby's face.

'Dear friend, for pity's sake . . .?'

But Patrick Norris hardly heard Adam's gentle pleading for the steel-cold eyes that blazed into his shocked and bewildered him, so eloquent was their unspoken contempt.

Three

Suddenly in that small bare room, Patrick Norris was a child again; a bewildered, restless boy who had looked at the confining walls of the court in Lace Street and felt, almost, that they were closing in on him. He wanted to push them back with his strong young arms and shout, 'No! I won't be shut in! I will not stay in this town. Nothing shall keep me here!'

He had determined then to leave the mean streets behind him for even in his youth he vowed that Liverpool should never be allowed to hold him.

That feeling possessed him again only now it was the white walls of Adam Carmichael's sick-room that closed him in; the hand that clasped his as though it would never let it go and the fierce, unspoken challenge in Sarah Rigby's eyes.

Why, Patrick fretted, had he let this happen to him? He had been a fool to respond to Adam's letter. And how could Adam expect all men to possess his own lofty ideals?

Patrick felt a pricking of guilt, for even as the thought was born his reason destroyed it. Adam was no knight-crusader. He was a compassionate and good man; he saw what needed to be done and quietly and earnestly tried to do it.

In their youth Patrick had loved Adam as a brother. It

had amazed him that in his unreasoning obsession to rise from the poverty of Lace Street he could ever have allowed himself the luxury of such a feeling.

'Patrick?'

He felt again the tightening of fingers within his hand and because he could not again expose himself to the utter destruction of Sarah Rigby's gaze he heard himself saying.

'Very well, I will stay – for just a little while . . .'

'God bless you, Patrick,' Adam whispered, the gratitude in his voice unmistakable.

Patrick raised his head and looked into Sarah's face and for a small moment he thought that relief had replaced the animosity in her eyes.

Then he was himself again, in command of his own destiny. He would give them two days and not one hour longer and during that time he would show them what he was made of. Sarah Rigby would have to admit he was no London quack!

'You are tired, Adam,' he said. 'I will give you something to help you sleep. Perhaps if Miss Rigby will be so kind as to help me . . .'

It took all his resolve to make the request. He had not thought any woman could have made him feel so inadequate.

'Certainly, doctor, if you will come with me?'

Patrick followed her downstairs to a passage-like room that contained rows of shelves and a stone sink with a brass tap.

She coughed, apologetically.

'This was once a butler's pantry; now, it is my dispensary.'

Patrick looked around him. Home-made bandages lay neatly rolled in boxes; crude splints stood in a corner; a mortar and pestle and a few assorted jars of powders and lotions looked strangely alone in the bareness of the room.

Patrick picked up a Bunsen-burner which seemed to him to be the only concession the so-called dispensary offered to the medical advances of the nineteenth century.

'There is gas-lighting in the house, Miss Rigby?'

Sarah shook her head. 'Only in this room and in the sick-ward.'

'You have sick *here*?'

'I will show you,' Sarah nodded.

She led him into a large lofty room that must surely have once known the polite gossip of crinolined ladies Patrick mused, as they sipped a glass of Madeira or nibbled daintily on a macaroon.

Now that room was stripped bare of its elegant past, its ornately patterned wooden floor scrubbed clean of stain and polish, its occupants the sick who lay in the narrow beds that were ranged arounds its walls.

Sarah allowed only the briefest glimpse before she closed the door.

'I will take you round later when you have seen to Adam. Some of the patients will be able to leave very soon. I shall be glad of their beds, if the fever gets worse.'

Patrick quirked an enquiring eyebrow.

'The fever, ma'am?'

'Surely you knew there is cholera in the port?' Sarah replied, tersely. 'It's taking a hold near the docks.'

'And you would nurse cholera *here*?'

'If it is necessary,' Sarah shrugged. 'We try not to turn anyone away who is sick – and poor.'

Patrick turned his back abruptly. Sarah Rigby, he realized, meant every word of what she had said.

Was she, he wondered, another of that rash of ranting

women who had ideas above the capacity of their brains? What right had any woman to imagine she could be anything other than what the good God had created her for? Why couldn't women be contented to be soft and gentle; to be a comfort to the men who had chosen them in marriage and bear healthy children to carry on their name. Women, it seemed, were getting strange ideas that would have been really quite amusing had they not been so outrageously ridiculous.

Take Miss Nightingale, Patrick reasoned; a lady of good birth, yet she was bothering everybody in the medical profession for help in the training of her lady nurses.

Lady nurses?

No lady would allow herself to be subjected to the filth and squalor of infirmary wards.

No decent woman could possibly enter those stinking places; no gentlewoman could ever be a nurse! Those who set themselves up as such were dirty, dissolute creatures, didn't Sarah Rigby know that? Many of them were hopeless drunkards or part-time whores.

A *lady* nurse? It was pathetic in its stupidity and now Sarah Rigby had exceeded the bounds of credibility by saying that she wanted to become a doctor!

He reached for the laudanum bottle.

Now, how different was his Arabella, thought Patrick, absently. Arabella Harrington was a credit to womanhood. She knew her place in life and accepted it gladly. She would make him a good wife and give him children as her duty demanded.

But he had often wondered about Arabella. There was a slightness about her; a fragility that sometimes made him doubt her ability to bear a child. She was a fairy thing – an elfin ornament to grace any man's home – but how would she fare on the child-bed?

Now Sarah Rigby, Patrick's medical mind supplied, would carry her children like a barefoot peasant and give them to the world with ease and dignity. Sarah Rigby had child-bearing hips and good breasts for nursing . . .

Patrick shut down his thoughts, becoming suddenly and acutely aware of two large grey eyes that looked questioningly into his.

He felt himself flush, ashamed of his thoughts. He was betrothed to Arabella and Sarah Rigby was obviously in love with Adam Carmichael. And anyway, he asserted silently, he had only been thinking of Miss Rigby in the purest of medical terms – it was as simple as that.

In two days he would leave *The Haven* and Sarah Rigby for all time. He doubted if he would ever think about her again.

Carefully he measured a sleeping-draught, meticulously replacing the glass stopper and placing the bottle back in its place on the highest shelf.

Two days, he assured himself yet again; for just two days he would stay and take Adam's surgeries and visit his sick then he would be up and away. He would leave Liverpool gladly and without a backward glance and be damned if he would ever return!

He had been foolishly sentimental to agree to Adam's pleading but for the sake of their friendship he supposed he owed Adam something.

True, Adam was sick and needed rest and nursing, but had it not been for Sarah Rigby and the mocking scorn in her eyes, he would never have allowed himself to be coaxed into the situation at all!

Patrick gave an exclamation of annoyance, pushing the thoughts of that unspoken challenge to the back of his mind. He didn't know why he allowed the woman to disturb him so. She was of no importance and he would not think about her. He would keep out of her way and communicate with her only when he must and when he boarded the train for Harrogate he wouldn't give her another thought. Why on earth should he?

Clearing his throat with unnecessary ferocity he walked past Sarah saying coldly, 'That will be all, ma'am. I will attend to Doctor Carmichael.'

Sarah flushed with amazed outrage. How *could* he speak to her so? What right had he to dismiss her from her own dispensary as if he owned the place? What was there about the man that made Adam speak of him so lovingly?

Why, Patrick Norris was nothing but an overbearing, self-opinionated, upstart London Dandy!

She drew in a deep breath, willing herself to be calm, refusing to let him see that he had succeeded in disturbing her still further.

'As you wish, doctor,' she said, more quietly than she could ever have given herself credit for.

After all, she reasoned, he would soon tire of the endless work at *The Haven*; would quickly come to realize there was little to be made by working for the poor. The gratitude in their eyes, the satisfaction of the giving of oneself to the utmost, of fighting and sometimes winning in the face of impossible odds were the only rewards anyone could hope for.

She looked round the little room. The dispensary had been her great pride until Patrick Norris's amused eyes had forced her to admit its utter inadequacy.

They had so little money with which to buy drugs and medicines. Adam had few instruments and those he had could well have been replaced by newer, more efficient ones.

Sarah recalled the day they had decided they could

afford to buy a stethoscope. How delighted Adam had been – a child with a Christmas toy.

If only she were rich, she yearned, there would be so many things she could buy; so much more they could achieve.

Sarah sighed. Tomorrow, she must get out the account books and go through them with Molly. Together they must sort out the bills and pay those that could no longer wait.

With luck perhaps, there would be a few pounds to come from the scattering of Adam's patients who could afford to pay for treatment. There were precious few of them left. They had sold or closed their houses and taken themselves off, away from the hot, dirty streets. Only the poor remained now and they couldn't pay.

Soon there would be a stream of women down the area steps that led to Molly's kitchens, begging water from her scullery tap. At least, thought Sarah, she must be grateful that the water supply at *The Haven* was never turned on and off at will.

Water, she thought, was what the town needed most; clean, pure water for drinking and washing in and swilling the choked, stinking gutters.

She wished it would rain. There had been none for weeks, now. A good downpour would flush out the filth that helped spawn cholera; cool the sweating streets. She wondered if any new cases of the fever had been reported.

'Dear God, let it not be,' she prayed for she knew that it would be to the house in Abercromby Square that the poor wretches would come to beg help. And if it got worse, how many sick could they take in? And, come to that, how would they manage with Adam so ill?

Dear Adam, who refused to acknowledge the fact and

would work for his poor ones until his last protesting cough.

If only Patrick Norris would stay, Sarah wished. Oh, she didn't like him, but at least it would give them the chance to get Adam into the country for a few months. Rest and good clean air might help – might even cure – the consumption that was choking his lungs.

She gave a short, derisive laugh. Patrick Norris would not stay with them, she was certain of it. She was surprised that she should even have hoped that he would.

And that, thought Patrick as the last patient stammered his thanks and left the surgery, has been a good morning's work. It was a long time, he realized, since he had dealt with such a varied and interesting number of ailments. Under normal circumstances he might well have enjoyed it.

'Come in,' he called, in answer to the loud knocking.

The door opened to admit a small, limping man.

'Good morning to you, doctor.'

The weather-beaten face creased into a genuine smile of greeting.

'Begging your pardon, sir, but I was hoping to find Miss Sarah with you. She usually helps Doctor Adam with morning surgery.'

'She's not helping *me*!'

'Then she'll be down in Molly's galley, for sure.'

Patrick scowled. 'Molly's galley?'

'Miss O'Keefe's kitchens, sir. A very worthy lady is Molly O'Keefe. It's generally about this time we all has a mug o' tea, so if you'd care to accompany me, I'll be pleased to escort you.'

'Might I ask, my man, who you are?' Patrick demanded

bluntly, noticing for the first time that the chirpy little body was balanced precariously on one leg and a wooden stump attached below the knee-joint of the other.

'You may, sir, you may!'

He gave a small, comic bow, almost overbalancing in his efforts at elegance.

'Richard Samuel Pickstock, at your service.'

'Then you must be Dicky-Sam?'

'I have that honour, doctor.'

Patrick smiled. He could not find it in him to resist the cheerful good-humour that bubbled out of the man.

'You work here, I believe?'

'That I does, sir, and proud to be of service. But then, I owes me life to Doctor Adam.'

He placed his hand on his heart in a dramatic gesture.

'Carried me off the *Cornucopia* a smashed and battered wreck, they did. Fell out of the rigging I had and not one unbroken bone in me body. "Dead he'll be afore nightfall," they said, but Doctor Adam patched me up a treat – cut off me useless old leg and fitted me with a new one!'

'I see,' Patrick nodded gravely.

'So I ended me sea-days and came to work for the good doctor. Glad to be rid of that packet, I was. She's a bad ship, the *Cornucopia*, a jonah ship if ever there was one. Bad luck she's been since the day her keel was laid!'

Dicky-Sam nodded his head, sagely.

'And I'm not the only one as thinks so. Miss Sarah thinks she's a bad 'un an' all!'

The little seaman sighed, volubly. 'But I'm keeping you, sir, and you a'thirsting for a mug of char.'

He limped to the door and held it open.

'If you'd care to come along o' me, doctor . . .?'

*

Sarah was sitting at the large table in the basement. Beside her sat red-cheeked, black-haired Molly O'Keefe whose long dress and snow-white apron seemed to have been padded out with soft, fat cushions.

'Good morning,' Sarah greeted them without raising her head.

Dicky-Sam took two mugs from the dresser then hopped over to the blue and gold teapot that stood beside the gleaming black cooking range.

'There you are, doctor. Strong and sweet and black as Hell's kitchen!'

Molly O'Keefe stared dismally at the collection of unpaid accounts.

''Tis a terrible sight to behold, Miss Sarah. That pile of bills gets bigger every day and myself in need of soap and bathbrick,' she sighed. 'I can't cut down on cleanliness, miss.'

'No Molly, you certainly can't though I think you must eat soap, you use so much,' Sarah smiled, gently.

Then she puckered her forehead into a frown.

'We *must* pay for the coal, Molly – we need it for cooking and hot water and the coalman is so good – he gives us good weight and never charges more than six-pence ha'penny a bag.'

They were totally immersed in their business, quite unaware of the two men who sat drinking tea.

Watching Sarah unashamedly, Patrick noticed the fleeting smile, admitting reluctantly that for an instant it had transformed her face into one of rare and startling beauty.

He dropped his eyes as Sarah shut the account book with a snap and picked up two half-sovereigns that lay on the table.

She handed one to Molly O'Keefe.

'Thank you kindly, Miss Sarah.'

Molly took the small gold coin that represented her wages for the month and turned it over on her hand.

'It would please me if you would accept my contribution to the housekeeping,' she said with dignity as she returned the coin to Sarah.

Sarah inclined her head gravely.

'Thank you, Miss O'Keefe,' she returned. 'I am obliged for your kindness.'

Patrick turned to Dicky-Sam, a look of bewilderment on his face.

'Molly always does that,' Dicky-Sam whispered. 'Always gives back her wages.'

Sarah turned to the little cripple, handing him the other coin.

Dicky-Sam tipped his forelock, then opening the purse at his belt he placed the money carefully inside it, smiling cheerfully as he limped from the room.

Sarah rose to her feet, gathering up her papers.

'I'll be in the sick-ward if you need me, Molly.'

Patrick set down his mug, following closely on her heels as she climbed the narrow stairs that wound upwards from the kitchens.

In the hall Sarah paused.

'Will you take a look at Adam?' she asked.

'I have already seen him. He seems much rested,' Patrick replied. 'On no account must he be allowed up, though. He needs sleep.'

'Very well,' Sarah nodded, her eyes on the toes of her boots, 'and now, if you will excuse me . . .?'

'Miss Rigby?'

Sarah spun round. 'Yes, doctor?'

'That business of the accounts – Molly's wages, I mean. Did you have to go through all that play-acting?'

'I don't understand you.'

Sarah's chin tilted defensively but Patrick blundered blindly on.

'Why did you pay Molly her wages then take them back?'

'It pleases her.'

'Ha! I didn't notice Dicky-Sam letting you take advantage of him,' Patrick laughed. 'He was off like a shot with *his* half-sovereign. Down to the ale-house, no doubt.'

Sarah took in a deep breath.

'Doctor Norris, can you really imagine what it is like to be poor? Dicky-Sam takes his wages to the tobacconist's shop and spends it on shag and twist. He gives it to the sailors in the infirmary. It gives him pleasure, you see.'

The stubborn chin was set at defiance, the wide grey eyes narrowed into suppressed anger.

'As for Molly, I accept back her wages because it helps her to maintain her dignity. Dignity, doctor, is a rare luxury amongst the under-priviliged. Molly and Dicky-Sam are poor but they have their pride – it is all that is left to them. Would you,' she whispered, her voice trembling, 'rob them of *that*?'

For a moment they faced each other unspeaking, then Sarah said quietly, 'We eat our dinner in the kitchen at noon. I must ask you not to be late,' and without waiting for his answer she turned her back deliberately and walked into the sick-ward.

For expediency's sake, Patrick carried his mid-day meal into Adam's room and sat beside the bed to eat it. He was pleased to see the patient looking more rested and the over-bright spots of colour that had flamed in his cheeks not so pronounced.

'I feel such a fraud,' Adam protested. 'I think I will get up when I have eaten.'

'If you do,' Patrick warned with mock severity, 'I swear I shall leave!'

Adam smiled. 'You are a good friend. You must have worked hard, this morning.'

'Indeed I did but I found it most enjoyable,' Patrick replied easily with the utmost truth.

He ate his meal with relish.

'This beef stew is very good.'

'Molly is a fine cook,' Adam acknowledged. 'She came to us, destitute, a little over two years ago. She can make a meal from next to nothing and she is obsessed with cleanliness. When she is not cooking she is washing or scrubbing.'

'And Dicky-Sam?'

'Dicky-Sam was brought here quite literally to die but we were able to save him,' Adam offered modestly. 'Now he works with us at *The Haven* and I don't know what we would do at times, without his good humour.'

'*The Haven*?' Patrick mused. 'It is a strange place.'

'Perhaps it is; certainly it is strange that we have been so lucky.'

Adam set his plate aside then turned to face Patrick.

'When I could no longer pay the rent of this house I appealed to the owner for a little time. Almost at once a letter came back, saying I need make no more payments.'

'So you live rent-free? Who is your benevolent landlord?'

'You'll not believe me, Patrick, but I don't know. Once, I believe, this house belonged to a shipowner. I have tried to find his name to thank him, but I cannot.'

'You have never met him?'

'No.' Adam shook his head. 'Always my business has been with a firm of notaries. But stranger than that, Patrick, is the *Bounty*.'

Patrick nodded.

'I heard mention of it, yesterday.'

'It arrives regularly,' Adam affirmed, 'on the twenty-first day of every month.'

'And how much is this *Bounty*?'

'It is always five guineas. At first, it worried me greatly but Sarah insisted that the time to worry was when it ceased to arrive. In time I accepted it. Somewhere there is a good soul who will never know how thankful we are to him. We need the money so very much, Patrick.'

Sarah, thought Patrick. *Always, it is Sarah!*

'Ah, and there, Adam, is another mystery.'

'Sarah, you mean? A mystery? No, not really, although she came to my door one day and said simply, "I want to work with the poor and I have decided that I can best do it here." I never questioned her coming and I have never regretted it for one minute.'

'But hasn't it caused a scandal?'

Surely it must be totally unacceptable, Patrick reasoned, for two people, unrelated and unmarried to live beneath the same roof?

'Not that I ever heard of, and besides, we were well chaperoned once Molly arrived,' Adam smiled. 'Had the whole town buzzed with gossip, I do not think Sarah would have worried over-much.'

No, thought Patrick, nothing would worry Sarah Rigby except the caring for her impoverished sick.

'Do you manage to get on well with her, Adam?'

'I do indeed. She has a splendid brain. She dispenses the

medicines and takes the worry of the running of the house off my hands.'

Adam smiled tenderly.

'Sarah is a rare creature, Patrick. She is kind and compassionate – she has changed my whole life.'

'But what do you know about her other than that? Why, she may be an erring wife who has run away from her husband!'

Adam laughed and for a moment Patrick caught a glimpse of the friend of his youth.

'I do not think she has a husband although I confess I tried, once, to find out more about her. But my enquiries were always blocked and as time went on I ceased to worry. I only knew she was our dearest Sarah and that we could never manage without her. I was always one to be thankful for my blessings, and Sarah is truly a blessing.'

There was a brief knock on the door and the subject of Adam's unstinted praise walked into the room without ceremony.

'It's Margaret-Mary Haggarty,' Sarah announced shortly. 'She's in labour.'

Adam made to throw back his bed-clothes.

'I must get dressed,' he whispered. 'I must go to her.'

'No, Adam!'

Patrick placed a restraining hand on his friend's arm. 'You must stay in bed – I order it. I will see to Mrs Haggarty.'

'But it isn't as easy as that, Patrick,' Adam protested, weakly. 'Margaret-Mary is not strong; she is worn out with child-bearing. I warned her and I warned Haggarty that another child would be the death of her . . .'

He shrugged helplessly.

'All we can do now, Patrick, is to give her what help and comfort we can. She hasn't a chance, God help her!'

Four

. . . *She hasn't a chance!*

Inexplicably Margaret-Mary Haggarty's wellbeing was of supreme importance to Patrick.

He rose to his feet, the thought of such a challenge setting his blood racing. He had been present at a great many confinements, some of them extremely awkward ones and he'd never lost a mother in childbirth, yet. What was more, he exulted, he wasn't going to lose one now without the fight of his life!

Of Mrs Haggarty's life, he thought, ruefully. He didn't know why suddenly an unknown woman who lived in obscure poverty should cause him even a second thought. Did he, perhaps, want to show them what he was made of; that there was more to Patrick Norris than his elegantly-cut clothes?

He shrugged. He didn't have to prove anything to Adam, did he? Surely then those grey, scornful eyes couldn't be the cause of his sudden charitable love for his fellow-men?

Pah! He was being ridiculous! He was a doctor and sworn to the care of all sick. It had nothing at all to do with Sarah Rigby – absolutely nothing!

Angrily he shut down his stupid thoughts.

'Adam,' he said gently, 'I am well able to attend to your Mrs Haggarty. There'll be a midwife there, I take it?'

'Yes,' Sarah interposed, doubtfully. 'But I think it might be better if I were to come with you . . .'

'I thank you, ma'am, but that will not be at all necessary,' Patrick retorted, more firmly than he had intended. 'But if you would be so good as to prepare a laying-in bag, however, I shall be obliged to you.'

Sarah spun round on her heel, biting back the angry words that sprang to her lips. Then she shrugged her shoulders briefly and walked resignedly from the room. She mustn't upset Adam, she thought. For his sake and for *The Haven*, she must do her utmost to prevent open conflict with Patrick Norris. Nothing else, she told herself firmly, absolutely nothing else mattered.

She was waiting in the hall when Patrick came downstairs with the laying-in bag packed and his street-coat and top hat at the ready to hand to him.

'Mrs Haggarty lives in Cable Street. I could come with you if you wished,' she said hopefully 'and show you the quickest way there?'

'Thank you, Miss Rigby. I am grateful to you, but I shall manage quite well alone.'

Damn the woman and her insistence he thought angrily as he walked in the direction of St John Street. Didn't she realize, he fumed, that he knew every alley and back street in the town?

Of necessity he slowed down his steps and breathed in the stiffling mid-day air, wondering what he would find when he reached the house in Cable Street. He turned as he heard he heard a familiar voice calling his name.

'Patrick! Wait for me!'

It was the first time Sarah had used his name and it added to his annoyance that he should feel pleasure.

'You need not have bothered yourself, ma'am,' he said formally. 'I assure you I am well able to manage.'

Sarah shrugged her shoulders.

'Nevertheless, I would like to be with Mrs Haggarty,' she said quietly. 'She knows and trusts Adam but you will be a stranger to her. It is best – truly it is – that I should come with you.'

Matching her step to Patrick's she strode easily by his side, neither of them speaking again until they reached Cable Street.

The wretched little huddle of houses was all Patrick remembered from his youth, built into a small, airless court with rubbish-strewn gutters and filthy pavements.

On the steps of the Haggarty house sat six children the eldest of whom – a girl – Patrick supposed to be not more than ten years old. She rose to her feet as they approached.

'Hullo, miss,'

Shyly she addressed Sarah.

'I'm glad you've come. I'm awful afeard. Me Ma's terrible badly.'

Sarah placed her arm round the thin shoulders.

'It'll be all right,' she comforted. 'Doctor Norris will take good care of your Ma.'

Large brown eyes looked unwaveringly into Patrick's.

'She didn't want you. She asked for Doctor Adam.'

'Doctor Adam isn't very well,' Sarah explained gently, 'but Doctor Norris is a fine London doctor, really he is!'

'He'll not let Ma die, will he, miss?'

'Silly girl, of course not! What an awful thing to think!' Sarah replied with more conviction than she felt.

She fished into the pocket of her skirt.

'See, here is a penny. How would you all like to share a bag of humbugs?'

'Oooh!'

For the first time the too-old eyes came alive and

hitching the youngest of the children onto her hip with an ease born of long practice the girl seemed momentarily to forget her fears.

'Thanks, miss,' she breathed, and calling the little brood around her she hurried them away in search of so rare a treat.

'Poor little wench,' Sarah sighed as she watched the bare feet skimming the hard, uncaring pavements. 'She's never had time to be a child . . .'

Margaret-Mary Haggarty was laid on a hard wooden bed, moaning softly into her pillow when Patrick pushed open the door of the downstairs room.

A small fire sulked in the hearth and a pan of water had been set there to boil.

Beside it, in the only chair, a woman rocked comfortably, a piece of knitting between her dirty fingers. By her side on the hearth stood a half-empty bottle.

She glanced up with disinterest as they entered.

'Good day to ye, Mistress Rigby. And who's the fine young feller ye've brought with ye?'

Insolently her eyes searched Patrick from head to foot.

'I am a doctor, madam,' Patrick replied stiffly.

The old woman bared her toothless gums in a gin-sodden leer.

'Well, my pretty, ye're wasting your time,' she nodded towards the bed. 'I'll have this stocking finished afore that one gets rid of her burden.'

'Who is this . . . creature?' Patrick ground, turning angrily to Sarah.

'She's the midwife, but if I had my way,' Sarah made no attempt to lower her voice, 'I'd not let her within a mile of a laying-in!'

Patrick walked quietly to the hearth and picking up the gin bottle thrust it at the woman.

'Out!' he rapped, jerking his head towards the door. 'Out, you dirty old rag-bag and take your bottle with you!'

His face glowered scarlet with rage.

' . . . And if I catch you again at a child-bed,' he yelled after the retreating figure, 'I'll fling you into the Mersey!'

Shaking his head he turned to Sarah.

'That's not enough water. Can you get more?'

'I'll try,' she replied doubtfully from the doorway, 'but have a look at Mrs Haggarty. I'm afraid for her,' she added, her voice low.

Patrick took off his coat then bent over the frightened woman who lay paralysed with pain on the rickety bed.

Taking her hand he said gently, 'Hullo, Mrs Haggarty. I've come to help you. Everything will be all right, now.'

'Doctor Adam?' The tired eyes registered apprehension. 'Where's Doctor Adam?'

'Doctor Adam has a sickness, ma'am, but Miss Rigby and I will take good care of you. I'm Doctor Norris,' he smiled.

The woman's reply was lost in a cry of pain. For a moment her body jerked and writhed then, gasping for breath she whispered, 'I'm terrible afeard, sir. You'll not let me die? For the sake of the bairns . . .?'

Patrick squeezed her hand reassuringly.

'If I do, Mrs Haggarty, you'll be the first mother I've lost on the child-bed.'

He smiled gently into her terror-filled eyes.

'Trust me?' he urged.

He looked at her frail, ugly body and cheeks sunken in a face made old before its time.

By God, he vowed, you shall *not* die, you poor creature.

He took a long sobering breath. He had never needed the Almighty's help more than he was going to need it now for Adam had been right, Patrick realized. Only a small miracle was going to save Margaret-Mary and her unborn child.

He tried to smile courage into her heart, to will his strength into her, to urge her to fight.

'All right, Mrs Haggarty?' he whispered. 'You and me together – we'll manage, eh?'

Sarah moved aside the pan and set the half-filled bucket precariously to boil.

'I couldn't get much water,' she apologized, 'there was barely a trickle from the tap but it'll do to be going on with.'

There had been three women waiting at the stand-tap but they'd gladly given her precedence.

'Here ye are, Miss Sarah.'

The precious liquid had been tipped into her bucket.

'Take my water, and welcome to it.'

'Bless you,' Sarah had whispered, grateful to be spared the agonizing wait.

Hell! she thought. This town is a small hell! No water, no food – no hope. It is a place to be endured for only as long as it takes a body to find the means to get out of it!

Where would it all end? she thought as she opened the laying-in bag.

She took out aprons for herself and Patrick then threw twinning-string and scissors into the pan of hot water.

'And please God we'll need them,' she prayed silently walking to Patrick's side.

'How is she?'

'The child should have been born hours ago,' his voice was low. 'Did you pack the instruments?'

Sarah shook her head.

'We have none.'

'No instruments? But the woman needs help! She is spent and her heart is . . .'

Patrick shrugged. He might have known it. He thought fleetingly of London and the women who were confined in comparative comfort and complete safety; women who could be helped through their pains with chloroform.

But this was Cable Street and there was nothing at all with which to help Margaret-Mary Haggarty. Why, oh why, he fumed, had he left his own bag in Harley Street? But then, he'd been going on holiday, hadn't he?

How on earth he wondered, did Adam achieve so much with so little to help him? Now, if something were not done quickly the patient would indeed die. It was as desperate as that.

Patrick spun round as a knocking on the outer door interrupted his angry thoughts.

'Here's another bucket of water for ye, Miss Sarah,' a voice whispered. 'And how is the poor woman doin'?'

'I hope she will be all right,' Sarah replied quietly. 'Doctor Norris will do all he possibly can.'

'Ah, but 'twould be a mercy if the good Lord took her so it would, for what's to become of her with Haggarty not cold in his grave?'

'Haggarty dead?' Sarah gasped.

'Did ye not know then, Miss Rigby? Got himself into a drunken fight on the quayside. Fished him out of George's Basin they did, four days back and the shock of it all starts Margaret-Mary in labour three weeks before her time!'

Sarah closed her eyes wearily, unable to trust herself to speak.

'Well, miss, there's one thing to be thankful for,' the woman continued. 'If Mistress Haggarty comes out of this with her life at least 'tis the last time she'll have to endure the child-bed! Haggarty was a lustful man when the drink was on him, God rest his drunken soul!'

Sarah was grateful for the water but she was impatient to be away.

'Thank you, ma'am, for your kindness,' she whispered, still shocked by the awful news.

'I'll fetch ye more, miss, if they don't turn the water off again!'

'Bless you,' Sarah smiled, quietly closing the door behind her.

She turned to Patrick.

'Did you hear that?'

'I did!'

Grimly he nodded his head.

By God, but the poor woman should not die! He took a deep breath, cold and calm again.

Desperate straits needed desperate measures, didn't they?

Squaring his shoulders he walked back to the bedside.

'Mrs Haggarty?'

Wearily the head turned on the pillow and fear-filled eyes looked pleadingly into Patrick's.

He closed his eyes briefly, flinching inwardly as he hit her. He felt his knuckles rasp against the defenceless chin and for an instant he wanted to vomit.

'Patrick!'

Sarah flung herself to his side, eyes wide with horror.

Dropping on her knees at the bed-side she looked up at him as if he had lost all reason.

'For pity's sake are you mad? You've knocked her senseless!'

Patrick grasped Sarah's shoulders, pulling her to her feet, shaking her roughly.

'Listen to me . . .'

He forced her to meet his eyes.

'You're right; she's unconscious and we've got just about three minutes before she comes round. Now, go to the other side of the bed and do exactly as I tell you!'

Suddenly Sarah felt calm, every vestige of tension gone. It seemed as if Patrick's personality had taken over completely, exuding confidence, silently urging her to have faith, to trust him.

'Take her legs,' he said quietly. 'Bend them towards the abdomen and press gently . . . gently . . .'

Sarah did as she was told, watching fascinated the probing fingers and hands that skilfully eased and manipulated.

She heard a muttered '*Good!*' and saw with relief that the tiny head was already supported on Patrick's hand.

For a moment it seemed that the whole of the world held its breath then unbelievably the child lay on the bed.

Briefly Sarah felt a surge of joy, searching with her eyes for Patrick's so that they might share his triumph.

But there was no elation in Patrick's face for the baby's body, Sarah realized, bore an unhealthy grey pallor and its limbs were limp and unmoving.

'String!' Patrick rapped. 'Two pieces – and scissors!'

Deftly he separated the child from its mother then held the prostrate little form aloft.

From the set of Patrick's face, Sarah knew that all was not well. Beseechingly her eyes met his, begging him silently to tell her that her fears were unfounded.

'I don't know,' he answered her unspoken question. 'The infant is in deep shock. The umbilical cord was wrapped round its neck . . .'

Gently he inserted a finger into the little mouth, hooking out mucus.

'I can't get a heart-beat or a pulse,' he muttered half to himself as he slapped the baby's back.

From the bed came a low moan as Mrs Haggarty struggled out of the blackness that had been her salvation.

'Lie still, Mrs Haggarty,' Patrick ordered sitting on the edge of the bed, suspending the child head downwards over his knee.

Gently, expertly, he began to massage the cold little back, helping and willing the lungs to start their breathing, urging as he did so the still and unresponding heart to beat.

For a while there was silence in the hot room, a quiet that seemed to scream out with tension and despair.

Patrick closed his eyes.

He is praying, thought Sarah, and it is all we can do, now.

Please God, she joined her unspoken entreaties to his, *let this little babe live?*

Desperately she watched, unwilling to lift her eyes from Patrick's hands.

Please, oh please try! she willed her strength into the inert little form. She couldn't bear it now if the child died. Not after Margaret-Mary had suffered so much; not after Patrick had worked so hard, so very skilfully.

She heard a small choking cough and Patrick's eyes jerked upwards to hers, his hands redoubling their efforts.

Then there was a cry, weak but unmistakable and Patrick felt a movement beneath his hands.

With a shout he grasped the little ankles, holding the child aloft again, slapping its back, its buttocks and its legs.

'Come on then, little one,' he coaxed. 'Try . . .'

The limp arms stiffened then flailed the air; the back arched protestingly, relaxed then arched again. The child spluttered and coughed, then gasping the life-giving air into its lungs, angrily bawled itself into life.

Patrick threw back his head and laughed out loud.

'Mistress Haggarty,' he cried triumphantly, 'you have a fine boy!'

Then he handed the child to Sarah and stood gravely looking down at the woman.

She grasped his hand in hers.

'I'm alive?' she whispered, tears spilling from her eyes. 'It's all over?'

Patrick nodded, smoothing the damp hair from her brow with gentle hands.

'I'm sorry I had to hit you.'

Expertly he ran his fingers over her jaw. 'We had so little time – I had to do it. Believe me, ma'am, there was no other way.'

Margaret-Mary smiled through her tears.

'God love ye, doctor, it's not the first time I've had a fist in me face,' she whispered, 'and never before in such a good cause; never at all . . .'

She took his hand and laid it to her cheek.

'Bless you,' she said simply then held out her arms for her son.

Slowly Sarah and Patrick walked home to Abercromby Square.

Patrick's body ached with fatigue. His shirt clung damply to his back, his coat hung carelessly over his arm and he had no idea what had become of his silk cravat. The elegant doctor from Harley Street looked more like a man toiling home after a hard day's labour but he was smiling.

'Imagine,' he said with undisguised pride, 'Mrs Haggarty calling the baby after me?'

Shyly she had asked his name.

'Patrick, is it? And 'tis a good Irish name. I'll be calling this bairn for you then, sir, for don't we both owe our lives to you?'

'Patrick Haggarty,' he grinned down at Sarah. 'It sounds good, eh?'

Then suddenly he was serious.

'I had to do it – hit Mrs Haggarty, I mean. That poor face will be black and blue before long!'

'You had no choice,' Sarah comforted 'and I think it hurt you more than it hurt Margaret-Mary.'

'I could have broken her jaw, though,' Patrick insisted ruefully.

'You could have but you didn't,' Sarah insisted. 'Forget it. The end justified the means and anyway, think how pleased Adam will be when we tell him the news.'

Then she frowned.

'Though what will become of them all now with Haggarty dead, God only knows.'

'Will she not go back to her own people in Ireland?'

'Ireland!' Sarah retorted bitterly. 'She can just as easily starve here! No,' she shrugged, 'it will be either the streets or the workhouse. Like as not it'll be the workhouse. Margaret-Mary isn't one to take to prostitution.'

Patrick noticed that Sarah's face was unbelievably sad as she spoke and he knew what she was thinking.

Against all odds he had snatched a mother and her baby from almost certain death. He had felt proud when she whispered, 'You've saved us both'.

But for what he wondered grimly as he walked up the steps of the house in Abercromby Square, had he saved them?

'I'll go and tell Adam,' Sarah called as she hurried up the staircase.

Patrick nodded briefly to the men and women who waited patiently on the benches ranged round the hall.

He had hardly taken his seat behind Adam's desk when there was a loud and urgent knocking on the door.

'I'll be seeing Doctor Adam, for it's life and death, so it is!' demanded a woman's strident voice.

Patrick rose to his feet.

'What is it? What is wrong?'

'It's Doctor Adam I'm wanting, sir. Would you be telling me where I can find him, for this poor old body here . . .'

She indicated the small, frail woman who lolled, eyes closed, on the bench.

' . . . she's powerful sick. How I got her here I'll never know for if you ask me she's dying on her feet!'

Patrick's eyes opened wide with horror. For a moment he was incapable of speech. Then he heard his voice, strange and far away, '*Aunt Hetty!*'

Desperately he scooped the pathetic form into his arms, his heart hammering loudly in his ears.

Aunt Hetty *dying*? he thought, wildly.

'Sarah!' he called as he ran towards the stairs. 'Sarah! Where are you?'

Her name had come easily to his lips but he did not notice it.

Five

Sarah ran along the landing; she had heard the brief commotion and sensed the urgency in Patrick's voice. Now, a glance at his face confirmed her fears.

'Miss Hetty!'

She looked at the frail old woman whose grey head rested beneath Patrick's chin.

'Patrick, what is the matter?'

'I don't know,' he panted, half turning towards the woman who had brought his aunt to *The Haven* and who now followed closely on his heels.

'Why did you bring her here?' he demanded, furiously. 'This place is a charity, for the *poor*!'

'And where else would I take her and what is she but poor?' the woman retorted.

Sarah held open the door of her own room.

'In here. Put her in my bed.'

Quietly and efficiently, as if it were an everyday occurrence, Sarah turned down the bed-clothes and Patrick was grateful that there was no accusation in her eyes, no triumphant condemnation.

He stood by silently as she gently removed his aunt's boots and unfastened the buttons of her blouse.

'What is the matter with Miss Norris do you think?'

Sarah turned to quietly ask the woman who hesitated

in the doorway still, anxious and curious. 'Why did you bring her here?'

'Who else would have taken her in will you tell me?' the woman asked, her face sullen. 'It was either *The Haven* or the workhouse!'

'What do you mean?' Patrick rasped, his fingers searching for the pulse-beat at the old woman's wrist. 'What do you mean, ma'am – the *workhouse*?'

Hostile now, the woman fixed Patrick with a long, cold stare.

'Have ye not heard of the place, my pretty?' she mocked. 'It's a house of charity where they take you when there's nowhere else for you to starve!'

'Starve?' Patrick jerked.

'Aye *starve*. Maybe you'll not know the meaning of the word but when an old woman goes without food she gets hungry and what with all the washing and Black Becky's tallyman . . .'

'See now, mistress.'

Gently Sarah took the woman's arm.

'I am very grateful for your kindness, but could you come downstairs with me? You can tell me all about it whilst the doctor sees to Miss Norris, can't you? I'd be very glad if you would,' she coaxed.

Patrick breathed heavily, fighting to control his anger, grateful for Sarah's intervention.

'Aunt Hetty?' he whispered, when they were alone. 'It's all right now. I'll take care of you.'

Desperately he rubbed the work-worn old hands.

Starving? His mind was bemused. Aunt Hetty paying money to the tallyman? It couldn't be true?

But a mere glance at the ashen face, the sunken cheeks and the thin, gaunt body told him his fears were stark reality.

With relief he saw a flickering of her eyelids and for an instant the old eyes gazed upwards then closed again as if they were unwilling to look on the bleak, uncaring world.

'Aunt Hetty?'

Patrick felt frail nervous fingers groping for his.

'Is it you, boy?'

'Yes, Aunt. Don't worry. You'll be all right, now.'

He lifted her gnarled hand, his fingertips searching again for a pulse-beat. It shocked him to find it was so very weak and irregular.

'What on earth have you been up to?' he asked, indulgently, his lips close to her ear. 'Is it true you've been neglecting yourself – not eating properly?'

'An old body like mine doesn't need so much inside it . . .'

Her voice trailed off into a tired whisper.

Guiltily Patrick remembered that not so very long ago his aunt had said those same words. She had said them as she sat at the table watching him eat. She gave me her supper, he thought, with a dull flush of shame. The plate of brawn, he remembered, that he'd forced himself to eat had probably represented the whole of her food for the day.

'If I can rest for a while I'd be grateful. It's the heat, you see . . .'

'You will rest until you are well, Aunt Hetty', Patrick asserted, firmly.

For an instant the ghost of the woman she had once been wraithed across Hetty Norris's face and she opened her mouth as if to protest.

But she did not. Nodding her head she said resignedly, 'Yes, I think I would like that.'

It was becoming obvious to Patrick that most probably there was little wrong with his aunt that bed-rest and good food would not eventually cure but his anxiety could still not be disguised as he asked, 'Do you think you could try to eat a little?'

'Yes, boy, just a little . . . I'll try . . .'

'I won't be long.'

Patrick walked towards the door.

'Now stay there, Aunt Hetty . . .'

He hesitated, his hand on the door-latch, fearful lest when he returned she would have vanished.

Hetty Norris smiled.

'I will, Patrick, I will.'

Gulping a deep breath of relief into his lungs, Patrick gently closed the door then hurried once more in search of Sarah.

'How could I have been so blind?' Patrick whispered, 'so inexcusably stupid?'

Sarah was in the kitchen, heating a pan of milk.

'How is your aunt?'

'Oh, I don't know what to think.'

Patrick shook his head wearily. 'I can't bring myself to believe what my own common sense tells me is true. How could she have got so ill? Why didn't I notice it the other day, Sarah? What was I about?'

He sat down on a hard wooden chair then jumped to his feet again, pacing the floor as he spoke.

'I mean, I had no idea – and there's the tally-man . . .'

He shook his head.

'How could she have got herself into Rebecca Solomon's clutches?'

'I don't know, Patrick. I can only tell you what her neighbour told me. It seems your aunt is deeply in debt and has to take in washing to keep up the payments. It's a terrible thing, but when Black Becky's tallyman gets a hold, a body might as well give up!'

'But why didn't she let me know? Do you think I'd have seen her in want?'

Sarah did not reply and Patrick had the grace to feel shame for his letters to his aunt had been few and far between, of late. And he should have known, he thought in savage self-condemnation, that those of Hetty Norris's breed didn't whine. Hetty Norris and those like her were a proud lot.

But for all that, Patrick conceded, his aunt was in need of nursing, now.

'Look, Sarah,' he hesitated, 'I'd be grateful if Aunt Norris could stay here for just a few days until I can sort things out.'

Sarah smiled.

'Of course she can stay. She must stay until she is well and strong again. Don't worry, we'll take care of her.'

Patrick stammered his thanks.

'And do you think you could find something for her to eat? A little beef-tea or some calves-foot jelly, perhaps? Something light and nourishing?'

Sarah shook her head.

'I'm sorry, Patrick, but we have neither of those things. I thought perhaps some bread and milk –'

She nodded towards the pan.

'You have nothing more suitable?'

'No, nothing at all. Tomorrow, perhaps . . .'

'But is there no meat at all in the house? Some of the beef stew we ate at dinner would be adequate?'

'It is all gone. Oh, we did have a little meat but we gave it to Adam because he is sick and to you, because you are a guest,' Sarah acknowledged, lamely.

'But what do *you* eat, then?'

'Oh, we manage. Some of our patients pay in kind, if they can. We eat well when the butcher's rheumatism bothers him,' she smiled impishly, 'or the flour-miller's gout plays him up. And there's a farmer who pays his bill in milk and eggs!'

'But is there nothing at the moment for my aunt, other than bread and milk?'

'I'm sorry, Patrick,' she shook her head, sadly. 'But tomorrow we may be lucky. Perhaps someone, somewhere, will give us something. I hope so, for the ward is full.'

Patrick's face flushed a deep and angry red.

'I'm going out for a while,' he jerked, tersely.

'But Patrick, your aunt,' Sarah stammered.

'Take her the bread and milk and stay with her, will you? I'll not be long!'

Angrily he brushed past her, his eyes downcast. How could he have been so stupid and selfish and utterly uncaring, he wondered, slamming the front door behind him.

Sarah's words spun giddily in his brain.

' . . . *once the tallyman gets a hold . . . only bread and milk – maybe tomorrow . . .*'

Tomorrow. Elusive tomorrow! Well, perhaps now, just for once he thought, he could do something *today*; something that might help even the score!

Still trembling with anger, with shock and shame, he strode purposefully towards Lord Street and Mr Gaunt's select emporium. And when, his conscience sitting a little easier within him he left the shop and set out for *The Haven* again, his thoughts were even yet in a turmoil of uncertainty and muddle.

He had always wanted to become a doctor, he mused, and a good doctor into the bargain. One day, he had vowed, he would take his place amongst the London physicians and surgeons, learned and respected as they were. And he had reached London far more easily than he could have hoped, for it had been offered to him on a plate.

Less than a month after facing a London Board of Examiners he had returned to the city of his ambitions, assistant to the famous Doctor Harrington and a whole new world of medicine within his grasp. He had achieved all that yet had failed to recognize that his own aunt was under-nourished, to say the least!

Shamefully he wrenched his thoughts away from the frail little body of Hetty Norris.

If only one small part of the resources of the London practice were available at Abercromby Square, he thought; if there had been even the barest of necessities at his command, the Haggarty baby need not have come into the world in so dramatic a way and at so terrible a risk.

Patrick thought again of Sarah, wondering how often she needed to go hungry.

Sarah had been magnificent; he couldn't have managed at Mrs Haggarty's without her help. Perhaps he had been wrong about her, he thought. Maybe she *was* one of the rare ones – a truly dedicated woman. Almost certainly she was, or why did she put up with the intolerable conditions that existed at *The Haven*? Could it be that she and Adam . . .?

He tried to wrest his thoughts away from what did not concern him but it was difficult not to think of Adam and his struggle against poverty and sickness and greed.

Adam had no well-stocked dispensary. His patients could not afford to pay large fees. Some of them could not pay at all . . .

Adam Carmichael made the best of the little he had and gave of himself in unstinted measure. He was a doctor against all odds and in the truest sense of the word.

Adam was also a very sick man. He needed rest, freedom from worry and above all he needed good, nourishing food.

'. . . *maybe tomorrow* . . .'

No, not tomorrow, Patrick insisted, quickening his steps into Abercromby Square. For just this one time, they would have food today!

'A sixpenny-piece for you lad,' he'd said to the boy with the handcart, 'if you can get this load delivered to number 13, Abercromby Square in five minutes time!'

The boy had earned his sixpence, Patrick exulted for Molly's excited voice could be heard exclaiming, 'Why, Miss Sarah, it's a miracle! Will ye look at that great pile? A sack of flour, eggs, bacon . . .'

'Tea, sugar, mutton, sausages . . .!' Sarah took up the chant.

'Potatoes, butter, oatmeal – oh, miss, there must be a catch in it. It's all a mistake – it must be?'

'No mistake,' Patrick said quietly from the doorway.

Sarah spun round, her eyes shining, her cheeks flushed.

'You, Patrick? You've paid for all this food? But why? *Why*?'

Her eyes danced with happiness.

'Because there was nothing in the larder,' Patrick shrugged, 'because Aunt Hetty is hungry and Adam is sick.'

He smiled into Sarah's eyes.

'See they are both well-fed, will you? See that all of them are!'

Then abruptly, as if ashamed of his generosity, he strode towards the door.

'I'll take another look at Adam then I'll be with Aunt Hetty if I'm wanted,' he said, tersely.

Without a backward glance, he left them.

Doctor Robert Harrington ate his roast beef with obvious enjoyment but his daughter toyed petulantly with the food on her plate.

'But, Papa,' she pouted, 'Patrick *promised*. He promised to join us within three days at the most. He should have been here, by now!'

'Three days, four days – what does it matter, Arabella?'

'It matters to *me*, Papa. It matters a great deal to me. I am bored. I am quite, quite bored!'

She waved away the waiter who removed her plate and offered strawberries and thick, whipped cream.

'I am becoming tired also of visiting the Pump Room and drinking that evil-tasting water!'

'That evil-tasting water, missy, is extremely beneficial. I am sorry you are bored and I am not a little hurt that you are not grateful for my concern for your health.'

There were times, sighed Doctor Harrington inwardly, when he found his daughter's behaviour a little trying.

True, there was no one to blame, he supposed but himself. He had spoiled her outrageously. His dear wife had never recovered from the child-bed and Arabella had been all that was left to him to lavish his riches and affection upon.

He had been pleased when young Patrick had haltingly asked for his daughter's hand in marriage. Patrick was a good doctor; he had indeed the makings of a brilliant physician. Robert Harrington had been glad to give the safekeeping of Arabella's future to so worthy a man.

But were they really suited, he pondered.

That Patrick was fond of Arabella Doctor Harrington did not doubt, but was Arabella ready for marriage to *any* man?

All her life she had been sheltered and indulged. Without so much as a thought she could spend on one gown what would have fed a family for a whole week.

Had he, wondered Robert Harrington, been too kind, tried too hard to make recompense to Arabella for the loss of her dear mama?

'You are not listening to me, Papa. You do not care that I am unhappy and pining away for Patrick.'

'Dearest child, Patrick will have good reason for his prolonged stay in Liverpool. He wished to see his aunt, remember, and no doubt he will have friends to visit. Be patient, little dove. Patrick will come soon.'

'I cannot be patient, Papa. My patience has become exhausted!'

Arabella's bottom lip trembled dangerously. She reminded him, thought her father, of a child who agitated for a toy, thinking she had only to snap her fingers and it would be hers. Arabella knew nothing of pain or suffering and the world outside her. She was like a small nestling, ever demanding food and it was he, her own father, who must accept the blame.

He had given in to her every whim and unless something were done about it and soon, there would be nothing but unhappiness ahead for Arabella. Patrick, decided Doctor Harrington, would not countenance such behaviour for long after they were married.

If only, he thought, he could find the moral courage to give his fledgling a push. Hadn't she been sheltered too long in the nest of love and indulgence he had so foolishly built around her?

Glancing up he saw that tears were imminent and knew at all costs he must avoid another of Arabella's tantrums in the crowded dining-room of the hotel.

'Well, little love,' he said with forced jocularity, 'if Doctor Norris will not come to Miss Arabella then Arabella must go to her beloved!'

Arabella blinked her tears away with a start. Surely Papa could not be serious?

How could she go to Patrick? It was not possible for her to travel without a chaperon to Liverpool and it would not be proper for a young lady to run after a gentleman, even accepting that gentleman was her bethrothed. Papa was teasing her again. He was humouring her as if she were a child and she *wasn't* a child. She was nearly nineteen and soon she would be a married lady.

Angry now, Arabella dropped her eyes to the table. If only her father would treat her as an adult, she wished. If only she could convince him she was no longer his little girl; that she had a mind and a heart and a will of her own.

If Patrick would not come to her?

Deliberately she folded her napkin.

'May I be excused, Papa?' she asked and walked purposefully from the room.

Robert Harrington gazed with affection at his daughter's retreating back.

Poor little Arabella, he thought. It had been wrong of him to say such a thing, even in jest, but at least Arabella had sufficient good sense to know he had only been teasing. And it had at least had the effect of drying her tears, of avoiding a most unpleasant scene . . .

He sighed. He would give her time to compose herself and when he had finished his meal and sipped a glass of port, Arabella would be her usual sweet self again and they would be the best of friends once more.

Smiling indulgently, Doctor Robert Harrington reached for the decanter.

Patrick tapped out his pipe on the heel of his boot, reluctant to return to the house but knowing he must.

He looked across the unkempt garden to where honeysuckle twined itself round a marble figure, where tufts of weeds choked once immaculate paths and roses ran a sweet riot of neglect.

Where was he now, thought Patrick, that benevolent owner to whom the rent of this great house meant so very little?

His gaze travelled beyond the decaying summerhouse to where Dicky-Sam had planted cabbages and potatoes.

How did a one-legged man manage to till a garden? What a painstaking labour of love the vegetable plot must be.

Patrick's mouth quirked into a smile. What a grand little character the ex-seaman was. Only that morning he had sidled into *The Haven* kitchens, his pockets stuffed with large green apples. He had found them by the canal basin. They had fallen, he explained, his face wreathed in innocence, from the back of a farmer's cart!

And Milly had called him a thievin' wee divil and promptly sprinkled the apples with sugar and popped them into the fire-oven to bake, thanking the good Lord for his providence as she did so and asking a pardon whilst she was about it for Dicky-Sam Pickstock and his itching fingers!

What a strange pair they made, Patrick mused; how great their simple hearts.

A soft footfall caused him to turn and Sarah stood beside him.

'I thought I might find you here,' she said quietly, sitting without ceremony on the stone steps at his feet. 'I often steal a few minutes in the garden at nightfall.'

She had been washing her hair and it hung loose and damp, almost to her waist.

Patrick had never seen her with her hair free for she always wore it in a severe utilitarian bun in the nape of her neck.

Glancing down he saw that the top buttons of her dark blouse were unfastened and with a surge of delight wondered why he had never before noticed the vulnerable curve of her slender neck.

Now, as she softly towelled the ends of her hair the gathering twilight gentled the care from her face and Patrick realized for the first time the serenity of her beauty.

For a moment he stood enchanted, a small pulse beating at his throat whilst the scent of honeysuckle drifted over them.

There was so much he wanted to say to her in this moment of tranquillity. He wanted to thank her for her help and support when he had been almost sick with worry at the Haggarty house; he wanted to thank her for taking in Aunt Hetty and for not censuring him for his callous neglect; he wanted to tell her of the turmoil that raged inside him, demanding that he choose between love and duty. Love for his aunt and Adam; duty to his employer and Arabella.

But he could not discuss Arabella with Sarah. It would be disloyal and he knew in his heart that he did not want to. He did not want to break their private little peace. He wanted to remember always the utter stillness that heralded the July night; a stillness so complete that he felt he could reach out with his hand and touch it as it folded itself like deep blue velvet over the harshness of the town. He wanted to keep in his heart for all time the earthy smell of grass touched briefly with evening dew, of honeysuckle scent mingling with the perfume of damask roses and of a woman who sat at his feet with newly-washed hair.

But Patrick's small moment of enchantment was not to last for Dicky-Sam's urgent call shattered the peace of the garden.

'Miss Sarah? Doctor Patrick? Be anybody there?'

'Here, Dicky,' called Sarah.

The little man tip-tapped down the path.

'Somebody'll have to go quick to Leather Lane, miss! Terrible carnage, there's been!'

'A fight?'

'Aye. Started over a street woman. Some seamen from the *Cornucopia*, so I heard tell.'

Patrick heard the quick hiss of Sarah's indrawn breath.

'Where is it?' he asked.

'The Compass, sir, and a right brothel of a place it is, begging your pardon, Miss Sarah!'

Sarah rose to her feet. 'Is it bad, then?'

'It is an' all! They've wrecked the tap-room. Whole thing seems to have got out of hand.'

'Right. I'll go!'

Even as he spoke, Patrick was making for the house.

'Wait for me! I'll come with you.'

'No, Sarah!' Patrick spun round in his tracks. 'It's no fit place for a woman. Stay and keep an eye on Aunt Hetty and Adam. And send the patients away unless there's something really urgent. Ask them to come back in the morning.'

Dicky-Sam limped out of the surgery holding Adam's bag in his hand.

'I'll follow behind, sir, if you don't mind. Can't keep up along o' you with me old peg-leg.'

'Thanks, Dicky.'

Patrick took the bag, his face grim.

Running into the square, trying to recall the alleys and short-cuts that would take him towards the river-front he saw a cab slowly clip-clopping its way across Oxford Street.

Thankfully Patrick hailed the driver.

'Leather Lane,' he called, 'and quick as you can make it!'

He leaned back against the soft upholstery, the smell of leather and saddle-soap strangely comforting. He closed his eyes. He had not realized how utterly spent he was.

How, he wondered wearily did Sarah and Adam endure it, day after day, after day . . .

Six

It wasn't hard to find the Compass tavern for the brawl had spilled out into the gutters.

Running up the narrow alley Patrick sidestepped the heaving mass of cursing, sweating bodies and made for the low doorway of the inn.

From nowhere it seemed, an arm shot out level with his eyes, blocking his way.

'Let me in!' he demanded looking up into the pock-marked face of a giant of a man. 'Let me pass; I'm a doctor.'

'Git!'

Tersely the man stabbed a thumb in the direction of the bottom of Leather Lane.

'We wants no doctors, 'ere!'

'I was sent for – someone is hurt! Will you please let me in?'

''Arry!' His eyes did not leave Patrick's face for an instant, 'There's a toff 'ere says he's a doctor!'

'Who is he?'

'Wot's yer name, me pretty?'

'Norris. I'm Doctor Norris.'

'Say's he called Norris,' called the ugly one.

'Never 'eard of 'im. Tell 'im to scarper!'

'You 'eard 'im, *doctor*. 'Arry don't know yer.'

The evil-looking face thrust itself dangerously close to Patrick's.

'So sling yer hook afore someone treads on yer toes!'

The small huddle of children that looked up at Patrick found him infinitely more interesting than the fight they had been watching, sensing his strangeness, wondering at the fine cut of his clothes. Then, as if some inbred gutter-instinct told them he was not of their breed, they simultaneously linked hands and ringed him round, prancing on dirty unshod feet, eager to join the ugly one in the baiting of the stranger who dared thrust himself into a private fight.

'*Cor, luk at 'him, luk at him,*
Chuck a bit o' muck at him!'

This is madness! thought Patrick wildly.

'Will you let me in, man?' he called, vainly trying to break the barrier of tightly-clasped hands.

'*Oh, luk at him . . .!*'

The derisive chant rose higher and louder.

'No, me fine cock-bird. You stay where you be an' play ring-o'-roses wi' the bairns,' he grinned, 'and keep yer nose out of what don't concern ye!'

Damn them then!

Patrick wrenched himself free of the chanting prancing urchins. They could batter each other to death for all he cared. Grimly, he hoped they would.

He spung round angrily and almost knocked Sarah Rigby to the ground.

Purposefully she walked up to the belligerent doorkeeper, pushing him aside with a sweep of her arm.

'Out of my way, Knocker White,' she demanded, her voice dangerously low, 'and get those children out of the alley before they get hurt!'

'Yes, miss!'

Obediently the man stepped aside to admit her then

the familiar fist shot out again and Patrick found his way blocked once more.

'This feller says he's a doctor, Miss Sarah.'

'That's right – let him in,' Sarah commanded. 'He's with me.'

The man stood aside.

'Sorry, me old mucker!'

He grinned sheepishly.

'Got to be careful, ye' see – there's some funny folks about, these days . . .'

Patrick ducked his head and entered the tap-room, an unaccustomed hurt pulsing inside him.

They hadn't wanted him! He had been reared in Lace Street but he wasn't one of them any more. He'd seen more street fights than Knocker White had had hot dinners, he thought grimly, yet for two pins they'd have spat in his face and sent him on his way again.

They were his own people and they didn't own him! It had needed the quiet authority of a slip of a woman they knew and trusted to provide his passport into the Compass tavern in Leather Lane.

He blinked his eyes through the haze of choking paraffin smoke. His breath hissed sharply between his teeth as he became aware of the devastation within and, pain and anger forgotten, he groped his way across the room to where Sarah stood.

If only he were not so very tired and confused . . .

The Irish immigrants had scrambled thankfully on deck to take their first look at Liverpool. They had blessed themselves and thanked the Almighty and Saint Christopher for a safe passage and for the tall beacon on

Everton Heights that beckoned them into the safety of the river.

But those who stood at the ship's rail were the lucky ones for there were many among their number who were ill and vomiting and none of the *Cornucopia's* passengers had been sorry to leave the creaking wooden ship and set their feet on dry land again.

Most of them had sailed from Dublin to Dumfries then south to Liverpool, spending three days and nights herded into the ship's hold, tight-packed and little better than ballast.

The *Cornucopia* had ridden low in the water and the voyage had not been a comfortable one. Those who were not ill stretched their cramped limbs thankfully. Some made off quickly to find relatives with whom they might stay; others lingered by the quayside, uncertain and apprehensive.

Already most of the crew had disappeared into the tangle of dockside alleys before their womenfolk could catch up with them and their pay, each man in search of his own particular delight.

But those who were ill cared little for anything save that they had arrived at last and it was those sick who found their way to the house in Abercromby Square and patiently waited for the help they had been told would not be refused.

'It's a long time ye'll be sitting there,' Molly O'Keefe told them, 'for the doctor is away to a fight and heaven only knows when he'll be back to see to ye!'

But they waited for all that because there was nothing else for them to do and nowhere for them to go.

'Sir, I sent the patients away,' Molly protested hotly to Adam, 'but a fresh lot has just come and and they'll not budge. Just sitting there they are, staring at nothing and saying nothing. Strangers they are to me. I'm thinking they're new in from the old country, God help the poor creatures,' she sighed.

'I'll get up, Molly, and see what I can do,' Adam tried to reassure her. 'They may only be trying to find a bed for the night and think that perhaps they can get one here.'

'Well they can't and that's for sure, Doctor Adam. Glory be, we're bustin' at the seams already!'

'I know, Molly, I know,' Adam smiled gently, 'but if there are any sick amongst them, perhaps I can help. I must not stay in bed any longer. Already Sarah and Patrick are strained to the utmost. At least I can attend to the sick.'

And not all Molly's pleading had been able to deter Adam Carmichael as unsteadily he walked down the stairs.

The sick from the *Cornucopia*, when he saw them, complained to Adam of stomach pains and vomiting and there seemed little that he could do for them but administer a dose of mixture.

Conditions on the immigrant ships were near intolerable, he knew. In all probability the sickness would clear up when they had adjusted to dry land again.

He was relieved when the last of them left for he had not thought he could become so weak and the exertion of leaving his bed had brought on spasms of coughing once more.

'Is that them all gone then, Doctor?'

Molly set bread and a bowl of soup on Adam's desk. 'Now drink it all up and then be back to bed with ye. What Miss Sarah is going to say when she gets back, I'd not like to think about!'

Adam smiled his thanks.

'Do you think we need to mention it to Sarah?'

'Maybe not, doctor, for won't herself be sure to find out anyway? 'Tis no use telling lies,' she sighed. 'So drink up your broth, doctor darling, and be away to your bed again,' she urged, "tis yourself that's in need of a physician, and that's for sure . . .'

Patrick Norris coughed in the choking fumes that hung heavy on the air in the Compass tavern. The oil lamp had been knocked over in the brawl and the rug that had been hastily thrown over it still smouldered and smoked.

'Open the window,' Patrick commanded the man at the door who seemed now to have accepted the stranger in their midst, 'and don't let anyone in here!'

But there was little fear of further intrusion. The men who fought in the alley would continue their sport until the children who kept watch at either end of the narrow way yelled 'Peelers!'

But the constable and his assistant – wise men both – would not appear until the rabble had all but exhausted themselves. Those worthy upholders of law and order knew better than risk a cracked head for a mob to whom a street brawl, from whatever cause it had started, was as good as a cock-fight.

Now the small, low-hung room contained only frightened women, some of them crying softly, some of them sitting quietly, stupefied by cheap gin.

The landlord set down candles and nodded towards the corner of the room.

'She's the only one that's hurt real bad,' he said. 'Best see what you can do for she's bleeding something 'orrible.'

A young girl lay on the floor, eyes closed tightly in a paper-white face.

She had been viciously slashed by a bottle or a knife and her injured arm lay awkwardly by her side.

'Quick!' Patrick demanded. 'A tourniquet!'

Deftly Sarah cut a length of bandage, knotting the ends with efficient, steady fingers. She handed it to Patrick with a small piece of wood the size of a lead pencil.

Expertly Patrick twisted the piece of cloth until it bit into the soft flesh of the injured limb.

'Now hold up her arm.'

Sarah took the blood-stained hand, looking down as she did into the bruised and shattered face of the girl.

Patrick wrung out a cloth in a bowl of water, gently cleaning away the marks of brutality.

'Who could do such a thing? She's little more than a child!'

He turned accusingly to the landlord.

'Why did you let her in?'

'Let her in? Lord luv ye, doctor, I can't keep 'em out! And anyway, they're good for trade. If they didn't tout here they'd do it somewhere else.'

'You mean this girl is on the streets?'

'Aye, sir.'

Patrick closed his eyes in disgust. At least, he thought, there appeared to be little damage to her face that time would not heal.

'It's only her arm,' Patrick turned to Sarah, 'but she's lost a great deal of blood and I'll have to stitch. Who is she, do you know?'

Sarah nodded, her face grave.

'She's Kate Tarleton. She comes of respectable folks but all her family died in the '47 epidemic. I suppose she looked after herself the only way she knew how.'

'I see,' Patrick nodded grimly.

His revulsion and disgust were not directed at the poor scrap who lay hurt and bleeding at his feet but at a society that allowed such circumstances to exist.

'There were these seamen came in from the *Cornucopia*, sir,' the landlord explained, anxiously. 'Kate Tarleton had dealings with one of them then there was trouble over money. Well, you know how one thing leads to another? Afore you could say "Wet Nelly" they'd wrecked the place!'

The *Cornucopia*!

Sarah tried to blot the name from her mind. There was the devil's thumb-print on that packet. She brought ill-luck with her every time she sailed into the Mersey.

Cornucopia. Jonah-ship. A packet that had once borne another name.

Sarah heard Dicky-Sam's voice at the doorway. Somehow it helped to pull her thoughts back to reality.

'Hullo, fairy!' chirped the little man as he gazed aloft at Knocker White's great hairy frame. 'You got Miss Sarah and Doctor Norris in there, then?'

'Here we are, Dicky-Sam,' Sarah called. 'Try to get a cab will you? Ask the driver to wait at the bottom of the alley.'

She turned to Patrick.

'We'll have to take Kate home with us,' she said.

'But Sarah, we can't. There's no room!' Patrick protested.

'There'll be room tomorrow. There's one due to leave the ward in the morning.'

Patrick saw the grim set of Sarah's lips. It would be useless to argue with her, he knew.

'We'll manage until then,' she asserted.

She would find a mattress, somewhere. They'd manage.

They always did and anyway she vowed, here was one poor creature who wasn't going back on the streets! If it meant her sleeping on the floor, Sarah asserted silently, Kate Tarleton was going back to *The Haven*.

Sarah smiled as the young girl's eyes flickered open.

'Hullo, Kate,' she said gently. 'Do you know who I am?'

'Aye, miss.'

The soft brown eyes brimmed over with tears.

'You'll not let the constable take me, miss? I'm not bad,' she whispered; 'not real bad. I wouldn't have started on the game if I could've got respectable work.'

'I know, child, I know.'

Sarah took the small thin hand in hers as the injured girl cried out in sudden pain.

'Hold on tight, Kate. The doctor won't be long, now.'

Patrick tied and snipped the last stich then smiled encouragement at Kate Tarleton. Not so very long ago he might not have shown such tolerance towards a street-woman but now he was remembering Aunt Hetty. Perhaps, thought Patrick, if he'd cared a little more his aunt might not be lying sick at *The Haven*.

Maybe, if someone had cared a little about Kate Tarleton, she might not be lying on the floor of the Compass tavern, a woman of the world before she had scarcely had time to be a child.

Sarah was right, thought Patrick. They would have to take Kate back to *The Haven*. She was a pretty child and fair game for the madams who provided young girls for lecherous old men. They would manage, he supposed.

Gently he helped the girl to her feet.

'Come along, little Kate,' he whispered, carefully gathering her into his arms. 'You're coming home with us.'

Sarah lifted her head then smiled tremulously into Patrick's eyes.

In that wordless moment of complete understanding he knew that however awful the day had been, however sickening and frustrating, Sarah's smile had made it all worth while.

Patrick lowered his body into the chair by Adam's bedside feeling that he would never again find the strength to leave it.

'You look utterly beaten, Patrick.'

Grave concern showed on Adam's face. 'Oh, I blame myself. I had no right to lay here while you and Sarah worked yourselves to a standstill.'

Patrick forced a grin to his lips.

'But you've been doing it for years, Adam, and anyway, it was only a fight that started over a prostitute. We brought her back with us. Sarah is settling her down, now.'

The door opened and Molly beamed her way into the room with a tray of tea and thick slices of bread and dripping.

'You'll be needing this I'm thinking, doctor!'

Gratefully Patrick accepted the mug of tea.

'Molly O'Keefe, 'tis an angel ye are!' he smiled.

'Now, there's no need for levity, sir, if you'll pardon me, for it's awful news I've heard from the lamplighter.'

'Bad news?' Patrick enquired, lazily, knowing that whatever it was he was fast learning to take one blow after another.

'Aye, Doctor Patrick. The *Cornucopia* docked on the late tide. There were sick aboard – a lot of them. They say it's the fever. They've brought more cholera into the port.'

Adam's face blanched.

'Is that true, Molly? Are you *sure* it's true?'

'Sure I'm sure,' Molly replied, bitterly, 'and some of the sick here at evening surgery as you well know, sir.'

Patrick felt his stomach do a somersault.

'You took a surgery this evening, Adam?'

Adam nodded reluctantly.

'And were there passengers here from the *Cornucopia*?'

'One or two, perhaps.'

'What were their symptoms?' Patrick demanded. 'Were any of them infected?'

'I think not,' Adam said quietly, willing his voice to be steady. 'I know cholera better than most, Patrick.'

But Adam's heart was thumping uncomfortably. He should have realized, he thought. He, above all, should have known. But he had been so tired; so very tired.

'It will be all right,' he said, softly.

But he was looking at his trembling fingers. Molly had brought him bread and broth when surgery had finished, and he had eaten it without thinking.

He, who should have known better, had not first washed his hands!

He clenched his hands tightly.

'Let it not be true?' he prayed, silently.

But how could he be sure? The symptoms of the *Cornucopia* passengers he had attended might well have been the result of the close-confining of bodies in an airless, crowded hold but they could have foretold something far more sinister.

With a gesture of near-despair Adam ran his fingers through his hair and felt the clammy sweat of fear on his forehead.

Gently Patrick's fingertips touched the pulse at Adam's wrist.

'You are more tired than you will admit. You should not have left your bed. Perhaps now,' he added gravely, 'you will listen to your doctor's advice!'

Adam reached for the comfort of his friend's hand, clasping it tightly with slender, anxious fingers.

'Patrick,' he whispered, 'I didn't want to ask this when Molly was in the room, but could I have been wrong? The symptoms of the sick from the *Cornucopia* – could they have been . . .?'

His voice trailed uneasily away and the dread question was left unspoken.

Patrick's hand tightened reassuringly round Adam's.

'Were you wrong, do you think?'

'I don't know.' Adam's voice betrayed a tremble of fear. 'God help me, I don't know!'

'Then tell me,' Patrick asked gently, 'if Molly hadn't told you that more cholera had come into the port, would you now be doubting your own diagnosis?'

'No,' Adam hesitated. 'No, I don't think I would.'

Patrick rose to his feet.

'Then let's leave it for tonight – sleep on it. We are both tired. Tomorrow it will all seem different, you'll see.'

Patrick smiled down into the pale face, realizing afresh how ill his friend was.

'You are right, Patrick. We are all tired and tomorrow is another day,' Adam smiled gently back. 'I think I would like to sleep, now.'

Patrick picked up the candlestick.

'Then I will wish you goodnight.'

A little of the tension left Adam's face and he lay back on his pillows.

'Goodnight, Patrick, and God bless you for all you are doing for us.'

Patrick nodded his head and then turning abruptly on his heel walked quickly away. He had wanted to find words that would give comfort but suddenly he found he was unable to meet Adam's eyes. It was something he could not explain. He only knew that for an instant he had known a feeling of awful foreboding.

Was it the fault of the flickering candleflame and the long, dark shadows it cast? Perhaps animal fear tingled its way down his spine because he was tired and hot and the smell of the tavern in Leather Lane was still foul in his nostrils.

He shook his head as if to clear it of such morbid thoughts. He was being foolish, afraid that if things got any worse he could no longer cope with the situation. A man felt like that, Patrick reasoned, when every nerve in his body screamed out for sleep.

Wearily he walked towards Hetty Norris's room and gently pushed open the door. He was almost relieved when her gentle breathing told him she was sleeping soundly.

Sarah blinked open her eyes in the unfamiliar room then realized she had spent what was left of the night in the small hot attic. Already the early morning sun was pouring through the fanlight in the ceiling and she knew that today would be no different from the other sultry days that had plagued the town for weeks on end.

She pulled her knees up to her chin and sat for a little while with her arms clasped round them, willing herself to leave her bed, uncomfortable though it was.

Across the room Kate Tarleton slept uneasily, her injured arm lying lightly splinted and awkward on the bed at her side. Her face showed the marks of the previous night's horror in angry bruises and lips that were swollen and distorted.

At least thought Sarah, the girl had youth on her side. Given care, her injuries would leave no scars. But the other kind of wounding, the degradation of the life she had been forced to lead; the loneliness she had known since her family died and the harshness of the world into which she had been thrust, might never heal and could only be eased by time and love.

Sarah lowered her feet to the bare floor, groping with her toes for her slippers.

Quietly and quickly she dressed then walked carefully from the room.

On the half-landing below she paused, remembering that last night she had not called in to see Adam before creeping thankfully into her attic bed.

Now, as she walked into his room, she knew at once that something was wrong.

'What is it?'

Instantly she was at his side.

'Adam, you are not well! Let me call Patrick?'

'No, Sarah.'

Adam shaped his lips into a small smile of reassurance. 'It is all right. I did not sleep, that is all.'

'But you should have asked Patrick for a draught.'

'I did and he gave me one. It didn't work.'

'Why not, Adam? What is worrying you?'

Adam's soft brown eyes clouded over. Anxiously his fingers plucked at the counterpane.

'Tell me about it,' Sarah urged, sensing that something inside him was crying out for help.

For a moment he lay quietly, his eyes closed, a small nerve flicking at the corner of his mouth. Then, as though it were an effort to say it he whispered, 'I think I was wrong about the *Cornucopia* patients. I diagnosed mal-de-mer when I should have known it was cholera.'

Sarah frowned. *The Cornucopia patients?*

Adam saw the doubt on her face.

'Have you spoken with Molly since last night?'

'No,' Sarah shook her head. 'I was on my way downstairs to the kitchen when I decided to look into your room.'

'Then you can't know. Last night, when you and Patrick were at the tavern in Leather Lane, some patients came to *The Haven*. Molly couldn't get them to leave so I attended to them. They were from the *Cornucopia*, Sarah. I thought they were only suffering from a bad dose of sea-sickness – at least until Molly told us there was the fever on the *Cornucopia* – cholera.'

Sarah's mouth went dry.

'And now,' she prompted, her suddenly-stiff lips forcing out the words, 'you think it wasn't sea-sickness? You think it could have been – something else?'

'I *know* it was, Sarah. The stomach cramps, high temperatures and sickness. I should have known!'

'Perhaps you were wrong?'

Adam turned his head and gazed into Sarah's eyes shaking his head wordlessly.

'Tell me what is to be done, Adam.'

The smell of fear was real in Sarah's nostrils but it was not for herself.

Adam had been in contact with cholera and already he was sick and weak.

'Tell me, and I will do as you say.'

Adam was grateful that Sarah did not assail his ears with easy words of comfort.

'First, I must talk to Patrick again. Last night, I thought

I had not made the wrong diagnosis. Now, when I have lain awake thinking about it, I am certain the *Cornucopia* patients who came here had cholera. I must do what I can to contain it within *The Haven* and if the worst doesn't happen then so much the better. But first it must be reported to Doctor Duncan.'

Sarah nodded. 'And then?'

'I must be isolated, Sarah. My food must be left at the door and no one here must come near me.'

'That is nonsense, Adam!' Sarah gasped. 'Do you really think I would agree to that?'

'It is the most sensible thing to do, Sarah, until we are sure I am not infected.'

'How long . . .?'

'Three days,' Adam shrugged. 'Perhaps less.'

There was a tremble in his voice.

'But is that absolutely necessary, Adam?'

'I think it is. A great many people come to this house. If we at *The Haven* got ill, how would the work continue? There would be no one to attend the sick. Think how many people would suffer.'

Other people, thought Sarah. It is always other people Adam thinks about.

'Couldn't you go to your family in Scotland, Adam? You would get rest and good food there and the country air would help your cough as well. I have asked this of you many times in the past. Will you not go, now?'

Adam shook his head.

'Once, Sarah, it might have been possible. Now, knowing what I do, I couldn't be responsible for spreading the infection and that is surely what I would be doing by going home.'

'But we are not sure there is any danger. We are not

even sure the *Cornucopia* passengers who came here were suffering from it, are we?'

She lifted her eyes to his, imploring him to tell her she could be right, but Adam shook his head.

'It is almost certain I am a cholera contact, Sarah,' he replied sadly.

'Then you shall not shut yourself away, at least not from me. I have nursed the fever before and I shall nurse it again, if needs be!'

With a sob in her voice she reached out and drew Adam's head towards her, resting her cheek on his hair.

'I will look after you, Adam,' she whispered. 'Do you think I could let you be alone at such a time? I will take care of you.'

Her voice broke huskily and her arms tightened round Adam's too-thin shoulders.

'I shall never leave you but it will all come right, Adam. I promise you *it will be all right.*'

Deliberately she emphasised each word, willing all the strength in her young body into his.

Desperately Adam clung to her. He was grateful for the comfort of her nearness for he felt utterly alone and very afraid. He must not be ill for there was too much still to be done; so many people who needed his help. If he were to die, who would be left to care about them but Sarah?

'Are you sure? Do you really believe it will be all right, Sarah?'

'I truly believe it, my dear,' she whispered, tenderly.

It was thus that Patrick found them. They had not heard his approach for he had walked quietly lest Adam should still be sleeping.

For a moment Patrick stood unmoving, almost unable to believe what he saw only too plainly. Then, scarcely breathing lest a creaking floorboard should betray his presence, he edged his way carefully back again down the long narrow passageway.

The sight of so tender a scene disturbed him and he was at a loss to understand why. He and Adam were friends of long-standing. They had talked intimately in the past of girls they had kissed and girls they had courted. Why then did the sight of Adam and Sarah in so loving an embrace make his body shake almost uncontrollably? It should have been obvious to him, he thought as he walked carefully back in the direction of Hetty Norris's room, that Sarah and Adam must be in love. Why else would a woman live and work in the conditions that existed at *The Haven*? Women would endure anything for the sake of the man they loved. Women were wondrous queer cattle!

Adam must find Sarah very easy to love. There was a quiet strength about her, a unique aura of gentleness that seemed to wrap her round wherever she went and whatever she was doing. And Sarah Rigby was beautiful, Patrick conceded. He had not realized it until last night when suddenly in the garden he had been only too well aware of it. He had felt an inexplicable peace in the gathering dusk with the evening scent of flowers around them.

Patrick jerked his thoughts back to reality. He was being foolish. He was making a fuss about nothing. He was betrothed to Arabella Harrington and Sarah and Adam were in love. It was as simple as that.

Purposefully, he knocked on the door of his aunt's bedroom.

Seven

Hetty Norris struggled into a sitting position and announced that it was time for her to return to Lace Street.

That she looked so much better was a profound relief to Patrick but he had no intention, yet, of letting her go back to her lonely house.

'You will do no such thing, Aunt,' he retorted firmly. 'You still need rest and a lot more of Molly's cooking.'

The little woman nodded her head in agreement.

'I will admit, boy, that I am tempted to stay a while but there are things I must do.'

'Like scrubbing floors and taking in washing?' Patrick asked bluntly.

Hetty Norris bit her lip.

She needed her work. To stay longer at *The Haven*, pleasant though it was, might mean the loss of her regular customers and that she could not allow to happen.

There was Rebecca Solomon to be paid, too, and Black Becky's clients knew full well that once they allowed themselves to fall behind with their payments they and the little they owned would be at the mercy of the tallyman.

'I would like to be where you are, Patrick. I see so little of you now and being waited on has been a rare treat. But I must go.'

'Why, Aunt? What excuse can there be for ignoring my advice?'

'Excuse, you young puppy! Since when did Hetty Norris need an excuse for anything she did?'

Patrick smiled. Aunt Hetty was indeed getting better.

'You may rant as much as you like, Aunt, but I shall tell Miss Rigby to hide your boots. See how far you get then!'

Hetty Norris conceded defeat.

'Now there,' she said, adroitly changing the subject, 'is a fine young woman for you. There's a real lady and no mistake.'

'Why do you say that? Do you know who she is?'

'No, Patrick, I don't but I know good breeding when I see it. I worked for gentlefolk for long enough.'

And who, wondered Patrick, had those gentlefolk been?

Tantalising memories of a large house came flooding back once more.

Were Aunt Hetty's gentlefolk his own kin?

'Who were they, Aunt?'

'Oh, fine folks who once lived in St Anne Street. They were good people and they treated their servants well.'

'Did they have a daughter?'

'Of course they had a daughter, boy. They had three daughters. What a question to ask!'

'Which house was it – what number . . .?'

Hetty Norris glanced sideways at Patrick.

The young whippersnapper was up to his questioning again. Some day, she decided, she would tell him. One day, he would have to be told; one day – when the time was right . . .

'Which number? I don't remember!' she flung back irritably. 'It was a long time ago; more than twenty years back. My memory isn't what it was. I can't carry numbers in my head!'

There was a knock on the door and old Hetty had reason to be grateful for Molly O'Keefe's timely interruption.

'Well then, it's better you're looking this morning, Miss Norris,' she beamed. 'And here's meself with some porridge and a nice plate of thin bread and butter.'

She arranged her plenteous hips on the bedside chair and settled down for a chat.

'See that she eats it all up, Molly,' called Patrick as he closed the door behind him.

Weak though she was he mused as he walked down the wide, bare staircase, Aunt Hetty was cunning as ever. It would take more than near-starvation to dull those keen old wits.

But he must find out who his real family were. Somehow he must make Aunt Hetty understand how important it was to him and to Arabella.

Arabella, his mind echoed. By now he should have joined her in Harrogate yet he hadn't even been able to find the time to write her a letter and beg her understanding.

He shrugged his shoulders moodily. Find time for letterwriting in Abercromby Square?

But today at all costs he must make the time to pay a visit to Hanover Street and one of the few of Adam's patients who could still afford to pay for treatment. And he could, whilst he was in the vicinity, pay Rebecca Solomon a visit for the old money-lender lived in nearby Paradise Street. Sooner or later Patrick knew, he would have to get to the bottom of the mystery of the tallyman's calls at Lace Street.

He sighed. It was something he wasn't looking forward to doing but it had to be done and who knew but that it might, perhaps, have some oblique connection with the *Private Matter*?

Rebecca Solomon, for all her undoubted wealth, lived in a small house at the meaner end of Paradise Street.

Carefully Patrick picked his way amongst men and women who lolled in small silent huddles in the hot July sun and tried to avoid the curious glances and satisfied smirks showing plainly their pleasure that yet another young buck seemed forced to seek the benefit of Becky's money-bags.

Patrick rapped on the shabby door with the head of his cane, outwardly affecting a confidence he was far from feeling.

'Come in. Come in, do!'

The room in which Rebecca Solomon sat was stiflingly hot and made the more so by a large fire that burned in the grate.

'Shut the door!' the old woman grumbled, hunching her shawl more closely round her shoulders. 'Can't abide draughts.'

Patrick looked round the cluttered room with distaste. The thick carpet that covered the entire floor was almost hidden by rich rugs and everywhere was evidence of the money-lender's squirrel-like mentality.

Ornaments covered the dresser and table and too many chairs, footstools and cupboards made it almost impossible to walk across the room in comfort.

'Well now, my dear, what can Rebecca do for you?' she croaked. 'Been playing cards? Got a little wench into trouble, maybe? Been a naughty boy, have you?'

With dignity Patrick removed his hat and gloves and laid them carefully on the edge of the table.

'I am Doctor Patrick Norris, ma'am,' he returned, stiffly.

'Oh?'

Clearly Rebecca Solomon was not impressed. She had

no need to be. She was rich beyond the dreams of most men and all else paled into insignificance beside that fact.

Patrick shuffled his feet.

'Sit down, my dear. Sit down, do,' Black Becky jabbed a wizened finger at the chair opposite, 'and tell me what I can do for you.'

'Ma'am, I will come straight to the point. How much money does Miss Hester Norris of Lace Street owe you?'

'That's a private matter between me and Hetty Norris!'

'Then now, madam, it is private no longer,' Patrick returned in his best London manner, 'and I will be obliged if you will answer my question.'

'She borrowed eighty pounds.'

'Eighty pounds!' *A small fortune!* 'When?'

'Oh seven, maybe eight years gone.'

'And how much does she give you each week?'

'Three shillings and sixpence.'

Patrick took his purse from his pocket.

'I would like to pay off what is owing.'

'And what if you can't, young sir? What if I'm content with things the way they are?'

'What do you mean by that?'

'Hetty Norris is a good payer – no trouble at all.' The black eyes narrowed. 'Maybe that's the way I like it.'

'Then I am sorry, Mrs Solomon, but I must insist. How much?'

'Thirty-five pounds.'

The reply was prompt and precise; the eyes that met Patrick's did not waver.

'*Thirty-five pounds?* But that is ridiculous! Why, the debt must have almost been paid, by now!'

'Ah, the loan perhaps, but what about the interest? What about compensation for the risk involved? What about the upkeep of me tallyman? Eighty sovereigns is a lot of money to lend a washerwoman! What about a little extra, eh, for me kindness and trust?'

Anger darted in bright red flashes before Patrick's eyes.

'You are a cheat and a trickster! You're a . . . you're a greedy old bitch!' Patrick spat, all pretence at gentility abandoned.

'Now then, young man, wait on! I miscalculated. It's thirty-seven pounds, now, for your impudence! And whilst we're about it, there was no one in at Lace Street when my gentleman called yesterday. Hopped it, has she?'

White-hot with seething rage Patrick spilled the contents of his purse into his hand then slowly counted out the money, slamming it onto the table.

'There you are,' he jerked, his words almost choking him. 'There's thirty pounds and you can take it or leave it! And I'll have a receipt, too, for the clearance of the debt!'

Rebecca Solomon pondered a while, then realizing the gentleman she thought might be easy-meat was hard as flint beneath the fine clothes, she reached for a quill.

'No justice, there ain't. Taking advantage of an old woman, it is,' she grumbled as she scratched pen to paper.

Patrick read the receipt carefully then folded it and placed it in his pocket.

The money he had paid Rebecca Solomon was almost all he possessed. Now he would be entering that most solemn state of matrimony with little more than ten pounds to his name.

'Now listen to me, you miserable old crow,' he spat. 'If your tallyman bothers Miss Norris again, I swear I'll break his miserable neck – in five places!'

Slamming the door behind him he walked back towards *The Haven*.

What had prompted him ever to return to Liverpool only God in His wisdom knew, but of one thing Patrick Norris was certain. The sooner he got himself out of it, the better!

Silently fuming he walked towards the Haymarket and the Folly Fair where farmers from the countryside around gathered to sell their produce and where, if they could afford it, housewives brought milks and eggs, cheese and butter.

Today, the fair was ill-attended. Farmers were loath to visit the town where it was known the fever was spreading with alarming rapidity.

But Patrick hardly noticed; he strode on blindly into Pembroke Place, remembering with a downward quirk of his mouth the old infirmary where once he and Adam had spent so many weary hours in the early years of their apprenticeship.

It had mattered then that those who entered such a place had little hope of leaving it alive. It had grieved him that infirmaries were places where a poor wretch was consigned to die with as much dignity as he could muster. In the small cold hours of the morning when most souls take leave of their earthly bodies, he and Adam had argued and debated and would have changed the world if they could, such had been the passion of their youth.

But London had beckoned to Patrick; only Adam had been true to himself. Adam had stayed in the mean streets and for his reward he had lungs that were choked with consumption and a heart heavy with fear because a sailing packet had brought more cholera into the port.

Angry with life though he still was, a small voice of conscience whispered in Patrick's ear that men and women would be waiting patiently at *The Haven* for surgery to commence and that Sarah would not be able to manage alone.

Crossing the road he walked quickly past the fever hospital, the oakum sheds, the workhouse and the lunatic asylum.

What a terrible collection of misery that street contained thought Patrick as he turned his back on Brownlow Hill and its macabre collection of buildings that stood high above the town and struck fear into the hearts of the poor.

Those were the places wherein hope finally died; but then – what hope was there for anyone in the festering port of Liverpool except for those who had the luck to land the means to get out of it?

As he walked up the steps to the open front door of *The Haven*, the resentment caused by the injustice of life in general and Rebecca Solomon in particular still throbbed inside him like an aching tooth. Perhaps it was because of this that when Sarah's anxious eyes told him silently that something was amiss, he gave an exclamation of annoyance.

'What is it *now*?' he asked brusquely, biting off each word as he fought to control the mixture of despair and anger that slapped a warning at the pit of his stomach.

Then, instantly contrite at the sight of her stricken face he asked more gently, 'Is something wrong?'

Sarah nodded and beckoned with her head for Patrick to follow her to the ward.

'It's the Hanson baby,' she whispered.

'Little Ben? But he's the only one in the ward who *isn't* sick.'

'I know, Patrick; I know.'

She had no time for explanations.

'Then what is it?'

As far as Patrick was concerned when last he visited the ward, the Hanson baby had been in perfect health, apart perhaps from the eye-teeth he was cutting. It had been his young parents, Tilly and George, who had been brought to *The Haven* with extensive burns when a fire had blazed their little home into a heartbreaking rubble.

Now they were well enough to leave and would have done so already had they been able to find some corner of a cheap lodging-house or empty cellar to live in. It was only Sarah's compassion, Patrick knew, that had kept the Hanson family at *The Haven*, for so long.

Sarah stirred the jug she carried.

'What is that?' Patrick asked, peeling off his coat.

'An emetic.'

'Salt and warm water?'

'Yes. I've got to make Ben vomit. It's our only hope.'

'What has he swallowed?'

'Laudanum.' Sarah's reply was terse.

'*Laudanum?* For God's sake, *how*?'

Patrick received no answer but he hadn't expected one, for a glance at the child who lolled like a rag doll in his mother's arms told him that time was precious.

'Bring him to the window and slap his face,' Sarah commanded Tilly Hanson, willing her voice to be steady.

'Do anything, but for pity's sake, don't let him go to sleep?'

'I'm trying, miss, but he keeps dropping off,' the young mother sobbed. 'He isn't going to die is he?'

'No, ma'am,' Patrick interjected, expertly forcing open the little jaws with his fingers, 'but you must help us. Ben must be made to drink all this salt and water. If we can make him sick, he'll be all right. Do you understand?'

Tilly Hanson nodded, her eyes dilated with fear. Beside

her, pale and anxious, stood her husband and in the corner Dicky-Sam sat unspeaking, his face white as chalk. There was no word from the other patients in the ward, merely a silent sympathy as they watched the water being forced into the mouth of the feebly protesting child.

'How much laudanum did he take?'

Patrick addressed Sarah but his eyes did not leave the child for an instant.

'A spoonful. A large spoonful.'

'A *what*?' Patrick exploded, doubling his efforts with frantic haste.

He turned to the child's father.

'Hold his nose. Make him gulp down air as he swallows. *He's got to be sick!*'

There was no anger in Patrick and this Sarah recognized. She was grateful for his presence. She had never been so glad to see anyone in the whole of her life as she had been when Patrick returned from his sick-visiting.

Now Patrick was icy-cold, working efficiently and without emotion but when the danger was over – if ever it *was* over – Sarah knew that the devil would have to be paid for what was happening.

For a few moments that stretched away into an eternity, it seemed that they were making no progrcss. Then, with a protesting cry from little Ben and a gasp of relief from Patrick, they knew that the danger was over.

'Good,' Patrick whispered, grimly. 'Now, if we can keep him awake for a few hours longer, I think he'll do.'

He turned to Sarah.

'Will you arrange to have this mess cleared up?' he demanded brusquely, nodding towards the floor and hating himself for what he was asking. He knew Sarah would have to clean the floor herself but he was still hurting inside.

It hadn't just been the finding of Adam in Sarah's arms or Rebecca Solomon's avarice; it was the happenings of the previous four days that he could still scarcely believe. The overdose of laudanum had only set the seal on his anger. He wondered how Adam – and Sarah, too – could endure to work at *The Haven* day after day, for years.

But that, he decided, was their business. Just as soon as he could he would be out of the place. He would be back with Arabella and Doctor Harrington and in the dignity and sanity of the Harley Street practice, he would be able to forget Liverpool entirely.

Patrick straightened his shoulders. First though, there were things to be done. Sarah must be told in no uncertain words that the dispensing of laudanum or any other such drug was not undertaken by meddling amateurs. What Adam permitted was between himself and his professional conscience but since he, Patrick Norris, had assumed responsiblity for *The Haven*, albeit for only a few days, it was his duty to see that she understood the enormity of her mistake.

Perhaps, he thought reluctantly, what he really wanted to do was to convince himself that Sarah didn't matter to him; that the unmistakably loving embrace he had seen hadn't stabbed into him like a knife. He wanted to believe it didn't matter, but that was not true. He knew that Sarah Rigby disturbed him deeply. He knew that if he let himself, he could love her and be in love with her. What he could feel for Sarah was not acknowledged in genteel society. It was the earthy love of a man for his mate; the kind of love that would want to make him defend her with his life. What he felt for Sarah was not part of a contracted, discreetly arranged match that would provide heirs with nicety. He wanted Sarah's lithe young body in his arms, with her hair tumbling the pillow. He wanted her to bear his children . . .

'Damn! Damn! Damn!' he swore, shaking his head as if to deny his thoughts.

He heard the clanking of a bucket and knew Sarah had finished her menial task of cleaning up the ward floor.

'Madam!' he yelled, the shame he felt for his surging thoughts finding release, 'Will you be kind enough to step in here?'

It was more a command than a request.

Patrick opened the dispensary door, deliberately walking through it ahead of Sarah. He closed it firmly then turned to face her.

She was drying her hands on her apron and he saw they were rough and cracked from scrubbing and washing. He wanted to take them gently into his and hold them to his cheek.

He said instead, 'Do you appreciate the seriousness of this morning's happenings, ma'am?'

Sarah nodded, her eyes still downcast.

'And are you in the habit of dispensing drugs?'

'Yes – yes, I am.'

'Then I would have deemed it propitious if you had learned a little more about their dangers and a lot more about their dosage!'

Sarah looked up quickly, her eyes meeting his.

'Oh, but I do . . .'

She dropped her glance, again.

' . . I do know,' she faltered.

'Then tell me what it is? What is the correct dosage, ma'am, for an infant of eighteen months?'

'One drop, in water.'

Patrick reached for the bottle of brown liquid and held it dramatically on high.

'One drop, Miss Rigby, not one *spoonful*!'

'I know. Oh, truly I know, but you see, the baby was teething and fretful and I had twice before given him a sleeping draught. I'd had to think about the others in the ward, as well. Ben was disturbing their rest.'

'So, this time you thought you'd give him a little extra.'

There was no mistaking the sarcasm in Patrick's voice.

'Well, ma'am,' he continued when Sarah did not reply, 'whilst I am acting as Doctor Carmichael's locum you will not enter this dispensary or administer any dosage whatsoever without my express permission. Do you understand?'

Sarah nodded.

'Now, miss, you will give me the dispensary key.'

He thrust out his hand and silently she passed it to him then turned on her heel and went quickly from the room.

For a moment Patrick stood, the laudanum bottle still grasped in his hand.

Other women would have protested, he reasoned. They would have found excuses for their carelessness or used their feminine ways to escape the consequences of their actions. Arabella would have done it – indeed most women would have used similar tactics.

But not so Sarah Rigby. She had not coaxed or tried to lie. She had accepted words that ripped from him like poison-tipped darts without protest because she had been wrong.

How many other women would have done that, he asked himself dispassionately.

Quietly she had given him the key then left the room

without any display of dramatics. He wondered what she was doing now and knew that somewhere she would be crying quietly. He had seen the tears that ran silently down her cheeks for all she had done to hide them and as she turned her back on him and walked quickly from the room, it had taken all the strength in his body to stop himself from taking her in his arms and kissing away those tears.

He had made her suffer for his own frustrations and every word he had flung at her tore at his heart like a vicious pain.

'Oh, Sarah, my love,' he whispered to the empty little room.

Like an automaton Patrick dealt with the patients who had waited on the hard wooden benches in the entrance hall of *The Haven*. He remembered little of it save that there had been no one with fever symptoms. For this at least he was grateful for he knew that the outbreak had reached almost epidemic proportions and that it could only be a matter of time before it burst like some filthy growth and paralysed the town with its evil.

Almost as the last patient left there was a gentle tapping on the door and Patrick was glad that in all the turmoil at *The Haven*, one thing did not seem to change.

Always after surgery, Dicky-Sam brought in a mug of tea. It was as if he waited and timed it to the last second.

'Come in, Dicky,' called Patrick.

'Your tea, doctor. To be sure, I thought it would be dinner-time before you finished.'

'I was late in starting.'

'Yes, sir. I knows that and it's on that matter I have something to say.'

'About the Hanson baby, you mean?'

'Aye, sir. It was me as did it.'

'*You*, Dicky-Sam?'

Patrick almost shouted the words.

'Aye. There was nobody about, you see. You'd gone out and Miss Sarah was seeing to Doctor Adam, so I took it upon meself to help. Only I didn't help, did I, sir?'

'No, Dicky. You didn't help at all.'

Patrick took a long, deep breath, trying desperately to be calm. 'Do you usually give out medicines?'

'No, doctor, never. But the little lad hadn't slept all night on account of his teeth. They hadn't wanted to bother Miss Sarah last night, knowing she was took up with Kate Tarleton. So the poor little shaver bawled and cried all night and looked settled for crying all day, too.'

'And you thought you'd set up as a doctor and prescribe yourself? Was that it?'

'No, doctor, that wasn't it at all. Only they knew Miss Sarah had given little Ben a dose of the brown stuff before; Mrs Hanson showed me which bottle it was. I was trying to do something that would help Miss Sarah.'

'And instead you caused her a lot more trouble?'

'Aye, I did and I'll never go near that medicine room again, I swear it! I'm only good at seafaring and lifting things and I'm sticking to that, now.'

Patrick knew he should have been enraged. He should have dealt more sternly with the distraught little man but all passion, indeed, all feeling had drained from him. Sarah had been his whipping-boy. She had suffered the brunt of his ill-temper and suffered it for Dicky-Sam's mistake.

'Then remember that, Dicky,' Patrick said, almost wearily. 'Remember that today you nearly killed a child.'

'I'll never forget it, doctor.'

The unhappy old face bore witness to Dicky-Sam's sincerity.

'And now if you please, sir, I'll take me punishment.'

'Do you want to be punished?'

'No sir, but I aught to be.'

'Then I will punish you, Dicky-Sam. I will tell you something that will hurt you very much. Before surgery I accused Sarah of your mistake. I was rude to her; I said most ungentlemanly things to her; I shouted and I made her cry. And for all that, she took the blame herself. She let me believe she had given the overdose. She shielded *you*!'

'Lawks, sir, then you've punished me all right. You've given me better than a keel-hauling. I'd as leave give up me good leg as have Miss Sarah suffer. I loves and respects her too much to hurt her and God's my witness to that!'

Patrick looked with compassion at the distress of the weatherbeaten little seaman for he understood his feelings only too well.

Dicky-Sam loved Sarah, too. They both loved her, each in his different way and were bonded by it. Patrick knew Dicky-Sam's punishment could not have been more complete and he knew exactly how sad the cripple felt.

I hurt her too; not because I wanted to help her as Dicky did, he thought, almost sick with shame. I hurt her deliberately because I loved her almost unbearably. It is I who must take the blame.

'What can I do, Doctor Patrick, to make amends?'

'Nothing, Dicky – I'll do it. I'll make amends for both of us.'

Silently, his face contorted with misery, Dicky-Sam limped from the room.

*

Sarah was crossing the hall as Patrick opened the surgery door. For a moment they faced each other and he saw that her eyes were still moist from weeping. She said quietly, her voice husky with emotion, 'Do you want something?'

'Yes, Sarah. I want something very badly. I want your forgiveness. Will you give it to me, please?'

He said the words softly and humbly.

'How did you know?'

Sarah raised her eyes to his.

'That it was Dicky-Sam? He told me himself.'

'He was only trying to help. You weren't too hard on him, were you?'

'No, Sarah, I wasn't.'

No, my darling, his heart supplied, I vented my anger on you. I hurt you because I love you and because you belong to Adam . . .

He clenched his fists in an effort to stop himself reaching out for her.

'Then I'm grateful to you, Patrick. Dicky's a good little man. He tries so hard to help us.'

Her lip trembled and her voice betrayed the tears that were still very near the surface.

'Sarah, don't be upset. I am so ashamed of my behaviour that I don't know what to say or how to apologize enough.'

Sarah shook her head wordlessly, covering her face with her hands and Patrick knew she was crying again.

'Please, my dear,' he pleaded, 'don't cry.'

'I'm sorry, Patrick. Oh, I'm so sorry. I don't often cry but I get so tired, sometimes and it's all piling up . . .'

Of course it was all getting too much for her, Patrick agreed silently. It wasn't the work or the poverty – Sarah could have stood up to that; but now Adam was really ill and Sarah loved him.

Patrick saw that her shoulders were shaking silently. She looked so alone and defenceless that he held out his arms and felt a fierce joy when she came to them.

'There now,' he soothed. 'I understand. Let the tears come if it will help you.'

He laid his head on her hair and with a shock of delight imagined that the scent of honeysuckle still lingered there. Her body near his felt just as he knew it would feel and he wanted to hold her closer and gentle the hurt out of her. He wanted her lips beneath his; he wanted to see her eyes close with delight at his touch.

But she didn't love him. She could not know what feelings surged through him. *Sarah loved Adam.* Patrick knew he must say it again and again until it no longer had the power to hurt him.

Sarah loved Adam and he, Patrick Norris, could only give her his comfort and a shoulder to cry upon. That much he could do for her; that much, and no more.

Vaguely through his pulsing emotions Patrick heard the click of a door-latch and a swish of satin.

In his arms Sarah stiffened then pushed her hands against him in a small protest. He felt her turn in his arms, heard the sharp intake of her breath.

Reluctantly he raised his head and blinked rapidly then as the shifting haze resolved itself, he felt a cold slap of apprehension in the pit of his stomach.

Before him the figure outlined in the open doorway stood rigid as a statue.

He saw a face drained white in anger, blue eyes wide with shock, lips set tight in unspoken accusation.

For a moment he was hardly able to believe what he

saw. It seemed almost that the voice he heard was not his own as he gasped,

'Arabella!'

Eight

'Arabella!' Patrick repeated, desperately willing his thoughts into some semblance of order.

He tried to hold out his arms in greeting but they hung like lead at his sides; he tried to step forward but his feet were incapable of movement.

He was not imagining it; Arabella was here, in Liverpool! She was wearing a blue travelling habit and tiny pink rosebuds nodded at the side of her bonnet. She was real yet now she was almost a stranger to him. She belonged in London, part of a life that now seemed so remote that it might never have happened.

Arabella was the woman he was soon to marry but she had no place in the house in Abercromby Square.

The quiet closing of a door told Patrick that Sarah had slipped away from them and it relieved a little of the tension inside him.

'I can't believe it,' he stammered. 'I had not expected . . .'

'No Patrick, it seems you had not!' Arabella whispered, each word a tight, sharp dart.

He heard the inward hiss of her breath and knew that soon the gates of shock and disbelief that held her would come crashing down before the torrent of her anger.

'But dearest,' he hastened, 'you misunderstand. What you saw –'

'What I *saw* Patrick seems to need no explanation!'

Patrick shrugged inwardly. He had been comforting Sarah – that at least was true – but the love he had felt, the wild upsurge of longing, the desire to never let her free from his arms were feelings he would never try to excuse.

But he could understand Arabella's anger for those feelings must have been mirrored only too plainly in his eyes.

'Sarah – Miss Rigby – was distressed,' he faltered. 'She and Adam are very close and Adam is ill.'

'I see.'

Arabella waited like a tightly-coiled spring for further explanation.

'You do not believe me,' Patrick accused, flailing blindly into the attack.

'I am finding it very hard!'

The reply was terse, each word bitten off sharply and spat out with venom.

'Look, Arabella, we can't talk here.'

Desperately Patrick played for time. Soon, if he were not careful, the full fury of Arabella's anger would release itself to be followed by tears and tantrums. He had witnessed such a scene before and he had no wish to see another. Nor had he, he thought grimly, the time or the patience to endure one.

He reached out for her arm.

'Come into the little parlour. It is cooler there, and quiet. We can talk – I can explain . . .'

But Arabella shook off his hand. Her body stiff with disapproval she reluctantly followed him. As he closed the door behind them she flung into the attack.

'A *few days*, Patrick! You said you would rejoin me within a few days. Almost a week went by without one word of explanation and I must come to *you*!'

Her eyes flashed like brittle glass and the paper-white cheeks now blazed red with uncontrolled temper.

'Things were not as I had expected to find them, Arabella, when I arrived here.'

'Nor, when *I* arrived, either!'

'You are determined to misunderstand. If you would listen to me, I could explain.'

'I do not doubt it for one instant, Patrick.'

'Arabella,' he appealed, his voice terse, 'I ask you to believe I am truly sorry.'

'Sorry? Sorry for what?' Her voice rose to near-hysteria. 'Are you sorry for what you have done or sorry I caught you doing it?'

Patrick let Arabella's anger wash over him. To protest further would only make a bad situation worse. She had, he acknowledged, cause for anger. If he were really truthful he must freely admit it. But at all costs, he must calm her.

Refusing to be drawn further, desperately trying to detach himself from her wrath, he stared grimly out of the window, seeing afresh the tangled garden that wilted now in the merciless shimmer of afternoon heat.

Could it have only been last night that Sarah sat there at his feet, her hair falling about her shoulders?

He jerked his thoughts back to the small sitting-room and waited for Arabella to continue to hurl her unhappiness at his back.

But his silence had the effect he desired. He heard a shuddering sob and a small sniff then waited as reluctant footsteps came slowly towards him.

She stood beside him, staring ahead. Presently, her voice stiff and dangerously quiet, she said, 'I want to go home to London. I want to go today, *now*, and I want you to come with me, Patrick.'

Had Arabella slapped his face she could not have startled Patrick more. He spun round to face her.

'I cannot,' he jerked. 'It is out of the question.'

The refusal spilled out without thought or effort and the realization staggered him.

Each day since his arrival he had vowed that the sooner he could leave the house in Abercromby Square the better he would be pleased, yet when Arabella was giving him the excuse he needed, he jumped like a scalded cat.

Was it for Sarah's sake he wanted so much to stay?

Surely not, he reasoned. It would have been the wisest thing he had ever done could he have removed himself from the despair of loving her.

'I cannot leave,' he repeated more calmly yet wondering still at his own perversity. 'My Aunt Norris is ill and I am very concerned about Adam, too.'

But it wasn't just Sarah or Adam or Aunt Hetty who kept him, thought Patrick. Something else held him; some secret truth hidden deep in his heart that defied recognition.

'Your aunt and your friend? Are they more important to you than me – than *us*?'

'Oh, my dear,' Patrick pleaded, 'you make it so difficult for me to explain.'

He took the dainty handkerchief she held and carefully patted her eyes.

'Look now; dry your tears and give me your hand. I will show you something. It will perhaps help you to understand.'

Reluctantly Arabella did as he asked.

'This,' said Patrick flatly as he opened the door of the small room nearest the surgery, 'is the dispensary.'

The brown laudanum bottle stood where he had left it little over an hour ago. The sun washed over it so that it glinted mockingly, reminding him of how he had hurt Sarah and in hurting her had driven a knife into his own heart.

'The dispensary?' Arabella repeated, glancing at its emptiness, sensing at once its inadequacy.

Patrick nodded, unspeaking, and urged her across the echoing hall and into the large room that ran from the front of the house to the back.

'This is the sick-ward,' he said, suddenly fiercely proud. 'Here, if there is an empty bed, no one is turned away. It is clean and sweet and a person may feel no sense of shame or indignity at being nursed here.'

He paused, startled by the depths of his feelings, willing Arabella to understand.

'The sick come to us not to die but to be made well. Often they are starving and penniless and their cares become our cares. There is little money here – Adam and Sarah depend upon the charity of many people – and there are few instruments or surgical aids to help them,' he said, recalling with a surge of happiness the triumph he and Sarah had shared when the Haggarty baby grasped at life with his tiny hands.

'Here at *The Haven*, a man is a doctor against all odds, Arabella. Here, Fate challenges a man to be a *real* doctor!'

Then suddenly and humbly Patrick realized the truth of his own dilemma. It came to him like a wild new awakening and it came in a blinding flash of truth.

No! he exulted, it wasn't just Sarah and Adam and Aunt Hetty who kept him at *The Haven*. Life had thrown him a challenge and he had picked it up because all his life he had been picking up challenges! He had unconsciously accepted the overwhelming odds against winning and he had so far survived because he had proved himself to be a good doctor. More than that, he had learned compassion. He had become a *real* doctor!

'Do you understand, Arabella?' he whispered joyfully, his eyes glowing with a happiness he could not explain but felt with delirious intensity.

'Could I leave *The Haven*? Could I leave these people?'

Arabella did not reply. Instead, she fought desperately to bite back the retort that sprung to her lips –

'*What about my father and the duty you owe to him? What about me, Patrick, the woman you are to marry? Do you expect me to share this existence with you?*'

She was about to fling those questions in his face but her instincts screamed out against it. She was treading on strange ground. Here was a different man, a man she had never known to exist. This was not the ambitious doctor eager to get on in the world and gather round him the riches that would loudly proclaim his success. This was not the polite genteel young doctor whose bedside manner was the delight of the rich old ladies.

Suddenly, it seemed, this strange new Patrick gloried in working himself to a standstill for little or no reward. He had become a crusader and seemed to find joy in it.

Take care, warned the woman in Arabella, *for this new creature will not be swayed by cajoling or tears*!

This man she must learn to know anew and suddenly she was aware that if she was to keep him she must fight for him and fight with every fibre of her being.

She turned her back on the sick-ward and walked towards the open front door.

'My trunks are outside, Patrick. Will you be so kind as to have them brought in for me?'

She gave him a sweet smile, womanly submissive, all traces of anger seemingly gone. 'If you will not come with me, dearest, then I must stay here, with you!'

The sudden about-face caught Patrick off balance. To realize in one wondrous moment that at last he knew his true purpose in life had left him in a state of tipsy elation.

But Arabella was about to thrust herself into that life and it was a sobering thought.

To stay at *The Haven* was all he wanted, now. To share the lot of Sarah and Adam, however much pain and heartache it might cause him to see them together, was one thing. To include Arabella in that life would be vastly difficult. But he realized that for the moment he was being offered a reprieve and much as it might complicate matters, he had no other alternative than to accept it.

'Very well, Arabella. I will let your papa know you are safe with me but I warn you that life at *The Haven* is not easy. There are no servants here, as such. We all serve, but only the sick. If you will accept those conditions you may stay here until other arrangements can be made, but you must expect no favours, Arabella. Life is rough, here – you can take it, or leave it . . .'

There was a small silence between them, then Arabella spoke.

'Thank you, Patrick. I will do my best not to hinder your work.'

Her reply was deceptively meek but inside her the turmoil of uncertainty raged with frightening intensity. Things would not go easily for her if she stayed at *The Haven*, she knew it only too well, for a glance at the Spartan bareness of the place confirmed that Patrick had spoken nothing but the truth and what was more, he meant every word of what he had said.

Life is rough, here . . . She accepted that and in doing so, realized with absolute certainty that if she did not accept such conditions and try for a little while to fit into the life of *The Haven*, she could lose Patrick forever. She must tread carefully and bide her time until she could make him see sense. When she had first arrived at the house she was sure that she had a woman for a rival but now it seemed to Arabella that Sarah Rigby could have been more easily disposed of than the intangible crusade that Patrick seemed determined to fight. No one, thought Arabella despairingly, could fight a *cause*!

So she smiled sweetly up at Patrick.

'Very well,' she affirmed, 'I am ready, dearest. Will you please have someone show me to my rooms?'

'But, Sarah,' Patrick protested as they sat together in the brief peace of the empty surgery, 'it is not right you should give up your bed yet again. You must take mine.'

'Thank you, Patrick, but no. You need your sleep and besides,' Sarah smiled impishly, 'the bed in your attic is the most uncomfortable in the whole house. I shall be quite happy sleeping in the kitchen. It will not be the first time I have slept on a mattress beneath the kitchen table. Miss Harrington is welcome to my bed.'

'It is so unfair,' Patrick persisted. 'Why must it always be you, Sarah, who is put out?'

Sarah gave a little shrug of her shoulders.

'Because I choose it to be so and anyway, I will be near the ward and nearer to Adam.'

Patrick smiled.

'You are right as you always are, Sarah Rigby. And you remind me that I have not made my round of the ward or visited my aunt, or Adam.'

'Your aunt seems much better and Adam was sleeping when last I looked into his room.'

She puckered her forehead into a worried frown.

'But I carried away his tray. He had not attempted to eat his food.'

'I am a great believer in the medicine of sleep, Sarah,' Patrick comforted. 'Don't worry. I will take a look at Adam as soon as he awakens.'

He rose to his feet, impatient to end their talk, be away from her disturbing presence, but Sarah remained seated.

'Is there something else?'

'Yes, Patrick, there is.'

Sarah dropped her eyes to the fingers that twisted anxiously on her lap.

'This afternoon – when I was crying and Miss Harrington arrived – I fear I caused you both embarrassment. I am very sorry about it and I am sorry I cried.'

She did not look at him as she spoke and Patrick was grateful for it. He did not want to see her troubled grey eyes, for to do so might release the words of love that were locked in his heart.

Instead he said, brusquely, 'That is all right, ma'am. Please do not mention it further.'

Sarah flinched inwardly, regretting almost that she had tried to thank him for his kindness. But Patrick was right to speak to her thus, she reasoned. Doubtless he was thinking that to offer more sympathy might encourage a fresh outburst of tears.

She shook her head impatiently. She would not cry again. No matter what happened, she could not and must not indulge in the luxury of tears. There was no time for weeping at *The Haven*.

She tilted her chin and said as brightly as she could, 'Miss Harrington is going to be a great blessing, Patrick. She is fetching and carrying and helping Molly in every possible way. I am truly grateful to her although it seems very wrong to allow a guest to work.'

Oh Sarah, Patrick's mind supplied, *you do not know Arabella as I know her. Today, this domesticity is just a game. By tomorrow it will have ceased to be a novelty and the friction between she and I will start again.*

'Arabella is hardly a guest, Sarah,' he returned tersely. 'She expressed a wish to stay and help us.'

'Then I am doubly grateful,' Sarah insisted.

Please, she pleaded inside her. *Please stay with us, Arabella. Don't go back to London for a little while. Don't take Patrick away from us – we need him so.*

She must try, she resolved, to make Miss Harrington's stay as bearable as she possibly could. She must show her gratitude to Arabella and try to see she did not work too hard and tire herself, for without Patrick's help Sarah thought despairingly, she could not carry on.

Arabella let her weary body sag onto the low, hard bed and fumbled to unfasten the too-large apron that covered her dress.

From the bed opposite she could feel Kate Tarleton's eyes upon her and wished there was a screen behind which she might undress in privacy.

Bending forward to unhook the row of buttons on her boots she felt her ringlets damp and limp against her face. Her feet throbbed and it would be good, she thought, to wiggle her toes and rest her aching leggs.

Arabella realized with a little smile of triumph that distressing as the work had been, at least it had caused the occupants of *The Haven* to take notice of her.

'Sure, it's not right for a dainty wee creature like

yourself to be doing the work of a serving girl!' Molly had protested.

And Patrick had smiled grimly as she hurried past him with gruel for the old lady in the corner bed in the sick-ward. Was he regretting his insistence that she should make herself useful? Had it startled him to realize that she could not be frightened away by the threat of a little housework? Patrick would give in, vowed Arabella, before *she* would!

A dainty white boot fell to the floor with a thump and Arabella recalled the undisguised admiration in the eyes of the funny little one-legged man as he called her a pretty little flower.

Sarah Rigby, too, had expressed her gratitude, imploring her not to tire herself and to take a rest and a dish of tea. Sarah Rigby, thought Arabella, had been the cause of serious concern to her. To see her in Patrick's arms had sent pangs of jealous anger stabbing through her.

But she need not have worried, she realized, for Sarah Rigby was plain and ordinary with her screwed-up hair and sad, grey eyes. It was almost feasible to believe now that Patrick really had been comforting her. Arabella was surprised that to recall the scene no longer made her angry; only regretful that she had been foolish enough to lose her temper and scream at Patrick like a fishwife.

Sarah Rigby was no threat; she did not, Arabella decided, have to fear the careworn, quiet woman she had found in Patrick's arms. She knew where the danger lay and she was at a loss as yet to know how to deal with it. Her real enemy, Arabella knew, was *The Haven*; the great bare house where the sick found health again or died with dignity amidst love and care. She knew that if she were not to lose Patrick she must fight not a woman but a way of life that she could not yet even begin to understand.

Perplexed and anxious she turned to face Kate Tarleton, forcing a small smile as she met the undisguised look of wonder.

The wide brown eyes dropped to gaze at the bedcover.

'Begging your pardon, miss; I know it's rude to stare but you've got me fair mystified.'

'Oh?'

'Aye, miss. Why's the likes of you doing servant's work and why aren't you creating at having to sleep in the same room with the likes of me?'

'Why shouldn't I help with the work here?' Arabella was immediately on the defensive.

Why, why, *why* must everybody presume that she was useless? They were all like her papa who teased and petted her as if she were still a child.

'And why shouldn't I share a room with you?' she flung at the startled girl.

Kate's pinched little face flushed. She dropped her eyes again and for a time there was an uncomfortable silence in the small, hot attic.

Then Arabella spoke.

'I'm sorry. I didn't mean to snap. Are you feeling better now after your accident?'

For reasons she could not explain, Arabella wanted to know more about the girl whose room she shared.

'Yes, miss, I thank you, but I'd have been dead in a pool of me own blood, now,' she supplied dramatically, 'if it hadn't been for Doctor Norris.'

Arabella blushed with pleasure.

'Doctor Norris and I are soon to be married,' she said proudly.

Kate Tarleton's eyes took on a wistful expression.

'Don't suppose anybody'll ever want to wed me.'

'Why not?'

'Well, on account of me being what I am – what I *was*,' she corrected hastily.

She looked pleadingly into Arabella's eyes.

'Did they tell you I was on the streets, miss? That's how I got knifed and battered last night. But Miss Sarah says I've finished with all that. Says as how she'll chain me to the table-leg afore she'll let me go on the game again. Miss Sarah's going to find me a position with a good family when I'm mended and then I'll be respectable.'

Her eyes shone.

'Just imagine that – being in gentleman's service; eating regular and sleeping in a bed . . .'

'Was it awful, doing what you did?' Arabella asked.

It was strange, she thought, but Kate didn't look like a street-woman – at least not what Cissy, her father's kitchen-maid said street-women looked like. Arabella had learned a great many of the unlady-like facts of life in whispered conversations in the Harley Street kitchens and Kate did not fit in with any of Cissy's lurid descriptions of wantonness.

Kate nodded.

'Aye, it's an awful life but at least I ain't got rot-gut. I'm thankful for that!'

Arabella tried hard to be shocked by such frankness but could not. She found instead a deep sympathy within her for Kate's misfortunes. It was a feeling that was new to Arabella Harrington and she was not at all sure she fully understood it.

'How old are you, Kate?'

'Thirteen or fourteen, I think. I've no way of knowing exactly, me Ma and Da being dead.'

Arabella swallowed hard. Kate was alone in the world; it must be a terrible thing, she thought.

She wondered how often in the past she herself, despite the luxury with which she was surrounded, had felt lonely, too. How often, she mused, if she had been given a wish, would she have asked for a sister or brother, perhaps?

Kate Tarleton had no one and no home; she had no money either, unless she got it *that* way.

Arabella was well aware of the fact that no young lady should begin to understand the plight of one so unfortunate. She should not even speak to such a person, let alone feel pity for her.

Yet she felt pity for Kate Tarleton; pity for her poor bruised face and the life she had been forced to lead, but mostly she felt sad at Kate's loneliness. Arabella could understand loneliness but she knew that if she lay awake the whole of the night she could not even begin to imagine the degradation of the life the young girl had been forced to lead.

Sarah Rigby and Patrick had brought Kate to *The Haven*. They had taken her from the Liverpool gutters and were caring for her with compassion. What had Patrick said?

'. . . *their cares become our cares*.'

And they would not allow Kate to go back to the uncaring streets. They would find her a position in a gentleman's household and the thought of it made Kate's eager young eyes shine with pride.

How dreadful must her life have been when the prospect of a life of domestic service seemed like the promise of Utopia? How could anybody like being a servant? she wondered. She had fetched and carried for just half a day and her body ached with fatigue. And tomorrow would be exactly the same. Tomorrow would be . . .

She shut down her thoughts and surrendered her body to the cool caress of clean cotton sheets. Her aching back did not feel the lumpiness of the mattress. Instead, she felt a strange thrill of achievement singing through her body.

Tomorrow would be a new day, she thought wonderingly; a chance to start again and make atonement; a day not to be allowed to slip by uselessly. Tomorrow she could, in some small measure, show gratitude for those things she had in such abundance. She could try to help those who were less fortunate than herself and less able to help themselves.

It wasn't really a question of showing them that Arabella Harrington could rise to a challenge and prove herself.

She wasn't quite sure just what she wanted of tomorrow so bewildering were the thoughts that spun with giddy joy in her head. She was certain only of one thing: that she felt pity and compassion and love within her for the first time and she wanted, most humbly, to be allowed to share them.

She hoped wistfully that she could give Patrick cause to be proud of her.

She leaned over and blew out the candle.

'Good night, Kate,' she whispered. 'God bless you . . .'

Nine

Through the thin partition wall, not a foot away from the sleeping Arabella, Patrick lay on his bed and looked up at the skylight above him into the dark of the night.

What a mess it all was, he thought. At last he knew that the only thing he wanted in life was to work at *The Haven* yet the realisation had come too late, he fretted.

His longing to care for the people of the alleys and back-streets was beyond all doubt but he had a duty to Doctor Harrington and to Arabella whom he had asked to become his wife.

Patrick knew now that he could willingly forsake the opulent life of Harley Street but how easy would it be for him to be free of it?

Doctor Harrington might well insist that he return and honour his agreement – he would be well within his rights – and Arabella was betrothed to him. A gentleman did not break his word, did he?

But Arabella could never fit into the life at *The Haven* no matter how she tried, his tortured mind supplied. True, he admitted as he thumped his hot pillow yet again, Arabella had surprised him by her willingness to help. He had never before known her to perform one menial task but then, she had never before had the need to.

What could be behind Arabella's actions? What, he reasoned, could she be trying to prove?

Patrick levered himself into a sitting position. Tonight, sleep evaded him. His body was weary but his mind buzzed with irritations and problems. Would it not be better, he thought, if he were to try to find one or two newly-qualified physicians who had not the means to buy their own practices yet would welcome the chance to gain experience at *The Haven*? He could return to London, then. He could afford to make an allowance to Aunt Hetty so that she never need work again and he would marry Arabella as he was pledged to do. He could try to forget Sarah; forget that she and Adam were in love. If he were away from it all he would not be tormented by Sarah's troubled grey eyes or feel the urge to lay her work-roughened hands to his cheek. If he could accept that there was no place in Sarah's life for him it would make it all the easier to leave.

But if there were no young physicians to be obtained, if Adam did not get well again, what then would happen to the poor ones? They would still need him, Patrick knew, just as desperately as he needed *them*. He was one of them; they were his own people. He had been reared among them in the tight, airless streets. It seemed that no matter who his real parents were the courts and alleys of Liverpool had set their mark on him and now they were calling him back. How could he have been so blind as to ever think he could forsake them?

With an exclamation of annoyance Patrick fumbled to light the candle at his bedside. The fingers of his pocket-watch pointed to three o'clock and soon it would be dawn and the start of another hot, dreary day. Soon the streets would be astir with people and the pathetic huddle of men and women would gather at *The Haven* once more.

He wondered how the cholera-ridden warehouses and

cellars had fared during the long-drawn night and how many more souls had departed their miserable bodies for want of care that might have saved them. Now the infirmaries were packed tight and Doctor Duncan had commandeered two ships and had them anchored out in the wide river to take the poor wretches who had nowhere to die and to prevent, if only in small measure, the further spread of the evil.

Patrick reached for his coat and slipped it over his nightshirt. He had not been happy when he visited Adam at bedtime. He had had the feeling that his friend had been holding back, deliberately trying to mislead him. Adam refused to let Patrick take his temperature saying that he had taken it himself and found it quite satisfactory.

But Patrick knew Adam had not eaten all day and when he suggested that Adam might like to meet Arabella there had been a too-hasty refusal.

'A sick-room is no please for pleasantries, Patrick. Leave it for a little while, will you? Perhaps tomorrow?'

But for all that, Adam had wanted to talk about other things. He had talked about *The Haven* and of his fears that one day there might be no one to care for the sick, save Sarah herself.

Patrick had challenged the statement.

'Why do you say that, Adam? Am I not able to run *The Haven* for a little longer? With rest you will get well again. If you would only give yourself a chance . . .'

'Patrick, we are not talking about my miserable consumptive lungs, now.'

'Then what?'

A dart of fear shivered through Patrick.

'Sometimes I think time is so short for me,' Adam shook his head wearily. 'It is then that I know only a desperate feeling of failure. I worry too, about Sarah. I know so little about her, Patrick. Until now it had not mattered to me who she was or where she came from, but if I were to die . . .'

'Stop it, Adam. Stop it, I say!'

'. . . *if I were to die,*' Adam insisted quietly, 'what would become of Sarah? I think above all I care about leaving her.'

'Then if you are determined to harbour such morbid thoughts, Adam, let me say at once that in my opinion Sarah would be able to care for herself.'

'But, Patrick,' Adam protested weakly, 'I am the tenant of this house. I live here only because some saintly person does not demand the months of rent I owe him. It would not bode well for Sarah and Molly and Dicky-Sam if I were not here. They might be tumbled into the street without a second thought. What would happen to Sarah, then?'

Patrick reached for Adam's hand. It was like the vulnerable hand of a small, trusting child and it shocked him it could be so cold whilst at the same time beads of sweat glistened on Adam's forehead.

'Listen to me, friend. You are tired and unwell. It is natural that you should feel despondent at times, but if it will comfort you I give you my most solemn word that you need never fear for the welfare of Sarah or Molly or Dicky-Sam. That at least I can promise you.'

Adam nodded his head and more relieved, smiled his sweet smile, a smile that tore at Patrick's heart. In Adam's beloved face was reflected all the sadness and gladness of their youth together. In it, Patrick was reminded of their burning optimism and of his own betrayal of those long-ago hopes. His voice unsteady with emotion he said, 'What are you keeping back from me, Adam? Why will you not let me examine you? Are you hiding something? I am your old friend and I know you almost as well as I know myself. Tell me what is really causing this brooding?'

But Adam closed his eyes against Patrick's directness.

'Leave me be, Patrick. Let me sleep?'

For the moment Patrick knew there was nothing more to be said but fear had coursed through him with ice-cold intensity.

He measured a strong sleeping-draught and was relieved that Adam took it without protest, whispering quietly, 'I shall sleep, now. Goodnight, Patrick, my dear friend. God keep you.'

So reluctantly and apprehensively Patrick had left Adam's bedside, fear nagging inside him that he could not explain.

Now suddenly in the small, cold hours of the morning, a feeling of animal terror gripped Patrick and he knew why sleep was evading him. Adam, he was certain, was in need of help. He would go downstairs to the sick-room and he would know at once if the morbid fears had any substance. Shielding the candle-flame with his hand he gently pushed open the bedroom door, sensing at once that Adam was not asleep.

'Patrick? Thank God you have come!'

'Adam – what is it?'

Fear surged afresh through Patrick, then wound itself into a tight ball in his throat so that he could hardly speak. He bent to light the bedside candle from his own and as it flickered then flamed into light he knew his most awful fears were realized.

Jerking in spasms of agony Adam lay flushed and sweating. His breath came in small painful gasps and Patrick wanted to puke with fear as a dreaded and familiar stench filled his nostrils.

Desperately he tried to raise the pathetic body into a comfortable position but Adam grasped his hands.

'Remember your promise, Patrick.'

Each word seemed an agony of effort.

'Take care of Sarah for me . . .'

The frail shoulders shook with a spasm of coughing.

' . . . take care of them all –'

Patrick wiped the fevered brow, bending low so that his lips were close to Adam's ear.

'Don't be afraid, Adam. I will awaken Sarah. I'll bring her to you.'

He did not remember his flight through the quietly brooding house or of groping with his hands for Sarah's shoulders in the unaccustomed darkness of the kitchen. He knew only that Adam was ill, desperately so and that Sarah must be with him.

'Wake up, Sarah. Wake up!'

Dimly Patrick saw her shake her head as if trying to remember where she lay but she did not cry out in alarm. Years of sudden night calls had schooled a discipline into her and her actions were almost automatic as she reached for the wrap that lay beside her.

Patrick turned his back on her and thrust a splinter of wood into the near-dead fire, blowing on it until it burst into sudden flame. Then, lighting the hanging oil lamp he turned again to Sarah.

She stood, endearingly vulnerable, her shawl clutched about her, blinking her eyes awake. She gave a little smile of recognition.

'Oh, it's you, Patrick. Is anything the matter?'

He placed his hands on her shoulders, urging his strength into her.

'Sarah?'

With an effort she raised her head.

'I am sorry, Patrick, but I am so tired . . .'

Compassion flowed through him as he realized that what he was about to tell her would send her small precious world crashing into smithereens at her feet.

'Sarah, I want you to come with me to Adam.'

He felt the sudden tremor of fear that ran through her body.

'What is it?'

Instantly she was awake, stumbling on bare feet across the stone-flagged floor.

'Is Adam worse?' she breathed.

For a moment Patrick was taken aback by her sudden wakefulness then instinctively he threw his body between her and the doorway.

'Listen, my dear. You must compose yourself before you go to Adam – you must be brave . . .'

Sarah's voice rose to a frightened sob as she struggled to get past him.

'Adam, oh, Adam! What is it? Tell me, Patrick?'

Gently Patrick restrained her frantic struggles, wanting with all his heart not to have to tell her. He sought her eyes then held them with the agonized intensity of his gaze.

'Sarah,' he whispered softly. 'Adam is worse; he's got cholera. I think he is dying.'

Dying? Adam dying?

For a moment in time that was no more than the blinking of an eyelid yet which stretched into a lifetime of horror, Sarah's world stood petrified.

'No! Oh, please, *please*, no!'

She was standing outside her body now and the agonized whisper she heard had surely not been hers?

But strangely her lips moved; stiff cold lips in a stiff, cold face. She looked into Patrick's eyes and read compassion there; read too that her plea was little more than a vain hope.

'I must go to him! Please let me go to him?' that strange voice whispered.

Now the lamp that hung from the ceiling had joined in the nightmare, casting shadowy, menacing fingers to a floor that rocked beneath her feet.

Desperately she clung for support to Patrick's hands willing her mind to control her shaking body, closing her eyes against the room that slid and spun around her.

She drew in a shuddering breath, fighting the darkness that threatened to engulf her and to which she so desperately wanted to surrender.

'Hold me? Hold me, Patrick?'

Once more Sarah felt the comfort and strength of Patrick's arms about her. With blessed relief she laid her head on his chest and heard his voice calling her back to sanity.

'It is all right, Sarah. You are not alone. I am here; I will help you.'

Oh, my dearest, his heart yearned, *I want always to help you. I want to care for you and comfort you and never let the world hurt you again. I would exchange destinies with Adam this instant if it could give you back your happiness.*

'I'll send Molly to you,' he said, instead. 'You are cold with shock and she will help you to dress.'

He held her at arm's length, looking into her eyes, willing his strength and love into her frightened heart. Perhaps, Patrick thought, the simple action of dressing, of pulling on her boots and pinning up her hair would give her the time she needed to compose herself a little, come to terms with the cruel truth he had just hurled at her.

'I must go back to Adam,' Patrick said softly, cupping Sarah's face in hands gentle with compassion. 'When you are ready, come to him. It is you he wants now. He needs your comfort and love. Try to be brave, for his sake?'

A small smile flicked on Sarah's lips and once again Patrick saw that familiar, endearing tilting of her chin.

'Thank you,' she whispered, drawing in a deep breath. 'I will be all right, now.'

Molly set down the teapot with a clatter, grateful that a new day was breaking, wishing at the same time that it were still yesterday and the events of the night had not happened.

She hesitated for a moment, reluctant to ask the question.

'It's cholera that Doctor Adam's got, then?' she whispered.

'Yes, Molly.'

'And he's bad?'

'Yes,' Patrick confirmed bitterly, 'he's very ill.'

'I tried to stop him!' Tears misted Molly's eyes and her lower lip trembled. 'I wanted him to stay in his bed when the sick from the *Cornucopia* came but nothing would do but that he should get up and attend to them.'

She sniffed and wiped the tears from her cheeks in an appealing, childlike gesture.

'Miss Sarah is afeard of that ship, Doctor Patrick.'

'I'm beginning to dislike it myself, Molly.'

Now, the *Cornucopia* had been turned into a hospital for the cholera sick, for infirmaries were turning away patients to die in the streets, so overcrowded were their wards. So Doctor Duncan had had the ship commandeered and towed out into mid-river where she now floated at anchor to take on yet more miserable victims of the dreaded fever.

Perhaps, Patrick thought, when the nightmare was over and the port returned to some semblance of normality, some sane person would have the sense to order the ship to be fired and exorcize for all time the evil that seemed to have seeped into her very timbers.

'You'll tell Dicky-Sam not to eat his food without scrubbing his hands, won't you Molly?' Patrick asked, 'and I'll make you a solution of calcium-chloride to act as a disinfectant.'

'A *disinfectant*, sir?'

'It will kill any cholera germs that might get onto your hands.'

It was hard for Patrick to explain to people like Molly O'Keefe such strange words as disinfect, or germ. Even the medical profession was only just beginning to acknowledge their existence and importance.

'I see, doctor,' Molly acknowledged doubtfully.

At least, thought Patrick grimly, simple though her heart was she had the right idea, for cleanliness was almost a religion with Molly.

'And you know that the house must be thoroughly cleansed? The hall, the surgery – wherever the *Cornucopia* sick have been – even the benches they sat on – all must be scrubbed, then scrubbed again.'

'Aye, doctor; Miss Sarah told me. She's away now, seeing to the sulphur candles you want lit.'

Molly sighed.

'You know, we're lucky at *The Haven*. At least there's always water in our taps. That's more'n some folk have got! At least we can keep ourselves clean here.'

She was right, thought Patrick. There just wasn't

enough water for everyone in the town. Even if people could be educated to understand the importance of cleanliness, it would do little good. How could people be clean in those miserable hovels and rat-ridden cellars when a communal stand-tap dripped water for one reluctant hour out of every day?

'Is Miss Harrington awake yet, Molly?'

'That she is, doctor, and up and dressed this last half-hour.'

It was only then that Patrick realized with apprehension the danger to which Arabella was now exposed. He wondered if he should demand that she leave for London immediately where she would be safe from the risk of infection.

He wished with all his heart she had not come to *The Haven*. There were difficulties enough without having the wellbeing of his employer's only child to add to his worries.

Patrick gazed upwards to the pavement outside the kitchen window, watching disembodied feet and the wheels of a milk-seller's cart as they trundled past.

Here was dawning another day. Not so long ago Patrick would have viewed it with trepidation. Now there was nothing he wanted more than to spend each day working at *The Haven* with Adam and Sarah.

But it could never be, for Adam was ill – dangerously so – and he, Patrick, had long ago chosen another path; one which eventually he would have to tread again.

Slowly he rose to his feet, reluctant to leave the saneness of Molly's kitchen but knowing it was time to visit Adam again.

Sarah would be sitting by his bed in that bare little room and the sight of her grief-stricken face would tumble his heart afresh. And Patrick knew he would have to listen to Adam's delirious mutterings and watch and wait helplessly until the crisis was reached.

Meantime, there would be another surgery to take, the sick in the ward to be visited and medicines to be dispensed. There was so much to be done at *The Haven* – too much – but then, thought Patrick grimly, there always had been and it had been done without complaint.

Now, Adam had driven himself to death's doorstep and with no thought for herself, Sarah was nursing him. The realization of Sarah's danger sent a shiver of fear surging through Patrick and he quickened his steps that he might be near her again.

A familiar acrid smell choked in his nostrils, causing him to cough violently and he realized that Sarah had already lighted the sulphur candles. Through the open door of the ward he could hear the steady rhythm of a scrubbing-brush against bare wood.

'Arabella!' he gasped.

She was kneeling beside a pail of steaming water, a bar of soap in one hand, an unwieldy brush in the other and determinedly scrubbing the floor of the ward. She rose to her feet as Patrick entered, her hair tied back in an unbecoming knot, her hands red and swollen from the unaccustomed immersion in hot suds.

'What on earth are you doing?' he asked, incredulously.

Placing her finger to her lips Arabella beckoned Patrick to follow her.

Closing the door of the ward behind her she wiped her hands on her apron before asking quietly,

'Doctor Carmichael has contracted cholera – am I right?'

Patrick nodded.

'Yes, Arabella, you are right and I am forced to the conclusion that *The Haven* is no safe place for you. I think it would be better if you were to return to London at once.'

'I see.'

Arabella set her lips in the way that was so familiar to Patrick yet now there was a sadness in her eyes, too.

'Are you in a position to send me back to London?'

'What do you mean?'

'Look, Patrick, there is cholera in the house. Miss Rigby is nursing Doctor Carmichael so cannot be of any help to you. There are sick to be cared for, a surgery to run and now the house must be thoroughly cleansed against the spread of the infection.'

She paused, seeking his eyes with her own, willing him to accept the soundness of her reasoning.

'Am I not right?' she demanded, quietly.

'Yes, Arabella, but I cannot let you stay here. I am responsible for your welfare – I have a duty to your father.'

'And I too have a duty, Patrick, to the man I am to marry. It entitles me to to stay by his side and share his cares. I will *not* go back to London!'

Patrick opened his mouth to protest then closed it again, unspeaking. Could this be Arabella Harrington who spoke such good sense so quietly? Was the woman who scrubbed floors that same person he had asked to become his wife? He had to admit to himself that all she said was right but he had expected a tantrum when he had suggested she should leave *The Haven* and there hadn't been one. She had completely mystified him.

'Very well, Arabella, you are right, I suppose.'

He gave a small shrug of resignation then chided himself immediately for his ingratitude.

'I will be glad of your help,' he hastened.

'Oh, Patrick, I will do anything . . .' she whispered eagerly, a new humility in her voice.

She raised her eyes to his, silently asking him to pull down the invisible barrier that seemed always to be between them now.

' . . . only tell me how I can be of help.'

Ashamed of his churlish behaviour, Patrick bent down and gently kissed her cheek.

'Thank you, my dear,' was all he could bring himself to say.

Lord, what a mess it all is, he thought as he watched Arabella walk back to the ward, the dejected droop of her shoulders telling him that she too was as unhappy and bewildered as he was.

'Where will it all end?' Patrick whispered to the emptiness of the hall. 'What in heaven's name has gone wrong with the world?'

Like a small child in need of comfort he made for Hetty Norris's room for there, he hoped, he could snatch a few moments in which to gather together his thoughts. Aunt Hetty always understood.

She was sitting up in bed like a chirpy little sparrow when Patrick entered her room.

'There you are at long last, boy! I thought you'd never come! I want to get up. It's time for me to go back home.'

'That is out of the question, Aunt Hetty. There have already been three deaths in Lace Street from cholera. To go back would be madness.'

'Is it so very bad, then?'

'Yes, Aunt – we have an epidemic on our hands and the heat is making things worse.'

It was obvious to Patrick that Hetty Norris had not yet

been told of Adam's illness. He said, 'Adam is very sick, Aunt Hetty.'

A look of fear fleeted across the old face.

'Cholera?' she asked, tersely.

Reluctantly Patrick nodded.

'I am going to visit him now. I came to see you first – to explain that it will be better if I don't visit you too often until the danger is over. Arabella will look after you and explain what is best to be done to stop the spreading of the infection.'

'I understand, boy. I understand,' Hetty Norris whispered quietly. 'Is there anything at all a useless old body like me can do to help?'

'No, Aunt, there is little any of us can do now but wait. But you can pray for Adam. Pray for him, I beg of you, with all your heart.'

But no prayers could help Adam Carmichael.

Quietly and gently as he had lived, so he slipped away from life as the first star of evening shimmered in a darkening sky.

Gently Patrick released the fingers entwined in Sarah's and closed the sightless eyes.

'Sarah?' he whispered fearfully for she sat as still and cold as marble, her face set in a mask of disbelief.

'So quick,' she whispered. 'It was so quick. He didn't have a chance . . .'

'It is often that way, Sarah,' Patrick replied, his voice thick with anguish and despair. 'It is the only blessing that cholera brings with it. Adam was already a sick man; he had little within him with which to fight.'

He waited for the torrent of grief to burst from Sarah's

lips but it did not come. Instead, she rose slowly to her feet and almost reverently drew the bed-sheet over Adam's face. Her actions were automatic as if some unseen manipulator pulled strings that gave movement to her wooden limbs.

Gently Patrick placed his arm around her shoulders drawing her from Adam's bedside and from the room wanting her to weep so that he might weep with her but she walked away from him, her head held bravely high, preparing herself to do those tasks that must be done with quiet dignity.

Perhaps she would cry later, Patrick thought. He hoped she would for it was not good to harbour grief. But Sarah's unhappiness was a private thing, he knew. In her own time and in her own way she would surrender to it and pity surged through him afresh for the quiet woman he had come to love.

Ten

It was long past midnight and Patrick's body ached with mingled shock and fatigue for the work of healing must take precedence over death.

Now, in a house hushed with grief, they talked sadly of Adam.

'There must be no public mourning,' Sarah said as she sat with Patrick in the surgery that had once been Adam's.

'He would not want fuss – he told me that. He said it with such certainty that now I think he must have known . . .'

Her voice trailed away into a desolate whisper and for a moment she did not speak but sat staring ahead, seeing nothing but a blank, black wall of misery.

'Adam was sometimes saddened by all the pomp and ceremony of a funeral,' she continued. 'He felt it was wrong to spend so much money in death when it could have done so much more good in life. "When I die," he once said, "give me a pauper's coffin and lay me with the poor ones, Sarah." '

She spoke softly, a slight tremor in her voice but her eyes were still empty of the tears that might have brought some small comfort.

Patrick nodded silently. He understood what Sarah was trying to say.

To be laid to rest with pomp and ceremony was the

burning desire of rich and poor alike. Those who had the means made a great pageantry of the giving back of their dead. Even the poor insisted upon their sad moments of glory, making beggars of themselves to the men who ran the infamous burial clubs.

Adam had been saddened at the waste of it all and now, Patrick vowed, Adam should have his wish.

'I know what he was trying to tell you, Sarah, and I agree with you. We will respect his wishes, you and I. We will lay him beside his poor ones as he would have wanted. There is no shame in a pauper's coffin – all men are equal in death. Adam tried to show that men are equal in life, too, but few cared to listen to him.'

Patrick shook his head wearily.

'I was one of those men,' he whispered, bitterly.

But even in the fever-ridden port where the sultry heat made the burial of the cholera dead an almost indecent necessity of haste, Adam's poor ones remembered. When the first shock of disbelief had given way to a despairing sorrow, their only thought was to honour their beloved Doctor Adam.

Not for him the indignity of a pit-burial, for dissolute and evil as the rum-sodden grave-diggers were, they showed their love for the gentle young doctor who had been their friend and set their spades grimly into the dry hard earth without thought of reward.

No city alderman or wealthy shipowner was borne to rest with more dignity than was Adam Carmichael as the people of the mean streets defied the order forbidding public gatherings and waited in silent misery outside the house in Abercromby Square.

And as Adam was laid on a simple carrier's cart that someone with love had bedecked with greenery, women wept and men set their lips in sorrow as he was borne away from the house from which no one in need had ever been sent away.

No fine carriages followed in the wake of the creaking little cart but men in rough working clothes and women, heads bowed in grief, walked sadly with their barefoot children to pay a last tribute of love.

No wailing mute carried his black-drapped staff but a one-legged little seaman with a grief-contorted face limped proudly at the head of the long, sad procession.

Head high, Sarah too walked with pride, fiercely glad for Adam's sake for the support of his loved ones.

Patrick stared ahead of him, his eyes not leaving the rough coffin and from all sides the soft sound of sobbing, of whispered prayers for the gentle young soul that was gone from them and small, unbelieving cries.

'What is to become of us, now?'

'Who can we turn to?'

'Who will care?'

I *care*, thought Patrick passionately. I want to try to take Adam's place. I want to do as he did and give as he gave but I am bonded to my master in London and held by a marriage-pledge I cannot but honour.

Adam was dead but the poor ones had a right to ask who would be left to care.

He wished that men were allowed to weep for his heart was bursting with unshed tears and his conscience was heavy as lead.

Adam was gone. He had forsaken the sweet Scottish island of his birth and made Liverpool his own and the brash, roistering port had taken him to its heart. He would rest, for ever a part of it now, in his pauper's coffin in the little cemetery by the Alms-houses, just two streets away from Abercromby Square.

'God keep you,' Patrick whispered as the earth received Adam Carmichael. 'Forgive me, dear friend, for breaking faith.'

Later that night as he sat alone in the darkening surgery and *The Haven* had settled down to a quietness born of sorrow, Patrick tried to take stock of the situation. His brain was so tired he could not think and his body ached, for the surgery had been more than ever crowded that night.

Many of those who came were not sick but had called to offer sympathy and to ask, timidly, what was to happen now that Doctor Adam was gone.

More than ever now Patrick knew how greatly Adam had been loved. Adam had been a champion, a shelter in a storm. Small wonder the house in Abercromby Square had come to be called *The Haven*.

Now Adam's poor ones were pleading for reassurance that his work would go on; that there should be someone else still to care.

Patrick set down his empty mug and walked slowly through the sighing house into the darkening garden. Outside, it was only a little less hot than in the oppressive atmosphere of *The Haven* but at least he could escape the choking fumes of the sulphur candles, the everlasting scrubbing of floors and boiling of bed-linen.

It was wrong of him to feel as he did when everyone was working until they were ready to sleep on their feet. It had been a bad day for them all but now Patrick knew he must come to terms with the future.

If only he could make Doctor Harrington understand how desperately important it was that the work at *The Haven* should go on, he thought.

But if by some miracle he should be allowed to have his wish, how would Arabella take to such a life? That he must honour his pledge and marry Arabella could not be denied but their marriage would be a sham because wherever he went or how far, Patrick knew that Sarah Rigby's sad-eyed wraith would always be at his side.

At first he tried to close his ears to the sound of Arabella's voice, needing as he did some time apart with his problems, wanting to be free from outside pressures and influences. He had come into the garden to be alone for a little while and stand where he and Sarah stood. Arabella's presence was an intrusion, he thought bitterly.

'Patrick?' she called again. 'Where are you?'

A sense of urgency in her voice made him call out, 'Here, by the statue!'

'Oh, please come. I don't know what to do but she's very sick, I'm sure of it. Sarah is ill now, Patrick!'

'Where is she?' he flung over his shoulder as he took the flight of stone steps in one desperate leap.

Sarah was standing in the hall, one hand grasping the newel-post at the foot of the staircase, the other stretched out to him in a gesture of supplication.

'Patrick?' she whispered, swaying on her feet as she tried to walk towards him. 'Help me, Patrick?'

Then her eyelids closed and she crumpled into a pathetic, unconscious huddle at his feet.

'Sarah!'

Anxiously Patrick rubbed her hands and patted her cheeks. Her flushed face, as he touched it, burned with a dry, intense heat.

'*Sarah?*' he pleaded as he gathered her into his arms, '*Oh, Sarah, my darling . . .*'

Her body was limp against him, her head rested beneath his chin.

Patrick stared unseeing into Arabella's eyes, knowing nothing and feeling nothing save that he had just plunged headlong into another nightmare.

How sick Sarah was he couldn't tell but his heart thumped against his ribs and his breath rasped harshly in his throat as he almost ran with her limp body to the sick-ward.

Gently he laid her on the one empty bed. Ahead of him the night stretched, long and desolate.

'I promise, Arabella, that as soon as I am able I will join you in London.'

Patrick looked despairingly at the litter of trunks and hat-boxes that were being carried to the waiting cab.

'You have said that before, Patrick,' Arabella replied sadly. 'How am I to believe that you mean what you say this time?'

Patrick winced, for the quiet finality of her reply hurt him far more than the most vicious of body-blows could ever have done. He looked into Arabella's eyes and saw that they were etched with tiny, tired lines. Her bobbing ringlets had been brushed straight and twisted into an unbecoming pleat in the nape of her neck. She looked older and suddenly strangely wiser as if she had faced life for the first time and was still reeling from the encounter.

Deliberately she avoided his eyes, pulling on her gloves with exaggerated care and Patrick saw that her hands were still red and swollen. He wanted to tell her how sorry he was that her stay at *The Haven* should have been so unhappy but there was a barrier of mistrust between them now and the words of explanation he tried to make came hard to his lips.

'Dearest, I give you my word that as soon as Miss Rigby is well enough to be left I will find another doctor to take charge here. I will come then and give an account of myself to your father. Believe me, Arabella, I will come.'

'And to me, Patrick? Will you give an account of yourself to *me*?' she whispered.

A flush of unease stained the back of Patrick's neck.

Not now? he pleaded, inwardly. He didn't want to provoke another scene. The night had been long and anxious and Sarah had tossed in a burning fever. He had not been able to diagnose her illness and he was in no mood for recriminations. And soon, he knew, Doctor Duncan might arrive. It wouldn't do for Doctor Duncan to witness Arabella in one of her moods nor, for that matter, see one of his old pupils in the throes of abandoned despair and that, he promised himself grimly, could take place at any moment.

But it was himself who shook with uncontrolled bewilderment; Arabella was composed and dignified. It seemed, almost, as if she had left her childish ways behind her and that he was looking for the first time at Arabella, the woman.

He said, uncertainly, 'Please Arabella, bear with me for just a little longer. All will be well, I promise.'

'And you will not return with me to London?'

'I *cannot*! In two or three days, perhaps, but not now. Try to understand, I beg of you.'

'I have tried very hard to understand, Patrick. I have tried to help, to make you proud of me.'

Her voice trembled and for a moment she fought to control her emotions.

'I can do no more, my dear,' she said, eventually. 'I cannot stay here another day. It is up to you, now.'

She lifted her chin and forced a small smile to her lips.

'What ever you decide to do, I will try to understand, Patrick.'

Gently she kissed her fingertips then placed them to his lips.

'Don't keep me too long in uncertainty, I beg of you,' she said softly. Then she turned abruptly and walked quickly away as though reluctant to prolong the pain of their parting.

Patrick stood in the open doorway. He should, he knew, have handed her into the cab but he was unwilling to risk even the slightest rebuff. He waited instead for some small sign, some quick smile of understanding or a nod of goodbye.

But it did not come. The cab door slammed with a dreadful finality and Arabella did not even turn her head as she drove away.

Suddenly Patrick felt the need for comfort. His world had turned a somersault and landed in fragments at his feet. It seemed as he stood there that he was no longer capable of coherent thoughts.

Arabella had left and Sarah was ill. He had never, he thought, felt so bewildered or unsure in the whole of his life.

But Aunt Hetty would understand. To her he could pour out his tangled thoughts and she would listen as she always did as he arranged them into some semblance of order again. Aunt Hetty was wise beyond understanding he thought gratefully as he walked slowly up the stairs, unhappy and bewildered as a small, whipped child.

'What is it, boy?' Hetty Norris asked gently, instantly sensing his misery.

Mutely Patrick shook his head, lowering his body into

the bedside chair, closing his eyes to shut out the madness of his world.

For a little time the old woman did not speak, her heart sad at the sight of Patrick's pale, tormented face. Then she said,

'How is Sarah this morning?'

'She's sick aunt, very sick,' he whispered. 'Her temperature is at fever point and I don't know what is wrong with her. *I honestly don't know!*'

She reached out in a a gesture of sympathy and patted Patrick's hand.

'Who's with her now?'

'Molly is there.'

Wearily he shook his head.

'I can't seem to get her temperature down. Sarah is in great discomfort. All night long we've been applying cold compresses but it's been of no use.'

He shrugged his shoulders.

'I'm beaten, Aunt Hetty. Dicky-Sam has gone to Doctor Duncan's house to see if he can spare me a visit.'

'Then all will be well, lad. Sometimes, when we are very close to a person, it is hard to see what's there before our eyes.'

'Perhaps you are right, Aunt,' Patrick conceded, his thoughts a little calmer, 'but soon I must talk to you. My mind is in such a turnoil. I am being pulled all ways . . .'

'And what do you think is causing all this upset, boy?'

Patrick smiled grimly.

'I am, Aunt. I'm reaping the rewards of my own stupidity. I went to London; I know now that I did the wrong thing and there's no way out for me that I can see.'

'Weren't you content in London, then?'

'I thought I was. I thought it was all I could ever want. If I hadn't decided to pay you and Adam a visit I suppose I'd have gone on quite happily working in Harley Street – marrying Arabella. But that's not enough, now. I want to work here, at *The Haven*.'

'Seems you want things all ways, Patrick, and that never makes for an easy solution.'

'I know. I've got myself into a bonny mess.'

'And what of Arabella? Was that her I heard leaving?'

'It was,' Patrick retorted, tersely.

'Was there an upset between you?' Hetty Norris asked anxiously. 'Did you have words?'

'No, not really. Arabella said she couldn't stay at *The Haven* any longer. She wanted me to go back to London with her.'

'And that was all? You're sure there wasn't anything else?'

Patrick straightened himself in his chair, something in his aunt's persistence ringing a small alarm in his mind.

'There was nothing else, Aunt – why do you ask? Should there be anything?'

Hetty Norris looked down at her tightly clenched fingers.

'I don't know, Patrick,' she prevaricated.

'Then what is the point in all these questions?' he persisted. 'What is wrong, Aunt Hetty? What are you trying to say?'

'I suppose I'm trying to tell you that I've been a foolish old woman. I've got myself into a pretty tangle as well as you. Perhaps, you see, it's what I told Arabella last night that made her go off to London.'

Mystified, Patrick did not speak, the sight of the anxious face before him warning him to tread carefully.

'I shouldn't have said what I did, Patrick. I'll never

know what made me do it. It wasn't right to tell her, I know that now.'

'What wasn't right?' Patrick whispered gently.

'It was after Sarah was taken bad. Arabella came in with my supper and I knew there was something troubling the lass. She talked about you – asked what you were like when you were a little boy. I think she wanted to say something. I couldn't find out what it was but she was uneasy and troubled.'

Something inside Patrick's brain clicked sharply into place.

'And what was it you told Arabella?' he prompted, his voice calm and soft.

There was a sharp tip-tapping in the passage outside and an urgent knocking on the bedroom door.

'Damn!' Patrick swore softly, jerking automatically to his feet.

'Be you in there, doctor?' Dicky-Sam called.

Swiftly Patrick opened the door.

'It's Doctor Duncan's carriage – just pulled up outside, sir.'

In an instant Patrick was gone from the room, his eager footsteps seeming almost to run down the stairs.

Hetty Norris lay back on her pillows, sighing with relief that the moment of truth had been postponed. But she would have to tell Patrick. He'd have to understand that she hadn't meant any harm in the telling of it. She'd been proud, in fact. She hoped that Patrick and Arabella had parted without anger. She would never forgive herself she thought sadly, if she had been the cause of Arabella's return to London.

'Lordy,' she whispered, 'but it's a funny old world and no mistake.'

'Sir, I am most grateful that you have come!'

Patrick held out his hand.

Carefully Doctor Duncan laid his top hat and gloves on the empty bench then looked long at the anxious face before him.

'Young Norris, isn't it? Patrick Norris?'

'Yes sir. I attended your lectures when I was apprenticed in Liverpool.'

'Ah, yes,' the older man nodded. 'I mind you well now and young Carmichael. Sad business that, very sad.'

For a moment the elderly Scotsman stood remembering then squared his shoulders and said briskly, 'I take it you want a second opinion, Doctor Norris?'

'Well, sir, not exactly,' Patrick mumbled, suddenly a student again. 'I am not able to diagnose Miss Rigby's illness at all.'

'I see. Then perhaps I can enlighten you, laddie.'

'I'd be most grateful . . .'

Patrick's mouth had suddenly gone dry.

' . . . if you'd come with me, sir –'

He threw open the door of the ward, indicating the screened bed where Sarah lay.

Molly rose to her feet.

'There's no change,' she whispered. 'The poor dear is rambling again and I can't make sense out of any of it!'

Patrick looked with compassion at the burning face that moved restlessly on the pillow and the dry, cracked lips that whispered endlessly in delirium.

'Miss Rigby has sudden surges of high temperature,' he said, 'followed by –'

Doctor Duncan held up his hand.

'Whisht!' he commanded, taking Sarah's hand in his, feeling the erratic pulsebeat with gentle fingertips.

'It's a sorry state ye've got into, Mistress Rigby,' he

smiled. 'Let's see what's to be done with ye, eh?'

Now Patrick felt relief that he was no longer helpless and alone. Beside him was his old tutor, learned and wise. If anyone could help Sarah, it would be he.

All was still in the sick-ward; so still that Patrick fancied his heart thudded loud enough for all to hear. He licked his dry lips, his eyes not leaving the old doctor's face, willing him to come to a decision – a merciful decision.

The long windows were open to the garden yet scarcely a breath of air penetrated the room. Outside, the day had dawned with an eerie yellow light and sullen, heavy clouds hung threatingly low. Perhaps it would rain at last, thought Patrick with an uplifting of hope; perhaps after all it was going to be a good day.

Trying to steady himself, to quieten the heaviness of his anxious heart, Patrick prayed as he had never prayed in his life before.

Let her be well? Only let her get well and I will ask no more of life . . .

Had he known how he would have conjured up the devil himself and struck a bargain there and then – his life, for Sarah's.

The seconds ticked swiftly into an eternity and the old Scottish doctor peered and poked and examined.

'H'mm,' he whispered, and 'Ah-ah,' as though he and Sarah were alone in the room.

Presently he straightened his back and nodded his thanks to Molly.

Patrick's throat was tight, his mouth parched. Hopefully he glanced at Doctor Duncan but read nothing in the face that was blank as a stone slab.

'I'd be obliged, Doctor Norris,' he said quietly, 'if ye would step outside with me.'

From the distance, thunder growled nearer. Inside, the strange yellow light cast an unreal glow on the empty, echoing hall. It seemed that the whole world was waiting with Patrick for what was to come.

The click of the sneck on the ward door vibrated like the crack of a pistol-shot through his brain. He heard himself asking – begging – in a strange, distorted voice,

'What is it, sir? Will she be all right?'

Doctor Duncan picked up his hat and walked unspeaking towards the front door.

Patrick swallowed hard and the action hurt his throat.

'Sir?' he pleaded, trying to control the feeling inside him that made him want to puke with fear.

The older man turned in the doorway, his face still a mask. Then he took a long breath.

'It surprises me, Doctor Norris,' he said, biting off each carefully enunciated word, 'that I should have once thought you had the makings of a fine physician!'

'I'm sorry – I don't understand . . .'

'Once upon a time, laddie, when yourself and Adam Carmichael attended my lectures I had the notion you were an arrogant young puppy but I put up with your daft ways because I had great hopes of you. In my stupidity I even hoped you might stay in Liverpool but to my sorrow you went to London.'

Glowering, he picked up his bag.

'Now, Doctor Norris, I could find it inside me to be glad that you did!'

Patrick had heard the clipped sarcasm many times before but he had never been so surely trounced in all his years as an apprentice.

'Sir,' he stammered, 'if I have called you needlessly I apologize but I still don't know what is wrong with Miss Rigby.'

'Then away back to her bedside and look into her mouth for little white spots and examine the backs of her ears for little red ones!'

'*Measles?*'

'Aye, Doctor Norris. Measles!'

'But she is so ill – her temperature, her delirium –'

Doctor Duncan shook his head wearily.

'The spots will show soon on the abdomen – the fever will quickly abate after that. Measles, in case you have chosen to forget what I tried to teach you, is a childish ailment and thrown off in most cases with impunity. But with an adult, and one who drives herself as Miss Rigby does, it is often a much more distressing matter.'

Then the dour face creased into a rare smile.

'So ye can stop acting like an anxious husband and let me be about my business. By the bye,' he added softly, 'I'd be willing to take back my past comments if I thought you might consider staying with us in Liverpool. Measles apart, young Norris, our need of you is great.'

'There is nothing I want more, sir, but it isn't possible. Now I know Miss Rigby can soon be safely left I must go to London and explain myself.'

'Your employer will not release you?'

'I fear not,' Patrick whispered sadly. 'It seems *The Haven* must close.'

Then as they stood there the little miracle happened and the rain began to fall. It came reluctantly at first making dark grey circles the size of halfpennies on the dust-dry pavement.

Then as the thunder rumbled ever nearer the storm-clouds let loose their precious burden and soon the road outside danced with raindrops.

'My, but that's a rare sight,' Doctor Duncan beamed.

'My, but it's bonny to look at. Now, ye may be sure, the cholera will soon be at an end.'

Rarely, thought Patrick, had he seen his old tutor so elated. Indeed, the sight of the road awash with the longed-for rain must have cheered him into making the offer of help.

'It seems wrong that this house should have to close its doors; there might yet be a way,' he acknowledged, cautiously. 'Perhaps for a while I might be able to loan ye a couple of students. The experience will be good for them and who knows, laddie, your employer down in London just might be more generous than you think, eh?'

So Patrick had accepted the well-meant offer, realizing that as he did so his last excuse for remaining in Liverpool had gone.

Doctor Duncan would ensure that the sick at *The Haven* would be cared for and Sarah was going to get well. It seemed that the Fates that had thrown the two of them together were now conspiring with capricious glee to tear them apart for ever.

Patrick held out his hand.

'I am grateful for all you have done to help us.'

The old doctor turned up the collar of his coat then grasped Patrick's hand firmly.

'Goodbye, laddie. I hope with all my poor heart that all goes well with you in London.'

Then amidst the clatter of horses' hoofs and a cascading of water from the carriage wheels, he was gone.

Patrick stood for a moment, breathing great gulps of cool, moist air into his lungs.

Now he must return to Harley Street. It would be no trouble, he reasoned. He need only acquaint the medical apprentices with their duties at *The Haven*, bid goodbye to his aunt and to Sarah, Molly and Dicky-Sam. Then he would take a ticket for London – it would be as simple and as easy as that.

But when he was in London, how would he fare with half of him still at *The Haven*? How did a man exist when his heart was elsewhere and his body ached with an impossible love?

'Sarah,' he whispered to the grey, uncaring skies. 'Oh Sarah, my dearest love . . .'

Eleven

Patrick placed his tall hat on the seat beside him and stretched out his legs, leaning back his head and closing his eyes, grateful that now he need not move one weary limb until the train stopped in London.

Three weeks ago he had left Harley Street, yet in that brief time he had lived a lifetime and learned a lifetime's wisdom.

He was no longer the self-possessed young physician complacently bound for a holiday in Harrogate. The man who surrendered himself to the rhythmic swaying of the train was another creature, a man who had learned humility, who had glimpsed his guiding star, sadly and too late.

The most he could hope for would be the granting of a few precious days in which to return to *The Haven* and do those things he had promised would be done.

Remember your promise, Patrick? Take care of Sarah for me? Take care of them all . . .?

Still Patrick heard the pathetic plea. He would hear it in every springtime and it would be borne to him on every gentle breeze. In the blaze of summer or the falling of a snowflake Adam's words would come to him. He would never want to forget them, or Sarah.

Sarah was part of him now. She was in his heart and in his mind and whilst his body still ached from wanting her, he knew he would honour his pledge and marry Arabella.

In time it might be easier for him to live with the certain knowledge that Sarah had loved only Adam. It might even become bearable. For Arabella's sake, he hoped it would.

You are a cheat, Patrick Norris, his conscience whispered. He knew now that even his name was a sham. *Norris*. Aunt Hetty's name; the one he had taken for his own; the one he would give to Arabella. Once, it had been important for him to know about his parents. In his early youth he was sure that his pedigree was long and noble, even though lacking the church's blessing.

'There's things you must know now that you're going back to London and they'll not keep any longer,' his aunt said as he sat by her bedside only that morning. 'I told Arabella, Patrick, and now I've got to tell you.'

'Well, Aunt,' he had gently asked. 'What did you tell Arabella?'

'I told her who you were and where you came from.'

'I see.'

The calmness of Patrick's voice seemed to take Hetty Norris aback and for a time there was silence in the little room. Then, unable to contain herself any longer she demanded,

'Well – ask me then – you've been trying to ferret it out of me for years! Ask me who your mother was!'

His mother? Strange, thought Patrick, he'd managed all his life without one. Aunt Hetty had been all he'd needed, truth known. Did it really matter who that unknown woman was? Could his flesh-and-blood mother have done more for him than Hetty Norris had done? Were there not more important things to be worried about, now?

'Very well, Aunt, I will ask you who my mother was but at this moment I care precious little, I am so tired.'

'You . . . *what*?'

'It doesn't seem to matter so much, now. It is more important that I should try to straighten myself out, think about my future – not worry over what is past.'

A smile of love and pride gentled the old face.

'Then I will tell you, boy, and gladly, because I reckon now you've grown up enough to be told!'

Taking his hands in hers she said quietly,

'Strange, for it's like giving my own son away . . .'

'Who am I, Aunt Het?' Patrick whispered.

'That I don't rightly know, Patrick. You see, I found you on the doorstep.'

'*Abandoned*, you mean?'

'Aye lad, by some desperate woman or a poor unwed lass, perhaps. All I knew about you was your name. It was pinned to your blanket – just that and the date of your birth.'

Patrick gave a small, mirthless laugh.

'You know, I don't know why, but I thought I was the love-child of some rich young lady. Sometimes, you see, I seemed to remember a large house and lofty rooms and rows of bobbing bells.'

'Aye, Patrick, you'd remember all that for you were left on the doorstep of my master's house. His three daughters took a liking to you and so did I. That's why my master let me keep you, provided you stayed below stairs with the servants.'

'But you supported me all my life? I had thought it must have been my mother's family or my natural father.'

'No, lad. My master and mistress left Liverpool shortly after that so I stayed behind and took the little house in Lace Street. I scrubbed and did washing to support us.

You've been the son I never had. I've been proud of you – so very proud.'

'But my education, Aunt Hetty? Did you pay for that as well? Did Black Becky bleed you dry so that your little foundling might have his chance in life?'

Hetty Norris's eyes filled with tears.

'I didn't want you to find out about that, but I had to go to Becky Solomon. It was the only way I could come by so much money. I'm sorry . . .'

'*Sorry?* It is I who am sorry, for my stupid pride!'

He fished eagerly in his pocket-book and took out the almost-forgotten receipt.

'Here,' he said, placing the paper in her hand, 'a present for you.'

Hetty Norris frowned.

'You know I can't read. What does it say?'

'It says you are out of Rebecca Solomon's debt for all time.'

'Oh, bless you, lad,' the old woman whispered. 'I've been fair worried lying here, thinking about the tally-man.'

Patrick reached out for her, holding her close, placing his cheek to hers.

'I was a child of the streets, Aunt, unloved and unwanted –'

For just a little time a feeling of indescribable sadness possessed him.

'No, boy, that's not true. You *were* wanted. *I* wanted you the minute I set eyes on you, and maybe your real mother loved you more than I did. Like as not she loved you too much to keep you. One day you'll understand what I mean by that.'

Then she placed her hands on his shoulders and held him at arm's length, looking into his eyes as she spoke.

'You know, deep down inside her, every woman wants a child in her arms. Like as not it doesn't matter how she gets it or even who fathers it. You have been *my* son, Patrick. You weren't of my body but you were the child of my heart.'

Her eyes misted with tears again and she could not hide the tremble in her voice as she whispered,

'Don't think too badly of your mother, Patrick. It must have been terrible to have to give you away. She left you at the bottom of the steps that led off the street and down to the kitchens. Like as not she thought you'd find more compassion there than there'd be at the front door.'

Hetty Norris sighed, remembering.

'But my master and mistress were good people. They didn't have you sent away. They could have given you to the *Ladies' Charity*. The *Charity* would have found some place for you – they'd not have put you in the workhouse – but it's hard for waifs, at times. Sometimes the wrong people get hold of them and they're often put upon – worked hard and cruelly used. I couldn't have risked that happening to you, boy.'

The old eyes pleaded for understanding. It was almost as if they were asking that he should forgive her for withholding the truth for so long.

'Oh you dear, stupid, wonderful old lady!' Patrick exulted. 'What can I say to you? I can only thank God that my mother, who ever she was, had the good sense to leave me on *your* doorstep!'

Then they were laughing and crying at one and the same time and Patrick's heart was suddenly a little less sad.

'Now, boy, we must talk seriously. Just what are your intentions, might I ask?'

'With regard to *The Haven*, you mean?'

'Aye, and to Arabella and your position in London. You've got to get yourself sorted out.'

'How did Arabella take it, Aunt, learning I was a nobody, I mean?'

'She took it very well. It seemed to me that it made very little difference at all. She had other things on her mind, if you ask me.'

'I haven't treated her very kindly, have I?'

Hetty Norris shrugged.

'Perhaps not, but maybe it's been good for the lass to stay at *The Haven*. It might have helped her to see the other side of life. She'll be all the better a wife for you, for the knowing.'

If you're still bent on marrying her. If you really loved her, Patrick . . .

'Look, lad,' she said when Patrick remained silent. 'I've tried to rear you to respect the truth and to act with honour. You've got a duty to your employer and to that poor girl. There's nobody can sort out your life now, but yourself.'

'I know,' Patrick shook his head miserably. 'I want so much to stay in Liverpool as Adam always wanted I should. But would Doctor Harrington release me and would Arabella live here?'

'I don't know, Patrick. I'd like you to come home but it's something you've got to work out for yourself. You'll do what's right, I know it.'

Aye, her mind supplied, *you'll stay with Doctor Harrington and you'll wed his daughter because I've brought you up to honour your word.*

'Yes, Aunt. I shall do what is right, I promise you.'

He had given her hand a little squeeze then, as he rose to take his leave of her.

'Thank you, dear Mother Hetty. Thank you for everything.'

Patrick Norris. Patrick Nobody.

The words chased round and round in his head. Funny, but he didn't care now; he really didn't care. In a strange way he was almost glad. He was a foundling. He had been spewed up by the Liverpool gutters and he wanted to return to the people who lived there – his own people. He needed them as much as they needed him.

Carefully he pushed tobacco into his pipe, staring unseeing from the window of the compartment, realizing that every second was taking him further away from Sarah.

He smiled gently as he recalled their goodbye. She had been sitting up in bed, her long hair tied back with a ribbon, her face covered with tiny bright-red spots.

'You look like a little girl,' he teased, desperately trying to make their moment of parting easier for himself.

'I don't feel like a little girl. I just want to stay here and sleep and sleep. Aren't I wicked?'

'Oh, very wicked and slothful, Sarah Rigby,' he smiled, wishing with all his heart that he too might be allowed to sleep for a week.

'Doctor Duncan's apprentices seem very keen to do their best to help,' Sarah said. 'I wish Adam could have employed students. We thought about it often and decided we couldn't afford even one.'

She smiled, ruefully.

'They eat so much, don't they, young growing men?'

They were making small-talk, Patrick had realized. Best he should get it over with as soon as he could.

'I must go now,' he said, tersely, 'but I will be back, Sarah, even if it is only for a few days. I must write again to Adam's parents and send them his personal things.'

'Yes, Patrick,' Sarah whispered. Then she smiled.

'I'm sure we shall be all right. You must not worry about us. Doctor Duncan has promised to look in, hasn't he, from time to time?'

Patrick nodded.

'Goodbye then, Sarah,' he said briefly. 'Take care of yourself.'

He strode from the ward without giving her his hand or permitting himself even one small backward glance, his body trembling with the effort of self-control. He had wanted to grasp her in his arms and hold her close; tell her that when he came back nothing would keep him from her ever again. He would have given a great deal to have been able to say that.

Dearest Sarah, his heart yearned. *Gentle, proud, beautiful Sarah. I know so little about you yet I love you so much.*

. . . *so much; so much; so much;* echoed the wheels of the train that carried him so relentlessly nearer to London.

The street lamps shone brightly as Patrick's cab swung smoothly out of Wimpole Street and into Harley Street, but for the first time Patrick felt no burst of elation as he drove down that famous road; only a feeling of guilt that was mingled with sorrow and regret.

The front door of Doctor Harrington's house was opened to him before he had scarcely had time to pull the bell. It was as if someone had been waiting breathlessly for his return.

Arabella ran lightly down the thickly-carpeted stairs as

Patrick handed his hat and gloves to the primly starched housemaid. Somewhere, it was certain, the footman would already be attending to his baggage.

For a moment Arabella and Patrick hesitated, strangely shy, each eyeing the other for some small sign of what was to come. Then Arabella held out her hands.

'My dear,' she whispered, softly.

Patrick bent to kiss her cheek, feeling a strange relief that the first awkward moments of their meeting seemed not to be tainted with the promise of bitterness.

'Did you have a good journey?'

'Yes, I thank you. The train made splendid time.'

Now they were talking to each other quite calmly, acting like distant cousins, polite and affectionate.

Arabella linked her arm through Patrick's, walking beside him to the first-floor drawing-room.

'I am glad to have this time alone with you, Patrick, but we may not have long. Papa is at the opera and will soon be home. Before he comes there is something I must say to you. It is important to both of us that you should know what it is before you speak to my father.'

Patrick frowned.

'It sounds very mysterious, Arabella.'

'Not really,' she shook her head, 'but I have told papa about *The Haven* and the conditions there. I think I might have helped a little. At least he understands now why you needed to be so long away.'

Patrick felt an unaccustomed surge of gratitude towards Arabella. He was amazed to see such a subtle change in her.

Now she no longer wore her hair in fashionable ringlets but had swept it into a chignon in the nape of her neck as Sarah did. There was a new maturity about her too, and an air of calmness.

Patrick lowered his tired body into a chair and closed his eyes, trying to shut Arabella out, to see instead Sarah's beloved face. But the lamps glowed softly, the chair cushioned him gently and try as he might that loved face eluded him in the richness and comfort of the room. Yet somewhere in the misty distance, tiny alms-houses stood by a cemetery and a gentle voice sighed insistent into the summer dusk,

'Take care of Sarah for me, Patrick? Take care of them all . . .'

Excitedly, Kate Tarleton burst into the kitchen.

'It's here, Miss Rigby! The waggon's come!'

Sarah set down the apple she was peeling.

'Very well, Kate,' she smiled, wondering afresh at the exuberance of the very young, for little more than two weeks ago Kate had lain bruised and bleeding, the cause and the victim of a brothel fight.

Now, her cheeks plump and rosy again, she had waited eagerly since sun-up for the arrival of the farm cart that was to carry her, along with Margaret-Mary Haggarty and her family, to the sweet, rich farmlands beyond Ormskirk. She was dancing with impatience at the head of the stone steps when the driver pulled the great Clydesdale stallion to a halt outside *The Haven*, and flinging her arms around Sarah's neck she kissed her cheek affectionately.

'God bless you, Miss, for what you and Doctor Patrick have done for me. I'll never forget you both, not ever!' she vowed fervently.

Sarah hugged Kate close, sorry that the lovable girl was leaving, yet glad she would now have a good home and a kindly mistress.

'Be off with you child,' she said, her voice husky with emotion and in an instant Kate was perched alongside the waggoner, her young face glowing with pure joy.

Sarah held up her hand to Margaret-Mary Haggarty who sat atop the waggon with her sparse belongings and her many children.

''Tis sorry I am not to be seein' Doctor Patrick for don't I owe my life to the dear man?' she whispered to Sarah. 'I'd have liked fine to show him his namesake,' she said proudly, looking down at the sleeping boy-child who had been born against the most fearful of odds.

Patrick had been magnificent that day, Sarah remembered. She had been proud to work by his side. She thought, too, of the night they had gone together to the tavern in Leather Lane and the compassion Patrick had shown for Kate, little more than a child yet forced into prostitution that she might exist. Now Kate would never need to go back to the Liverpool streets.

There was so much goodness still in the world, Sarah thought as she waved goodbye to the waggon-load of happiness. Now the Haggartys and Kate Tarleton were beginning a new life in the peace of the countryside, the heartbreaking circumstances of their old lives behind them.

Sarah thought with gratitude of the promptness with which the friend of her schooldays had answered her plea for help, offering a farm cottage to Margaret-Mary in exchange for sewing-work, and the job of dairymaid to Kate. Now, as the waggon rumbled out of the square, Sarah turned once more to *The Haven*, trying desperately to ignore the fact that slowly and surely it was becoming an empty, silent shell.

George and Tilly Hanson and little Ben had already left for Macclesfield at the promise of regular work in the silk mills there and now Kate had gone.

The sick-ward was almost empty and the dispensary almost bare of medicines and drugs for it was another week before the *Bounty* was due. Almost all the food Patrick had bought was gone too and there was no money left with which to buy more. Soon the medical apprentices would return to Doctor Duncan and the doors of *The Haven* would finally close. Then there would be just the three of them; Molly, Dicky-Sam and herself to remember the good days when Adam had been alive and hope had run high.

Slowly Sarah walked down to the kitchens, wondering yet again how Patrick was faring and how much longer she would have to wait before there was news of him from London.

It was strange, she mused, that she had not liked Patrick when first they met yet now she found herself starting hopefully at the sound of an approaching cab or a sudden knocking on the front door.

But Patrick too had gone and with him all hopes that *The Haven* could continue for Sarah knew how difficult it would be for him to return, even for the few days he had hoped to be given.

' . . . and I'll tell ye, Dicky-Sam Pickstock, that there's not much time left for us all at *The Haven*.'

Molly's voice floated disconsolately from the kitchen.

'I'm thinking the landlord will be setting the bailiffs on us now that Doctor Adam's gone, God-rest-him.'

'No, Molly, the landlord won't do that,' Sarah spoke quietly from the kitchen doorway. 'At least I can promise you both that we shall have a roof over our heads until we can decide what is to be done.'

'But how can ye be so sure?' Molly demanded, doubtfully.

'Because *The Haven* belongs to me.'

'To *you*, Miss Sarah?'

Molly's teacup dropped with a clatter.

'You mean that it's been yourself that hasn't taken a penny rent all these years?'

'Yes,' Sarah nodded. 'I am the mysterious landlord and Adam never knew,' she whispered, sadly.

'And the *Bounty*, miss?' Dicky-Sam asked. 'Has that been of your sending, an' all?'

'It is sent by the notaries of my late aunt. She left me shares that allow me an income of five guineas a month. That, and this house is all I have, but I wanted to give it to Adam to help run *The Haven*. To have it sent secretly was the only way I could find to make him accept it.'

Sarah shrugged her shoulders, anticipating Molly's next question.

'Don't talk about it any more, Molly, there's a dear soul. I'll tell you – in my own good time – I promise. But not now . . .'

'Why, to be sure, Miss Sarah,' Molly retorted, blushing to the roots of her hair, 'such a thing never entered me head, so it didn't, but you'll be fine, now. You'll be able to sell this great barn of a place and find a nice snug little house, somewhere.'

'No, Molly, I want us all to stay together. I promised Doctor Adam it would be like that. We'll manage, the three of us.'

She tilted her chin and smiled.

'Why, who knows, perhaps even now Doctor Patrick is on his way back to us!'

Dicky-Sam and Molly nodded but their eyes were empty of hope. They knew as well as Sarah knew that Patrick had been gone for almost a week and time was running out.

Sarah rose abruptly to her feet.

'Will you give Miss Hetty her breakfast then help her to dress, Molly? I am going out for a little while.'

'But, Miss Sarah, you've not long been out of your sickbed,' Molly protested. 'Let Dicky-Sam go with you?'

'No, Molly; you are kind and I thank you, but I must go alone.'

The kitchen door closed behind Sarah and Dicky-Sam shook his head sadly.

'Poor lass,' he said softly.

'Oh? And why do you say that, Dicky-Sam Pickstock,' Molly demanded. 'And why is herself the owner of a house such as this yet as poor as a churchmouse, God love her?'

Carefully avoiding the little man's eyes she filled her teacup afresh.

'Not that it's any concern of mine, mark ye. Never let it be said that Molly O'Keefe's a busy-body . . .'

She shrugged her shoulders and pulled up a chair to the table.

' . . . And another thing,' she continued, now in full spate, 'where's the girl going that's so secret we can't be told? Will ye tell me that, Dicky?'

'Aye, I'll tell ye for I'll wager a year's pay I know where she's a'going.'

He paused, dramatically, savouring his moment of importance.

'They're going to sink the *Cornucopia* this forenoon, aren't they?'

'They are, too, and a good riddance to the evil ship, says I.'

'Well, don't you see, Molly? Reckon Miss Sarah's going to be there to see the last of the packet.'

Molly shrugged her shoulders doubtfully.

'And why should she want to do that?'

'Eh, woman, don't you understand? If Miss Sarah owns this house then she's old Mad Jonathan's kin, ain't she? Like as not Miss Sarah once owned that jonah-ship!'

'I'll not believe that!'

'Then believe what you want, Molly O'Keefe. You've not lived in Liverpool all your days like I have. I was a seaman remember afore I was nearly killed on the *Cornucopia*. I knows all about Liverpool ships and ship-owners.'

'Then who was Mad Jonathan, will ye tell me?'

'He was Jonathan Rigby, a shipowner. He was all respectable on top, but there's some as knew all along where he got his money from. It came from slaving, Molly, and that's a fact!'

'God help us! Tainted money!'

'Aye, and old Jonathan made sure his wealth stayed in the Rigby family. He only had one child – a daughter he called Sarah and he married this Sarah off to her cousin – name of Rigby, too. That way he kept an eye on his investments, see? Well, talk had it that this daughter and her new husband made a sea journey on the *Cornucopia* and they never came back; died at sea, both of 'em and buried at sea, an' all. They left a child behind them, little more'n a babe and that little lass was our Miss Sarah, like as not. I don't know what become of that little one. Folks said she was packed off to some school in the south as soon as she was old enough. Old Jonathan couldn't stand the sight of the poor little thing – reminded him over much of his dead daughter.'

'Poor lonely little wench,' Molly sniffed. 'Poor Miss Sarah.'

'Aye, I reckon old Jonathan Rigby took a turn for the worse when that ship docked and the Master had to break the news to him. Stood on the quayside and cursed something awful, he did. Then he cursed the ship, an'all and had her name changed, there and then. He'd called that ship for his daughter, see? That slave-ship was once called the *Sarah*. Funny, I've known that all along but I never connected old Mad Jonathan and his packet with *our* Miss Sarah.'

He shook his head sadly.

'Changing a ship's name ain't good you know. Calling her the *Cornucopia* was bound to bring ill-luck, I'm thinking.'

'And this ship's Master? What happened to him, then?'

'Don't know, Molly. Didn't even know his name. You see, I didn't sail on the *Cornucopia* until she changed hands; she had a different Master, then; one as kept his mouth shut tight, an' all.'

'But I thought shipowners were rich, grand folk, Dicky,' Molly hazarded, doubtfully. 'Poor Miss Sarah ain't rich.'

'No, she's not and that's a fact. Old Jonathan went from bad to worse. Died of drink, in the end, in a dock-side gutter. They said he left nothing but a pile of debts and the *Cornucopia*. All his money went on cards and dicing and drinking. You see, they'd stopped slaving by that time. There was no more money coming in. Jonathan Rigby wasn't a good merchant. All he dealt in or knew anything about, for that matter, was black ivory – slaves.'

Molly carried the cups to the sinkstone.

'Poor Miss Sarah. No wonder she feared that ship. And she'd be mortal shocked I'll not doubt, when she found out where the money came from that paid for her fine upbringing. Imagine the shame of slave-trading? And 'twas the *Cornucopia* sick that brought cholera into this house, never forget that,' she whispered, sadly.

'Aye, Molly and maybe it would be as well if *The Haven* was to close its doors. Miss Sarah has worked herself to a shadow here and it's my belief she's done it on account of being a Rigby, I'm thinking. She's ashamed of her past kin and being reared on bad money. She's been trying to even things up, if you ask me.'

But for once, Molly O'Keefe had nothing to say. She turned her back on Dicky-Sam and busied herself with the washing of the breakfast crocks. She wished he'd take himself off to the market. Molly O'Keefe wanted to be alone; she wanted to weep for Miss Sarah and poor young Doctor Adam. She wanted to weep until she was sick for the wickedness of the world . . .

Sarah sat down on a hummock of grass, surprised that she felt so tired but realizing it was important that she should come to the jutting arm of land that reached far out into the wide River Mersey. People called it the Wishing Gate and today Sarah would wait with other women who kept vigil there and bid farewell to a part of her life.

Women who waited at the Wishing Gate were often seen to weep for there they watched the passing of the ships that bore their men away and they wished them God-speed and a safe landfall, standing there until the mast-tops had merged into the distant horizon where the river poured itself into the sea.

Sarah waited too for the passing of a ship. She awaited the jonah-ship, the condemned *Cornucopia*. The packet was old and unsafe and her timbers rotten. She had housed cholera victims, tied up there in the middle of the river, and no mount of limewashing would ever cleanse her of the disease. Now the Port Authority had demanded that she be packed with explosives and floated downriver to the open sea, there to be sunk. It gave Sarah a strange satisfaction to know that soon all the ill-luck and evil the ship had attracted to itself would be gone for ever. Perhaps, with the sinking of the *Cornucopia*, everything would come right.

So much was going out of her life, Sarah thought. Since she could remember, she had been lonely; it seemed that Fate had decreed it should be so. Dear, gentle Adam was gone and still she had not wept for him for her grief was too fierce for tears.

Now Patrick had left, taking with him that feeling of safeness she had come almost to depend upon. If only he had been able to stay at *The Haven*, she yearned, and take up where Adam had left off. Patrick was such a fine doctor, Sarah thought sadly; so skilful and confident. What could they not have accomplished, he and Adam, at the house in Abercromby Square?

Sarah hugged her shawl around her, straining her eyes for signs of the Cornucopia's approach. She would know that ship at once, even from a distance. She would sense its coming, that ship that had once been named the *Sarah*. She knew every mast and spar, every inch of rigging.

'Dear God,' she prayed, silently, 'will I never be free of the curse of my forebears? Shall I ever rid myself of the shame of it all?'

How could her grandfather have done it? How could he have sold his fellow-creatures like dumb beasts? Surely that was the devil's work, she thought, grateful that now men could no longer live by such evil.

A rough but kindly voice pulled Sarah's thoughts away from the past.

'Are you all right, lass? Trembling something awful, you are.'

'Thank you, ma'am, but I am only a little cold. I have not been well –'

Her voice trailed away as the *Cornucopia* hove into sight.

The packet's sails were tightly furled and lashed; her masts, yards and bowsprit sticking out like skeletal fingers as two of the new steam-tugs, importantly belching coal-smoke, nosed and fussed her down-river. And as the ship a madman once cursed went slowly to her destruction, the woman with the sad grey eyes who stood at the Wishing Gate said goodbye to so much of the unhappiness in her past life.

With her solemn passing, the *Cornucopia* took with her a mother and father Sarah had never known, an old man driven mad by misery and remorse, the bewildered crying of poor negro souls and the soft sad sighing of a gentle young doctor.

'May God forgive the evil you have had a part in,' Sarah whispered to the ship that would soon lie in a million pieces beneath the sea. 'May I live long enough to right some of the wrongs those before me have caused.'

If only there could be a way, she wished desperately, to keep *The Haven* open. For Adam's sake she must try. Adam's sacrifice must not be allowed to have been made in vain. She would remember the promise she made to him; keep his face before her as a talisman.

'Oh, Adam, my dear,' she whispered.

Then the tears she had denied for so long began to fall and she sat with the arms of the kindly stranger around her and wept for Adam until she could weep no more.

'There now,' soothed the woman, her rough hand

gently stroking Sarah's hair. 'There now, lass, stop your weeping. He'll soon be back.'

But you don't understand, Sarah thought desperately. *He won't be back. He's never coming back!*

Twelve

Sarah walked slowly homeward, looking across the fields at the end of Vauxhall Road to the slowly-turning sails of the tall windmill, remembering clearly the day Great-aunt Polly had said,

'Well, he's dead at last. You'll have to know now, for you've inherited a fair load of trouble, Sarah girl!'

Sarah had been just seventeen then and old Polly Rigby had only two years left to live, had they known it. She had been happy in the little house set deep in the Cheshire countryside; glad to be rid of the select boarding establishment for young ladies and live in a real home at last. She hadn't known a great deal about her parents except that they had died young within two days of each other and had been consigned to the waters that washed the African shores. It was a mysterious ailment, Aunt Polly said and tight-lipped had left it at that.

Then *He* had died and Sarah came to know of the existence of Mad Jonathan – Jonathan Septimus Rigby, her grandfather.

'Why didn't you tell me, Aunt Polly? I didn't know that all this time I had a grandfather.'

'Best you shouldn't know until you had to, girl.'

'But he's dead now and I'll never know him. I'd have liked to have known him – talked to him about my parents, about my mother . . .'

'That you wouldn't! The mention of your mother's name would have set him ranting like the mad creature he was. And he wouldn't have you near him; he said so, the day the *Sarah* docked and they told him your mother was dead. Jonathan Rigby was twisted with hatred; he was rotten to the core.'

'How can you say that, Aunt Polly? Why are you so bitter, and he your own brother?'

'I didn't own him. Rather to have no one left in the world than to be kin to a slave-trader!'

'A slaver? Oh, no! I won't believe it! I'd have known; I'd have heard about it, somehow . . .'

'No one knew, save a few. I knew it and the Master of the *Sarah* knew it –'

'But no one has ever seen slaves in Liverpool, it's a well-known fact. It must be a lie about my grandfather, it must!'

'It's no lie, Sarah Rigby. There weren't any slaves came into the port but that's not to say slaving didn't go on. No ship's Master ever dared bring blacks into the place. He'd have had them all thrown overboard before he'd have done that. No, my girl. On the surface of it, my brother was a merchant. He loaded his ship with guns and cheap gin and took them to the African coast. The ship's Master traded them for negroes and those poor creatures were shackled like animals in the hold and taken straight to America. They were traded there for cotton and tobacco and molasses and sugar – all very respectable. Everybody knew it went on yet nobody admitted to working the triangular run, as they called it.'

'Dear God,' Sarah whispered. 'My mother, my grandfather – even *you*, Aunt Polly – lived on bad money.'

'Aye, we did and we shall pay for it, just as your grandfather and your mother before you paid for it. Us

Rigbys'll never be free of it, make up your mind to that, Sarah!'

And when it was all over and done with, when the creditors had been paid and the debts settled there was only the re-named *Sarah* left and the empty, neglected house in Abercromby Square.

The *Sarah*, named for her mother and on which her mother had died was sold to continue its evil as the *Cornucopia*, and the house in Abercromby Square had been leased by her notary to a young doctor, a gently-spoken Scotsman named Adam.

That had been little more than six years ago and like Great-aunt Polly, Adam too was dead. It seemed to Sarah that as soon as she learned to love a person she was fated to lose them. Were the Rigbys truly cursed or dare she hope that now the curse lay at the bottom of the sea with the remains of the *Cornucopia*?

She had tried so hard. Surely things would go right, now?

Dicky-Sam was waiting outside the surgery door, a large mug of tea in his hand when Sarah walked wearily into *The Haven*.

'Lord bless us, miss, ye've been away so long I was off to find the Town Crier!'

Sarah smiled at the little man's concern. Dicky-Sam never changed, she thought. No matter what happened, he always made it his duty to take in a mug of tea as the last patient left the surgery.

'I'm sorry I caused you to worry, Dicky,' she said, eyeing the mug longingly. 'Do you think Molly might have any tea left in her pot?'

'To be sure she will, Miss Sarah. If you'd like to take this mug in to the doctor, I'll bring up another for you.'

'Bless you,' smiled Sarah, knocking gently before opening the door of the surgery.

Then she stood transfixed, willing her hands to stop their sudden trembling, holding the mug tightly lest it hurtle to the floor. She took a deep, steadying breath,

'Your tea, doctor,' she smiled, tremulously, not knowing whether to laugh or to cry, wanting desperately to shout with joy at the sight of his face.

He was back! Patrick had come as he said he would! Now she knew, her heart beating joyfully, that she could tell him all her worries and he would help things to come right. Now, for just a little time, she could feel safe again.

Gravely Patrick rose to his feet.

'You are looking much better, Sarah,' he said quietly, willing himself to be calm. 'It is good to see you again.'

'Patrick! It is good to see you, too! How much time do you have? Two days? . . . three? Oh, I have so much to ask you. I need your advice on so many things.'

She perched herself on the edge of the desk, laughing joyfully.

Patrick sat down again, urging himself back to normality, clenching his hands on the arms of his chair so that he might not reach out and touch the cheek flushed pink with excitement.

A pulse beat in his throat at the beauty of her. How wonderful it would be if she could always look at him with eyes that shone like summer sunlight. But she was only relieved to see him, of that he was sure. Women like Sarah only loved once and Adam had been Sarah's man. Patrick knew that all he could have hoped for would have been second-best and that he would never have accepted.

'I will be glad to help you in any way I can, Sarah. I have been giving a great deal of thought to the running of *The Haven* – the two unused bedrooms, for instance.'

Sarah puckered her forehead.

'Yes, Patrick?'

'Hmm. I often felt it was wrong that they should stand empty. Had you never thought of putting them to better use?'

'Yes, of course we had.'

Sarah was completely mystified.

' . . . but we could not afford even to furnish them, let alone run them. Perhaps if we had had apprentices it might have been possible. But why are you saying all this, Patrick? Far from taking on more work, I'm afraid we shall now be able to do very little here, at all.'

Patrick smiled gently.

'But had you not thought,' he persisted, 'that with those two rooms made available, there could be separate wards for men and women and there could be a laying-in room for mothers in labour? Women should not suffer in child-birth. They should have the benefit of chloroform when they are confined. Chloroform has been in use in Edinburgh now for three years and more and more London doctors are acknowledging its great advantages.'

Sarah's head buzzed.

'Stop, Patrick! You know all this is not possible.'

Patrick reached out and took Sarah's hands in his, smiling into her bewildered eyes.

'But it *is* possible, Sarah, and I intend to make it so.'

'How? With the best will in the world, Patrick, I cannot follow your reasoning.'

'We will take an apprentice,' he replied, triumphantly. 'We will take *two*!'

'*We?*'

It cannot be possible, thought Sarah. Patrick cannot be teasing? Surely he couldn't be so cruel?'

'Yes Sarah. *We!*'

Patrick laughed with delight, no longer able to keep the news from her. '*I've come home, to The Haven!*'

'To *stay*?' she whispered, incredulously. 'Oh, I can't believe it. I'm asleep! I am dreaming the loveliest of dreams!'

She turned to Dicky-Sam who stood in the doorway, a mug of steaming tea in his hand.

'You didn't tell me, Dicky!' She was laughing and crying at one and the same time. 'Why didn't you say that Doctor Patrick was back?'

The weatherbeaten face creased into a thousand happy wrinkles.

'Why, Miss Sarah, 'twould have spoiled the surprise, wouldn't it?'

'But he's staying with us. Doctor Patrick isn't going back to London and I can't believe it. It isn't true!'

'Well, if the doctor's only here on a fleeting visit then all I can say, miss, is that we've lugged and tugged an awful lot of baggage up to the attic,' Dicky laughed as he closed the door behind him, leaving them alone again.

'Oh, Patrick, I'm so glad.' Sarah hugged herself with joy, 'but you must have a better room. It would not be proper, when you are married, for Arabella to have to sleep in the attic.'

'Arabella won't be coming to Liverpool, Sarah,' Patrick replied quietly. 'She has released me from our pledge. We are not to be married, now.'

'Oh, Patrick, what can I say?' Sarah whispered. 'I am so sorry. If anything that happened at *The Haven* was the cause of, I shall never forgive myself.'

'Perhaps, indirectly,' Patrick acknowledged, '*The Haven* had something to do with it, but you must not blame yourself, Sarah.'

The Haven, Patrick thought, had just been the start of it. At *The Haven*, both he and Arabella had found themselves, had recognized the selfishness of the lives they had lived, the falseness of the opulent world they had created about themselves.

Patrick smiled. 'Indeed, I have to thank Arabella that Doctor Harrington agreed to release me from my bond. It was she who made her father realize I was needed here; that my heart was here, too.'

'And you?' Sarah whispered. 'How do you feel about it?'

'A little sad,' Patrick acknowledged, 'but glad we found out in time. We were not truly in love, Arabella and I.'

'But your good living at Harley Street? You have given up so much to return to Liverpool.'

Patrick smiled and shook his head.

'No, Sarah. If you knew the truth of it, I shall be the richer by far for coming home.'

He threw back his head and laughed aloud.

'Don't you realize that my roots are here, deep and secure in the back streets of this town? I was an abandoned child – forsaken by my parents. I was a doorstep baby, Sarah, and I am not ashamed of it. I only want to be with my own people. What more is there to ask of life?'

Perhaps only you, Sarah, his heart whispered dully. *Just you, my dear one.*

'And was it because of that – because of your beginnings, I mean – that Arabella decided not to marry you?'

'No, Sarah. I thought at first it might have been the reason, but it wasn't. Strangely enough, it made little difference to her.'

How could he tell Sarah, he thought, what Arabella had really said?

'I love you, Patrick. In my own way, I love you as much as I am capable of loving any man. But I don't love you enough,' she had said, *'to give up my life in London and follow you to Liverpool.'*

Arabella had laughed then; a brave, sad little laugh.

'I have persuaded papa, you see, that your future lies in Liverpool and that is true, Patrick, in more ways than one.'

'What do you mean, Arabella?' Patrick had whispered apprehensively.

'Oh, Patrick. If you had once looked at me as you looked at Sarah, I would have followed you to the ends of the earth!'

Arabella had known, he realized dully. All that time it must have been plain for everyone to see. Everyone of course, but Sarah. She had loved Adam . . .

'Then I am glad for you, if you are not unhappy. Do you know,' she laughed, 'I went to the Wishing Gate this morning. How long I was there I don't know – hours and hours, I think – and I made a wish.'

'Yes, Sarah?'

'I wished there could be a way to keep *The Haven* open. In my wildest dreams, I could not have expected it to happen, but it has. You are back!'

So that is all I mean to you, Sarah, Patrick thought, sadly; just a means of keeping *The Haven* open.

But it didn't matter. He was back in Liverpool and there was much to be done. At least he would be near Sarah and he must be content with that. For once in his life he conceded, he must take second-best.

He said, 'I am concerned about Aunt Hetty. Do you think it would be possible for her to remain here? Had I stayed in London I could have afforded to make her a comfortable allowance and she could have returned to Lace Street. But now –' he shrugged.

'But of course she must stay with us, Patrick. She is a dear old lady and she will be most welcome. Already she and Molly are firm friends.'

Relieved, Patrick nodded his thanks.

'There is another thing too, Sarah. The tenancy of this house was in Adam's name, wasn't it?'

Sarah nodded.

'Then before I make any more grand plans, I think it would be wise if I tried to contact the owner of *The Haven*.'

'What good would that do, Patrick?'

Sarah felt a small shiver of fear. If Patrick got in touch with her notaries, the past she wanted so much to live down might become evident. She had managed when Adam was alive to keep it to herself. Perhaps with Patrick it might not be so easy. She didn't want to admit that she was the grand-daughter of the notorious Mad Jonathan; that she had lived in comparative luxury when Patrick had lived in Lace Street.

Now she only wanted to serve humanity; to give back to life a little of what her greedy forebears had wrenched from it.

'Perhaps it would do no good at all, Sarah, but the owner of this house chose not to accept rent from Adam. If I were to ask him for the tenancy, things might take on a very different light. First, I must make sure that we can all remain at *The Haven*.'

'Oh, Patrick, let us not worry today about such things. Tomorrow, as Molly always says, is always the best day to look for trouble!'

Please, begged Sarah silently, *let me not have to tell him just yet who I am?*

'Perhaps you are right, Sarah. Today is special, but tomorrow I must really set to work.'

He laughed, his eyes shining at the thought of each wonderful new day and the challenge it would bring. With the help of apprentices Patrick knew he could take on more patients who were able to pay well for medical treatment. Rich men and women, he reasoned, could help pay for the treatment of the poor ones. He grinned, happily. He'd never before thought of himself as a latter-day Robin Hood.

'I must go out, Sarah, for a little while. I want to see Doctor Duncan and I must call upon the good ladies of the *Charity* and prevail upon their generosity. I need not only apprentices but beds and blankets for our new wards.'

Sarah stood at the surgery window and watched Patrick's jaunty walk and the debonair set of his hat as he set off in search of his old tutor.

Foolish tears of happiness pricked her eyes. There was a warm glow inside her and all around her; the safe-feeling she had never expected to know again.

'Oh, Adam,' she whispered, turning her face upwards, 'Patrick is back. He's home again to take care of your poor ones. It's going to be all right.'

Patrick stood by the moss-covered statue in the tangled garden behind *The Haven* and looked into the gathering dusk of late summer.

The scent of moss roses and honeysuckle was all about him and with it came memories of the first time he stood there, the night he had known the hopeless discovering of his love for Sarah.

Now, in the cool of the rain-washed August gloaming, he felt again that same forlorn desire.

Impatiently he wrenched his thoughts to other things; to the Ladies' Charity who had promised him the beds with which to furnish the new laying-in ward for women in labour and Doctor Duncan who had grasped his hand with nothing short of delight and offered all the apprentices he could use.

Life would not be easy, Patrick acknowledged. For a time there would be little money with which to keep *The Haven* out of debt but he knew that one day he could do all that Adam had done for the poor people he had loved so much. Perhaps, Patrick thought, he and Sarah might even begin to instruct women in the skills of nursing – women who were gentle and compassionate; women like Sarah.

If only, he yearned, there could be some small hope that one day Sarah might come to care a little for him then he would walk proudly indeed in the mean streets, poor as a church-mouse though he may be.

It had pleased him that morning when Sarah seemed glad to see him, but surely it was only relief and gratitude that had made her eyes shine and her face take on a beauty that caused his breath to catch in his throat. She could not have felt as he felt; could not have known how he ached inside at the sight of her and the sound of her voice. It would not be easy for him to live at *The Haven*, so bittersweet to be near her yet so very far from her love.

He wanted her beside him now, knowing that just the nearness of her presence would be enough to set his pulses racing once more and his heart pounding with desperate longing.

If he willed it strongly enough, would she come to him? Would she come as she had come that first night with her hair loose about her shoulders?

Come to me, his heart yearned out to her. *Come to me again, my Sarah.*

And so it seemed that drawn by his intangible longing she came gently to his side and her footsteps were so soft that for a moment Patrick could only sense she was there.

For a little time they stood unspeaking, something in the magic around them forbidding almost that they should breathe.

Then Sarah said softly,

'I hoped I might find you here, Patrick.'

I wanted you to come, Patrick's heart exulted. *I called out to you with my love and you came!*

Sarah gazed ahead of her to where the first star hung low in the sky.

'There is something I must tell you, Patrick. I cannot keep it inside me any longer. There must be no secrets between us.'

It was inevitable that soon Patrick must find out that she owned *The Haven* and that he need have no fears for its security. But in telling him that, he would have to know too how high a price in human anguish it had cost. She would need to tell him that all she had known in her youth – the elegant establishment at which she had been educated, her clothes, the jewellery she had worn and the luxury into which she had been born was paid for by the misery of others – by the buying and selling of human life.

Then Patrick would learn she was Mad Jonathan Rigby's kin. Would he have the charity, she wondered, to believe that in her innocence she had known nothing of her grandfather's wickedness or indeed of his existence?

Patrick had once been very poor; it would likely give him satisfaction to know that in the end her grandfather's vast fortune had gone, she thought dully.

Sarah felt Patrick lay his hands gently on her shoulders, turning her to face him. He did not speak and Sarah drew courage from the familiar strength of his nearness.

'It would be unfair that you should not know, Patrick.'

He looked down at her troubled face and his heart contracted with pity. What could there be about Sarah that should cause her such anguish, he wondered. And whatever it was, did she imagine it could ever be so enormous as to make him stop loving her for one small second?

'Sarah,' he whispered gently, 'I do not know what it is that troubles you so and I do not care. To me you are Sarah and the dearest person I know. That is all that matters and all I care about.'

'But Patrick . . .'

'No, Sarah.'

He placed his forefinger tenderly on her lips for he was confident that there was only one thing he needed to know about her past life.

Once, he and Adam had talked about Sarah.

'*But have you made no enquiries about her background? She may be an erring wife who has run away . . .*'

Not that, he shuddered; anything at all but that.

But still he made himself ask the question of her.

'There is just one thing I want you to tell me, Sarah. I would not ask but it is important to me. All else doesn't matter.'

Even as the words tripped from his tongue, he cursed his stupidity. Why couldn't he let well alone?

'What is it?' Sarah whispered, her lips stiff.

'Are you a married woman, Sarah? Is there, somewhere, a man who has claim to you?'

Sarah's eyes jerked wide open.

'Married, Patrick?' She shook her head. 'Of course I am not married. Why should you think I was?'

Relief washed over Patrick. He heard his voice saying,

'I was certain you must be. What other reason could there have been to prevent you and Adam from marrying?'

'Adam and I? Marrying?'

She gave an embarrassed laugh.

'There was never any thoughts of marriage between us,' she said, incredulously.

'But you were lovers.'

He hated himself for what he was saying, but he had to know. 'I saw you in each other's arms, when Adam was ill. I wasn't spying, believe me Sarah; it was accidental –'

Sarah shook her head sadly.

'Adam and I were not lovers, Patrick. I loved him – I am proud to admit it – but the love I felt for Adam I would have felt for my brother had I had one or my mother, had I known her.'

She made a small, helpless gesture with her hands as though lost for words.

'You see, I loved Adam for what he tried to do. I respected him for his great compassion. If you saw us together in such a way I can only think I was trying to comfort him.'

'Oh, my dear, I have gone through unspeakable torment thinking you could never love me –'

'Love *you*, Patrick?'

'Yes, Sarah. Is it so very strange? I have loved you almost from the moment we met.'

'But I cannot believe it.'

She dropped her eyes, suddenly shy of him.

'I am Sarah – poor, plain Sarah. I have no dowry, Patrick; I am not beautiful.'

'You are beautiful to me!'

Triumphantly he reached out for her, cupping her face in his hands, forcing her eyes to meet his.

'You are the most beautiful thing in my life, Sarah. Can you understand what I have endured, loving you?'

'Forgive me, Patrick,' Sarah stammered. 'I didn't know.

Perhaps I should have, but I didn't. You were betrothed to Arabella and she was beautiful and rich and everything a man could want in a wife. I didn't so much as think you could ever have wanted me.'

'Everything I want is standing just the distance of a kiss away. She sat at my feet one night with her hair falling to her waist and from that moment on I loved her.'

Gently he removed the combs from the nape of her neck and her hair scattered about her in a gleaming fire-tinged fall, slipping and sliding like silk over his wrists.

'Now we are at the beginning, Sarah, with no misunderstandings or pledges to come between us. I shall teach you to love me!'

He buried his face in the red profusion of her hair and knew with a thrill of triumph that her body was trembling as crazily as his own.

'Now I can say what I wanted to say that first night we stood here together.'

Her body grew soft and yielding as he pulled her into his arms.

He wanted to tell her of his longing, of the fierce surging inside him that made every pulse in his body throb out a mad tattoo; he wanted to kiss her cheeks, her eyes, her lips; to tear down the stars and scatter them at her feet.

But his throat was tight and he could hardly breathe.

'I love you,' he whispered instead. 'I shall love you, Sarah Rigby, until the end of time.'

He felt her mouth near his. She was trying to speak his name but no sound came. Her lips, as they moved, felt like the brush of a butterfly's wing.

'Sarah,' he breathed as her arms stole round his neck.

Then his mouth was on hers. It was just as he had

known it would be and her body trembled with delight as he had so often dreamed it would.

'Oh, Sarah, my love, I want you so,' he whispered.

She did not reply but in the shyness of her eyes that mirrored the soft grey twilight, he saw the love for which he had been longing.

There was a star in the sky; bigger and brighter than all the rest, that seemed to glow above them, casting its light upon them like a benediction and suddenly Patrick knew with utter certainty that he would hear no more sighing. Now the gentle friend of his youth could rest beside the little Alms-houses with a peaceful soul.

'We will call our son Adam,' Patrick breathed as he looked with love at the star.

'The *first* of our sons,' Sarah whispered as her lips searched trembling again for his. 'The first of our sons, my darling.'

Mistress of Luke's Folly

One

'Just wait until I tell them!'

Instantly it seemed as if the sun was shining and every bird in creation singing fit to burst its little throat. Sarah Makin was going to be a lady-clerk! She was on her way up in the world and, by Old Lud, she'd show them!

But who would have thought it? Who could possibly have imagined such a thing could happen? She had awakened to the same grey morning, she reasoned breathlessly, to the same hopelessness that each day brought. There had been the same insistent rattling on the window pane from Ned's five o'clock pole. So how could she possibly have known something so wonderful was just around the corner?

There were no alarm-clocks in Canal Street. The mill-workers of the Three-streets put their trust instead in Limping Ned. Six days a week Ned rattled his pole against the windows of Canal Street, Albert Court and Tinker's Row, shattering dreams, calling young and old to face another day, a day as drab as yesterday that was gone and tomorrow, still to come.

Sarah had opened her eyes then quickly closed them. Why couldn't today be Sunday so she might sleep on, lie quiet in her bed until the ache was soothed from her bones and the mill noise that beat inside her head was silenced?

Folk here in Hollinsdyke swore God Himself was a mill-owner but Sarah knew for sure He wasn't. If God had owned Low Clough mill there'd have been no day of rest.

The rattling came again.

'Coming!' She threw back the blanket, pattering barefoot to draw aside the blind.

In the street below Ned waited patiently for a sign that she was awake. He was a good knocker-up; always waited until he was sure, and all for tuppence a week.

Sarah raised her hand and the little man nodded, then dragging his withered foot across the gas-lit cobbles, limped on to the next soot-blackened window.

'One day,' Sarah whispered, 'I'll get back into bed and Luke Holroyd and his looms can go to the devil!'

But not this morning, for today was reckoning-day at the mill, the day that made sense of the rest of the week. Tomorrow she would be penniless again, but tonight, for just a little while, there would be ten silver shillings shining bright in her pocket.

From across the landing she heard the creak of her father's bed. Like Ned, her father was lame, but Ned had been born that way and Caleb Makin had not. Caleb's wasted leg and twisted shoulder were not the whim of the Almighty but the bitter outcome of a mill-master's meanness. True, Luke Holroyd's unguarded machines were breaking the law, but the knowledge sat easily on his conscience. Luke Holroyd was also a magistrate; he *was* the law in Hollinsdyke, so if his workers didn't watch what they were about it was their own fault. If a man tangled with a great iron cog or a child's hand was slashed by a power-strap, it was nowt to do with him!

It was sad, Sarah sighed, to see her father so. Since the accident, he would often sit unspeaking, staring into the past, remembering when his body was whole and his wife alive. But those days were long gone, she reasoned. Now she was the breadwinner and Luke Holroyd owned her soul for twelve hours a day, six days a week.

She poured water into a bowl and splashed herself awake. She never ceased to marvel about the other world, that faraway place where people had rooms especially to wash in. She knew it was true. Her mother had told her about such things. There had been three bathrooms at Ainderby Hall, with violet-scented soap and soft, white towels. But Ainderby was a fairy-tale palace, set in that other world, something they had talked about on winter evenings.

'Tell me, Mam,' Sarah would plead, snuggling close. 'Tell me about Ainderby.'

The Ball had been one of her favourites, she recalled; the coming of age of Ainderby's eldest son and half the gentry in Lancashire dancing the night away.

'*Real* gentry,' her mother insisted. 'Gentlemen born, not mill-owners.'

Her mother's voice had been soft and low. It was the way you learned to speak, it seemed, when you entered service in a gentleman's house. Mary Makin had been a parlourmaid and worn soft boots and long, warm frocks and starched aprons, bleached white. And all the servants at Ainderby slept in beds with counterpanes on them and nobody, not even the tweenies, set a foot out of bed until six-thirty.

Half-past six. By that time, Sarah thought dully, she had walked the mile to Low Clough mill and put in thirty minutes work.

She hated the weaving-shed. Since she could remember she had wanted to work at a great house like Ainderby, but such positions went to the favoured few. Most Hollinsdyke women ended up in one or another of the mills around and wedded a mill-worker and produced unwanted bairns to work in the mills, too.

'I'll not get married,' Sarah whispered, cutting savagely at the bread loaf. 'The man hasn't been born who'll entice me into misery.'

For that was all marriage was. A mean wage and a mean little house. To marry was to change one weary way for another. Best stay as she was and strive for better things, hope that one day Luke Holroyd would get his comeuppance, that his mill would fall down, that a lady would drive up in a carriage and take her off to work in a house like Ainderby.

'Cut a cob for me, lass.'

Startled, Sarah saw Caleb standing in the doorway.

'You're up early, Father. Not poorly, are you?'

'I'm right enough, but I couldn't sleep,' Caleb nodded. 'I've a mind to go to Moor Top woods, see if the celandines are out. We're into March now.

March. Springtime. Sarah hadn't noticed. There were no seasons in the Three-streets, no trees or birds or flowers. The chimneys that dominated the town shut out the sky with their smoke and spread a blanket over the sun. Only if she walked to the hills that ringed Hollinsdyke around could she feel grass beneath her feet and breathe air that was sweet and cool. Now, for all his misfortune, she envied her father. He would spend the day in the woods and fields, searching for celandines to make into salve and wild pansies for eye-wash. Local folk relied on Caleb's lotions and potions. His mugwort tea was without equal for an upset stomach and his wood-sorrel syrup had soothed most of the street's teething babies. Caleb had even been known to cure warts, when the mood was on him, though it was for his raspberry-leaf infusion that he was most famed, and the pregnant women who drank it swore it dulled their labour pangs.

'It's a fair step to Moor Top,' Sarah cautioned.

'I'll take it easy. I've got all the time in the world.'

There was a note of bitterness in his voice, but she chose to ignore it.

'I'll take Billy-Boy a couple of pieces,' she murmured, reaching for the dripping-jar.

'Aye, lass. Likely he'll be hungry.'

Billy-Boy was always hungry. Billy-Boy was a workhouse child, abandoned as a baby on the chapel steps. Now he was nine and worked in the weaving-shed at Low Clough, running errands, sweeping floors, cleaning machines. Against her better judgement, Sarah had come to care for him and the child sensed that reluctant affection, clinging to it jealously, for it was the only tenderness he had ever known. Each morning he waited for her at the mill gate, wearing boots too small and trousers too large, his fair hair cropped short, brown eyes large in a pale, thin face. Seeing him there like a small, unwanted puppy aroused feelings in Sarah she had never thought to admit to and she would take his hand in hers and walk with him to the hot damp weaving-shed.

All Low Clough was damp. It had been standing for a hundred years and was fast falling into disrepair. Once Luke Holroyd had been a spinner in that very mill and had managed, though God alone knew how, to rise above himself and buy the place. It had been the talk of Hollinsdyke for months with everybody saying that here at last would be a mill-owner who cared.

But he had done nothing to improve it, forgetting the men he'd worked with, as easy as falling off a log. Nobody in Hollinsdyke liked him, yet they allowed him grudging respect for what he had achieved. He was the master now, so they tipped their caps to him as he passed in his carriage. It was the way of the world. No use fighting it.

Sarah wrapped her mid-day bread in a cloth then filled her water-bottle at the backyard pump. Imagine water in taps. Imagine a world where there were no mill-masters, no orphans like Billy-Boy or men like her father. Imagine clean streets and clean air and sunlight.

'I hate you, Luke Holroyd,' Sarah whispered. 'I'll never own you've got the right to set yourself up as God Almighty, thumb your nose at the law, work children for a pittance.

But at least he couldn't employ a bairn under nine years old, now. And he had to see to it that the children in his mill got three hours schooling a day, for this was 1870 and the world's slow conscience was stirring. Black slaves were a thing of the past. Soon, maybe, there'd be no white ones either.

When would he come, she sighed, the long-promised Messiah who would fight for their rights? One day, happen, when she was too old to care. And until then she had four looms to tend and a sick father to feed. So stop your imagining, Sarah Makin, she chided silently; stop sighing for what might have been . . .

'I'm off, then.' She draped her shawl over her head and shoulders and pinned it firmly beneath her chin. 'Mind what you're about on Moor Top. Don't go tiring yourself.'

'I'll think on. And watch yourself, an' all.'

They didn't kiss. Words of caution and grave admonitions were the only affections that passed between them. There was no love now in the little house in Canal Street. Just a kind of hopeless caring. And it was better that way, Sarah accepted, slamming the door behind her. Loving laid hearts bare and weakened resolve. Loving was a luxury in the Three-streets.

It was still dark and lamplight streamed like a beacon through the open doorway of the end house in Tinker's Row. An open door on a cold morning signalled trouble and Sarah slowed her steps and called: 'Anything the matter, Liza?'

'Eh, lass. I've been waiting for you to come along.' Liza Nuttall grasped Sarah's arm. 'Can you slip back and fetch your father? I'm worried half to death.' She nodded toward the corner of the room where her husband lay in the shadow, coughing quietly. 'He's gone on and on, all night, and now he's spitting blood. Happen Caleb can help – mix him a dose?'

But Sarah had seen consumption before. 'There's nothing my father can do for that,' she retorted grimly. 'It's a doctor you need now, Liza.'

But doctors cost money. They even insisted on cash in advance in places like Tinker's Row. A shilling it would cost and Liza was penniless.

'I'll lend you the money. I get paid tonight,' Sarah offered rashly, knowing it could never be repaid. 'And don't fret,' she comforted. 'I'll call at the doctor's on my way in. When he comes, tell him Sarah Makin'll pay.'

The church clock chimed three times the quarter. Fifteen minutes to starting time! She picked up her skirts and ran.

The yard gates were shut when she arrived, breathless, at Low Clough.

'You're late. Three minutes,' the timekeeper pronounced, pushing a book at her and a stub of pencil.

'But I've been for the doctor!' Sarah protested.

'Three minutes late. Three pence fined,' the man persisted. 'Better sign sharpish, or it'll be four!'

She reached through the gate and scribbled her name in the Fines Book.

'Rot your clogs!' she flung, as he let her in. Deep in trouble already and the day hardly begun!

The overlooker stared meaningfully when Sarah clattered into the weaving-shed, but made no comment for she usually kept good time. No sense in causing a rumpus. Caleb's lass had a peppery temper, when roused.

Billy-Boy smiled, relieved to see her, peering anxiously at her apron pocket for the tell-tale bulge that meant bread and dripping at dinnertime.

Sarah threw aside her shawl then abandoned herself to the noise of the shed. She had long ago ceased to fight it. Now there were even times when she hardly noticed it. At first the thunderous roar made her afraid and she had wondered what would happen if ever she had cause to scream. No one would hear her. If the chimney-stack fell, none would know save those it fell on, for the crash and clatter of a hundred looms would drown the blast of the Last Call, when it came!

She smiled at Billy-Boy and mouthed 'Hullo', setting her looms into motion, checking bobbins and shuttles, breathing deeply to calm the anger that bubbled inside her. Three pennies fined and a shilling to Liza for the doctor! Precious little left to last the week on. Oh, damn Luke Holroyd! Damn all mill-masters!

She looked up and saw the nodding heads of Poll Clegg and Belle Birtle. They were talking about her, gloating over her fine. Belle was a troublemaker with a quiet way of talking that made everybody listen. Belle put words into the mouths of others, then sat back with pleasure to enjoy the upset. She didn't care that Sarah was watching the exaggerated moving of her lips, reading the words as clearly as she read a printed page.

Sarah stared dully across the shed. Belle, she decided, was in the mood for a bit of trouble to start the day with. She turned her back on the taunting face. Let her find it somewhere else. Sarah Makin had had bother enough for one day!

But Billy-Boy was not so cautious. Confronting the gossiping women he took up the cause.

'You're talking about my Sarah,' he stormed, his small face flushed. 'Sarah's my friend and you're a wicked old woman, Belle Birtles!'

'Why you – you cheeky little shaver!'

Poll's hand flashed out, catching the child a blow to his ear, sending him sprawling. Belle smiled, well satisfied.

Anger blazed red on Sarah's cheeks. Jamming her hands on her hips she marched into battle.

'Do that again!' she challenged, sticking out her chin.

She had thought her show of protest would be the end of it, that Poll would withdraw. She hadn't bargained for the stinging slap that was delivered to the side of her face.

'Aaaah! Why – you . . .'

Honour demanded that Sarah should retaliate. If she didn't, there would be no living with Belle Birtle's smugness. She returned the blow with venom.

'That'll be all, now!'

The overlooker was quick to drag the gasping women apart, marching them roughly toward the doors.

'Fighting in t'mill isn't allowed. You should both know that!'

Fighting in the shed was dangerous too. It could end in one or the other of the participants being hurled against a moving machine and that was a messy business, to say the least. The yard was the place for such things. And they'd be fined a shilling apiece for brawling, so why not let them get their money's worth? he reasoned.

'Out! If you've got to fight, then do it in the gutter!' he bawled, slamming the doors on them. And may they claw each other to pieces, for all he cared!

David Holroyd arrived at Low Clough in time to bear witness to the set-to. At first he was taken aback, wondering what he should do. It would, he supposed, be wisest to ignore it. No one in his right mind tried to come between snarling dogs and the same applied to fighting women. It would be a brave man who got himself embroiled in that heaving tangle of black-stockinged legs and thrusting, steeltipped clogs.

And then he saw the face of the young one, the face of the girl who walked barefoot on Moor Top hill with the wind in her long, black curls and her fine-boned face held high to the sun. He'd seen her there often, remembering her beauty, wondering who she was. Now, sadly, he knew. She was a Low Clough weaver, fighting in his father's yard and getting the worst of it too.

'Stop it! Stop it at once, I say!'

The authority in his voice surprised him and that the brawling should instantly cease.

'You!' he jerked, glaring at Poll with all the dignity he could gather. 'Get back to your work, and *you*,' he jabbed his walking-stick at Sarah. 'Come with me!'

Dejectedly Sarah rose to her feet and dusted down her skirts. Fighting was one thing; getting caught at it by the master's son was another. At the best it would be another fine and at the worst it could bring dismissal. Panting with exertion, her head throbbing with pain she followed despondently, remembering her father's words.

'That temper'll be the ruination of you, my lass. Mark my words if it won't!'

Now her father had been proved right and she was deep in trouble. Backed up by Belle Birtle, they would believe what Poll Clegg told them. Poll was a valuable six-loom weaver. Poll who was never absent, never late, would get the benefit of the doubt, Sarah argued silently, and Belle Birtle would laugh for a week at the trouble she'd caused.

'What is your name?' David Holroyd asked, closing the door of his office behind him. 'And why were you fighting?'

'My name is Sarah Makin,' she said slowly, tilting her chin, trying to speak the way her mother had spoken. 'I'm a four-loom weaver and I always make my yardage,' she added defiantly.

'And?'

'And I was fighting because Poll Clegg slapped Billy-Boy. He's a child. She'd no right to do it!'

A warning bell rang stridently in her head, telling her to stop while there was yet time, but she was angry now; she'd say her piece, by Lud, and go down fighting!

'Do you ever give a thought to the children in your mill, Mister David? Do you ever stop to think how cheaply your money is made?'

She paused, breathless, and looked into his face, seeing for the first time the clean-shaven cheeks, the deep blue eyes that looked calmly into her own.

This was the end. She had gone too far. Dry-mouthed, suddenly afraid, she stared back, waiting for the blow to fall.

'Sit down, Sarah,' came the quiet reply. 'Please?'

Startled, she did as he asked. Sarah, he'd called her. 'Please?' he'd said.

So that was his game! He was the master's son and she a mill-girl and a mill-girl was easy pickings! Oh, but she knew all about mill-owner's sons and the girls they'd had their way with then left at the workhouse door, their trouble hidden beneath their pinnies.

Lowering her eyes, she began to think desperately of a way out.

Perhaps if she told him she was sorry for what she had said he would let her off with a fine. It would be better than losing her job? Maybe, if she was to squeeze out a tear or two, put on an act, it would help. It was worth a try. She had nothing to lose. Tremulously she sighed and raised her face to his.

'I'm sorry for what I said, sir . . .'

David stared fascinated at the girl with the brown, pleading eyes. She was far more beautiful than he had first realized; even with her tangled hair and grimy face and a bruise on her cheek that grew redder as he watched.

'I'm sorry you had to say it,' he heard himself retort. 'Is it so very awful, working at Low Clough?'

Anger flamed afresh inside her. Just one week in that shed and he wouldn't need to ask! She opened her lips to fling scorn into his face again, then remembered the danger wasn't over. Breathing deeply, blinking a tear from the corner of her eye, she whispered:

'It's worse than awful. I'd do *anything* to get away from Low Clough.'

'But where would you go, Sarah, except to another mill?'

'I could go to a place like Ainderby,' she retorted. 'Be a parlourmaid. Work for a gentleman and be treated decent.'

'A *servant*?'

'Oh, yes. I'd like that.'

She lifted her head and he saw real animation in her face. A servant, indeed! She was worth better than that! Caution cast aside, he said,

'Tell me about yourself, Sarah. How old are you? Where do you live?'

'I'm twenty and I live in Canal Street.'

'And are you married?' She wasn't wearing a ring, but that meant nothing.

'Married? That I'm *not*!'

'And have you brothers, or sisters?'

'No, sir. There's just me and father. Mam died of typhoid when I was twelve, then father got lamed in the mill.'

She said it, he thought, as if such tragedies were commonplace, a part of life to be accepted without question.

'Can you read and write, Sarah Makin?'

'Course I can,' she said scornfully. 'And figure too.'

'So you went to school?'

'Until I was twelve. I'd have been as good as Maggie Ormerod if I could have stayed on,' she added hastily.

'Miss Ormerod who teaches the mill apprentices, you mean?'

'Aye,' Sarah nodded, amused. *Miss* Ormerod indeed! Why, Maggie was from the same mould as herself and lived in Albert Court, not a spit away. But Maggie had done well at school and been singled out by the Minister to teach Luke Holroyd's mill children. Maggie went to her work in a bonnet and gloves.

'And can you add and subtract and multiply?'

'Set me some sums, and I'll show you,' she challenged eagerly, wondering for all that what sums and schooling had to do with fighting.

'I'll take your word for it,' he said quietly, wondering what madness was putting ideas into his mind. Sarah

Makin was a weaver and used to nothing else. Wouldn't it be fairer to leave her where she was, tell her to mend her ways and send her back to the sheds?

But she had long fascinated him. There was a wildness about her that excited him as none of the young ladies of his acquaintance had ever done.

'Sarah,' he smiled. 'There is a position for a lady-clerk in the counting house, here at Low Clough. Would you like it?'

Would she like it?

In that instant Sarah's world exploded deliriously about her. Stars cascaded before her eyes and a thousand mill-hooters shrieked inside her head.

But there had to be a catch to it. Nobody did anything for nothing, least of all a Holroyd. Yet here was the chance she had been waiting for, the chance to get out of the shed, to better herself.

'*Me?*' she whispered.

'Why not?' he retorted, delighted by her reaction. 'Unless you're determined to be a servant, that is?'

'How much?' she countered. 'What'll you pay?'

'Ten and six a week. Eight o'clock start.'

'And no fines?'

'No fines – well, not unless you're caught fighting again.'

'Then it's a bargain,' she replied solemnly, holding out her hand. 'When do I start?'

'Monday morning. Report to Mr Dinwiddie.'

He took her hand in his as was the way with sealing a bargain and suddenly the full realization of his rashness struck him. He'd been an utter fool and his father, when he heard about it, would tell him he was out of his mind. Usually he bowed to all his father's wishes, but in this, he vowed, he would stand firm. Sarah Makin fascinated him and this time he would do as he pleased. He would have her near him and nothing his father or Dinwiddie might say would change it!

Head spinning, heart thumping, Sarah clattered across the yard to the shed.

'Imagine!' she exulted, the full force of her good fortune hitting her for the first time. 'A lady-clerk!' Imagine going to work in the daylight. Imagine Sarah Makin in a bonnet and gloves and slim, soft boots.

'Oh, my Lord,' she whispered, because she didn't have any boots. She had never worn anything but clogs.

The noise of the shed stretched out to meet her, eager to enfold her, claim her back. But it didn't matter. After Saturday the sheds would be nothing more than a miserable memory. No more noise, no more weariness, no more fines. Come Sunday she would be free of it all.

Straightening her shoulders and throwing back her head she gave a great shout of joy.

Who cared about boots? There'd be time enough to worry about such things tomorrow. This moment, this wonderful, *wonderful* moment, the only thing that mattered was Belle Birtle's face.

'Just wait until I tell her!' Sarah thrilled. 'Only wait!'

It seemed, suddenly, as if the sun was shining and she was walking barefoot on Moor Top hill, with every bird in creation singing fit to burst.

Sarah Makin was on her way up in the world and by old Lud she'd show them!

But her joy was short-lived for it was obvious, as she neared her home that night, that death had walked the

Three-streets. At every window of every house curtains had been closed in unspoken respect.

'Was it Will Nuttall?' Sarah asked, filling her bowl from the broth-pan that hung above the kitchen fire.

'Aye. Two hours gone.'

'And how is Liza taking it?' No use grieving for the dead, Sarah reasoned. Best by far to have a care for the living. 'I'll go round and see her.'

'I wouldn't. There's folk a-plenty there, weeping and wailing,' Caleb supplied. 'I took her a draft for her nerves . . .'

'How will she manage?' Sarah hazarded.

'God alone knows,' he shrugged. 'Liza's proud. She'll not plead poverty.'

'Then I'd best take the tin round.'

This morning Liza hadn't had the price of the doctor in her pocket and it was unlikely things could have changed meantime. Best make haste with a collection while there was still some money about, Sarah decided, gratified that Will Nuttall had had the good sense to choose pay-day on which to breathe his last.

No one in the Three-streets refused a contribution and money rattled into Sarah's tin. At the Black Bull ale-house, unusually busy with Friday night spenders, the landlord gave Sarah permission to collect, opening his drawer, taking out a shilling. Will Nuttall hadn't been a drinking man, he reasoned, but doubtless Liza would buy the funeral ale from the Bull.

'My condolences to Mrs Nuttall,' he said.

'Aye. I'll tell her you gave,' Sarah acknowledged dryly.

'Here, lass!' Someone tugged at her shawl and Sarah spun round, tin extended. A man held a sixpenny piece aloft. 'Who's it for?'

'Who's asking?' she demanded bluntly. The man was a stranger, to be treated with caution.

'Robey Midwinter.' The reply was equally brusque.

'Are you from the Parish Relief?'

'That I'm not! And don't worry – I'll not let on you're collecting,' he assured her, dropping the coin into the tin. 'Who's dead?' he asked again.

'Will Nuttall,' Sarah supplied reluctantly.

'A mill-worker?'

'Aye. From the card-room at Low Clough, before the coughing took a hold.'

'Luke Holroyd's mill? And how much will *he* be giving?'

'Nothing,' Sarah replied flatly. 'Mister Holroyd doesn't believe in charity.'

'But surely it was his cotton-dust that caused the trouble?'

'Happen it was,' she snapped, suddenly angered by the stranger's questioning. 'But Luke Holroyd'll not lose any sleep over that!' Confronted, he would swear it had been Will's fault for breathing it in. 'He'll not care!'

'Then he should be made to care!'

Sarah shrugged. The man wanted to know too much. Let him find the answers to his questions elsewhere.

'Then maybe you're the right one to do it, Robey Midwinter!' she flung, turning away abruptly, annoyed with herself for noticing that his shoulders were straight and broad and his mocking eyes black as the night.

'Happen I am,' he whispered to her indignant retreating back. 'Happen I am, at that!'

It wasn't until almost midnight that Sarah was able to tell her father about the goings-on at the mill.

'Just like that?' Caleb questioned. 'Young Holroyd

catches you fighting then offers you a job in the counting-house? Is it likely?'

'It's the sober truth,' Sarah retorted. 'I thought you'd be pleased.'

'I might have been if there was any sense in it. A Holroyd giving favours? What's behind it?'

'Nothing's behind it, Father!' She jumped angrily to her feet then shook her head in despair. Since his accident her father had looked on the world with distrust. Nothing pleased him nowadays. If Luke Holroyd were to fall head first into the workhouse midden, it wouldn't bring so much as a smile to her father's lips, she thought wearily. Yet maybe his suspicions were not entirely without foundation? No use denying she had used her wiles, wept a little. But who could blame her for that? Her job had been at risk and, if David Holroyd had got wrong ideas into his head, then that was his fault!

'You've tired yourself out, tramping all that way to Moor Top,' she scolded, giving way to compassion. She found it impossible to be angry for long and a wave of pity for her father washed over her, just as it did when she looked at Billy-Boy. She had to try to be more patient. Once Caleb had been a strong, well set-up man. Small wonder then that sometimes he should give way to despair.

'There was a stranger in the Black Bull tonight,' she offered cheerfully. 'Asked a lot of questions, but he gave me a sixpence for Liza's tin.'

'Aye – that 'll be Robey.'

'You know him?' Trust her father to keep such news to himself.

Caleb sucked at his empty pipe and stared into the fire looking almost, Sarah thought, as if he were sorry to have told her.

'He's taken a bed at Ormerod's,' he said eventually.

'Since when has Maggie's ma taken in lodgers?'

'Since this morning. I met Robey on the hill road, on my way up to the tops. He asked if I knew of any lodgings and we talked awhile.'

'And where is he from? What's he doing here?'

'He didn't say. To hear him talk he's been to most parts, though what there is in Hollinsdyke for the likes of him is beyond me.'

'Happen he's looking for work?'

'Happen.'

Caleb shrugged and jammed the stem of his pipe between his teeth again, indicating that the conversation was over. Anything else she wanted to know about Robey Midwinter, Sarah conceded, she would have to learn for herself.

But weren't there more important things in her life? Men were of small concern to a girl who was busy getting on in the world. And, besides, Robey Midwinter was far too proud, much too handsome. And his eyes were full of mockery and mischief.

His arrogance she could accept, his good looks she could shrug aside, but a stranger who asked questions was altogether another matter. So best forget him?

Sarah bid farewell to the weaving-shed at Low Clough with undisguised pleasure. Every hour of that last day had seemed to stretch itself into a lifetime but now she was free of it she could feel nothing but relief. Saying goodbye to Billy-Boy caused the only sadness, for the child had clung to her, crying quietly, begging her not to leave him.

'But I shall only be across the yard, in the counting-house,' she whispered. 'And I'll wave to you, from the window.'

'You'll forget me, Sarah.'

But she wouldn't forget him. That was why she was on her way now, to see Maggie Ormerod. Maggie was Billy-Boy's teacher and it seemed a good idea, Sarah reasoned, to ask her to keep an eye on the child, tell her at once if he got sick. She chose to ignore the faint voice of her conscience that suggested the visit to Albert Court might not be entirely concerned with the child's welfare. She really wasn't interested in Ormerod's new lodger. Admitted, he made her curious, but the tallness of him, his blatant masculinity and his tantalizing smile meant absolutely nothing, she insisted yet again.

Maggie greeted her warmly.

'Come in, Sarah lass. It's grand to see you.'

Plump, pretty Maggie, with corn-gold hair, an angel smile and a mind free from any kind of malice.

'Sit you down,' she smiled, setting the kettle to boil, arranging tea-cups on a tray.

Maggie had pretty manners. She could pass for a lady any day of the week, Sarah acknowledged, noting the long full skirt, the white, high-necked blouse and soft, highly-polished boots. Sarah Makin could do a lot worse than copy the school-teacher. Sarah Makin could –

Robey Midwinter strode into the kitchen as if the place were his own, crashing into Sarah's daydreams, sending a reluctant flush to her cheeks. But she collected herself sufficiently to incline her head when Maggie introduced them, making no mention of their meeting in the Black Bull, pretending surprise that he should be there.

'You're a weaver, aren't you, at Low Clough?' he demanded abruptly of Sarah. 'What are conditions like?'

'Like anywhere else,' she replied, taken aback.

Questions. Always questions.

'I heard they were bad,' he insisted flatly. 'Talk has it that Luke Holroyd's mill is the worst in these parts, and damp too.'

'It's damp,' Sarah acknowledged, 'but show me the cotton-mill that isn't? If you knew anything at all about it, you'd not need to be told that cotton needs moisture in the weaving.'

'Oh, I know about cotton-mills, all right,' he flung, 'and woollen-mills too. And I can tell you about coal-mines and tin-mines –'

He broke off abruptly, shrugging his shoulders.

'Robey's a deep thinker,' Maggie interrupted gently. 'Things bother him. Tell him about your good fortune, Sarah. Cheer him up.'

Sarah hadn't meant to be flippant about it, turn it all into a joke, but a desire to impress Robey Midwinter arose strong inside her and the mischief in her soul urged her on. She took the centre of the floor as if it were a stage.

'Oh, I thought I was in for the sack!' she gasped, laughter dancing in her eyes. 'There we were, Poll Clegg and me, rolling in the muck. And wasn't it just my luck to get caught?'

Impishly delighted by the sound of her own voice, Sarah gave a dramatic account of her pleading, her crocodile tears and David's Holroyd's gullibility.

'Fell for it, he did – daft as a brush!'

Then she gave an exaggerated impression of the mill-owner's son, mimicking his voice, turning it all into a farce; a farce, she realized suddenly, that wasn't funny.

No one was laughing. At any other time Maggie would have been amused, taken her performance with a pinch of salt and told her, smiling, she was a right caution. Maggie understood her, but not Robey Midwinter. Slab-faced, he watched her antics, waiting until her last whispered word hung still on the uneasy air before saying,

'And I suppose it makes you proud? Is that the way to better yourself – simpering and smiling and degrading your womanhood? Oh, there's nothing like a bit of lick-spittling to the master's son, is there, especially if he's pretty to look at and has an eye for a mill-girl that's easy? You did well for yourself, Sarah Makin. It'll be interesting to see the price you pay for your grovelling!'

It would have been wisest, Sarah knew, to have bowed out gracefully, to have left well alone and allowed his sneers to ride over her. After all, she had gone too far; she'd asked for it. But his eyes were mocking her again and anger was quickly replacing her dismay.

'All right – so it was wrong of me to do what I did,' she flung. 'But what would you have done in my place? I was sick of the shed and so would you be too! You've never stood on a mill floor until your legs turned to lead and you don't know what it's like to work in that noise, day after day. So don't presume to judge me, Robey Midwinter!'

Snatching up her shawl, near blinded by tears, she slammed out of the house, walking blindly, rage and shame writhing inside her. She'd made a fool of herself in front of Robey Midwinter. She'd been impetuous again, rushing in without thought like she always did, and this time the joke had misfired. Her father was right. One day her unthinking ways would land her in real trouble and she would spend the rest of her life being sorry for it.

Why couldn't she be more like Maggie? Maggie was of mill-stock like everyone else in the Three-streets, yet she had a way about her that commanded respect. But it was all Robey Midwinter's fault, rot his clogs! She would never have done it, but for him! There was something about him that disturbed her, turned her into a show-off. Why had he needed to come to Hollinsdyke and how long would he be staying?

But maybe tomorrow he would be on his way again, she reasoned hopefully, for he'd soon find there was no work in Hollinsdyke for strangers who asked too many questions.

Mollified, she looked upwards to the hills. Oh, be damned to Robey Midwinter! Maggie Ormerod could have him, and welcome!

Sarah's temper was spent and her natural optimism restored when finally she reached the budding trees of Moor Top woods. Kicking aside her clogs, pulling off her stockings, she thrust her feet into the beck that flowed, ice-cold, down the hillside. Here, where there was nothing to stop her reaching up and touching God, the grass was soft and green and the pale Spring sun shone gently. Here, high above the town, all was stillness and, if she didn't look down, there would be nothing at all to remind her that Hollinsdyke existed.

Leaning back on her elbows, closing her eyes, she breathed deeply. Tomorrow work began in Luke Holroyd's counting-house. Soon she would be able to buy soft leather boots and dainty gloves. And she would try, she really would try, to think before she spoke and keep a hold on her temper, be more like Maggie.

'Good-afternoon, Miss Makin.'

Sarah's eyes flew open and, startled, remained open, gazing upward with dismay. Oh my goodness, she'd done it again; got herself caught with skirts above her knees and up to the ankles in beck water.

'Mr David!'

David Holroyd smiled and squatted beside her,

searching his brain for something to say, wondering why the sight of her tied his tongue so.

'Not in church, then?'

'No, sir.' Of course she wasn't in church!

'Do you often come here?'

'Only on Sundays and nights, if it's light.' All other days she worked – didn't he know that?

'You surprised me, Sarah – meeting you here, that is.' Liar. He had come here especially.

'You surprised *me*, Mr David.' Gravely she held out a dripping foot.

She was very beautiful, he conceded, fixing a picture in his mind to take away with him. Barefoot Sarah, with flowing hair and cheeks whipped rosy by the wind.

And there was a waywardness about her that sent excitement thrashing through him, set him searching for words as if he were a pimply youth.

He wanted more than anything to stay and talk. Tomorrow, at the mill, it might not be so easy.

Unbidden, a fleeting vision of another Sarah flashed before him; Sarah in velvet and satin, with silk stockings clinging to her ankles and dainty shoes on her pretty pink feet. And it was useless to deny it any longer – he wanted her for himself. She was exquisite. She set his blood racing yet he couldn't even offer his arm, walk back with her to the outskirts of town. To have done that would have proclaimed, to a mill-girl's way of thinking, that they were walking out and pledged to wedlock. There was a strange, strict code of behaviour among the working classes, he acknowledged, that was almost prudish. Best tread carefully. Sarah Makin was a fey creature; one wrong move and he'd lose her.

Abruptly he raised his hat. 'Bid you good-day, ma'am.'

*

Sarah watched him go, her forehead creased. He had called her Miss Makin and raised his hat and if she could only forget he was a Holroyd she was sure she could find him very agreeable.

But mill-owner's sons needed a lot of watching. They were like their elders who had got rich because they'd never done anything for nothing. David Holroyd had taken her out of the mill and her father had demanded to know what was behind it. And Robey Midwinter had given his unasked opinion, telling her she would have to pay.

But would she? Only wait, and she would show them all who would be doing the paying! David Holroyd wouldn't have things all his own way and as for Master Midwinter – why, she wouldn't care if she never saw him again! In fact, there was only one thing about him that bothered her. He irritated her so much that she couldn't get him out of her mind!

She shook her head, wondering why it was that suddenly her life should have become so vaguely complicated, why it seemed she was waiting, breathless, for something to happen. It was a feeling she could not explain. It frightened and excited her at one and the same time. It was rooted in the past yet seemed to be beckoning her on to a turbulent tomorrow. And bound up in it were David Holroyd and Robey Midwinter; the one she mistrusted and the other she disliked.

Where in heaven's name was it all to end?

Two

'Tell me about the counting-house.' Billy-Boy's voice was hushed with reverence.

Sarah looked thoughtfully at her last piece of bread then handed it to the child.

'It's very nice, Billy. Very genteel . . .'

She puckered her forehead, searching for words, for the counting-house at Low Clough mill had proved to be something of a disappointment and not the holy of holies she had imagined it to be. The long-legged desks were old and worn, the wooden floors bare and the smell of musty paper sickened the air.

'Of course, it's nothing like the weaving-shed. As I was saying this morning to Mr Dobson –'

Joshua Dobson was the gentlest of men, and patient to a fault, for which blessing Sarah had quickly found reason to be thankful. The bothers that beset a lady-clerk were beyond belief. The mastering of four temperamental looms had been child's play compared to the pitfalls and mantraps of the Order-by-Post department. But give her time and she would get the better of that too.

'As I was saying to Mr Dobson when we had our tea and biscuits –'

'*Biscuits*, Sarah?'

'Yes, indeed! Currant biscuits and tea in china cups.'

Such pretty little cups, thin as could be and sprinkled

with pink rosebuds. They had belonged to his mother, Mr Dobson explained, and Sarah had flushed with pride, sticking out her little finger in a lady-like gesture as she drank.

She was well aware of the existence of such luxuries, of course. They had used china cups at Ainderby. Every day. Imagine such a thing.

'And is it better than working in the shed?'

'It is, Billy-Boy. It is,' she nodded, begging silent forgiveness for such a downright untruth. Indeed her first impressions of the counting-house had been those of distinct hostility. Two gentleman clerks with slicked-down hair and hurt expressions had gazed right through her, and as for Mr Dinwiddie! Well, he had been most unfriendly, declaring loudly that as soon as Mr Holroyd got himself back from Manchester there'd be trouble! He'd have an explanation, Dinwiddie would, or he'd know the reason why! And as for Mr David! *That* young man had taken leave of his senses, bringing a mill-lass into the counting-house without so much as a by-your-leave!

After which show of protest Dinwiddie had retreated to his office, wondering out loud what the world was coming to. Thank the good Lord, Sarah had sighed, for Mr Dobson. He at least had been kind.

'Come in Miss Makin, do. I'm glad you're here.'

Small and elderly and much overworked, his welcome had been genuine and Sarah warmed with remembered pride at being so addressed.

Painstakingly he had explained the workings of the Order-by-Post department.

'It was Mr David's idea, you see. The country housewife likes being able to order her linen by letter. The Master and Mr Dinwiddie were both against it, at first. New-fangled, they said it was and doomed to fail. But it's doing well – so well that sometimes I can't keep up with all the invoicing and packing.' He smiled timidly. 'I was glad when I heard you were coming. Trouble is,' he sighed, 'Mr David didn't think to tell Mr Dinwiddie about you and I'm afraid the gentleman is somewhat piqued. But I dare say it'll all get sorted out before long.'

The counting-house at Low Clough mill, Sarah discovered, consisted of four rooms. One for Luke Holroyd, one for his son; a large, musty room where the clerks worked and a small cubby-hole into which Mr Dinwiddie retreated in times of stress. The Order-by-Post department, being something of a novelty, was housed in a storeroom at the end of the corridor. Its window was very small, its ceiling very high, its walls a drab green. But the room had the benefit of a small, iron firegrate on the hob of which Mr Dobson's little black kettle bubbled constantly.

'You'll feel strange at first, Miss Sarah, but they leave us alone, this being Mr David's experiment, so to speak,' he smiled, handing her a cup of tea, offering a biscuit from a tin with the Prince Consort's picture on the lid. Joshua Dobson's kindness had cheered Sarah enormously and before long she was singing happily as she packed pillow ticking, tea-towels and unbleached sheeting into neat, brown-paper parcels.

The knocking-off hooter blared and Sarah looked up, surprised that dinnertime had come without further interference from Mr Dinwiddie. Picking up her bundle she hurried to the mill-yard, suddenly lonely for Billy-Boy.

'Said I wouldn't forget you, didn't I?' she smiled, unwrapping her bread, giving him half. She had tried not to love Billy-Boy. Loving people, gathering them close, was a luxury she could not afford. If she was to get on in the world she had to be free, so that when her chances came she could move on without encumbrances, without regret. But for all that she had come to care for the child. Against her better judgement she had let him gentle his way into her heart. She felt protective towards him, responsible for his wellbeing. He was the child she would never bear, she supposed, for marriage did not rate high in her plans. Bringing innocent babes into the world was downright sinful. There aught to be a law against it.

The hooter invaded her thoughts with lungs of brass.

'It's one o'clock, Billy. Be off to school with you.' She hugged the child briefly. 'And learn your lessons like a good lad.'

Dipping into the pocket of her skirt she took out the biscuit she had slipped there earlier.

'Here you are. I saved it for you.'

The child regarded the unexpected treat with awe.

'Go on, lad. Eat it up afore somebody takes it off you!'

'You'll come again tomorrow, Sarah?'

'I'll come. Promise.'

She watched him go, shaking her head with disbelief that a child could be treated so. Billy-Boy lived his life between the confines of the mill and the workhouse orphanage; six hours in the weaving-shed and three hours schooling. Always ragged, always hungry. Nine years old and ninety years wise.

Oh imagine, Sarah yearned, a world without unhappiness. Imagine a world without hunger or cold, without mill-owners or workhouse-masters, a world of rosebud china and water in taps.

But Maggie was kind to the bairns in the mill-school, Sarah owned, and made sure her classroom was as warm and bright as she could make it. Nor did she, in her compassion, ever awaken a child who fell asleep, exhausted, over his slate.

Tonight, Sarah decided, she would call on Maggie. There were matters to discuss with her friend – matters of importance, like the buying of shoes and how to brighten up her clothes. Before this her appearance had mattered little. Mill-girls wore skirts and blouses and pinafores and to have tried to ape their betters would never have occurred to them.

But Sarah Makin had gone up in the world. A lady-clerk wore a cape and bonnet and shoes or button-boots. Small wonder they had looked down their noses at her, Sarah sighed. There had been the stamp of the Three-streets on her and it wouldn't do.

But come next reckoning-day she would be rich. There would even be money over to spend on herself and then she would show them! She'd walk the Three-streets as proud as Lucifer and as for that bothersome Robey Midwinter – well, just let him wait! Next time he sneered at her she would draw herself up, all haughty-like and look at him down her nose. He'd not get her flustered again, be sure of that!

She shook her head, angry with herself for even thinking about him. But he bothered her. Try as she would, she could not get him out of her mind.

Who was he? Why had he come? But such matters had to wait. The hooter had gone and it simply would not do to be late back. Not on her first day. Not ever.

Luke Holroyd had spent a very profitable morning at the Cotton Exchange, eaten a delicious cold luncheon at his Manchester club and returned to Low Clough well pleased with himself. Then, just as he had been about to settle down for a doze, the counting-house manager burst into his office.

'I'll have to have words, Mister Holroyd, for I'm fair beside myself with grievance!'

'What is it, Albert?' the mill-master clucked testily. 'Can't young David see to it?'

'That he can't, Master. It's on account of Mr David I'm here. He's the cause of it – him and that lass!'

'What lass?' Luke sat bolt upright in his chair. 'What's our David been up to, then?'

'He's gone behind my back, that's what. Without so much as a word to me he takes a lass from t' weaving-shed and sets her up as a clerk. I wouldn't care, but lasses like her upset the tone of the place. Only last week she was brawling in t'yard and ever since she's come she's been singing at the top of her voice and clattering up and down the passage. I tell you, Mr Holroyd, you'll not have a floor-board left come reckoning-day, with them clog-irons of hers!'

Luke Holroyd sighed annoyance, his mellow mood gone. Albert Dinwiddie's petulant outbursts were enough to cope with; he could do well without young David's adding to the bother. Banging loudly on the partition wall, he nodded placatingly.

'All right, Albert. Say no more. Let's see what the lad has to say for himself!'

When David Holroyd answered his father's summons he was greeted tersely.

'Now then – what about this lass you've taken on?'

'Josh Dobson's assistant? Sarah Makin?'

'Makin? Caleb's lass, is she?'

'Yes, Father.'

'Aye, and without so much as a by-your-leave, Mr

David! Without telling me!' Dinwiddie interrupted. 'Undermined my authority, you have . . .'

'You surprise me, Mr Dinwiddie.' David raised an eyebrow. 'As I recall, you said you wanted nothing to do with the Order-by-Post department. "Don't come running to me," you said, "when you find you've bitten off more than you can chew, when you've bankrupted the place and the bailiffs are in."'

Dinwiddie regarded the highly polished toecaps of his boots, momentarily deflated. True, he had spoken out loudly against the idea of postal ordering, but who could have told it would do so well?

'It isn't that,' he grumbled. 'It's the principle of the thing, Mr David. You're forgetting my position.'

'And you are forgetting *mine*!' David flung.

'Come now, gentlemen!' Luke shook an admonishing finger. 'Let's not get upset! Happen you'd best leave the matter with me, Albert. David and me had best straighten it out between us, eh?'

Dinwiddie rose to his feet, well satisfied. As soon as the door closed behind him, he gloated, Luke Holroyd would put things to rights. Just a few well-chosen words from the Master would soon settle young David. And Sarah Makin would be back in the weaving-shed as fast as her rackety clogs would carry her.

He smiled a secret, malicious smile, gratified that his position had been upheld, his honour defended. A weaver from the Three-streets in his counting-house indeed! Whatever next?

'Right, lad. What've you been up to?' Luke demanded. 'Can't have you upsetting Albert, can we?'

'He's an old woman, father. What's more to the point is what about *me*? Dinwiddie treats me like a boy still. He seems to forget that Low Clough will be mine, one day.'

'Well now, you *do* surprise me, David. I'd never have thought you were all that concerned about the mill. Somehow I seemed to get the impression it was of no interest to you where your money came from.'

'Of course I'm interested. Didn't I start up the Order-by-Post department? And isn't it doing well, in spite of all you and Dinwiddie said?'

'Aye, I'll grant you that, but there's a way of doing things. You've got to learn, son, that you can't go stepping on people's toes without a thought. Dinwiddie's a faithful servant and I get him cheap, an' all.'

'I know that,' the younger man conceded quietly, 'but it's time I had more responsibility here.'

'And by responsibility I suppose you mean that you want to do things *your* way,' came the dry retort. 'Want to show off your fancy schooling and spend all my brass on new-fangled ideas?'

'Low Clough is old, father. If you spend money on it now you'll be glad, later on.'

'To get back to this lass,' Luke changed the subject adroitly. There were two things certain to give him indigestion; parting with money and the knowledge that someone other than himself could be right. As far as he was concerned there was only one opinion at Low Clough, only one master, and that was the way it would be until Luke Holroyd JP made his peace with the Almighty.

'Well, Father?'

'Well nowt! She'll have to go back to t'shed and that's all there is to it. There's a right way and a wrong way of doing things and –'

'And the right way is *your* way, sir! You said I could run the new department yet as soon as I hire another clerk I am called into your office for a lecture!'

Luke Holroyd drew in a deep breath then let it go in a strangled snort. On the face of it, his son was right. The hiring of an extra clerk was nothing to get het up about. But the lad had stepped out of line and gone over Dinwiddie's head. He had taken on a mill-lass who clattered about and sang songs at the top of her voice. Well, he wasn't going to stand for it, nor for his son's defiance!

'Get rid of her,' he ground. 'Either send her back to the shed or sack her. I don't care what you do, lad, but either way I want her out of my counting-house!'

'Then you can sack her yourself, for I won't!' came the icy retort. 'Or better still, tell Dinwiddie to do it. He'd enjoy that!'

The mill-master opened his mouth then closed it, speechless. His son's show of defiance should have made him angry but it hadn't. Luke was a bully, had clawed his way to the top by walking over those too weak or too afraid to stand up to him. Once he had worked at Low Clough. He had laboured, barefoot and half-naked, in the heat of the spinning-room, but with guts and guile and the luck of the devil, he had become Master. And had remained Master, an' all, and prospered too, because he'd never forgotten what it was like to be a spinner. He knew how to push a man to the ends of his endurance, when to threaten, when to give in. And now, he acknowledged warily, was a time to give in. Or to appear to. He forced a smile to his lips.

'Very well, young man. Nobody can say Luke Holroyd isn't as fair as a summer's day. I'll go to the post department and see this lass for myself. If she seems willing to learn and Josh Dobson speaks well of her, then I'll reconsider the matter.'

And if he could bait her into anger, he thought cunningly, force her into a situation that showed her up in a bad light, then he would have no alternative but to sack her, would he?

There were more ways than one of skinning a cat, Luke smiled grimly, and he knew them all!

'Well, son?' he demanded. 'Are we agreed?'

Sarah knotted the string around the brown paper parcel and snipped off the ends.

'There now, Mr Dobson, that's the last of them. All packed and ready for the postman to collect,' she declared triumphantly. 'I think we deserve a cup of tea, don't you?'

'Then if you're making tea wi' *my* coal and in *my* time, you'd best get out an extra cup for me!'

Joshua Dobson spun round gasping to face the man whose great bulk blocked the doorway.

'Afternoon, Mr Holroyd,' he whispered, his voice shaking with apprehension. 'It's an honour – a *great* honour – to have you visit our Order-by-Post department.'

'I see you've got yourself an assistant, Joshua.' Luke raised an enquiring eyebrow. 'This couldn't be the lass who was fighting like an alley-cat t'other day?'

'Aye, Master, it was me.' A dull flush coloured Sarah's cheeks.

'Then I hope you're not going to make a habit of it, Miss Makepiece? I hope we all in the counting-house may consider ourselves to be reasonably safe from your unladylike brawlings?'

'There'll be no bother. I only fight when I'm attacked,' Sarah flung meaningfully. 'And my name's *Makin*, Mr Holroyd. Caleb Makin's my father. You and him worked together in the spinning-room, if you remember.'

'I remember, lass. Caleb got himself lamed.'

'Aye, and you got yourself the mill, Mr Holroyd.'

'That I did,' he retorted comfortably, 'and there's some who'd do well to remember that, Sarah Makin!'

Drat it, he fretted. The lass was looking at him bold as brass, challenging him with her eyes when she aught to be cringing.

'And some should try to remember what it's like to be poor,' Sarah flung. 'And they should bear in mind that it's not a sin to want to get on in the world!'

For a moment Joshua Dobson's timid little world trembled under the impact of two stubborn wills in close combat. Clasping and unclasping his hands he looked from one contestant to the other; from Sarah's defiantly tilted chin to Luke Holroyd's angry eyes. And then he beheld a little miracle. A small smile flickered on the mill-master's lips as he said quietly:

'So you want to get on in the world, Sarah Makin?'

'That I do!'

'By fair means or by foul, eh?'

'I reckon so, Master, though I'd rather fight clean.'

The smile on Luke's lips gave way to a throaty chuckle.

'By the heck, Miss, but you've got the makings of a gradely lass, be blowed if you haven't!'

Then the laughter died and the smile faded and he was the Master again, the man who ruled his little kingdom as of God-given right.

'Josh Dobson,' he ground, glowering down at the man who wavered beside him. 'I'm holding thee responsible for this lass's good behaviour. We'll have no more brawling and a bit less caterwauling – is that understood?'

'Oh yes, Mr Holroyd. I'll mind what you say.'

'And tell her from me to get herself a pair of shoes. Them clogs of hers'll be the ruination of my floors!'

Anger sparked in Sarah's eyes. Oh, the arrogance of the

man! Did he think folk fished money out of the canal? Rounding on the trembling Dobson she spat:

'And tell *him* I'd like nothing better! Ask him if he thinks I like looking as if I've just crawled out of the gutter! Tell him all I want is a chance!'

'I'm giving you a chance, Sarah Makin, but you'll do things my way, in this mill,' Luke rasped. 'And don't think for a minute that I've forgotten what it's like to be hungry, either. And there's summat else I'll tell you for nothing. As far as I'm concerned, there are worse tribulations in life than the wearing of clogs! Remember that, Miss, when you're on your way to the top. Remember it was Luke Holroyd told you so, an' all!' And, turning on his heel, he slammed from the room.

'Eh, Sarah,' Josh breathed as the banging of a distant door confirmed that all was well again. 'Eh, but that was a close shave, all right.'

'Aye, Mr Dobson, I can't say I wasn't worried – for a time.' Then she grinned impishly. 'Happen I'd better put the kettle on! I think we deserve that cup of tea!'

The stock-pot was bubbling on the kitchen hob when Sarah reached Canal Street that evening.

'I've just put the dumplings in – won't be long,' Caleb Makin smiled.

Sarah returned the greeting warily. Her father was in a rare good humour and that should have pleased her. But Caleb's small upliftings often heralded long bouts of blackest depression, and that wasn't good.

'Been busy, then?' she asked, settling herself at the fireside, wriggling her stockinged toes into the clipped cloth of the rug.

'Aye,' he nodded. 'Paid my last respects to Will Nuttall, heaven rest him. Sold a couple of bottles of parsley tonic, an' all. Folk always seem to get fearful for their health, after a funeral. I said as much to Robey.'

'Robey Midwinter?' The name caught Sarah unawares.

'Aye. He was at the graveside.'

'Why? What has Will Nuttall's burying to do with him? He doesn't even live in the Three-streets.'

'He does now. But happen you'd better talk to him about it, if it bothers you, lass.'

'Oh, it doesn't.' Sarah shook her head airily. 'I don't like that man, that's all. It's as if there's trouble all around him. I just wish he'd go back to wherever he came from.'

'There's no trouble around him that honest men need fear. Robey Midwinter talks good sense. Why, he sat here today and –'

'He was *here*?' Sarah demanded. 'What have you and him got to talk about, Father?'

She felt a tingling of apprehension. Her father had not meant to tell her he'd had a visitor, she was certain of it. Yet the meeting seemed to have cheered him and for that she should be grateful.

'*Why*, Father?' She had to ask it.

'Oh, he had an aching tooth. I put some clove-oil in it for him.'

'I see,' Sarah nodded, wondering why a feeling of unease was buzzing inside her head like a trapped bee, why she couldn't be glad that for once her father appeared to have had a good day. Then she shook herself impatiently. No sense in looking for trouble. She would worry about it tomorrow, if needs be. Today she had things to do and, oh, there was such news for the telling.

'I thought,' she remarked as she ladled out the steaming broth, 'that I might go to Albert Court, to Maggie's. I want to have a talk with her.'

'You can go, but you'll not find her in,' Caleb supplied. 'Maggie's going to the Mission Hall – playing the piano for the Band of Hope singing tonight. I know she'll be there. Robey's going with her.'

'Why, the cheek of him!' Sarah gasped. 'Is he going to sign the pledge then, or does he fancy himself as a preacher?'

'Happen he does. Happen he doesn't,' Caleb retorted flatly. 'But there's some in these parts are going to have reason to remember him coming, be sure of that!'

'What do you mean? Just what is this Midwinter up to?' For he *was* up to something. '*Tell me!*'

But Caleb had said all he was prepared to say and began to eat his broth with exaggerated concentration, staring into the fire as if the answers to Sarah's probings were written in the flames.

But his eyes held a strange kind of triumph, Sarah pondered. There was the light of excitement in them as if he were waiting, breathlessly, for something to happen. And in his eyes too there were dark depths she couldn't fathom. And in that instant she was afraid, for those mocking deeps held secrets too.

It was strange, Luke Holroyd mused, how much louder a clock ticked in an empty house, for this barn of a place he'd once called home *was* empty.

Tonight, as he had driven up his carriageway, there had been no thrill of elation, no pride of achievement as he regarded the house that once gave him so much pleasure. High Meadow, he'd called it in his long-ago dreams, then watched it grow, stone by stone, a tribute to his success. He had hired a gardener to bring order out of the wildness around it, then filled the rooms with good, solid furniture, the finest linen, the best silverware. When it was complete, High Meadow had been a house to be proud of, waiting for the woman he would one day bring to it as his wife.

The parlourmaid tapped gently on the door.

'Cook asks if you're ready for your dessert, sir.'

'Nay, I'm not hungry.'

'But it's roly-poly pudding, Mr Holroyd. Cook did it special.'

He didn't doubt it. Cook always served him with homely victuals when Charlotte was away; hotpot, tripe and onions and puddings that stuck to a man's ribs. All the things, he sighed, that Charlotte regarded with amused scorn.

'I don't doubt that cook'll find somewhere to put it,' he retorted dryly, reflecting on the amount of food that went begging, day after day. It was a sin to waste food, he sighed inwardly. No good ever came of it.

But no one listened to his forebodings. Why should they? They'd never known adversity. Charlotte had been born into a world warm with plenty and David thought his father's pocket was bottomless.

What would become of it all when he was gone? Luke fretted. Would David's children spend fecklessly until there was nothing left? Would Low Clough fall into the hands of money-lenders? From clogs to clogs in three generations, that's what folk said when he'd become master of Low Clough, Luke recalled grimly. He had started with nothing and that was what the third generation would end up with, they'd whispered behind his back. There were some, even yet, who would like to see him fail, he brooded, and if David didn't shape himself it would be clogs to clogs all right!

Life was very unfair. That one day he would have to leave it all behind was bad enough to contemplate; that David seemed set to marry a simpering creature and rear a generation of drones was beyond thinking about. If only, Luke grumbled silently, David would find himself a spirited lass, one who could be relied upon to fill High Meadow with lusty sons, lads with a bit of the devil in them, who could be taught to care for Low Clough. It was little enough to ask.

But it would never be, for Charlotte had other ideas. David, she asserted, had been brought up a gentleman and had to marry a lady, one who would be hand-picked by her. Already there were several lined up in the marriage-stakes, one of them linked to half the nobility in Lancashire. Charlotte's grandchildren, she vowed, would have nothing of the commonplace about their pedigrees. Give her another generation and there'd be some real thoroughbreds in the Holroyd stable!

Luke shuddered. Just to think of it made his blood run cold.

He was still brooding on the underhanded ways of Fate when his son came home.

'You're late, lad,' he growled. 'Supper's finished.'

'I'm sorry, sir. I had some business at work that kept me.'

'Oh, aye? Monkey business, was it? Now I'm warning you, David –'

'Don't worry, Father. I was quite alone. As a matter of fact, I've been going through the ledgers and what I've learned is very pleasing. The post department is doing well.'

'You think so, lad?'

Luke reached for the decanter and refilled his glass. Could it be that David was beginning to care for Low Clough?

'I do, Father, and it will do still better.'

Mollified, Luke permitted himself a fleeting smile. If only Charlotte would stop her meddling, he yearned, their son might even yet turn into a mill-master.

'Where's Mama?' David sliced into the cheese. 'I thought she'd be back.'

'Well, she's not,' came the flat retort. 'There was a letter waiting when I got home. Your mother's decided to stay on in London for a while. It seems that the Prince of Wales is attending some charity performance at the opera and nothing would do but that your mother should be there too.'

He winced afresh, just to think of the expense of it all, for Charlotte wouldn't dream of hobnobbing with royalty in anything less than a new gown.

But he had learned to suffer his wife's improvident ways in silence. Protests only served to drive her into a tantrum. She would storm and rage, telling him he was mean, that he didn't care for her. Then she would pack her bags in high old dudgeon and take herself off to London where she would spend more money than ever. He wondered at times what had gone wrong with their marriage, why Charlotte always seemed to get the better of him. He had been so careful in his choice of a wife. He had approached her only after the greatest deliberation. Her father was a baronet and her great-uncle, on her mother's side, had been a peer. Proudly he brought his bride to High Meadow and within a year she had given him a son. His cup of glory was full, until she slammed her bedroom door in his face, declaring her duty to be done.

'You've got your son,' she shrugged. 'Be content.'

Selfish, Charlotte was.

Now Low Clough was his love and he had stood by and watched Charlotte rear that son in the ways of the gentry with never a thought for what was to come. Or so it had seemed, until David had come up with the idea of an Order-by-Post department. Nonsense, of course, but Luke had been so grateful for his son's sudden interest in the mill that he had gone along with the idea.

And now it was making money and David had taken on another clerk – that dark-haired lass of Caleb's. Full of fire, Luke mused; an ambitious wench. He'd enjoyed sparring with her. She was handsome too; a lass that by the looks of her would bear her children with ease. What a pity she couldn't have had a duke or two in the family instead of a morose and crippled father! But that was the way of the world. You couldn't argue with what the Almighty decreed, not even if you were Luke Holroyd JP you couldn't.

'It was good of you, sir, to give Miss Makin a chance. I appreciate it.' David pulled out a chair and settled himself at the table. 'Josh seems pleased with her.'

'But spirited,' Luke nodded cagily. 'Looks as if she could be headstrong.'

'Maybe,' David shrugged.

'And she'll have to compose herself a bit. Can't have mill ways let loose in the counting-house. Decorum, David. Decorum.'

'She'll be all right, Father, once she settles down. I'm sure she must feel different. I thought,' he hazarded, glancing sideways at his father's blank face, 'that I might offer to buy her a pair of shoes –'

He closed his eyes, trying to choke back the reckless slip of words, but it was too late. Already the damage had been done.

'Shoes? By the heck, I knew you were up to something!' Luke roared. 'As soon as Dinwiddie told me how you'd sneaked that lass in, my nose started to twitch!'

'Sir! It's not what you think. I gave Miss Makin the job because –'

'Because you had designs on her!' the irate man supplied. 'Damn it, lad, do you take me for a fool? Do you think I came to earth with the last fall of soot?'

'Father – if you'd let me –'

'I was beginning to think you were showing a bit of backbone at last, but I was wrong!' Luke thundered, refusing to be interrupted. 'I'll not have carrying-on at *my* mill with one of *my* workers! I'll not have a local lass weeping and wailing all over the town that she's been wronged by a Holroyd! I don't want a workhouse brat for a grandchild. Sow your wild oats if you must, David, but don't do it in Hollinsdyke. Take yourself off to t'other side of the Pennines and do your rampaging there, but –'

'Father! Be *quiet*!' David Holroyd brought down his fist with a force that set the cutlery dancing on the table-top. His face was dark with anger, his eyes flashed danger.

Luke's mouth sagged open. Never before had his son spoken so. Never, ever, had he shown such spirit. It was unbelievable. It was magnificent!

'Sir – please hear me out.' The anger was gone, now, but the voice was quietly resolute. He had not intended showing his hand yet, the young man mused, but this was the time! 'Yes, I do admire Miss Makin. I think she is spirited and beautiful and I find her most desirable. But I don't wish to seduce her.'

'No?' Luke gasped.

'Oh, no! When Sarah bears my sons, they'll be Holroyds, not nameless chance-children for the parish to rear. I've given the matter a great deal of thought. I intend to marry Sarah Makin if she'll have me and there's nothing that you or Mama can say will stop me! Do I make myself clear, Father?'

Three

The meeting had already started when Sarah arrived at the Mission Hall in Tinker's Row. It was so quiet that at first she thought it must have been over, but as she pushed open the door the silence was ripped wide by a sudden great cheer. Hands clapped and clogged feet stamped out a storm of approval.

'He's right! The mill-masters are evil!'

'Speak for us, Robey? Help us?'

The atmosphere in the crowded room pulsated with life and the drab walls seemed to take on a reflected glow as the man on the platform acknowledged the applause of his audience. His lips were parted in a half-smile and triumph blazed in his eyes. Robey Midwinter had wooed the men and women of the Three-streets with whispered sympathy, demanded their allegiance with words of fire, then rising up like a giant had mocked their apathy.

'Do you want to live forever on this muck-heap, work for a pittance until you drop? Isn't the labourer worthy of his hire? Did not our Lord say, "Suffer little children to come unto me", yet you stand by and see your bairns exploited!'

The dark eyes swept the room with unhurried contempt.

'You stand like sheep, bleating silently, tipping your caps to the mill-masters, grovelling . . .'

The words ripped into the astonished silence like bullets and each one found its mark. Women dropped weary eyes and men shuffled uneasily, unable to deny the truth of the words that wrapped them round in a lash of scorn.

'Your women grow old before their time and your children never know childhood. Your bellies are empty and will stay empty until there is such a fire in them that you can stand it no longer. And when that day comes, my brethren, you will rise as one man from the midden of your misery and speak with one voice, a mighty voice to be heard all over this land. I pray God,' he whispered, 'I may live long enough to see it!'

Men looked at Robey Midwinter that night and saw themselves reborn in the glow of his aura and women drank in his manliness, thrilled to the challenge in his eyes.

Could this be the Messiah, the promised one who would fight for them, uphold their dignity? Who he was, where he had come from, none cared. Sufficient that he was here, this mountain of a man, pawing the ground like a lusty buck, eager for a fight. They were with him to a man.

The cheers rose and swelled, filling the room like a battle hymn and as she stood there amid the heady tumult Sarah feared that Luke Holroyd must surely have heard the wonderful noise at faraway High Meadow. He'd hear it and come tearing down the valley with the Constabulary at his heels and the law in his pocket, eager to keep the Queen's peace and uphold the authority of every mill-master in Lancaster County.

Words were wonderful, Sarah thought bitterly. Words were cheap, like ale-house gin, and any fool could drink them in.

But Robey Midwinter's words were heady with promise. He believed, so you believed. You closed your eyes and saw a golden world where men walked with dignity and no one went hungry; a world in which it was no sin to be old or lame.

Sarah clucked with annoyance. Such things could never be. Men could talk until Judgement Day if they were so minded and it wouldn't make a ha'porth of difference to Hollinsdyke. Even God had turned his back on the place.

But imagine. Imagine green-cool woods and fields of buttercups. Imagine winding lanes and soft sunsets and snow in winter that never got dirty.

Oh, why had this man come to their town? What was there about him that brought out the worst in her? Why did she want to impress him, make him notice her? And it was all so stupid because there was no room in her life for men. She was too busy getting on in the world to be bothered with such things.

But imagine what it would be like to be Robey Midwinter's woman, to walk beside him proud as a queen, to look into his eyes and see love there, and desire.

'Come on, Sarah. Give a mite for the speaker?'

A small boy grinned up hopefully, rattling the coins in his cap.

'Here y'are, cheeky.' Sarah tossed over a penny. 'And keep your thieving fingers to yourself. I'm watching you!'

Watching as the man at the back of the room was watching, the man who stood unmoving in the shadows, eyes downcast yet missing nothing; the same man who only this morning had looked at her with contempt in the counting-house at Low Clough. Aaron Silk, one of Dinwiddie's clerks, taking in every word, every gesture, storing them in his maggoty little mind to tell to his betters.

By tomorrow morning Luke Holroyd would know all about Robey Midwinter.

'And what did you make of it all?' Caleb Makin demanded of his daughter as they walked home. 'Didn't it fire your blood, lass?'

'I don't rightly know,' Sarah hazarded, slowing her steps to match those of her father. 'I got there late and didn't hear much of it. What's Robey Midwinter trying to do? Set the streets alight?'

'It'd be a blessing if he could!' Caleb flung. 'I'd give what was left of my life to see Low Clough go up in smoke!'

'Aye, but Low Clough'll be standing long after you and me have gone,' Sarah added dryly, 'so don't take on so. It's not right of Robey to raise people's hopes. What's his business here? What is there in Hollinsdyke for the likes of him?'

'His business, my girl, is righting wrongs. He's a thorn in the flesh of the Masters. He preaches against injustice.'

'Talk costs nothing,' Sarah spat, annoyed that even for a moment she had let her guard slip, had looked at Robey Midwinter through the eyes of a woman. 'And what's more, I'm surprised at Maggie's mam for taking him in,' she added, glad she had come to her sober senses again. 'Just wait until Luke Holroyd hears about what's going on. Your precious Robey'll be on his way so fast his toes won't touch the cobbles and Maggie Ormerod'll be out of a job,' Sarah prophesied darkly.

Men like Robey were trouble. They were tall and good to look at and their eyes held mischief. They had soft words to command and when they smiled it was fit to charm the birds from the trees. But they were *trouble*.

*

They said little else that evening, the man whose mind was sick as his body and the girl who had no time for love, for the meeting in the Mission Hall had touched them both.

It left Sarah more certain than ever that first impressions are often right. She had sensed unrest about Robey Midwinter, known that his easy smile masked a pitiless heart. Now, as she watched her father, she was even more sure she was right.

Crouched by the hearth, bellows huffing, Caleb blew life into the dying fire, watching intently as the coals reddened, then blazed high. And there was a hardness in the eyes that gazed into the licking flames. It was as if he saw the blazing streets of Hollinsdyke there and in the middle of the carnage Low Clough burning in fierce retribution. But even the fire that flamed in the old man's eyes could not hide the secret triumph that smouldered there.

Sarah saw it plainly and her blood ran cold.

'Sit yourself down, Albert.'

Luke Holroyd reached for a cigar. Albert Dinwiddie's face wore a confidential look and when the counting-house manager had confidences to impart, it could be a wearisome business.

Dinwiddie hitched his trouser creases delicately and settled himself. What he had heard seemed hard to believe, but Aaron Silk usually spoke the truth so it was only proper the Master be told.

Silk had a nose for goings-on. If bother threatened, he could be relied upon to sniff it out.

'There was speechifying last night at the Band of Hope meeting,' Dinwiddie offered. 'From what I heard, I'm afraid there's trouble afoot, Mr Holroyd.'

'And who told you, Albert? Was it that ferret-faced little clerk with the fancy hair?'

He did not like Silk, but it was necessary at times to heed his tittle-tattle.

Dinwiddie sniffed, ignoring a question that needed no answer.

'There was a stranger at the Mission Hall, preaching anarchy and inciting the mob. By the heck, your ears must have been burning last night, Mr Holroyd, for he fairly had it in for you.'

'Oh, aye?' Luke's right eyebrow lifted a fraction. 'And who is he, this splendid apostle, and what makes him think that *my* mill is any of his business?'

'They call him Robey Midwinter. He's got lodgings in the Three-streets. A big fellow he is – handsome, so I'm told. Had the women eating out of his hand.'

'And the men?'

'They were listening, sir. Stamping and shouting and agreeing with every word he said. Called you the world's worst, Midwinter did; said half the cripples in Hollinsdyke had you to thank for it. Said he'd see to it that you put guards on the machines.'

'Aye? Pray continue, Albert.' The voice was steely-soft.

'Said you didn't do right by your apprentices either. He reckoned as how half of 'em were nowhere near nine years old and shouldn't be working.'

'Well now, isn't that strange? Since most of 'em are foundlings and without a birth certificate, I don't see how anybody could blame me for that. Were any of my workers at that meeting?'

'Aye, Mr Holroyd. Just about all of 'em. There was a collection, afterwards, and everybody gave, including Miss Sarah Makin.'

'Oh, but we're living in an ungrateful world.' Luke shook his head sorrowfully. 'I give them work and they bite the hand that feeds them. They plead poverty yet they throw their money away like drunken sailors.' He raised his eyes heavenward. 'May the Lord have mercy on the undeserving poor.'

'Amen to that, sir.'

'Thank you for warning me, Albert. You're a good and faithful servant. I'll be mindful of your loyalty, at Christmas.'

Dinwiddie rose, duty done, and minced toward the door. Poor Mr Holroyd. Ingratitude was a terrible thing, he thought, well satisfied.

At the clicking of the door-sneck, the sorrowful mask fell from the mill-master's face. His eyes narrowed into slits and his jaw shaped itself into a trap. Fury raged briefly inside him, then his expression softened into one of cunning.

There was nothing to worry about. A nod to the constable and the rabble-rousing Robey would be hustled out of town if he as much as spat on the cobbles. And as for his ungrateful, ungodly workers, as for those wretches in the Three-streets –

A smile softened the craggy face. Those wretches in the Three-streets could follow their Pied Piper to perdition if that was what they wanted. And they could toss their pennies into his hat until they starved. A fool and his money were soon parted. That was why he lived at High Meadow and owned the mill. That was why they, the miserable fools, lived in the Three-streets, and owned nothing.

He puffed on his cigar and watched the smoke drift wraithlike to the ceiling. The settling of Master Robey could wait. At this moment there was a far more interesting matter for his attention. His son's sudden fancy for Caleb Makin's lass, for instance. Now there *was* something to chew over . . .

David Holroyd was restless. He had refused his father's invitation to luncheon then spent the past half hour gazing down into the mill-yard like a love-sick idiot. And that was exactly what he had become, he thought grimly, envying the child who seemed so close to Sarah, wishing it was he himself who sat beside her, received her smile.

'But why *her*? Why a mill-lass, when you could take your pick of half Lancashire?' his father demanded.

'I don't know, sir,' he had hesitated. 'I think I wanted to marry her the first time I ever saw her. This isn't a sudden decision.'

He would have to take a wife, it was expected of him, but not a girl of his mother's choosing, not one of the languid young ladies who were persistently paraded at High Meadow. There had not been one of them as lovely as Sarah. Sarah was so exciting. There was a turbulence about her that roused him. He was beginning to dream about her now and always in those dreams she was walking on Moor Top hill. She would smile and beckon to him, then, just as he reached out to touch her, she'd be away like a wild thing, her hair flying, bare feet skimming the grass.

'And what,' his father demanded, 'makes you think she'll have you? Caleb Makin's a proud old cuss and likely he's reared a proud daughter. She might laugh in your face, lad.'

And that was all his father would say on the matter. He hadn't ranted or raved. He had just raised a quizzical eyebrow, then lapsed into maddening silence. And when that happened, David acknowledged uneasily, he knew to tread carefully. Luke Holroyd angry was something to beware. Luke Holroyd silent was crafty as a waggon-load of monkeys and you avoided him, if you'd the sense, as you avoided the plague.

But, desperate, David had decided that now was the time to bring things into the open.

'Ask Miss Makin to come to my office when she gets back from her dinner-break,' he'd told Joshua Dobson. 'Nothing to worry about,' he hastened. 'Just want a chat . . .'

Then he had fled from the room lest Dobson should see the flush that crimsoned his cheeks. He was acting like a lad in the bonds of calf-love, but he didn't care. He wanted Sarah for his wife and to that end he would agree to any conditions she might care to impose, anything she asked, so long as she took him. He would even marry her without love and wait, if he had to, until she came to care for him. But, by God, he would have her!

When he heard Sarah's footsteps in the passage outside, David took a deep gulp of air, then settled himself uneasily behind his desk.

'Josh said you wanted me?'

She smiled and closed the door behind her.

'Yes, Miss Makin.' Jumping to his feet, he offered a chair, taking her elbow, handing her into it. The feel of her warm, bare skin sent need flaming through him and he allowed his hand to remain on hers.

'Is something wrong, Mr David?'

He felt her body stiffen as she pulled away her arm, her eyes instantly guarded. Her withdrawal was intended and obvious. It acted as a sharp, silent reprimand, a sobering reminder that she was not for touching.

'No, Sarah. Nothing's wrong.' He sat down heavily again, damning his stupidity.

The eyes that levelled with his sparked defiance, demanding he keep his right and proper place. He read the message clearly. He was a Holroyd and she a spinner's daughter. The gulf between them was wide and deep, so think on!

'I wanted to ask you,' he floundered, latching on to the first thought that drifted into his muddled mind, 'about the Band of Hope meeting last night.'

Sarah's chin shot out and up, her eyes narrowing.

'What makes you think I can tell you anything about it?'

'Because you were there, Sarah, and I hoped you'd tell me what happened.'

'I got to the meeting late, so I don't rightly know what went on. But why don't you ask Aaron Silk?' she flung, her lips tight with distaste.

David Holroyd's head jerked upward. 'I know nothing about Silk,' he rapped. 'My father told me about the meeting, then asked me to get to the truth of it.'

Liar! His father had asked no such thing. His father had told him about the meeting then laughed defiance. Let them listen to Midwinter until their clog-irons rusted! he'd said. Empty heads made empty bellies. If that was what his workers wanted, they were perfectly free to choose.

'Tell me, Sarah – who is this man Midwinter? I heard he has lodgings in the Three-streets.'

'Happen he has, but it's of no interest to me. And as to who he is,' she shrugged. 'Then your guess is as good as mine.'

Sarah wriggled uneasily. She didn't like being questioned or having to meet and return David Holroyd's stare.

'Then I'd guess he's nothing but a rabble-rouser,' he flung, 'who thinks he can teach my father his business. Don't the workers at Low Clough know that if they've got a grievance they have only to see Mr Luke?'

'You mean nobody's ever told the Master about the bad lighting in the spinning-mill and the cold in the weaving-shed?' Sarah mocked. 'He'd put it to rights, would he, if he knew? And fix guards on the machines and free the apprentices?'

'*Free* them? You talk as if they were caged! We give them work, pay them a wage –'

'Which goes straightway to the ale-house or is grabbed by the workhouse-master to help pay for his charity. Either way, those bairns are losers!'

'You feel strongly about the children, don't you, Sarah?' Here could be a way to her heart. 'Tell me what I can do to help.'

'I don't rightly know,' she shrugged, caught off guard by the abruptness of such an offer.

'Then put yourself in my place. If you could, how would *you* help the orphans?'

'I'd feed them, poor little souls.' Her eyes were gentle again. 'They're always hungry. They work nearly seven hours in the mill then go straight to school. Their insides must ache with emptiness.'

'Is that why you give food to the child, every day in the yard?'

'Billy-Boy? Yes,' she smiled. 'I share what I have with

him but it's only a drop of charity in a sea of want. Bairns should be fed regular. It's their need and their right. Either that, or people shouldn't bring them into the world!'

'But Sarah – having children is Nature's way of things. Children are a fact of life.'

'Then more's the pity. A child should be wanted, not a burden. Aye, sir,' she flung. 'That's what most bairns are in the Three-streets. *Burdens!*'

The animation had left her face and in its place was a yearning sadness. David saw that look and knew there was hope.

'Sarah,' he said gently. 'I want to help. I know how much needs to be done, but Low Clough isn't mine yet, and I must make haste slowly.'

'You truly care, Mr David? Enough to want to do something about it?'

He nodded silently, amazement bursting inside him, realizing that whatever Sarah wanted he wanted too. It was merely that the thought had never crossed his mind before. And until now, if he dared to be honest, he hadn't much cared either. But to love Sarah was to look at the world through her eyes.

The hooter blared and Sarah jumped instinctively to her feet.

'I must go, but – but if you really care, Mr David, couldn't you put it to the Master? A bowl of broth costs next to nothing, but it would mean a lot to a hungry child.'

'Sarah!'

Her hand was on the door latch. Any moment she'd be gone and a chance lost. He had to ask her! *Now!*

'Wait, Sarah. There's something else!'

'Yes?'

'Marry me, Sarah? Say you'll marry me and I'll do anything – anything at all you ask!'

The words sounded strange, as if other lips had formed them. What had he done? He waited, his heart pounding.

Sarah turned slowly, her eyes wide with disbelief, and then, as if her legs were suddenly useless, she leaned heavily against the door.

'Did you say *marry* you, Mr David? Have you taken leave of your senses?' Her words came in a whisper of anger. 'Or is it a game, a joke?'

'No! I mean it. I love you.'

'Love me? You don't even *know* me! A week ago we hadn't even met!'

'That isn't true,' he urged. 'I've known you much longer than that, but you didn't realize it. All last summer, when you walked on Moor Top, I was there watching you. I'd go almost every night, hoping to see you, wanting to speak to you, wondering who you were . . .'

'Then you'd only to ask,' she retorted bitingly, 'and I'd have told you!'

'I realize that now,' he admitted. 'But I was afraid if I approached you you'd run away.'

'I'd have told you,' she continued doggedly, 'that I was Sarah Makin, that I lived in Canal Street, that my mam was dead and my father only half alive, that –'

'I know all that,' he interrupted softly.

'And?'

'I only know I love you and want to marry you. Nothing else matters.'

'Oh, Lordy,' she breathed. 'What a mess!'

'A mess, Sarah? Would it be so very terrible to be married to me?' he gasped. 'Wouldn't you like a fine home, a carriage of your own, all the dresses you could dream of, pairs and pairs of shoes?'

'Of course I would,' she whispered, wide-eyed. 'But to take all that without having anything to give in return wouldn't be decent.'

'Give me yourself. That's all I ask.'

'No, Mr David. It wouldn't be right. Oh, I reckon I could be a wife to you, but I'd be cheating, for all that and it would be wrong. Even a mill-girl has her pride.'

'I don't understand you, Sarah. What has marriage to do with pride?'

'It means that if I took all you offered I'd be sinking to the level of the gutter,' she whispered, her eyes downcast. 'I'd be selling myself, wouldn't I, because there'd be no love in it – not for me, anyway.'

'But many a young lady marries without love, then comes to care for her husband.'

'It wouldn't work.' Solemnly Sarah shook her head. 'And even if I loved you there'd be your parents to think about.'

Oh, think of it, she fretted. Think what the proud Mrs Holroyd would say to a mill-girl for a daughter. And think about the rumpus there'd be an' all in the Three-streets. They'd say Sarah Makin had gone off her head and they'd laugh themselves silly. Then, when the laughing was over, they'd turn their backs on her because she wouldn't be one of them any more. They'd hate her more than they hated the mill-masters because she'd be a turn-coat.

But, oh, imagine living in a house as grand as High Meadow. Imagine riding in a carriage, having shoes of softest leather and little pink slippers. And lazing each morning in a soft, warm bed; her *husband's* bed.

'I'm sorry,' she heard herself say. 'I'm mindful of the honour you do me, but I can't marry you, *sir*.'

She laid great stress on the last word, so it should

emphasize the divide between them, but he chose to ignore it.

'I won't give up, Sarah. I shall ask you again. I'll ask until you say yes.'

Lost for words, bewildered and dismayed, Sarah fled.

'What is it, lass?' Josh asked. 'What's upset you? Mr David's not found fault with your work?'

'No, Mr Dobson. Nothing like that. Nothing to worry about,' she whispered, forcing her lips into a smile.

Nothing at all to worry about except that somehow she had landed herself feet first in trouble again. Oh, Lordy. Why did it always have to happen to Sarah Makin?

Dismissing a problem, Sarah discovered, did not guarantee that it would go away. She had firmly decided to forget what had taken place, disturbing though it had been. She would forget it as if it had never happened.

But it had not been as easy as that and the vexed question was still there, niggling inside her head as she lay wide-eyed in her bed, counting the quarters that chimed from a distant clock.

Why had Mr David spoiled things? She had been so happy about her promotion. Joshua Dobson was a kindly soul and there were no overlookers to watch her, no machine noise crashing inside her head, no fines. Just to think about buying her first pair of shoes had stood out like a milestone in her life, yet now she was being promised pairs and pairs of them.

She wished she could have shared her problem with her father, but mill-masters in general and Luke Holroyd in particular brought out the worst in him. Caleb Makin was the last person she could confide in.

But share her worry she must and it had to be Maggie she would tell. And even if her friend could not help, she reflected, a trouble shared would be a trouble halved. Nor would Maggie shout her confidences all over Hollinsdyke, for being proposed to by a mill-owner's son wasn't a thing to be bandied about. For the most part, mill-owner's sons were slippery customers and a working girl remembered that if she didn't want to end up in trouble.

Without a doubt, her secret would be safe with Maggie, but wasn't it a pity Robey couldn't know about it? Not that he mattered, of course! But to have seen the amazement on his face would have been nothing short of wonderful. And when he had recovered from the shock he'd be glad she had said no, look at her in a new light, show her a bit more respect, like as not.

And that was a puzzle, if you like, because she didn't like the man at all and it didn't matter one bit what he thought of her.

Sarah sighed and pulled the blanket over her head. There would be time for a chat before she went to work. Maggie would know what was best to be done. Maggie would straighten things out for her.

There was a softness about the early morning that made Sarah look up to the distant hills. High on Moor Top there would be birdsong and fat little leaf-buds ready to burst. And the spiky blackthorn that grew beside the beck would be a froth of white blossom.

Undaunted, she swung into Albert Court and stopped at the third house down. She felt almost happy. Strange, this churning inside her. She shouldn't, she supposed, be feeling so light of heart and there shouldn't be a kind of breathlessness inside her, as if she were a child again and this were Christmas Eve. It wasn't, it really wasn't anything to do with Robey Midwinter. The giddy feeling was nothing to do with his being there. Robey was a rabble-rouser. He had a tongue that could wound and eyes that mocked. His sort were best left alone and she knew it. Then why, she thought irritably, was she getting herself into such a state?

She didn't tap on the back door or even call out. There was no need. No 3, Albert Court was open house to Sarah Makin.

At first everything seemed so still she was sure the kitchen was empty, then in the dimness she caught a movement, heard the whispering of a sigh.

Robey stood there and, in his arms, Maggie. They did not hear the opening of the door or Sarah's gasp of alarm. They were kissing. Their embrace was long and passionate, their bodies touched. Robey, his arms cradling Maggie's waist; Maggie, pink and pretty, her hair disarranged, so small beside him that she reached on tiptoe to meet his lips.

Sarah backed out of the room, cold with shock, stunned and disbelieving.

No! Not Maggie and Robey? Maggie wasn't his kind. She was too gentle, too trusting. And she had no right to him when Sarah Makin wanted him. Oh, it was useless to deny it. In that small moment of realization she had wanted to sink her nails into Maggie's face and draw blood; had felt a sickening urge to tangle her fingers in the pale yellow hair and, screaming, pull her from his arms.

Rage danced before Sarah's eyes. She picked up her skirts and ran blindly.

She was late arriving at the mill for she had walked aimlessly, unthinking and uncaring. The shock of her anger had lessened but the agony of her friend's betrayal had not.

But see if Sarah Makin cared! Let them have their stolen kisses, if that was what they wanted; it was nothing to her. Only let them wait, and she would show them!

She clattered up the staircase and along the counting-house passage. Outside David Holroyd's office she stopped, tossed back her head, then knocked loudly on his door.

'Sarah!' He rose quickly to his feet. 'My dear, what is wrong?' Gently his finger touched the tear that lay on her cheek. 'You've been crying!'

'No! I was late, that's all. I was running . . .'

She drew in a shuddering breath, then dropping her eyes to her hands she said slowly:

'I came here to say something. I'd be grateful if you could spare me a minute, Mr David. I'd like to get it over with.'

For just a moment it seemed she could not go on, then straightening her shoulders, staring at the wall above his head, she whispered,

'Yesterday, sir, you asked me to marry you and I said I couldn't. I'd like to change my mind. I'm saying yes.'

'Sarah!' He stared at her bemused. 'I can't believe it. You turn me down, then out of the blue you say –'

'I see. You've thought better of it?' she demanded harshly. 'It was a joke. You don't want me?'

'Of course I want you, but –'

'But you don't want to *marry* me?' she supplied. 'I'm a mill-girl and gentlemen don't marry the likes of me. They only –'

'Sarah! Sit down, and shut up – *please*! Of course I want to marry you. It came as a shock, that's all. Yesterday I cursed my stupidity for flinging it at you so clumsily. I thought I had lost you. Now, you've turned completely about face. Why, Sarah?'

'I don't know,' she shrugged. 'Happen I've had time to think about it.' What was she about? Cutting off her nose to spite her face, that's what! And it was Robey Midwinter's fault; his and Maggie's! 'Happen I've come to realize the honour you do me –'

'Honour? Oh, my dear,' he said gently, 'that's a silly word!' Then he shrugged and smiled and taking her hands in his own said softly, 'It doesn't really matter what your reasons are. Just so long as you'll marry me that is all I want to hear you say.'

'I'll marry you, Mr David,' she whispered. 'And I *will* try. If you'll put up with my ways, teach me how a lady should act –'

'No. You mustn't change. All you must learn is how to love me. Oh, you've been honest with me,' he hastened, silencing the protest that sprang to her lips. 'But you will come to love me, Sarah. And I shall never give you cause for regret.'

She didn't speak. She couldn't. There was a great pain inside her and tears in a tight knot in her throat. She tried to smile, but her lips were stiff with misery.

'We'll be married at once, my love. I'll see the Bishop, get a licence to have the banns waived. I won't give you time to change your mind.' He squeezed her hands gently, realizing for the first time how cold they were, how they trembled. 'You'll not change your mind, Sarah?'

She shook her head, her eyes downcast. *Never have cause for regret?* But already she was filled with remorse. She had been stupid again, blundering in without thought. Blinded by jealousy and anger she had excelled herself this time. Already she regretted her rashness, and serve her right too. Only Sarah Makin could be so foolish, promise herself in marriage to one man whilst every small part of her cried out for another.

Oh, damn Robey Midwinter! Maggie was welcome to him! Let her wed him and see if Sarah Makin cared! And she wasn't weeping, she really wasn't.

Then like a frightened child she went blindly into David's waiting arms and sobbed as if her heart was ready to break.

Four

Sarah walked moodily, kicking the grass with a petulant toe, trying to ignore the feeling of panic that surged inside her each time she allowed herself to think about the day to come.

The air was warm with the scent of awakening earth and tender growing things and here, on Moor Top hill, Hollinsdyke seemed far away. But for the drift of church-bells ringing out below her, she could have imagined herself into another world.

She willed the bells to stop. They reminded her uneasily about tomorrow, the day she was trying hard to forget.

She hadn't told a soul yet; not even her father. How would he react, she fretted, when she said:

'I'm going to be married, Father. Tomorrow I shall wed Luke Holroyd's son.'

He would be bitterly angry and it would take him a long time to get used to the idea.

Why was everything in such a turmoil? Why had Mr David rushed things so? Had he thought she would call it off with the first reading of the banns? Had he really believed that to be married quickly by special licence would save her from three weeks of wagging tongues and sly nods?

It wasn't the talk she was worried about. More than gossip she feared her father's fury, for sometimes she thought it was only his hatred of Luke Holroyd that kept him alive.

'One day,' he had said, 'Luke Holroyd's going to get his comeuppance and I want to live long enough to see it. I want to stand there, and laugh.'

'We'll make it a quiet wedding, if that's what you want,' David had said and nowhere, Sarah acknowledged, was quieter than the parish church at nine on a Monday morning. There was almost an air of furtiveness about it.

But at least it would not be raining tomorrow, she thought gratefully, looking up at the rosy evening sky. She wouldn't feel so badly about it, if the sun shone.

David had said she had to have a wedding-dress.

'Buy something blue,' he said, offering her a handful of sovereigns.

'When we're wed, Mr David, you can buy my clothes,' she retorted, more sharply than she had intended, 'but until then you'll take me as I am, or not at all!'

It had been a deliberate act of defiance. Had he protested, she could have walked out of his life. But he was careful not to give her the chance.

'I'm sorry, my darling. I'll not care what you wear – only come?' He had smiled then and chided her gently. 'And when we are married you must learn to call me David. I shall put you across my knee and spank you if you call me mister!'

He had said it kindly, yet Sarah bristled with indignation. Spank her indeed? Only let him try, and he'd feel her clog-irons against his shins! But it mattered little, she shrugged, for David Holroyd's like didn't do such things. With Robey Midwinter, now, it would be a different matter. Robey wouldn't take nonsense from any woman. To be spanked by him would be an altogether different experience and to kiss and make up afterwards would be nothing short of wonderful.

But Robey didn't love her. Angry for letting herself think about him again she tried to force him out of her mind. That he belonged to Maggie was beyond doubt. When a man and woman kiss as they had kissed, marriage must surely follow.

Yet it isn't easy to dismiss a man when suddenly he is there, not a hundred yards away, walking the hillside with great swinging strides.

Sarah gasped, not wanting to believe it, her heart pounding with happiness because it was undeniably true. Scrambling to her feet she took a deep, calming breath.

'Good-evening, Mr Midwinter,' she called, marvelling at her primness, glad he could not see the tightly-clenched fists thrust deep into her pockets.

'How-do, Sarah Makin? Come up here after some fresh air, have you?'

'Aye,' she nodded.

'My, but it's good to get away from the muck.' He threw himself to the ground then patted the grass at his side. 'Sit down, lass, and talk to me.'

The familiar arrogance was gone and as she looked into his eyes Sarah saw they were without scorn.

'What about?' Cautiously she dropped to her knees beside him. 'Want to ask questions again?'

'Not today,' he smiled. 'I know all I need to know about Hollinsdyke, for the time being.'

He settled his hands behind his head and shut his eyes as if to announce the subject was closed.

Sarah shifted uneasily. She wasn't at all sure how this different Robey should be handled.

'How is your tooth?' she ventured, trying to keep her voice even. 'Father said you'd had a bad ache.'

'*Me?*' He opened his eyes and laughed up at her. 'Sure you're not mistaking me for someone else?'

'N-no. Father said he'd put oil of cloves in it.'

Instantly the suspicions she had felt took substance. Her father had acted strangely, as if he had not intended telling her that Robey had been to the house. Now it was obvious he'd had a reason for lying.

'I called on your father, but not with an aching tooth,' Robey admitted easily, closing his eyes again.

Oh, but he was handsome, Sarah acknowledged. Just to look at him sent small sinful shivers tingling through her. She wanted to touch him, trail her finger across the outline of his face, brush his lips with her own. What would it be like, she wondered, to feel his arms around her?

'What are you thinking about, Sarah Makin?'

His voice crashed into her secret thoughts and she flushed, angry he had caught her looking at him so intently.

'I was wondering who you are,' she lied, 'and why you are here.'

'You were at the meeting,' he shrugged. 'You should know what I'm here to do.'

'But it won't be any use!' she protested. 'You'll never change things. Men have tackled Luke Holroyd before, and come to grief.'

'I can try,' he retorted amiably. 'At least I can say I cared.'

'And I care too,' Sarah cried. 'I care about the children, anyway.'

'And your father – crippled by wilful neglect? Doesn't he matter?'

'Of course he matters,' Sarah flung, trying not to be goaded into anger. 'But he had a choice, and the children haven't. My father could have walked out of Low Clough any time he'd a mind to. But the bairns are different. They're little and weak and they don't have a choice. They can't fight back. Bother about *them!*'

For a moment he didn't speak, leaving Sarah to fume inwardly that he had succeeded in upsetting her yet again. Then slowly he said:

'So you do care? There *is* something other than self inside that head of yours?' He reached over and took her hand in his. 'I'm glad, Sarah. I'm glad.'

She closed her eyes helplessly, for the sudden delight of his approval was almost more than she could bear. She felt the pressure of his hand, his cheek close to her own. Tilting her head, breathless with joy, she parted her lips to receive his kiss.

But he did not kiss her. He laughed instead and pulled her to her feet.

'Come on, lass. I'll walk you home. I promised Maggie's mother I'd not be late for supper.'

With a gasp of dismay Sarah's eyes flew open. His words were like cold water thrown carelessly into her face and they had the same shocking effect. Trying to collect her reeling senses she stood bemused as he turned his back on her and strode towards the path that led down to the town.

Damn the man! Damn him for making her care! But he was in for a shock, she fumed. She would show him how little he meant to her! Tomorrow she was marrying David Holroyd and Robey Midwinter could go to the devil, for all she cared!

'Wait for me,' she called, loving him so much it was like a fire raging inside her.

He stopped and held out his hand and she placed her own inside it, thrilling as an exquisite pain shot through her.

They walked without speaking and then, where the path crossed the beck on large, flat stones, he stopped, dropping to his knees at the foot of the blackthorn.

'Look, Sarah – primroses. Now there's a sign that summer's a-coming.'

Gently he gathered the pale little blossoms, then, binding them together with a wisp of dried grass, solemnly gave them to her.

'Flowers for my lady,' he smiled.

Pain stabbed at Sarah's heart. Didn't he know what he was doing to her? She wanted to crush the flowers, fling them away, but she cupped them tenderly in her hands, for they were the most precious things she had ever beheld. She knew she should thank him, smile into his eyes as if the giving and receiving of flowers was a commonplace thing, but she could not. A smile comes hard to a woman's lips when her heart is weeping.

'Let tomorrow come quickly,' she prayed, 'and let it pass quickly too. You see, Lord, I'm cutting off my nose to spite my face. I love Robey and I can't have him and it's all such a mess . . .'

And then, as if her prayer had been heard, Sarah knew where the answer lay.

She would tell her father about it, just as she had intended telling Maggie. She would ask his advice and she would act on it too. Marriage was a serious thing and her father was older and wiser by far than she. Caleb Makin would know what was to be done.

Decision taken, she smiled into Robey's eyes. It was as if a great unhappiness had been banished, as though in a twinkling she were free of her own foolishness, for she knew exactly the advice her father would give.

Caleb Makin was sitting by the fireside, staring fixedly

into the flames when Sarah got home. He didn't move as she entered and she knew that the previous day's elation had turned, as it always did, into black depression.

'See, Father,' she coaxed. 'Primroses from Moor Top.'

Slowly Caleb raised his eyes, his face blank and bitter. His shoulders lifted in a small shrug and Sarah knew that this was not the time to tell him her secret or ask his advice. It was as if he had pulled a curtain of resentment around himself and there was no way through it.

She knew there would be no help for her now. She could talk to her father all night and he would not hear a word she uttered. He would just sit there, in his little private hell.

'And I,' she thought, 'will marry David Holroyd as I said I would, because there's no getting out of it.'

She filled a cup with water, then tenderly placed the flowers in it.

'They were growing by the beck,' she whispered to the uncaring room. 'Pretty little things, aren't they?'

Flowers Robey had picked for her. Flowers from her love.

Sarah awoke long before Limping Ned knocked on the windows of Canal Street. Reluctantly she stretched and sat up in bed, looking round the little room, knowing she was doing it for the last time.

Where would she sleep tonight? They hadn't talked about it, she and David, but there had been so little time. Five days ago he had asked her to marry him yet only last week she had been looking forward to her first day in the counting house.

It was her own fault they had not talked. She had been deliberately vague, shutting it out of her mind as if to ignore it was to postpone its coming.

But this was the day on which she was to marry a mill-master's son. This drab, half-awake stillness was her wedding-morning and a small breath of fear caught in her throat. Then realizing there was nothing to be gained in delay, she wrapped her shawl around her shoulders and slipped silently downstairs.

She was surprised to see the kitchen fire blazing and the kettle puffing steam on the hob. Usually her father lay abed until the clatter of clogs outside proclaimed a new day. But today he too seemed restless.

'Good-day, lass. You're up early.'

'I couldn't sleep.'

Her father seemed better. Now, thanks be, she could tell him. Soon she would have to be at the church. The matter had been put off for long enough.

'Tea?' Caleb asked.

'Please. And, Father – come and sit by the fire. There's something I want to tell you.'

'Bad news, is it?'

'No.' Her father always expected the worst, but he couldn't be blamed for that. 'It's just that I'm getting married –'

The old man looked up sharply, his eyes questioning.

'Well?' Sarah demanded. 'Aren't you going to say anything?'

'What is there to say?' Caleb's eyes narrowed. 'You didn't even think to mention you were walking out, so why should it matter all that much when suddenly you tell me you're thinking of getting wed?'

'Not thinking, Father. It's decided. It's this morning, at nine o'clock.'

Caleb set down his mug, splashing tea on the hearth-stone.

'I see,' he jerked. 'Since you've waited this long to tell

me, I can only reckon you've got yourself into trouble.'

'If you mean am I going to have a baby,' Sarah cried, 'then I'm not. Certain sure I'm not! I didn't tell you because I knew you'd be upset.'

'Upset?' he ground. 'Why should I be upset? Doesn't every lass get wed, sooner or later? But I thought you had more sense, Sarah Makin. I thought you were going to get on in the world.'

'Then happen I just might be,' she whispered, tears pricking her eyes. 'Only it's a sad day when I can't ask my own father to give me away.'

'And why not? If you've got your heart set on it, then I'll come with you to the chapel, lass.'

'Will you?' she choked, her voice a whisper of torment. 'When I tell you I'm marrying David Holroyd, will you come, Father?'

For a moment the silence in the little room was so complete that Sarah could feel it screaming a warning. Then, with a terrible cry, Caleb lifted his hand and brought it crashing into his daughter's face.

'Trollop!' he hissed. 'I see it all, now! Setting you to work in the counting-house, giving you ideas above your station. *My* lass, marrying a Holroyd! I never thought I'd see the day,' he spat, his eyes burning hate, 'when I'd take my hand to my own girl. But as from this day, Miss, you're no longer mine. I'm going out, for the sight of you sickens me. Go to your fine lover! Go anywhere, only don't be here when I come back! Don't *ever* come to this house again, my fine lady. You'll not be welcome!'

With a cry that was almost a sob, he dashed his hand across his eyes and snatching up his jacket slammed out of the house.

Sarah stood still as a statue, listening shocked to the

dragging of his foot on the cobbles outside until she could hear it no longer.

Tears rose in her throat in a great choking lump and she bit hard on her fist to prevent herself from giving way.

Why had her father done this to her? He had only needed to forbid the marriage and she would have obeyed him. Gladly she would have obeyed him.

But she wouldn't weep, not on her wedding-day. It was unlucky, wasn't it, and she had had all the bad luck she was prepared to take.

Why had her father made it necessary for them to part in anger? But perhaps, she sighed, when he came to realize he could not keep himself without her help, he might make her welcome again.

Would he though? Caleb Makin would beg for parish relief, end up in the workhouse even, rather than take Holroyd money. And from this day on, she conceded, it would be Holroyd money she would be offering him.

Suddenly she could stand it no longer. She wanted to be as far away from the Three-streets as she could get. She wanted to be away from her father's house, no matter what her future held. And she would marry David Holroyd, and be damned to them all! What lay ahead she could only wonder about and fear, a little, but there was nothing she could do now to change things. She had given her word and she would keep it. She had made her bed, hadn't she? Well now she would lie on it!

Rounding the corner into Church Street, Sarah stopped short. Now, if she was to do it, was the moment to call a halt, the time to say no. Even yet, it was all slightly unreal. It was as if she had stepped, unthinking, on to a roundabout, a gaudy prance of wooden horses, rotating so quickly that it was impossible to get off and run back to the dreary safety of the Three-streets.

But she had passed the point of no return when quietly she closed the door behind her and, crying inside herself, walked away without so much as a backward glance.

Now, grouped around the church gate like an unreal tableau, was her future. David Holroyd standing erect, his morning-coat immaculate, his top-hat set at a stiff, anxious angle. And by his side the verger fidgeted, looking at his pocket-watch, wishing, she shouldn't wonder, he had not been called upon to witness this hole-and-corner wedding.

Only the coachman seemed at ease as he waited beside Luke Holroyd's best carriage, soothing the restive horses.

David looked up and saw her standing there.

'Sarah!' he called, running to meet her, taking her hand in his lest even now she should turn and flee. 'Dearest, you've come.'

'Of course I've come,' she choked. 'I said I would, didn't I?'

'I know,' he smiled. 'But I was anxious.' He entwined his fingers in hers then tucked her arm beneath his own.

'Nervous, Sarah? I know I am.'

'Me too,' she nodded. 'But it isn't too late, Mr David. If you've thought better of it, now's the time to say so.'

'Oh, no,' he jerked. 'There's no getting rid of me now.' Then his forehead wrinkled into a frown. 'Your father isn't coming?'

'No,' she whispered, colouring deeply. 'He had one of his turns. Does he have to be here?'

Maybe they couldn't be wed if there wasn't someone to give her away, she thought wildly. She didn't understand church ways. She had been Band of Hope all her life.

Maybe, without her father, the wedding couldn't take place?

'No, Sarah. It needs just you and me and two witnesses – and the vicar, of course.'

'All right, then,' she said, tilting her chin. 'Happen we'd better go.'

The church clock began to strike nine. It was too late now for regrets. For better or worse, Sarah conceded, this was her wedding-day, and nothing would ever be quite the same again.

Their steps echoed loudly in the empty church. Before them on the chancel steps stood the vicar, his book open at the ready. He nodded a reluctant greeting, then, nervously clearing his throat, began to speak the words of the marriage service.

'Dearly beloved. We are gathered together here in the sight of God and in the face of this congregation – in the er – presence of these witnesses . . .'

What a mess he was making of it! But it was upsetting, a Holroyd getting married in such a way. Nor did the vicar care for special licence affairs. He wondered uneasily if Mr Holroyd knew about this morning's goings-on and he didn't dare even begin to imagine Mrs Holroyd's thoughts on the matter. But there was nothing he could do; he sighed and, squaring his shoulders, resumed the chant.

' . . . to join together this Man and this Woman –'

The verger stood rigid, staring ahead at the sombre purple of the altar-cloth, wondering why they couldn't have waited until Easter to get themselves tied. Didn't they know Lent weddings were unlucky, the silly young things?

The scrubbing-woman who was cleaning the church porch when the vicar asked her to stand witness wiped a tear from her eye and smiled gently. She loved a wedding, even a wedding like this one without kith or kin or well-wisher present. She hoped the bride would have no regrets. Such a bonny, sad-eyed lass . . .

David Holroyd looked with love at the woman who stood beside him.

With this ring, I thee wed and with all my worldly goods I thee endow.

All he had he would gladly give her. Soon he would be able to buy her everything she could want. Soon. When she was his.

Those whom God hath joined together, let no man put asunder.

The vicar's voice droned into his thoughts. It was almost over. She was his wife now. Dear, wide-eyed Sarah whose face was pale and whose hand trembled in his. Sarah in a drab grey skirt and cheap white blouse with a bunch of primroses pinned bravely to her shawl. Dear God, how he would cherish her!

'Happy, Sarah?'

'Happy?' she echoed, gazing around her at the breath-taking litter of boxes and parcels. 'Why, yes – yes, I am . . .'

But it couldn't be happiness, this churning inside her. Bewilderment, excitement, agitation like as not. But happiness – no.

Since the church clock struck nine she had been in a half-dream, unwilling to awaken to face up to this fateful day. She had become an ostrich, she thought. All fine feathers and head in the sand.

Vaguely she remembered the church, cold and musty-smelling, the vows she had made, David's kiss. Out of the shadows came fleeting recollections of the drive to the railway station, the journey to Manchester and the shock of her first real encounter with David's world.

'Now I shall take you shopping,' he smiled.

They had stopped at the store to buy the dress he was so set upon and ended up by buying the entire place, or so it seemed to Sarah.

The gown David chose was of silk, the colour of the first forget-me-not, its skirt pulled back into the newly-fashionable bustle, its cuffs and neckline edged with matching lace.

Bemused, she fondled its rustling folds. It was the most beautiful dress she had ever seen; just to touch it made her want to weep.

But her husband's generosity had not stopped at the purchase of a single gown. They bought house dresses and street dresses, petticoats, ribbon-threaded under-pinnings, bonnets and gloves. And cotton stockings and silk stockings, button-boots, shoes, slippers trimmed with swansdown.

'Please – no more,' Sarah begged, guilt thrashing inside her. It was downright sinful. They had spent so much she had lost count. Pounds and pounds. More than the whole of the Three-streets could earn in a month.

He was trying so hard, she thought miserably, willing herself to respond to his kindness, wishing she could shake herself out of the dream.

'I love you so much,' he whispered. 'Please, my darling, don't look so sad. Everything will be all right. I promise.'

'I know,' she choked, 'and I'm grateful. Truly I am.'

But gratitude was the last thing he wanted of this woman who was now his wife. He wanted her love, wanted her to say the words he so longed to hear.

But one day she would say them, he vowed. He would

make her so happy she wouldn't be able to help herself. Only let it be soon, he yearned. Let it be soon.

Sarah hung the last of the gowns in the massive mahogany wardrobe then closed the drawer on the dainty undergarments. Soon she would awaken. Soon she would open her eyes and find she was sitting by the hearth at Canal Street, wondering about the dream she had just had.

'What am I to do with these?' she hesitated.

Only one box remained unpacked. In it were her mill clothes. They looked almost comic, laid carefully between crisp tissue paper, folded as painstakingly as the most luxurious of her dresses.

'Will Madam be needing *these*?' the shop assistant had asked, holding the skirt and shawl between a disdainful finger and thumb. Sarah was about to ask her to throw them away, but David had told the girl to pack them in a box, if she pleased, and have them delivered with the rest.

'Why did you want to keep them? The lady in the shop looked at them as if they'd bite her. They're poor things, worth nothing.'

'You wore them to our wedding. I want them to be kept,' he said firmly.

'Why?' she insisted. 'I'd have thought you'd not want reminding of what I was, where I came from. I thought you'd be ashamed . . .'

'Then you thought wrongly, my Sarah.'

She shrugged, not understanding. But if that was what he wanted then so be it. It was fair exchange for all he had given her.

They dined later in the privacy of their room. It was surely the most magnificent room in the world, she decided. Ainderby must be exactly like this, she marvelled as they were bowed through the glittering glass doors of the Manchester hotel. There had been potted palms and greenery everywhere and gilt chairs, plush-covered, and the grandest staircase she had ever seen, smothered in thick red carpet.

Their rooms were even more opulent, but after the first shock had passed the richness faded and became one more part of the unreality.

Sarah wore the blue silk and coping with the bustle would have been a near disaster if David had not had the sense to ring for a maid to help her into the dress.

Shyly she watched as a small army of servants set a table with silver and glass and little posies of pale pink rosebuds. Waiters followed to serve their meal, then coughing discreetly had left them alone in the flickering candlelight.

Sarah ate little but drank the wine because it was cool and the champagne because of the novelty of it. But for the most part she sat with hands clenched, tension coiled inside her like an overwound spring, her head growing lighter, her eyes growing heavier.

She looked again at the gold ring that made her hand feel odd, proof beyond doubt that she must surely have been married. She still walked in the mists of make-believe but the ring could not be ignored. It was very solid and very real.

The candles burned lower and a chambermaid tapped on the door, asking to be allowed to turn down the bed.

'Sweetheart,' David smiled when they were alone again. 'Don't be afraid?'

'I'm not afraid – not really,' she whispered, 'but it's like a dream, Mr David, and it's happened so sudden-like that I can't seem to catch up with it.'

She glanced through the open door of the bedroom. The pink-shaded lamps had been lit, the satin bedcover removed. Folded neatly on one pillow lay her husband's nightshirt and draped mockingly across the other was the new white nightdress. It was decorously styled with long, full sleeves and a high neckline demurely frilled, but it was so flimsy, so blatantly transparent that she blushed just to look at it.

One by one, the candles flickered and died and the mantel clock chimed midnight. David pushed back his chair and rose to his feet.

'Sarah?' he said gently, holding out his hand.

The room tilted slightly, then righted itself and she walked with him to the bedroom.

By the dressing-table she paused. Lying forlorn beside the silver-backed brushes was the little bunch of primroses, fresh still, as though they had just been gathered.

Without another thought she took them, then, shuddering at the wickedness of it, tossed them into the glowing coals.

'Sarah!' David cried. 'Your wedding flowers!'

She watched unspeaking as they shrivelled, burned briefly, then were gone. Only then did she say:

'It doesn't matter. They were dead.'

They had been Sarah Makin's flowers. Sarah Holroyd had no right to them.

Lifting her chin she smiled and crossed the room to stand beside him, trying not to look at the sinful nightdress.

The dream was giving way to reality. She was David's wife now and the big bed mocked her.

Turning her back, lowering her head, she whispered, 'Unhook my dress, will you?'

Five

The great gates swung open, the lodge-keeper's wife bobbed a curtsey as they passed, and the fear that had smouldered uneasily in the deeps of Sarah's mind blazed into naked panic.

Now she had to face the music and it would assail her from all sides; from the people of the Three-streets who didn't easily forgive those who stepped out of line and from her husband's kind who didn't take gladly to a mill-girl with ideas above her station.

The train journey from Manchester in a first-class compartment had been most enjoyable. Indeed the whole morning, until this moment, had passed agreeably enough. Even awakening to the sight of her husband's head on the pillow beside her had not been unduly perturbing and to sip tea in bed as she watched him shaving was, she had had to admit, almost pleasant.

David had been kind to her last night, she conceded gravely, treating her gently, soothing her fears. For that at least she was grateful.

'I shall visit your father,' he called from the dressing-room, 'and beg his pardon for stealing his daughter so shamelessly.'

'No!' she cried harshly. 'He'll not see you. He took it badly when I told him about us.'

'You didn't tell me that.' David appeared in the

doorway, thoughtfully fastening his cravat. But there was a lot, he shrugged inwardly, they hadn't talked about. 'Is that why he didn't come to the wedding?'

'It is,' she admitted. 'I didn't say anything because I thought it would be the same for you too. I didn't expect your parents would be overjoyed either.'

'I see what you mean,' he admitted. 'To be honest, my father was away yesterday, in Liverpool. He'd get to know about us when he got back, I shouldn't wonder. A bit of a shock, I suppose, hearing about your son's marriage second-hand.'

'From the coachman, an' all,' Sarah added soberly. 'And what about your mother?' she whispered, wishing London were on the other side of the world.

'She'll get over it – they both will,' he smiled. 'Just give them time.'

He kissed her gently and she closed her eyes, trying not to think of what might await them. It would not be easy, no matter what David said. Elders had contrary ways and there was no reason to suppose her husband's parents were in any way different. But best not dwell too deeply on such matters. Life had taught her never to court trouble since it could always find her with no bother at all. Later she would worry, not here in this unaccustomed place where everything had a dreaming air about it. And there was, she brightened, pushing aside her doubts, padding barefoot to the wardrobe, a most pressing decision to be made. Which, for instance, of these beautiful new garments to wear this morning? Would it be the fawn serge street-dress with its little matching cape or the velvet-trimmed skirt and jacket?

It should all, she yearned, be wonderful and exciting and dizzy-making. Then why, her head demanded perversely, was it not so? It was a question to which her heart could find no answer.

Now the unreal honeymoon was over and they were bumping up the drive to High Meadow in a hansom-cab.

Sarah had often seen the great house, but distantly, through locked gates, wondering what it would be like to have more beds than anybody could decently sleep in and fires that burned the whole day long in rooms that were never used.

Now it was her home and she was seeing it close-to for the first time, this solidly built house of stone with a roof of no-nonsense slate and high, wide windows, a house little more than a quarter of a century old, yet which was mellow and perfect.

Sarah gasped at its beauty. Daffodils rippled in golden drifts in the woodland gardens and fat-budded rhododendrons made ready to greet the spring.

'Welcome to High Meadow,' David smiled, helping her to alight.

She smiled uncertainly, walking catlike on the rough gravel. The sharp stones bit into her dainty shoes and she winced, wondering why she had so despised her solid clogs.

'It seems,' David smiled wryly, 'that we are expected.'

A black-gowned figure appeared at the top of the stone steps, her hands clasped in front of her, a bunch of keys swinging from a belt at her waist. She inclined her head.

'Good afternoon, Mr David.'

Sarah gazed dumbly at the housekeeper, then felt a shiver of dismay as she looked beyond the rigid shoulders and into the vastness of the entrance-hall.

Luke Holroyd stood there, thumbs pushed belligerently into his waistcoat pockets, feet slightly apart, his jaw clamped tight.

'Father!' David smiled easily, holding out his hand. 'I didn't expect to find you home.'

'I'll wager you didn't,' came the dry retort, 'but there's things to be said that won't keep, so I'd appreciate it if the pair of you would step inside.'

He held open the door of his study, a room he had never learned to feel at ease in. It was a grand place, furnished with pieces wished on him by Charlotte's parents and packed with books no one ever read. He kept his study for brooding in and for occasions he found unpleasant, and his son knew it.

Placing his arm protectively round Sarah's shoulders David murmured:

'My dear, this is Parkes who looks after High Meadow for us. She will take you to my room.'

His voice was firm, indicating that the altercation his father seemed set upon was men's business only.

The woman bowed stiffly and lifting a finger to summon a passing housemaid, gave clipped orders for Sarah's bag to be carried upstairs.

'Now, Father,' David said quietly, closing the door behind him. 'Which of us is to start this discussion?'

Luke's face crimsoned. He had not expected this quiet defiance although secretly he found it not unpleasing. The old man liked a fight, the more so when the protagonists were evenly matched. He had no time for men who cringed – never had – but his son had made him look a fool and for that he'd have satisfaction.

'This isn't a discussion,' he said aggressively. 'I want an explanation, lad, and it had better be a good 'un!'

'Then if that's all, sir, you shall have one. I told you, a week ago, that I intended to marry Sarah. I did just that, yesterday morning, in the parish church.'

'That you did!' Luke roared, 'without either your mother or me there, without family or friends or –'

'Or business associates and half the county set who

couldn't give a damn, anyway,' David finished mildly. 'Be honest, Father. I did it the only way possible. Sarah wouldn't have countenanced a big wedding. She'd never have married me if I'd asked her to face up to such a ridiculous charade. And that's exactly what such a wedding would have been!'

'Then why marry the lass at all, if you're ashamed of her? Is there some reason for this hole-and-corner affair? Have you got the lass into trouble, then? Is that what folk are to think?'

'People may think what they like!' David jumped to his feet, his eyes flashing anger. 'If it's any of their business, I suggest they be patient and time will answer them. But get this clear, sir. I am *not* ashamed of Sarah. I love her dearly and I will not have her reviled by anyone. If you and Mama reject her, you reject me too. If she is not to be made welcome here then I will take her away!'

'Oh, aye? And what will you live on, the pair of you? Will you live on love, in a garret?'

'No, sir,' came the steady retort. 'I shall be well able to manage. There are mill-owners who would welcome my knowledge of postal selling. I could offer my services to Gideon Hindle.'

'Hindle? That – that charlatan!' Luke gasped. 'Have you taken leave of your senses? Work for my rival, for a man who'd sell his old mother's boot-laces if he thought it would turn a quick penny?'

'Gideon Hindle has a fine mill, father, with new machines and a sick-club for his workers.'

'And you'd desert your poor old dad for him?'

'If needs be, sir.'

The truculence melted from the mill-master's face and his eyes took on the gaze of a downtrodden spaniel.

'Oh, the hurt of it,' he moaned. 'Was there ever anything so wounding as an ungrateful child? After all I've done.' He swept his eyes heavenward. 'After I've –'

'Schemed and slaved, worked your fingers to the bone?' his son suggested, eyes dancing. 'Oh, Father, you should go to London, work the music-halls. You could render East Lynne to perfection. You'd have them weeping into their beer.'

'By the heck, but you're a tough one under all that polish,' Luke sniffed, abandoning his hurt, changing tack again. 'You drive a hard bargain. You fight unfair.'

'Yes, I truly believe I do,' David admitted softly. 'But I've learned it in the best of schools, haven't I? I'm a Holroyd.'

A Holroyd? It dawned on Luke like the sun after rain. Of course the lad was a Holroyd! It had taken a time to show itself, but here was a new side to his son's nature.

Hope wrapped the old man in a warming glow. Happen marriage was going to be good for the lad.

'Ha!' he grunted, mollified.

'You'll receive Sarah kindly, then?'

'Aye. It might well be,' Luke conceded, 'that she'll do very nicely.'

'She will,' David smiled. 'Oh, she *will*, I promise you.'

'Then I suppose we'd better drink the lass's health.'

Luke poured sherry, well pleased. By gum, he pondered, shaking with silent mirth, but this situation had the makings of a fine old to-do, be blowed if it hadn't. Caleb's lass versus Charlotte? Whatever the outcome, he decided impishly, life henceforth would not be dull. And on that he'd lay his last shilling!

The housemaid who carried Sarah's bag was pert and pretty and bursting with the importance of being the one to gain first-hand knowledge of the new Mrs Holroyd.

'Will you take tea, ma'am?' the housekeeper asked stiffly, 'or will you wait until later? Mrs Holroyd will be taking hers in the drawing-room at three-thirty.'

David's mother – back from London?

Sarah shook her head miserably. She didn't know how to speak to servants. They were so superior, so sure of themselves. Servants were not reduced to despair at the sight of a dinner-table or frightened silly at the prospect of fine living.

'Very well.' The woman withdrew, motioning to the housemaid to follow.

Left alone, Sarah prowled uneasily around the room, picking up objects, putting them down again. She tried to interest herself in the photographs that lined the walls, but could not. They were all a part of David's past, a life about which she knew nothing.

Drawing aside the heavy lace curtain, she peered across the lawns to the parkland beyond. Down there, she supposed, lay Hollinsdyke, shut out from the beauty of the day by a blanket of smoke. And down there, straggling the canal-bank, were the Three-streets where her father lived and all her friends. Tonight they would go to the Mission Hall. They'd sit there as one and listen to another outpouring of Robey's anger. Folk stuck together in the Three-streets, Sarah yearned, wondering if she would ever dare set a foot there again.

Then she sighed impatiently and stuck out her chin. At this moment it was more important to know what was being said in Luke Holroyd's study. David had ordered her upstairs and she was grateful to him. She had not relished being the butt of Luke's anger.

Carefully opening the door, glancing either side of her, she walked softly to the head of the stairs, leaning over the banister-rail, listening intently, but there was no sound save the ticking of the clock that stood on the half-landing.

A door-latch clicked and Sarah spun round, flushing guiltily at being caught eavesdropping by a servant. But it was not one of those superior beings. Better by far if it had been, for there was no mistaking the tall figure standing in the doorway.

Sarah pulled her frozen lips into the shape of a smile, wondering if she should offer her hand or merely incline her head.

She was given no choice. Charlotte Holroyd swept along the corridor towards her like a galleon with full sails.

It would have been prudent, then, to have disappeared behind the safety of a closed door, Sarah considered, but wisdom had deserted her as she stood there, courting disaster, waiting for the fury to break around her.

But Charlotte Holroyd had better ways of dealing with the girl who had married her son. Satisfaction she would have – vengeance had to be slow and sweet. Drawing herself up with dignity, tilting her head so she was able to gaze down her nose, she stopped and faced her son's wife. For a moment she glowered down, then, lifting her lorgnettes to eyes that were little more than slits, swept her gaze over the trembling girl from top to toe, then back again.

'Tsk!' she clucked, as if she had beheld a troublesome insect. 'Tsk!' Then brushing an imaginary speck of dust from the sleeve of her gown, walked on as if the younger woman did not exist.

Instinctively Sarah bobbed a curtsey, wishing the floor would open up and swallow her, then, picking up her skirts, fled to the shelter of David's room.

Tears pricked her eyes. She could bandy words with the

best of her opponents and she could, if need be, give a good account of herself in a fair fight. But against open contempt she had no defence.

Miserably she slammed shut the door, then, throwing herself face down on the bed, pummelled the pillows with angry fists.

But she wouldn't cry! She *wouldn't*!

Uneasily Sarah dressed for dinner. Twisting her hair into a pleat she secured it with combs, then, patting her face with rosewater, dabbing lavender scent at her wrists, pronounced herself to be ready.

'You look very beautiful,' David whispered, brushing the nape of her neck with his lips. She had chosen to wear the blue silk gown again and it pleased him.

'I'm afraid,' she whispered. 'I'll not know what to say and there'll be all those knives and forks to sort out.'

'Then watch me and you'll be all right,' he smiled, 'and as for my mother – well, if you ask her about London, she won't stop talking, I assure you.'

He made it all sound so easy, he who had been born into such luxury. And as for Mrs Holroyd, as for that formidable woman who had reduced her to a jelly with a glance, well, the likes of her didn't bear thinking about.

Sarah had not told her husband about the afternoon's encounter. It would have sounded childish, complaining about a look. But what a look it had been! She trembled, just to recall it. It embodied bitterness and dislike and total contempt. It had made her want to find a crack in the floorboards and squeeze into it.

David offered his arm. 'Shall we go down?' he asked comfortably.

*

Luke was standing beside the drawing-room fire and his eyes showed admiration as they entered.

'Well now. At last I get a chance to greet the bride.' Placing his hands on Sarah's shoulders, he kissed her cheek. 'Hullo, lass. That's a bonny dress you're wearing.'

'David chose it,' Sarah whispered, blushing at the unexpected compliment.

'Aye. David was always a good picker,' he retorted obliquely, then turning to his son remarked:

'Cook's done us proud tonight. I believe the table looks a real treat.'

Sarah accepted a glass of Madeira, grateful that Luke Holroyd at least seemed to have accepted the marriage. His attitude had thrown her off balance, for she had expected him to offer dire warnings of the perils in store for those who went to the altar without thought. She had not believed David when he assured her that all was explained and the explanation accepted. The mill-master was known for his guile, Sarah acknowledged apprehensively. Best she should take care. She made a mental note not to drink too much wine. Until last night she had never tasted alcohol. She had sighed the pledge almost as soon as she could write her name. The champagne they drank had made her lightheaded and this evening she had to keep her wits about her.

Instinct directed her glance to the open door and she caught her breath fearfully. Charlotte, splendid in lavender satin, was progressing down the staircase.

Sarah's stomach contracted painfully and she gulped hastily at her wine.

'Here's Mama at last,' David smiled, taking Sarah's hand in his.

Charlotte paused in the doorway of the room, then, walking to her husband's side, tilted her cheek to receive his kiss.

'Evenin', my dear,' Luke nodded amiably. 'You look very smart.'

'Tut! This old rag?'

She turned to greet her son, permitting him the smallest smile and a stiff inclination of her head. Totally ignoring Sarah, she said:

'Kindly tell Parkes we are ready, David.'

'In a moment, Mama,' he retorted softly. 'I want you to meet Sarah. Please wish us well.'

Shaking in every limb, Sarah offered her hand, but the older woman declined to take it.

'Sarah *whom*?'

'Sarah Makin, Mama,' David supplied.

'One of the Lancaster Makins, perhaps? You'll be related to Sir John?'

'No,' Sarah spoke slowly and quietly, remembering the softness of her mother's voice. 'I live – lived – in Canal Street. My father is Caleb Makin and I was a weaver at Low Clough before David wed me.'

The words ended in a breathless whisper and she felt David's fingers tighten comfortingly around her own, heard him saying:

'Isn't she beautiful? Aren't I the luckiest of men?'

Charlotte stared down her nose, drew herself up tightly and murmured:

'Perhaps you will take me in to dinner, David?'

She laid her fingertips possessively on her son's arm, turning her back on the girl at his side.

'Mama!' His face flushed dully.

'A very good idea!' Luke intervened hastily. 'And maybe Sarah will do me the honour.'

His eyes met those of his son and signalled a warning. 'Not now. Not here. *Leave it!*'

'Of course,' Sarah choked, finding it hard not to throw her arms around him and hug him from sheer gratitude. 'I'd be delighted, sir.'

Slowly the tension in the room dissolved and Luke let go his indrawn breath as the head-on collision seemed to have been averted.

'Drink up your wine, then we'll follow the others. Go on,' he urged when she hesitated. 'It'll calm you down – put the roses back in your cheeks. And if I may say so,' he whispered, 'I think that round went to you, Sarah Makin, so don't look so doleful. Chin up, eh, lass?'

The meal, as Sarah had feared, was a complete disaster. Not, surprisingly, because of the bewildering array of cutlery, crystal and fingerbowls, but wholly because of Charlotte Holroyd's studied rudeness.

At first Luke's wife declined to speak at all, concentrating on the food before her so there should be no doubting the strength of her displeasure. Then suddenly she laid aside her knife and fork.

'Well, husband,' she pronounced in a high, clear voice. 'I said it many times before and you made light of it, but I knew I was right.'

'Right about what?' Luke growled, realizing from years of experience that the tone of his wife's voice signalled trouble.

'About that quaint Lancashire saying, my dear,' she said lightly. 'How does it go, now? *From clogs to clogs in three generations*. Is it not about to come true?'

'Mama! Just what do you mean?' David's fork hit the table with a clatter.

'What I have in mind, I think, is something to do with

the making of a silk purse.' She stared meaningfully at Sarah. 'From a sow's ear, of course. Pretty well impossible, I would say.'

Sarah closed her eyes and shook with shame. How could David's mother be so cruel? Even in the Threestreets, folk didn't behave like that. They said what needed to be said without fear or favour, but they never used words as weapons.

From the serving-table came a gasp of amazement. The parlourmaid stood, ladle poised, her eyes popping, and the under-parlourmaid's mouth sagged open. The room was very still as, with an icy calm, David said slowly:

'Mama, I must ask you not to speak so to my wife. Your rudeness is most uncharitable.'

The older woman gasped.

'How dare you?' she hissed, her cheeks flushing crimson. 'I will not be reprimanded by my own son in front of servants!'

'And why not?' Luke demanded mildly. 'Since everybody seems set on forgetting their manners, let's all join in. I think you've gone a little too far this time, Charlotte.'

From across the room came the crackle of starched aprons and a hurried patter of feet. The servants at High Meadow knew when their presence was an embarrassment. The door opened and closed quietly.

'Well, madam?' With an exaggerated calm, Luke blotted his lips. 'We are alone now, so maybe we'll hear your apology.'

'No!' Sarah gasped. 'Oh, please, *no*!'

But Charlotte was already on her feet and making for the door, her back stiff with indignation. She knew when to retire with dignity.

'Well, son?' Luke smiled wanly when his wife's retreating footsteps could no longer be heard. 'There's a lesson in self-preservation, for you. Nine times out of ten, a woman's instinct is a very reliable phenomenon and best deferred to, but every so often a man has to assert himself. Tonight, lad, was one of those times. And maybe,' he sighed, 'it was as well to get things straight, right at the onset.'

'I'm so sorry,' Sarah choked. 'It's all my fault. If I'd not come here, there'd have been none of this upset.'

Her voice trembled and she stared miserably down at her hands. It was part of a nightmare. There was no other way to describe it.

'Oh, darling, it wasn't your fault,' David hastened. 'I never thought my mother could be so – so thoughtless. Please don't be upset.'

'Upset? Of course the lass isn't upset!' Luke boomed. 'I'll wager it'll take more than a tantrum to nettle Sarah Makin!'

Sarah tilted her chin. He was right. She wasn't made of pink sugar. She had married David for better or for worse. Tonight, she reasoned, was one of the testing times.

'Aye,' she nodded, feeling the tension slowly slipping away. 'I'm not easily put down. And if you don't mind, Master, let's get another thing straight. Sarah *Holroyd* isn't upset by tantrums either.'

'By the heck, David lad,' Luke roared, his shoulders shaking with laughter, 'but you've found yourself a gradely lass, be damned if you haven't!'

Never, thought Sarah as fear slowly loosed its grip on her trembling limbs, had she ever thought to find an ally in Luke Holroyd. Strange, but if he hadn't been a mill-master, she'd have been prepared to swear he was almost human.

But everything was strange now. Nothing, she told herself silently, would ever be quite the same again. Nothing.

Sarah awoke with an uneasy start and peered, blinking, at the bedside clock.

Lordy! She'd overslept! Instinctively her hand touched David's pillow and it was cold beneath her fingers. This wasn't, she brooded, going to be a very good day.

Dressing quickly, she fought the panic that nowadays seemed never very far below the surface. She would be late for breakfast too. They would all be waiting there, drumming their fingers on the table, their eyes accusing.

She was pinning up her hair when she saw David's note and gasped with pleasure as she tore it open.

Sweetheart, she read,

I needs must work today, but I will be home early. Why not visit your father?

Please miss me a little.

D.

She smiled, strangely comforted, then ran hurriedly down the winding staircase. A maid in a blue cotton dress bobbed a curtsey as she passed and unnerved by such servility Sarah gasped:

'Am I too late?'

'For breakfast?' The girl sounded surprised. 'Why, no, ma'am.'

She indicated a door and bobbed again as Sarah nervously pushed it open.

It was a room she had not seen before, small and cosy with a fire burning brightly in the iron grate. Luke Holroyd sat alone, a napkin tucked beneath his chin.

'Hullo, lass. You've just missed David.'

'I overslept,' Sarah mumbled. 'I'm sorry, but I seemed to lie awake till daybreak, almost.'

'Deary me. Brooding, were you?'

'No. Just thinking, I suppose.'

'Aye. It was only a storm in a teacup, last night,' Luke said comfortably. 'Nothing to fret over. Get yourself something to eat – we serve ourselves at breakfast.' He nodded towards the side-table. 'The kippers are very good.'

Carefully Sarah lifted the lids of the silver dishes that stood on a warmer. Scrambled eggs, bacon, kidneys, kippers. Enough to feed a regiment.

Cutting a slice of bread she buttered it thickly then sat down at the table.

'Well, Sarah, and what'll you do with yourself today?' Luke demanded.

'I don't know,' she admitted dubiously, realizing that for the first time since she could remember she had nothing to do but please herself. 'Maybe I'll go out, if I'm not needed here, that is.'

'Which means that you intend keeping out of Mrs Holroyd's way,' Luke commented dryly. 'Well, I'd not worry overmuch, if I were you. Like as not she'll spend the day in her room, making plans.'

'Plans?' Sarah whispered.

'Planning how to spend my brass. When David's mother is aggrieved, it comforts her to spend money. Likely she'll be off again tomorrow, either to her sister Clara's in Cumberland or to visit the cousin who's married to a Scottish earl, or back down to London again. Charlotte isn't fond of Hollinsdyke society,' he sighed.

'But this house is so beautiful. If it were mine, I'd never want to leave it!'

'Wouldn't you, lass?' Luke's eyes gleamed with pleasure. 'You like High Meadow, then?'

'Like it? Why, it's like something out of a storybook. But it's a big place,' she added dubiously, 'for such few folk to live in.'

'You're right,' he admitted. 'But I didn't think so, when I built it.' His eyes took on a faraway look. 'I built this house for a family, Sarah. I wanted sons in it and bonny little daughters. I wanted to fill it with noise and happiness.' He shrugged, looking down at his plate. 'Folk in Hollinsdyke used to walk up here on Sunday afternoons to watch it being built. Luke's Folly, they called it behind my back, but I took no notice because I knew one day they'd envy me my big, roistering family. But I worked my fingers to the bone for a dream.' He laughed shortly. 'I should have known that in real life, dreams have no substance.'

Sarah glanced at the rough-hewn face. The hardness was gone and in its place lay sadness. Could this man be misunderstood by those who lived in Hollinsdyke's small streets? Could he, underneath, be deserving of pity?

Pity for a mill-master? From Caleb Makin's daughter?

'Had you considered, Sarah,' Luke broke into her thoughts, 'that one day this house will be yours to care for? Will it bother you that likely they'll call you Mistress of Luke's Folly?'

'I hadn't given it a lot of thought,' she hesitated, taken aback. 'This marriage came about so suddenly that sometimes I still can't believe any of it.'

'You mean you've never wondered what it would be like to be lady of this house?' He looked at her quizzically, one shaggy eyebrow raised. 'I'm surprised, yet I'm inclined to believe you. I'll admit, though, I thought you'd had an eye to the main chance. But, if you didn't, then why did you marry David? And in such a hurry too.'

Sarah shrugged and regarded her fingers, as if, somehow, the strange gold band there would provide her with an answer.

'I don't rightly know,' she hesitated.

She really didn't know. She had done it in a fit of pique. She had rushed in, unthinking, like she always did.

'Do you love him, Sarah?'

'No,' she whispered flatly. 'No, I don't think I do. But I respect him and I'm grateful for his kindness,' she hastened. 'I promised to be a good wife to him and I'll stand by it.'

She hoped her answer would satisfy him, even though it might not be the one he wanted to hear.

'Then tell me – are you truly a wife? Are you wedded and bedded, Sarah?'

The question was startling in its directness and she floundered for words.

'If you mean can you hope for grandchildren,' she whispered, 'then the answer is yes. One day there'll be the bairns you want about the place. Does that please you?'

'Aye, Sarah. It does. It pleasures me a lot,' he replied huskily. 'I'd give most of what I own to know there'd be Holroyds in this house when I've been called to my Maker. Only give me grandchildren, lass, and you shall have anything your heart could want. I swear it.'

'I want nothing, Mr Holroyd,' she said evenly, 'except maybe an apple-pie.'

She was rushing in again, but the Three-streets had taught her to grasp every passing chance.

'*An apple-pie?*'

'The one left over from dinner, last night. There was a large dish of trifle too and a fruit-cake. All those things for afters and all sent back to the kitchen, untouched. What will become of them, do you think?'

'I don't need to think,' Luke replied darkly. 'I *know*. They'll be eaten in the servants' dining-room, that's what.'

The appetites of his servants had always been a thorn in Luke's flesh.

'And how many of them are there?'

'Eight in all, counting outside.'

'So they do pretty well?' Sarah reasoned. 'They'd not miss that pie, I shouldn't wonder.'

'Now see here, Sarah,' Luke exploded, unused to such quizzing. 'Be blowed if I know what you're getting at. What do you want with an apple-pie?'

'I want to take it to the mill-school, Mr Holroyd, *your* school. I want to give it to your apprentices. And I want soup for them, every working day and bread to eat with it.'

'Soup and bread? Free? *Out of my own pocket?*'

'If needs be. Those children are hungry.'

'But I give them work,' Luke fretted. 'They get their money, regular, every settling day. And tell me, whose was the only mill in these parts to keep working during the American troubles? When they were fighting each other and there was no cotton grown, who alone but me gave work to the people of Hollinsdyke?' he demanded triumphantly.

'The American War's been over for years,' Sarah flung disparagingly, 'and cotton's cheap again. Think about it,' she wheedled softly. 'Why, word of your generosity might even reach the Queen's ears. And you'd be spiking Robey Midwinter's guns,' she added slyly. 'He's got it in for you, Robey has. Says you work your apprentices –'

'I know what he says,' Luke ground. 'And I haven't lost any sleep over it.'

'All the same,' Sarah persisted. 'Soup and bread and

leftovers from your table? It's nothing to you, but you'd be blessed by those children every day. And it'd please the good Lord, I shouldn't wonder . . .'

Luke pursed his lips and narrowed his eyes. Happen she was right, at that. *Do unto others? Suffer little children?* And the Lord might indeed be pleased, bless him with grandchildren of his own.

'How much,' he hesitated, rubbing his chin thoughtfully, 'will all this frivolity cost me, do you suppose?'

Sarah laughed triumphantly. Maybe it wasn't going to be such a bad old day, after all.

'Wait for me,' Sarah instructed the coachman. Her heart was beating uncomfortably, but sooner or later, she had reasoned, she had to show her face in Hollinsdyke. Besides, she had pressing business to see to and news she was bursting to impart, so best get it over with.

The mill-school was housed in a side-street, well away from the mill. Once it had been a run-down weaver's cottage, but Maggie Ormerod had scrubbed its floors and whitewashed the walls and even persuaded Luke Holroyd to supply coal for its iron stove. She was cleaning the blackboard when Sarah pushed open the door. For a moment she hesitated, then, holding out her arms cried:

'Sarah! Oh, how grand you look!'

Then they were in each other's arms, hugging and laughing as old friends do, with no barriers of class or riches between them.

'It's good to see you, Maggie love,' Sarah whispered huskily, delighted by the warmth of her welcome, wishing she could dislike Maggie, glad she could not.

'You'll take a cup?' Maggie set a kettle on the stove top. 'The children aren't due until one o'clock.'

'It's about the children I've come,' Sarah hastened, anxious not to be sidetracked into talking about the wedding. 'See what I've brought.'

She nodded towards the basket and from the folds of crisp white napkins took an apple-pie and a fruit-cake.

'These are for the children, Maggie. There was a trifle too, but I wasn't in time to rescue that. They'd got it eaten,' she said sorrowfully.

Maggie flushed with delight. 'Oh, Sarah. They'll think it's Christmas!'

'Then from now on it'll be Christmas every day,' Sarah laughed, 'because, starting tomorrow, there'll be soup and bread for all the apprentices and anything else I can find. What do you think to that?'

'Every day?' Maggie gasped. 'It's so good of you, so kind . . .'

'Nay, it's on Mr Holroyd's orders,' Sarah smiled, knowing the more credit she gave to Luke the better the apprentices would eat. 'It was him told me to arrange it. I'll try to bring it myself, each day. It'll be good to have a chat, see Billy-Boy. And, Maggie,' she hesitated, 'will you keep an eye on Father for me? He's a stubborn old cuss and he'll have nothing to live on now but the few shillings he makes from his potions.' She held out a sovereign. 'Here's some money. See that he gets a meal now and then. No need to let him know it's come from my purse.'

'I'll do that gladly,' Maggie promised, 'and I'd let you know at once if ever he got sick. Did he take badly to the wedding?' she ventured.

Sarah nodded. 'Nothing pleases him these days. But I'll visit him on his birthday. Maybe he'll have got over the worst of it by then. After all, he can only turn me away.'

She smiled, but there were tears in her voice. Her father was old and sick in body and mind, but she remembered when he had been the handsomest man in the Three-streets and her mother the most ladylike of women. They had laughed a lot in those days.

'I'll have to go, Maggie. We can have that tea some other time.'

She was worried, truth known, about the coachman. It was past dinnertime and he'd want to get back to High Meadow. It wouldn't do, she worried, to keep him waiting.

'Tomorrow I'll stay longer and have a chat with Billy-Boy. I miss him,' she sighed. 'Give him a hug sometimes, Maggie.'

Another minute and she would have missed the man. She would have been driving up the street in the carriage and she could have pretended not to have seen him. But it isn't possible to ignore a man who's tall as a tree, with shoulders so broad they block the doorway. Oh, why had he come here?

'Robey,' she whispered, her heart quickening at the sight of him.

'Why, if it isn't the lady from the big house, Mistress Holroyd herself, come slumming in Hollinsdyke!' He touched an imaginary forelock then bowed with an exaggerated gesture. 'Or has Sarah Makin come to show off her fine feathers in the Three-streets?'

'Robey!' Maggie admonished. 'That's not fair! Sarah came with food for the apprentices and they're to have soup regularly now – every day.'

'Is that so?' He raised an eyebrow, his lips pulled down in a smile of disbelief. 'Is Milady Bountiful trying to ease her conscience, then? Is she sorry for deserting her own kind? By the stars, Sarah Makin, I thought you'd more about you than to creep off and sell yourself cheap to a mill-master's son!'

Sarah stood as one who has turned suddenly to stone. To see him so unexpectedly had been shock enough. To have to withstand his derision was almost unbearable.

The man who smiled into her eyes and gave her primroses was gone. The Robey in whose arms she had wanted to lie no longer existed. To her eternal shame she had longed for that man, yet now he lashed her with contempt, looked at her as though to touch her would soil his hand. He made her want to clench her fist and lash out blindly. She wanted to hurt him as he was hurting her but he had rendered her incapable of such passion. White-faced, she walked to the door, then, turning, heard herself whisper:

'I'm sorry, Mr Midwinter, if I've upset your plans, but from now on I promise you'll have no cause to complain about the way in which the apprentices are treated.'

She said it softly with a ladylike calm her mother would have been proud of and she walked to the carriage with a dignity Charlotte could not have bettered. But there the deception ended. Safely out of sight, she gave way to the tumult inside her.

Damn the man! Why did she find him so good to look at? Why did she want a man who despised her so?

Closing her eyes tightly, she bit on her clenched fist until she winced with pain. She hated Robey Midwinter! She loathed and detested him! Be damned if she would let him make her cry!

But, for all that, the tears that streamed down her cheeks were hot and bitter and all the way back to High Meadow her body shook with silent sobs.

Would she never get him out of her mind?

Six

Maggie Ormerod placed her hands together and bowed her head.

'Bless our food, Lord, and make us humbly grateful for the charity of our betters.'

'Amen.' The response was ragged and impatient.

'All sit.'

The apprentices needed no prompting. Spoons clattered, eyes closed blissfully. The soup was thick and hot, the bread plentiful. Such bounty was almost unbelievable and they ate quickly, lest it should be snatched from them.

'A hungry bairn is a terrible thing,' Sarah choked.

The school-teacher nodded soberly. She worried about her orphans constantly. That Sarah proposed to feed them made her dizzy with delight, so who cared if folk in the Three-streets muttered that Caleb's lass was heading for a fall? Sarah could rub shoulders with the devil himself, so long as Maggie's pupils reaped the benefits.

'There's more to follow,' Sarah smiled as each bowl was polished clean.

It was fortunate, she admitted, that Charlotte Holroyd's cook was one of twelve children whose artless concept of heaven had been stew and dumplings four times a day and bread and jam between times, doled out by a smiling Archangel Gabriel. Cook had not only provided soup, she had made a large currant pasty too.

'You're a good soul,' Sarah whispered soberly, silently thanking Providence for a woman who still remembered the pangs of a hungry childhood.

The pasty was eaten with sighs of delight and when every crumb had gone, every finger licked, Sarah prepared to leave. Here, in the little classroom, she had been able to forget the vague worries that preyed upon her mind. She had felt at ease, and grateful that Maggie had not asked one curious question about the secrecy and haste of the wedding.

'I'd like to talk to Billy-Boy,' Sarah said as she packed the hamper. 'But not here, not in front of the others.'

'Then leave your gloves behind,' Maggie suggested. 'I'll send him out with them.'

When the door opened and Billy-Boy stood hesitant, gloves clasped in a small, thin hand, Sarah held out her arms, smiling happily. She had missed him and the sudden luxury into which she had been pitched served only to emphasize the dreariness of the little boy's life.

He came to her reluctantly and Sarah felt his body stiffen as she hugged him to her.

'Don't you love me any more?' she teased. 'Have you forgotten your Sarah already?'

'You went away,' he choked. 'You didn't tell me. I waited and waited . . .'

'I went to get married,' she smiled gently, 'but I'm back again. I shall see you almost every day. It'll be the same as it was before, won't it?'

The child nodded dubiously. Sarah was a fine lady now and rode in a carriage. He'd liked it better when they worked together at the looms. Now he had to share her and it worried him that one day she might stop coming.

But the food she brought had been good and he felt duty-bound to tell her so.

'I liked the soup,' he said shyly. 'Will there be more tomorrow?'

'Of course there will,' she choked. 'Sarah won't forget you.'

Anger and compassion struggled inside her as she climbed into the carriage. She must do something to help Billy-Boy. She must take him out of the workhouse and out of the mill, see him apprenticed to a craftsman who would give him a home and treat him kindly. David would arrange it. David, who refused her nothing, would make it possible.

The idea pleased her. Where was the sense in marrying into money if she was to forget those she was in a position to help? She could help her father too, if only he'd bite on his cussed pride and let her.

Oh, imagine, she yearned, if the bogey of Charlotte's resentment could be banished and her father would give his blessing to the marriage, how pleasant life could become. But her mother-in-law's displeasure was as real as Caleb's stubborn hatred of anything that bore the name of Holroyd and it would not be easy, she sighed.

But she had made a start. The mill children need never go hungry again and soon she would have Billy-Boy's future settled. If only Robey Midwinter would take himself off, out of Hollinsdyke, out of her thoughts.

She shook her head impatiently, angry with herself for thinking of the man as she did. But his mocking eyes haunted her constantly and even in the private darkness of their bedroom, with David's arms around her and his lips gentling hers, she could never quite shake herself free of that dark, handsome face.

She was a fool; a complete and utter fool and one day,

she prophesied darkly, she was going to be sorry for her self-inflicted stupidity.

Oh, why, she sighed, had she been born so perverse? Why did she have to complicate her life so?

Life was becoming complicated for Luke Holroyd too. He had awakened to a bright spring morning and felt near-contentment as he drove to Low Clough. He had been pleased that Sarah had given him full credit for the providing of the apprentices' victuals and mildly grateful that Charlotte appeared to be staying in her room to nurse her injured pride. He had just filled his pipe and taken out last month's Profit and Loss Account – the most pleasurable reading he knew – when Albert Dinwiddie appeared at the door, wearing a face that foretold trouble.

'Have you a minute, Mr Holroyd?' The counting-house manager's face was flushed and it was obvious he was the bringer of news. 'Nay, I'll not sit down,' he gasped as Luke indicated a chair. 'I've not got long. They'll be here any minute!'

'*They*?' Luke scowled.

'Aye. They've stopped work in t'spinning-room to discuss it and likely the weaving-shed'll join 'em afore long. They're drawing lots for a spokesman. They've got a grievance and they're coming to see you.'

'They've alus got a grievance,' Luke growled as his bright spring morning darkened. 'What is it this time, Albert?'

'I don't rightly know, Master. Silk seemed to think it's over the to-do last night. I suppose you know there was another meeting at the Mission Hall and –'

'And Midwinter was crying stinking fish again,' Luke supplied. 'Don't tell me any more!'

He raised his eyes heavenward, sending smoke to the ceiling in short angry puffs, silently imploring his God to bear witness to the tribulations that beset a mill-master.

Robey Midwinter was becoming a nuisance, he brooded, wondering whether to stand firm on his dignity or whether to accept the challenge the rabble-rouser seemed intent upon hurling.

'Get back to the counting-house, Albert,' he advised, 'and say nowt. Leave it to me.'

Dinwiddie scurried along the passage, duty done. Closing the door of his little office he mopped his face. Normally he was never unduly alarmed by day-to-day upsets that were only to be expected in any cotton-mill, but this time he had sensed unease when Silk brought details of the gathering in Tinker's Row. Mill-workers always grumbled. Some of them had even joined the trade union, but their resentment usually blazed fiercely and burned out quickly.

Now it was different. Midwinter had come to Hollinsdyke with a great deal to say. And they listened to him. He was a man's man that women sighed over; he was dangerous, and best left to Mr Holroyd, Dinwiddie decided, popping a mint humbug into his mouth and champing it furiously. And may the best man win!

The deputation straggled across the mill-yard and clattered up the counting-house stairs. Luke saw them coming from his window and calmed his ruffled feelings by breathing in deeply then exhaling through stiff, indignant lips. It made a hissing sound that put him in mind of an angry gander. The simile pleased him and added to his determination not to yield an inch.

One of the tacklers had been elected leader. Pulling off his cap he wished Luke a respectful good-day.

'And what seems to be the trouble?' Luke demanded, when the five men had arranged themselves around his desk.

'I'm come to tell thee, Master,' the man cleared his throat awkwardly, 'that there's grievances in t'mill. We want guards putting on t'machines and more money for our pains. And there's bairns in the shed not nine years old –'

'Then they are the most fortunate of infants to be working at Low Clough,' Luke smiled smoothly, 'because from now on they'll be given good victuals, every working day. And entirely at my own expense, mark you!' Luke delivered his trump card with relish. 'What have you to say to that, eh?'

'I say that soup for fifteen childer costs nothing!' a sallow-faced spinner took over the discussion. 'I say it's been done to pull the wool over our eyes.'

'It was done out of the goodness of my heart,' Luke protested mildly, 'and shame on him that doubts my good intentions.'

Again the cunning old eyes implored the heavens to mark his sincerity.

'And shame on you, Master! You pay us starvation wages. The men over at Syke Mill get a ha'penny an hour more'n us and we want the same!'

'Then you'd better walk the three miles to Syke and see if you can get taken on,' Luke suggested amiably. 'Be reasonable, now. A ha'penny an hour?' He swept the men with disbelieving eyes. 'Have you stopped to work it out? Don't you realize that to do as you ask would raise your wages by three whole shillings? Can't you see that that would cost me an extra thirty pounds a week?' He spread his hands in a gesture of bewilderment. 'Now where's a man to find money of that magnitude?' he appealed.

Blinded by such calculations it appeared that no one could provide the answer until a small, wizened man suggested:

'Happen the women-folk'd make do with a farthing.'

'A farthing an hour to all the females I employ?' Luke gasped, 'when they're already on a bonus on their yardage?'

'And which most of them are hard put to it to make,' flung another. 'We can't manage on what we get and that's the truth, Master. Some of us have a lot of mouths to feed.'

'Then there's the answer to all your problems,' Luke smiled as though suddenly all was explained. 'Don't have so many bairns!'

Slowly he rose to his feet and, taking his top-hat from the peg behind the door, placed it firmly in position.

'And now, if you'll excuse me, I have a pressing business engagement.' He gave a good-natured nod of his head to the gaping assembly. 'And rest assured that I shall instruct Mr Dinwiddie not to make any deductions on settling-day for time lost this morning. Bid you good-day, gentlemen.'

He walked sedately along the passage, head erect, then crossed the yard to where his carriage waited, his countenance radiating goodwill to all men. He sustained the expression until he was well away from Low Clough, when anger stained his cheeks scarlet and evil intent swept the benevolence from his face.

A ha'penny an hour, indeed! Damn Robey Midwinter and his interference! Who was he, this trouble-maker who refused to be ignored? Where did he come from and who was behind him?

The Master of Low Clough did not know, but he'd find out, so help him, and before very long, an' all! Master Midwinter had gone too far this time!

*

David smiled reassuringly at Sarah across the dinner-table. He never tired of looking at her and tonight, with candleglow reflected in her eyes and the anxious little hollows in her cheeks accentuated by the flickering flames, she was so beautiful that his heart ached dully.

She had seemed happier, more relaxed, as they dressed for dinner, chattering about her plans for the mill-school, but when he suggested the time had come to visit her father the animation left her face and her body tensed visibly in protest.

'Not yet, David. The time's not right. Leave it to me.'

'But, Sarah, it is impolite of me to make you my wife and not acknowledge your father. I want him to know I shall take care of you. And he must be lonely now. He likes the lanes and the hill tops, you say, and there are empty cottages on High Meadow land. Why don't we offer him one?'

'Oh, please *no*! He's a bitter man,' Sarah pleaded. 'He'd sooner live in the workhouse!'

'Very well. We'll leave it for a time,' David yielded. 'But sooner or later I must visit your father. Civility demands it.'

He regretted having upset her, the more so since without warning his mother had chosen to leave the confines of her room and take her meal in the dining-room.

Sarah's eyes showed alarm as the older woman took her place at the head of the table, accepting the formal bows of the men with a small smile, inclining her head in Sarah's direction as if acknowledging an unwanted guest to whom she must needs be polite.

From then on the conversation had become brittle and forced and Sarah ate little, praying for the meal to end.

But by some miracle, or maybe it was Luke's meaningful gaze in Charlotte's direction, the tension at the table did not explode into bitterness and Sarah's misgivings became a little less acute.

There could be no denying, she conceded, that Charlotte was a remarkable woman. Born into the ruling classes, she was only exercising, Sarah supposed, her divine right to rule. She had no warmth or tenderness as her own mother had had, but she was real, nevertheless. Somewhere inside her had surely to be the capacity to love.

Sarah sighed, self-pity washing over her. She had never ceased to miss her mother, even though such longings had been kept in check, and it would have been nice, she yearned, to have been able to talk to David's mama, learn from her.

The doors opened quietly and the housekeeper rustled the length of the room to stand beside Luke's chair, her hands in the familiar clasped position.

'What is it, Parkes?' Luke demanded, slicing irritably into the cheese. He disliked having his meals interrupted and his shaggy brows met in a frown.

'There is a person asking for you, sir. He came to the back door. I told him you were not able to see him but he insisted I inform you of his presence. His business, it would seem, is urgent and confidential.'

'Oh, aye?' Luke glowered. 'And does this person have a name?'

'It is a Mr Silk, sir.'

'Something's wrong?' David looked up sharply.

'It wouldn't surprise me,' Luke conceded. 'Trouble and Silk are never far apart. I don't know why I bother with him,' he sighed, reaching for the decanter. 'All right, Parkes.' He dismissed the housekeeper with a nod. 'Show him into the study when I ring.'

'What do you suppose he wants?' David demanded. 'Could it be anything to do with this morning's upset, or could it be the gypsy?'

'The gypsy?' Charlotte arched her slender brows.

'That's what they're calling the rabble-rouser, it seems. There's a man,' David explained, 'who is telling our workers how badly done-to they are. It seems that nothing will content him but the complete disruption of Low Clough. Midwinter's his name. He's a born talker and a bit of a mystery package, by all accounts.'

Sarah drew sharply on her breath and looked down at her fingers.

'And the gypsy is worrying you, husband?' Charlotte's laugh tinkled falsely.

'Not so's you'd notice,' Luke growled, 'though I don't take any too kindly to being told how to run my own mill.'

'Then how providential it is that I have decided to visit my sister,' came the smooth reply. 'I do so dislike trouble and perhaps by the time I return, Luke, you'll have sent this gypsy fellow packing.'

'I don't doubt that I shall,' Luke retorted dryly, rising to his feet. 'Perhaps you'll excuse David and me. We'd better see what Silk has come about. After all, my dear, he might have come to tell me that Low Clough's on fire!'

'No! Oh, please never joke about such a thing!' Sarah gasped.

She closed her eyes as an icy finger touched her. Her father had used similar words, but Caleb had not joked.

I'd give most of what was left of my life to see Low Clough go up in smoke!

Her father meant every word, Sarah thought, dry-mouthed. They had issued from his lips like a prayer to the devil.

'Don't worry, Sarah.' David was on his feet in an instant. 'Father's sense of humour takes a little getting used to. Drink a glass of wine; it'll do you good. Silk's visit will be a fuss over nothing, you'll see.'

'No thank you.' Sarah waved away the decanter. 'And I'm not upset, David. Not really . . .'

It wasn't true, but in no way would she wilt or wither in Charlotte Holroyd's presence.

'Then happen you'd like to come with us,' Luke suggested. 'After all, it's mill business and the sooner you see the other side of the coin, Sarah lass, the quicker you'll grasp what you've taken on. There's more to being a Holroyd wife than living up here in splendid isolation!'

The words were uttered with resigned bitterness, but Sarah was quick to catch that Luke directed them at his wife, for she saw the flush that stained the other woman's cheeks and the slight flaring of her nostrils.

'That's a fine idea!' David enthused, grasping at any excuse to separate his mother and his wife. 'Sarah's opinion might be useful, Father.'

And so it was that Sarah sat uneasily in a corner of the study, preparing to learn mill-business from the other side of the divide.

Aaron Silk sidled in, his hat clutched between his hands.

'It's good of you to see me, Master,' he gasped. 'I came at once. I thought you should know before morning what was afoot. I took the liberty of acquainting Mr Dinwiddie with the facts and he agreed that forewarned is forearmed, as they say.'

'You make it all sound most alarming,' David remarked. 'Is something wrong at Low Clough?'

'Not yet, Mr David, but there will be. There was another meeting at the Mission Hall tonight. Most of Low Clough was there, although the ringleaders came mostly from the rabble of the Three-streets.'

Sarah bit her lip angrily, marvelling at Silk's impudence. Either he didn't know that she herself was sprung from that rabble or he was a very stupid man. Her eyes met David's and she saw with relief that his own were filled with laughter. Taking her cue from him, she relaxed. Silk was a fool, anyway. Old Luke would use him only as long as it pleased him. When his tale-telling lost its value he'd be thrown aside for the parasite he was.

'And?' Luke prompted. 'Get on with it, man!'

'They're going to give you one more chance, Mr Holroyd. Midwinter says they must ask you again to raise their wages and if you won't they'll strike.'

'Will they, by heck? And where's that going to get them? Where's it going to get any of us? What'll they use for sustenance? Is this man going to work a miracle? Is he going to support them with fine words when they've nowt in their pockets? Haven't they realized that talk is cheap?'

'I think you should have Midwinter arrested, Father,' David flung impatiently. 'He's inciting people to disobedience, maybe violence . . .'

'Nay, lad. Not so fast. Don't get carried away. Nothing was said about violence, was it, Silk?' Luke questioned pointedly. 'Midwinter'll not counsel anything like that. From what I've heard about him, he'll not overstep himself. If he hasn't incited law-breaking, there's nothing I can do about him.' Luke knew what he was about. 'Oh, if only once he'd step outside the law.'

'I can't say he did anything wrong,' Silk admitted. 'The man seemed reasonable.'

Silk had seen or heard nothing that could be used against the gypsy. Tonight there had been no mockery in his voice, no derision, no challenges. They were no longer necessary. His audience had long since been captivated. They were ready now, to follow every whispered suggestion, latch on to the smallest innuendo. Robey Midwinter had stormed the citadel. Now the people of the Three-streets were eating from his hand.

'Mr Holroyd will listen to you,' he had urged with sweet reason. 'Of course he's refused your request. They always do, the first time. But ask again, and ask humbly. Luke Holroyd was a spinner once. He'll remember.'

'He'll remember nothing!' had come the angry reply. 'Luke Holroyd's forgotten the likes of us. He lives up there in that great house of his and thinks he's almighty God!'

'Then remind him,' Robey insisted gently. 'Appeal to his better nature. No man can be so base that he turns his back on the roots he sprang from.'

'That man'ud turn his back on St Peter at the Gate, if it suited him!'

'Oh my friends. Be charitable. You *will* prevail.' The man they called the gypsy had held out his arms in a gesture of benediction. 'You, my hungry ones, will inherit the earth!'

My, but he was clever, Silk thought. He would give old Luke a run for his money, all right. It would be a wise man who could forecast the outcome of this to-do. A wise man indeed . . .

'So what's to be done?' David demanded when Silk had left. 'This Midwinter is dangerous.'

'I know it,' Luke grumbled, 'and it isn't the only thing I'm bothered about. There's five mills in this town and heaven only knows how many more, all over the county.

So why did he pick on *my* mill?' He thumped the desk-top angrily. 'And who's harbouring him? If we knew that, it would be a start.'

He looked directly at Sarah and she met his stare blankly. It wouldn't help any to tell him and anyway Silk would find out soon enough.

'Sarah – I know this must be painful to you,' David placed his arm around her shoulder, 'but have you any knowledge of this man?'

No knowledge, husband, her heart cried. Only an upset inside me whenever I am near him, only the need to gain his approval, the need, if I am truthful, to feel the touch of his hands on my body, his lips . . .

'No!' she replied sharply. 'Why should I? Does anybody know who he is?'

'It's all right, lass. I reckon you're as mystified as we are,' Luke nodded, 'only I've got to say this, Sarah. You're a Holroyd now. You'll bear it in mind, won't you?'

Ah, yes, and in return for such a privilege, she accepted silently, she would outwardly conform. She'd play fair, but in her heart she would be Sarah Makin, still, the weaver who tended four looms and fought like an alley-cat at the dropping of a challenge. The secret Sarah would always be there.

'I'll bear it in mind, Father-in-law,' she whispered.

And I will be two people, she thought fearfully. I will be torn apart by duty and inclination. No matter what happens, I shall always understand the people of the Three-streets. If Life should scratch any one of them, Sarah Makin's foolish heart will bleed.

She was up early next morning.

'Can I ride with you into Hollinsdyke?' she asked her husband over the breakfast-table.

'Indeed you may,' he smiled. 'But why so early?'

'I'm going to see my father,' Sarah hesitated.

'Then I heartily approve. It will pave the way for my own visit. Do you want to take him a gift, Sarah? Have you sufficient money?'

'I'll take him some tobacco, and I've more than enough money.'

Guilt squirmed inside her at his trusting goodness. True, she was going to see her father but for what purpose she couldn't have told. She genuinely wished to see him. Her conscience had not ceased to plague her since the day he stormed, hurt and bitter, out of the house. But there was more to it than that, even though she couldn't decide exactly what it was.

'I've seen Cook. If I'm not back in time, she'll see the food is taken to the school. It's barley broth today,' she smiled, 'and jam buns for a treat. Cook is a good woman. She doesn't complain at the extra work.'

'And you are good, Sarah.' He reached for her hands and held them tightly. 'I love you so much, my darling,' he whispered. 'But you know that, don't you? You know I'd die for you . . .'

'David! Please? You mustn't say things like that! Maybe I'm a superstitious mill-girl, but *please*, never say that again.' Suddenly the room had lost its brightness and warmth. There was a heaviness in her heart, a suffocating weight on her chest as if someone danced a jig on her grave. 'Promise me?'

'I promise, my funny Sarah.'

Could it be, he wondered, that she was beginning to care a little?

Sarah waved to her husband as the carriage drew away. She had asked that she be set down at the top of Tinker's

Row. It wouldn't have done, not this first time, to be seen arriving in so grand a manner.

She carried gifts – a twist of tobacco and a packet of peppermints, but her heart beat uncomfortably and she had to school herself to walk with indifference.

No one called out a greeting. It was as if they had known she was coming, she thought miserably, and shut their doors on her.

Her father was pounding roots for boil-salve when she walked into the kitchen. Its smallness shocked her. She had been left the little house for less than a week yet by comparison with High Meadow's loftiness it seemed even more mean. Caleb knew she was there, but he did not look up.

'So you've come, my proud lady?' he mocked.

'Aye, Father. Sarah's come.'

'To show off your fine feathers, I don't doubt. Had you forgotten I said you'd not be welcome here?' His lips were twisted with bitterness.

'No, I hadn't forgotten,' she whispered, willing her hands not to tremble so. 'But I was passing the top of the street. I couldn't walk by –'

For the first time Caleb raised his head and looked directly at his daughter. His face was blank as a slab, his jaws tight with distaste.

Meet me halfway? Sarah's eyes pleaded.

'Why have you come?' the old man muttered. 'Do you want to shame me?'

'I've done nothing to be ashamed of, Father. I'm decently wed.'

'You call bedding with a Holroyd decent? You allow yourself to be kept by the man who brought me to *this*?' He flung out his arms in a gesture of hopelessness, his twisted limbs grotesque. 'You can forget my sufferings?'

'Father, it's done now. Let the past take care of itself. I'm married too and that can't be changed either. Accept it.'

'Are you happy, then?' The question was reluctantly asked.

'I'm happy enough. David wants to come and see you. If you'd accept him I'd be a lot happier.'

Caleb resumed his pounding, turning his back as if there was nothing more to be said.

'Tell me – what is Robey up to?' Sarah whispered. 'He doesn't know what he's about to start. Tell him to go, Father. Ask him to leave us in peace.'

'Us? Who do you speak for, daughter? Have your new masters sent you? Are they getting worried?'

'No-one sent me,' she retorted wearily. 'Luke Holroyd can look after himself without any help from me. I wanted to make sure you were all right. You're my father. It worries me that Robey Midwinter is out to cause trouble.'

'Then don't worry about me. Don't worry about any of us in the Three-streets, Mistress Holroyd. The only trouble there'll be will be for you and yours. Robey'll take care of the likes of me. It'll be the mill-masters who'll be screaming for mercy, afore much longer!' He spun around, laughing, yet his face was set in a mould of triumphant hatred. 'Take yourself back to the fine folk on the hill. We've no liking for turncoats in these parts. Go back to that folly Luke Holroyd built. And may he burn in hell!'

'Father,' Sarah pleaded, suddenly afraid. 'There's enough unhappiness in the world without you and me adding to it.'

But Caleb was staring into the fire, deaf to her pleading. Placing her gifts on the table she choked:

'I shall come again on Monday. I haven't forgotten it's your birthday.'

Tears stung her eyes and she dashed them angrily away. She had been wrong to come. Her visit had served no purpose but to widen the chasm between them and to prove beyond all doubt that her flimsy fears had taken on a frightening substance.

Her father was beyond help, there was no doubting it, and his last bitter words rang in her ears as she strode the road that led her back to High Meadow.

May he burn in hell! It was the curse of a madman.

Seven

The Holroyd pew in Hollinsdyke parish church was carpeted and cushioned but Sarah wriggled with discomfort for every eye in the congregation was turned in her direction.

Once, when she was little, she had sat beside her mother in this very church and gazed upward in awe at the fine family who sat in isolation to the left of the altar, rubbing shoulders, or so it then seemed, with God Himself. She had wondered about the mill-master and his high-born wife, weaving fantasies around them, imagining how grand it would be to sit there in glory beside the fair-haired boy who was as beautiful as the cherubs on the painted ceiling.

Now, amazingly, that boy was her husband, and rubbing shoulders with the Almighty, she found, was an unnerving experience. Indeed it was so discomfiting that she was glad when Matins was over and she was able to seek refuge in a corner of the carriage.

'An enlightened sermon, don't you think?' Charlotte enquired of her husband.

Luke grunted and leaned back in his seat. The message from the pulpit had been too long by half and he'd been hard put to keep his eyelids from closing.

'The vicar enjoys the sound of his own voice,' he grumbled, 'and he's forever begging. Asked me only yesterday for money for the orphanage. As if there aren't enough demands on my resources,' he added petulantly, remembering the demands of his workers for a rise in their wages. 'I told him he'd better put the matter before the Ladies' Charity.'

'Which means he'll be asking *me*,' Charlotte flung tartly, 'and just when I had almost decided to send the proceeds of the Charity Ball to the fund for Missionaries.'

The Charity Ball was the great event in Hollinsdyke's smug social calendar. To be summoned to attend was the next best thing to shaking the hand of the Prince of Wales and those who were favoured to receive Charlotte's gold-edged invitation counted themselves fortunate and gave gratefully to her Charity Fund. Everyone whose pedigree was acceptable to Charlotte and the ladies of her committee, and could be relied upon to give generously, attended the ball in the Assembly Rooms. Sarah knew all about the Charity Ball; she should do, for she had always watched the arrival of the guests from behind the broad shoulders of an officer of the law. To witness the comings and goings was an event never to be missed by the women-folk of the Three-streets. It was the next best thing to the mayor's parade.

Now, Sarah realized, she too would go to the ball. She would arrive in a carriage with a maid in attendance to fuss over her gown; she would walk up the broad sweep of steps to the Ohs and Ahs of onlookers.

Sarah Makin had come a long way, she thought soberly, since she had fought Poll Clegg in the Low Clough yard. It was almost unbelievable and very frightening. It was as if she were still seated on the roundabout, still riding the prancing horses, only now they were whirling faster.

The ball was a grand occasion and she would make a

fool of herself, she thought miserably as the carriage swung into the drive that wound through the trees to High Meadow. She would say the wrong things and do the wrong things and David would be ashamed of her. She wondered if she might plead indisposition on the night, have a sudden attack of vapours or a make-believe fever. Unfair perhaps, and deceitful too, but better than facing the slanting stares, the raised eyebrows, the heads that would nod behind fluttering fans.

Later she spoke of her fears to her husband. They were walking in the garden, the smell of newly cut grass heavy on the air, the sun warm in the sheltered corner where already a white magnolia bloomed.

'I don't think I want to go to the ball,' she announced. 'It's got me bothered, thinking about all those grand folk.'

But David had laughed and taking her hand in his, squeezed it tightly.

'Don't worry, my darling,' he whispered. 'You'll be so beautiful that the men will envy me and the ladies turn green with jealousy.'

'But I shall do something wrong,' she insisted. 'I don't have fine manners and I use all the wrong words when I get flustered.'

'Oh, my lovely Sarah,' he shook his head in fond exasperation. 'Don't try to be something you're not. Be your dear self, and everyone will love you. And you shall have the grandest gown of them all. We'll go to Manchester and order one. In the palest pink and scattered with rosebuds, I think it must be; cut low to show your shoulders.'

Sarah sighed. There was to be no getting out of it. For some strange reason David thought she was beautiful, imagined that all men desired her as he did. She would have to attend, if only because of his kindness. And he *was* kind and good, her conscience stressed and she *didn't* deserve him. She should be married to a man who would beat her regularly and make her polish his Sunday boots, a man like –

She shut down her thoughts at once. She wouldn't think about Robey Midwinter. He wasn't the only man who was tall as a tree and so handsome it disturbed her, just to look at him. The world was full of men like him and they all added up to trouble. Those who were stupid enough could listen to his silver tongue – he wasn't fooling *her*!

'What are you thinking about so earnestly?' David demanded, breaking into her guilty thoughts so that she blushed scarlet.

'Oh, I – I was thinking about the Charity Ball, I suppose,' she floundered. 'I was thinking about speaking to your mother, asking her if she'd tell me what was right and wrong,' she flung, off balance. 'She could teach me how to act like a lady,' she rushed on, warming to her lies, 'how to speak –'

But David pooh-poohed the idea, then traced the outline of her face with the tip of his finger.

'No one,' he whispered, 'need teach you anything. Anyone as beautiful as you needs no social graces.'

His eyes searched hers, loving and desiring her and she turned her head away sharply as he bent to kiss her.

'Not here, David!' she hissed tartly. 'The servants might be watching!'

It was a pompous thing to say, she knew it at once, seeing the sudden alarm in his eyes. She didn't know why she had said it. As if a kiss mattered.

'Sarah,' David ground as, embarrassed, she turned to walk away. 'Never speak like that to me again!' His voice was sharp with reproach and she knew she had hurt him.

'You sounded,' he said, shaking his head as if lost for words. 'You sounded just like Mama!'

They laughed about it afterwards as they walked arm in arm toward the house.

'Minx!' David scolded after she had kissed him until he forgave her. 'I really thought you meant it.'

But she had almost meant it, Sarah admitted. She had wanted to copy Charlotte Holroyd's manners and social graces, to know what to say and when to say it, be proud and haughty, as she was. She needed to be able to ape the older woman's brittle coldness, shield herself from attack, if needs be. There was much she could learn from the proud lady of High Meadow, Sarah decided, if only it could be possible to break down the coldness between them, talk together as women so that in time they might at least call a truce. It was up to her herself, she thought, to make the first move. What could be lost by offering her friendship to David's mother? Wouldn't it be worth a try?

'Now what are you thinking about so secretly?' David demanded. 'What new notion is buzzing in that head of yours?'

'Why,' Sarah retorted, wide-eyed. 'I was only thinking about my beautiful new ball-gown.'

She closed her eyes briefly, disliking herself, promising tonight when she said her prayers to have a good long chat with the Lord about her impious ways. It was becoming alarming, she brooded, the way untruths seemed able to spring unbidden to her lips.

'And I was thinking about your mother too,' she added. 'Just a little . . .'

Luke dismissed the carriage then picked his way across the puddled yard. He was not in the best of spirits. Monday was his least favourite day, a wet Monday even more so. And that was not the least of it, for the moment he entered the mill-yard he had felt the unrest. The mill was working as it always was when he arrived, punctual as the clock, at half-past eight each morning. The chimney belched smoke and scattered soot, the looms clattered and cotton bales swung high on the spinning-room hoist. To an outsider it was normal enough, but the man who owned Low Clough, who understood every stick, stone and mood of it, knew better. He sensed the tension, smelled the discontent as if it were a slow-burning fuse. It was as if eyes pricked into the back of his neck, as if the mill itself had joined the brooding displeasure and marked his passage from a hundred watching windows.

Luke tensed his shoulders and walked with deliberate slowness toward the counting-house stairs. It was no surprise that Dinwiddie was waiting there, changing feet like an agitated sparrow, hands twisting.

'Mornin', Albert. What's up, then?' Luke slammed his hat on the peg. 'What's bothering you?'

'It's nowt to do wi' me, Mr Holroyd,' the counting-house manager exploded. 'It's that yellow-faced tackler from the spinning-room, him as came to see you, wanting more money. Told me to ask if you'd see the deputation –'

'I've seen 'em,' Luke barked. 'The answer was No, then, and I've had no cause since to change my mind!'

' . . . if you'd see the deputation *again*. Said as how they wanted to do things fair and square, like. Said you'd reconsider, he was sure, you being a reasonable-minded man,' Dinwiddie finished with a gasp, the message delivered.

The silence in the room was thick. Luke rested his elbows on the desk-top and glowered at the wall clock.

Dinwiddie mopped his brow and moistened his lips. The upset was not of his making yet he was being growled at by both sides.

'Well, Master?' he croaked. 'What am I to say?'

'Say I'm busy, Albert. Tell them you delivered the message but that I'll be busy all week – oh, you know what to say!' he finished testily.

'Aye, Mr Holroyd, I do. In a word, the answer's *No*!'

Luke smiled grimly and nodded, then settling his spectacles on his nose, unfolded the morning paper with exaggerated calm. The interview was over.

Dinwiddie sighed and left, closing the door behind him with a kind of gentle fatality. At the clicking of the door-sneck, Luke pushed aside the paper and cocked his head, listening to Dinwiddie's retreating footfalls, then, taking out his watch, began to count.

A minute would be all it would take for Dinwiddie to tell Silk and for Silk to scuttle across the yard with the reply. In just a few seconds it would all be over and done with and they could forget the nonsense.

Footsteps in the passage outside caused Luke to smile and he walked to the window in time to see Silk heading at break-neck speed for the spinning-room door.

Luke snapped shut his watch and replaced it in his waistcoat pocket with seven seconds to spare.

'By gum,' he chuckled, 'but bad news travels fast!' Then settling himself in his chair again, filled his pipe with tobacco.

A ha'penny an hour indeed? Whatever was the world coming to?

Charlotte Holroyd made her final choice of dinner-dresses from her wardrobe, added a mere half dozen tea-gowns, then declared herself satisfied. Now her clothes could be packed and she could set out for Cumberland and the home of her sister Clara. Charlotte had considered visiting her cousin, the countess, but the Scottish castle in which she lived was damp and dark and the earl's table frugal. Cumberland would suit her better for a few days, she decided, and then she would be back, to approve the final arrangements for the Charity Ball.

She clucked impatiently as the door-knob rattled, then stiffened visibly as her son's wife entered the room.

'Can I talk to you?' Sarah whispered.

'Have we anything to say to each other?' Charlotte demanded.

'Yes, ma'am, I think we have. This is a barn of a house but no place is big enough for two women at odds with each other,' Sarah said quietly. 'I want us to be friends. Won't you give me a chance? Help me?'

She held out her hand, willing her mother-in-law to take it, pleading silently for one small act of kindness, one charitable word. She had known that at first there would be difficulties, but surely every woman wanted a daughter just as she, Sarah, had never ceased to want a mother. A truce would make life so much more easy.

But the hand she offered remained unclasped and the older woman turned coldly away.

How dare she? How *dare* this girl set her cap at David, inveigle him into marriage then expect to be treated as an equal? And how dare she wreck the carefully laid plans of a mother who wanted only the best for her son?

'Help you?' Charlotte flung. 'I would suggest you are well able to help yourself!'

'But I only want you to teach me a few airs and graces so I'll not let David down at the ball,' Sarah frowned. 'I don't want to let anybody down,' she added hastily, 'but I'm not used to such grand affairs, you see, and –'

'Then you should have stayed within your own habitat,' Charlotte ground, 'married someone of your own station in life and left the choice of my son's wife to *me*! Oh, I dread to imagine what people must think.'

Sarah's cheeks flamed as she fought down the anger that blazed inside her, praying silently that just this once she might not lose her temper.

'You mean they'll say the marriage was forced on your son, that I'm having a baby?' she demanded.

'And aren't you? What other reason could there be for so disastrous a marriage?'

'No, ma'am, I'm not. Life's hard enough in the Three-streets. We don't look for trouble.'

'Then why did you come here? Why did you force your way into this family and by what right do you demand I should even acknowledge you, let alone try to make you into a lady?' The words were acid, for she had grown bitter with discontent. At odds with life, she had seen no reason over the years to add to the happiness of others. 'I don't wish to speak to you,' she added flatly and finally. 'Please leave my room!'

It would have been better, Sarah thought miserably, if David's mother had struck her; such an injury would have been easy to forget. But words could wound deeply and their hurt lingered longer because they left no bruise or scar. Suddenly she felt alone and defenceless and the bewilderment that screamed to be heard burst out in an indignant torrent.

'Oh, I'll go,' she flung. 'It was foolish of me to come. I wasn't trying to ape my betters, act like I'm a lady born like yourself, but I did want you to like me. Is that so very wrong? And I wanted a mother again – someone to share woman-talk with, someone I could turn to if I was bothered. I wanted it so much,' she choked.

For a moment the tears inside her welled into a constricting lump in her throat and she stood trembling, unable to speak. Then the girl from the Three-streets tossed her head in defiance. Wrenching open the door she hurled her parting shot.

'But don't think *I* care! If my mother'd been alive she'd have taught me. My mother spoke like a lady and she knew how to behave in genteel company. *She* worked for the gentry, at Ainderby!'

'What's that, girl?' Charlotte's head jerked round. 'Did you say Ainderby?'

'That I did!' Sarah retorted. 'My mother mixed with better folk than this town'll ever know. Lords, ladies – she served them all. She'd have taught me how to conduct myself in company. Why, they had such grand balls at Ainderby, just to hear about them would make your hair curl! You'd never believe it, if I told you!'

'Oh, but I would,' came the whispered reply.

How *could* she? How *could* this girl awaken memories, Charlotte fretted, conjure up days long gone? By what right did she reach into the shadows, remind her of a happiness she thought she had forgotten?

Unwillingly she looked afresh at her son's wife. Standing there, she admitted, was she herself almost thirty years younger, a girl sick with delight at the thought of an Ainderby ball; a girl young, brash, heedless of her elders' advice and desperately in love with William – penniless William who had asked her to marry him in the rose garden at Ainderby. It had been at the coming of age of the eldest son, she remembered, with everyone there. They had danced until morning came and she'd given her heart into William's keeping.

'You've heard about Ainderby too?' Sarah whispered. 'Then it wasn't just a fairy story my mother made up?'

'It was real, child, and it's like a fairy story remembered, a dream . . .' Charlotte mused, her eyes faraway, her heart suddenly young, beating as it had done so many years ago with the love of being alive.

'And was there a grand ball like my mother said, and did all the young ladies creep away from their chaperons and meet their sweethearts in the garden? It did happen, didn't it?' Sarah pleaded.

She wanted so much to hear it again, for just a while to be a little girl again, with a gentle-voiced mother who knew so many lovely things.

'It happened,' Charlotte nodded. 'I know it, for I was one of those young ladies. I remember that we always prayed for our chaperons to nod off, so we might escape. On the night of the ball my old chaperon drank too much wine and fell asleep in her chair and I ran down to the rose garden . . .'

Dear William, who had sailed for India to seek his fortune so he might marry her and who died there, of cholera, the man who still held her girlish heart in his hands.

'I can't believe it,' Sarah gasped with delight. 'You were at that ball? You were truly there? Oh, it *was* a wonderful place, wasn't it, just like Mam said?' She couldn't bear it, if it hadn't been.

'Your mama was right, Sarah. It was an enchanted place and nightingales sang that night and the world was so very beautiful . . .'

Tears trembled in her voice as the past became the present and she recalled that young, heartbroken Charlotte who was bullied into a marriage she hadn't wanted, and memories of the heartache faded from her thoughts as she remembered again that past love.

Sarah closed the door and walked slowly to the side of

the woman who was no longer to be feared. Sinking to her knees, she was a child again in the kitchen at Canal Street, listening to her mother's gentle voice. And the kettle bubbled on the hob, ready for when Caleb, her handsome father, came home from the mill.

'Tell me,' she pleaded softly. 'Please tell me about Ainderby.'

David found them there in the firelight, his mother and his wife, sharing something too special to be interrupted. Mother and daughter you'd have thought they were, he mused, closing the door gently again, walking quietly away.

Dearest Sarah. She had charmed his father and now she had found her way into his mother's unhappy heart. She was irresistible and lovely and so dear to him that it hurt when she wasn't near him. She gave herself to him without protest, lay passive in his arms, yet he knew she did not love him as he loved her.

Something, someone, he pondered, was keeping her from him. If only he knew, he frowned, what or who it was.

The problem was still with him that evening as they sat together in the small drawing-room. It was a cosy, lamplit room and they had taken it for their own.

'Mama's good humour seems to have returned,' David remarked, relieved that the barriers between the two women seemed at last to be coming down, wishing he could have shared, or even understood, the closeness between them.

'I think,' Sarah retorted cautiously, 'it is because she is pleased to be visiting her sister.'

'And I think not. You have found your way into Mama's affections just as I knew you would. What mischief were you plotting? You were so engrossed, the two of you, that you didn't even notice me.'

His voice was teasing but his heart was uneasy. He too wanted to be close to Sarah, share small intimate confidences with her. As a wife, she could not be faulted. She was obedient, eager to please him, and he should be the most contented of men. But some part of her eluded him, he brooded. The Sarah he had first loved, that exciting creature with her hair blowing free and a wildness about her that flamed his senses, evaded him even yet.

'Mischief?' she smiled. 'It was only gossip, woman-talk.'

She couldn't explain that they had been brought together by longing, that the past had reached out and linked them. She couldn't admit that deep inside them they had both searched for affection. She, Sarah, had yearned for a mother's love, but for Charlotte it was the remembered kiss of a long-ago love that gentled her heart into compassion.

'Talk,' Sarah stressed. 'About the ball.'

'I see. You were planning what to wear? You'll have to hurry. It's little more than two weeks away and you haven't yet seen the dressmaker.'

'I shall wear pink, as you suggested,' she retorted, unwilling to explain it had been another ball she and Charlotte had talked about. 'Will you help me choose a style? Shall we go tomorrow?'

'We shall indeed.' He could refuse her nothing, and the familiar longing for her swept over him again. Without doubt, she would be the most beautiful woman at the Charity Ball. With her black hair pulled into the nape of her neck and the exquisite whiteness of her shoulders enhanced by a low-cut gown, she would captivate every man in the room.

'She is mine!' he would want to shout. 'This lovely creature is my wife!'

And she was truly a wife, he frowned, yet, even as she lay gentle in his arms, there was still a part of her that remained impassively remote.

'Do you realize,' he demanded, pushing aside the thoughts that disturbed him so, 'that you will be the belle of the ball? Men will rush to sign your dance-card. It will be filled twice over, I shouldn't wonder and I shall be the most neglected of husbands.'

'Oh, but you needn't be,' she retorted. 'Just to think of it sends me into a bother. What will I say to all those grand folk? And another thing –' Her lips tilted in a half-smile. 'Did you ever stop to wonder if I could dance!'

'But *can't* you, Sarah?' he gasped. 'I thought everyone could dance.'

'Now how,' she flung, 'could the likes of me learn such things? Mill-girls don't go to balls and anyway dancing was frowned on at the Band of Hope. Downright sinful, they said it was although I often thought I'd like to try it. But how can you dance the waltz,' she sighed, 'in clogs?'

'Oh, my dearest Sarah,' David laughed, gently cupping her face with his hands. 'You are such a contradiction, such a joy to know!'

His lips found hers, his gaze unashamed in its desire.

She closed her eyes at his kiss, caring for him yet ill at ease. Why did her heart have to be so wayward? Why couldn't she love him, just a little, in return?

'And you, David,' she retorted gravely, 'are a good and kind man and I am grateful for all you have done for me.'

It was not the answer he wanted, the sudden pain in his eyes told her that, and she disliked herself at once for hurting him so. Why was she so stupid, so unthinking;

why couldn't she count her blessings and thank heaven for the love of a good man?

Impulsively she sank to her knees before him, then taking his hands in hers she whispered:

'Please give me time. I'm trying so hard. Be patient, David.'

He smiled and kissed her again, knowing he would never cease to want her. Gratefully she melted into the shelter of his arms. And she would try, she vowed silently. *She really would try.*

They were walking hand in hand up the staircase when the urgent ringing of the front door-bell caused them to pause.

'Who can it be?' Sarah whispered, apprehension tingling through her. 'It's late . . .'

The footman who always answered after-dark calls walked slowly across the hall below them as the bell clanged again.

'Wait here,' David ordered tersely, running lightly downstairs. 'I'll see to it.'

When the door was opened Sarah was unable to distinguish the man who stood there, but her doubts were dispelled when a voice demanded:

'I'm here to see Luke Holroyd. Tell him it's Robey Midwinter!'

She caught her breath in a gasp as the familiar weight pressed down on her chest and ghouls danced on her grave again. Here was Trouble, searching them out.

The footman stood aside as David called:

'Come in, sir. My father isn't here, but if I can help . . .?'

'Nay, I'll bide where I am. I'm not here on a polite errand and I'll not hand you the satisfaction of having me thrown out. But if the organ-grinder won't see me, then I'll make do with his monkey. I take it I'm speaking to the young master?'

His words were thick with sarcasm and Sarah's apprehension turned to anger. She disliked people who used words as weapons and Robey Midwinter was altogether too good at it. Clenching her jaw, she ran quickly down the stairs and took up her stance at her husband's side.

'What do you want, Robey Midwinter?' she demanded, her voice low with outrage. 'You're not welcome here. Go back to wherever you came from!'

'Leave us, Sarah!' David's voice was harsh as he pushed her behind him. 'This man's business is *my* concern!'

'Aye, Sarah. Do as you're bid,' Robey mocked. 'He's right. My business doesn't concern you any longer, though maybe you should stay and hear what I've got to say. Happen then you can persuade your new masters to heed my warning.'

His eyes swept her from head to toe, flashing contempt, his lips slanting derisively, then, turning to David, he said:

'The workers at Low Clough have asked for another ha'penny an hour. They've asked it twice and been refused. I'm serving notice that unless the master sees fit to grant that request inside seven days, the workers will withdraw their labour, as is their right!'

'Strike, you mean?' David ground.

'Call it what you like,' came the comfortable retort. 'It'll all be the same in the long run. There'll be no more yardage, come Saturday night.'

'And no more money either – had you thought of that?' David flung. 'How long can they live without money?'

'As long as it takes,' came the arrogant reply. 'Just as long as it takes to convince you that God is not a mill-master!'

The seconds stretched into eternity as they faced each other in brooding silence, then, pulling off his cap, Robey touched his forelock in an exaggerated gesture of servility and, sweeping a low bow, smiling as he said it, wished David a pleasant goodnight.

'And you too, Mistress Holroyd,' he whispered. 'May your dreams be sweet and your conscience rest easy beside you!'

Then throwing back his shoulders he turned abruptly and strode away.

The darkness instantly wrapped him round and they stood, unmoving, listening to the crunch of his feet on the gravel of the drive. Only then did Sarah give way to the pent-up emotion inside her.

'Oh, David,' she whispered, her voice harsh with fear. 'Please do as he says. It isn't much they're asking and it'd be a small price to pay.'

'Pay, Sarah? For what? Are we to be blackmailed by this gypsy, give in to his whims without a fight? Who is he?' he demanded, 'and by what right is he so familiar with the use of your name?'

'By no right at all,' she retorted wearily, 'except that he knew me by that name before I married you. It means nothing. It's just the way he goes about things, that's all.'

'You seem to know a great deal about him.' His voice was cold. 'How long has he been in Hollinsdyke? How long have you known him?'

'About as long as I've known you,' came the whispered reply. 'I met him the day you offered me a position in the counting-house though it seems, sometimes, like a lifetime ago.'

'Is that the truth?'

'I give you my word.' She raised her eyes to his and her gaze was steady.

And she *had* answered him truthfully, she urged as they walked once more up the broad sweep of stairs. She had first met Robey the day she'd fought with Poll Clegg in Low Clough yard. Thank the dear Lord David hadn't asked her why she had stood there trembling at the sight of the man, or why her heart had turned over at the sound of his voice. To have answered such questions truthfully would have been another matter.

'Please believe me,' she urged, taking his arm, hugging it tightly. 'You mustn't get strange ideas into your head. I'm your wife, David, and I care for you.'

'Do you, Sarah? But how much do you care and how much of yourself do you keep hidden from me?'

For the rest of the evening there was an unkind silence between them. Bewildered, Sarah prepared for sleep behind the closed door of the dressing-room and when she crept into the bedroom her husband did not open his eyes or turn his head on the pillow.

'Good night,' she whispered to his unyielding back as she turned down the lamps and pinched out the bedside candle. But he remained uncompromisingly aloof and he did not whisper to her in the darkness or reach out for her.

A noise in the courtyard below awoke Sarah and she jumped guiltily out of bed, peering through the curtains to see Charlotte's trunks and boxes being loaded into the carriage.

'Lordy! This would happen!' she fretted, splashing her face with cold water, dressing hastily. Yesterday David's mother had unbent and shown kindness and it would be uncivil, Sarah reasoned, not to be there to wish her goodbye.

Charlotte was sitting in the breakfast-room when Sarah burst in, red-faced and flustered.

'Good morning, ma'am,' she gasped, praying fervently that the goodwill of the previous day still held good. 'I'm sorry – I slept late.'

Charlotte nodded stiffly to a chair, then pouring a cup of tea and handing it to Sarah said:

'I am afraid that yesterday we allowed ourselves to be carried away by sentimentality which is rarely a good thing, and not to be encouraged. Nevertheless I enjoyed our chat and when I return next week we will talk about the Charity Ball. And Sarah – never, *ever*, come down to breakfast with your hair undressed!'

Sarah let go her indrawn breath in a gasp of relief. It was going to be all right. Given time, they might yet become friends.

It was only later, when she sat alone, munching bread spread thickly with Cook's special lemon conserve, that Sarah was able to take stock of the situation.

Last night, for the first time, David had shown jealousy. There had been a coldness between them and this morning he had left for the mill without awakening her.

And it was all Robey Midwinter's doing. Robey had no right to come to High Meadow, threatening a strike, using her name with deliberate familiarity, making a downright nuisance of himself. That she found him disturbing was a matter only for her conscience, but the man had become a threat to the people of the Three-streets and something had to be done. For everybody's peace of mind, he had to be persuaded to leave Hollinsdyke.

She said as much to Maggie Ormerod as they ladled soup into the apprentices' waiting bowls.

'You should know, Maggie – what's behind it all?' Sarah demanded. 'There's been upset in the place ever since Robey came. Doesn't he realize the damage a strike will do?'

'Mister Holroyd wouldn't stop the children's food, would he?' Maggie asked anxiously. 'If the mill came out, he'd not be so cruel as to take it out on the apprentices?'

'No.' Sarah shook her head firmly. 'The bairns won't suffer, I promise you. I only wish, though, that Robey would leave us in peace.'

'He'll not do that,' Maggie sighed, cutting thick slices of bread. 'His mind's set on getting something done at Low Clough. It's not just the wages – he's right about the machines too. They're dangerous – but you know that, don't you?'

Tight-lipped, Sarah nodded. She didn't need reminding. The day her father had been carried home still lived vividly in her memory.

'I'm not defending Luke Holroyd,' she whispered, 'but there's better ways than striking to get things done. Surely they know the old man won't be pushed?'

She patted Billy-Boy's head as she prepared to leave and slipped a twist of humbugs into his pocket, brooding guiltily that she still had not spoken to David about taking the child out of the workhouse, finding him a kindly home. But there had been so much to do. Folks would never believe what a time-consuming business it was, being rich and idle.

But speak to David she would, she resolved, as the sad brown eyes gazed up into hers.

'Will you come again tomorrow, ma'am?' Billy whispered solemnly.

'Aye, child. Sarah'll look after you.'

She would too. She would speak to David about Billy this very night. Setting the world to rights wasn't easy – miracles never were – but at least she must find the time to make one small boy happy. Whatever happened, she must not fail Billy-Boy.

Kissing Maggie warmly, Sarah sighed and picked up her basket. She wasn't at all sure what she would say when she got to the Three-streets, for her heart had begun to beat uncomfortably just to think about it. But today was her father's birthday and it was the excuse she needed to warrant another call at the little house that backed on to the slow-moving canal. She knew she would be greeted coldly, treated with contempt, even, but it would be worth it if it enabled her to talk sense to her father, get him to warn Robey Midwinter that his actions could lead to nothing but trouble.

She called out cheerfully as she entered the house, despite the foreboding that warned her to turn and walk away. Her mouth was dry and her heart thumped so loudly she feared her father must have heard it.

But it wasn't Caleb who rose straight and tall from the fireside chair and she bit hard on her lip to prevent herself from crying aloud.

'Why, good-morning, ma'am. If it isn't the young mistress from the Big House come spreading her bounty again!'

Sarah turned away, fighting down the tumult that thrashed inside her. Playing for time, she placed tobacco, bacon and a freshly-baked loaf on the table top.

'Bid you good-day, Robey Midwinter,' she whispered. 'I'm here to wish my father the compliments of his birthday,' at once furious with herself for stooping to explain her actions. 'Where is he, do you know?'

'Gone to Market Street to deliver a potion for whooping cough,' he supplied. 'I'd not wait, if I were you, Sarah. You'll not be welcome.'

'But you are *not* me!' she flung, trepidation giving way to anger, 'and I'll thank you to mind your own business. What's more, I'll wait in my father's house as long as I've a mind to and, if my being here bothers you, you've only got to leave!'

'Do you want me to leave, Sarah? Do you *really* want it?' His voice was low and indulgent and his eyes challenged her to tell the truth.

'Of course I want it!' she gasped. 'I want you to leave this house, this street. I want you to go away from Hollinsdyke and never look back! Oh, why,' she pleaded, 'did you have to come here?'

He took a step toward her and stood so near that she could hear his rasping breath. Dismayed, she dropped her head, tensing her body in an effort to still the trembling that shook it from head to toe.

'I came to right a wrong,' he whispered. 'I told you that, the night we walked together over the hills, the night before you wed the mill-master's son.'

'And what wrong might that be?' she jerked.

'You know it as well as I do, Sarah Makin. Oh, why are you so contrary? Why is every word you utter a nonsense of cussedness?' He grasped her arms roughly and swung her to face him. 'And why didn't you think on before you wed David Holroyd?'

His eyes blazed into hers, his nearness sent her giddy with longing and she wanted to feel his arms around her, his mouth hard on hers. But he had called her contrary and cussed and besides she was David's wife. Breaking from his grasp she rounded on him like a wild cat.

'Then why did you let me?' she sobbed. 'You knew you had me bothered. You picked me flowers, that night. You'd only to say –' She stopped, her breath shuddering in her throat.

What was the use? Robey was Maggie's and she, Sarah, wasn't free to love him.

'Go away, Robey,' she moaned. 'There'll be no peace for this town while you're here.'

'And for you, Sarah?'

'No peace for me either,' she choked.

'I'll go when my work is done and be glad to,' he jerked, 'for you torment me as I never thought to be tormented again. But before I go I swear you'll remember me!' and gathering her into the circle of his arms he held her close, kissing her eyelids, her cheeks, gentling her body until her resistance was overcome and she relaxed, crying softly against him.

'I want you, Sarah Makin,' he choked. 'I wanted you the moment I laid eyes on you.'

His mouth found hers roughly and she was too weak to resist him. He kissed her again and again, until her head reeled and every small pulse in her body beat madly with need of him.

'Robey, oh, Robey . . .'

A little keening sob escaped from the secret deeps of her heart and the cry shocked her. It was the cry of a wanton, the animal mewl of unbridled need. Through the mists of her madness she heard her husband's voice, '*Dearest Sarah, you are such a joy . . .*' and self-disgust swept over her. Tensing her body against him, tearing herself from his arms, she stood like a cornered animal, panting and weak, her eyes flashing a warning. Pulling the back of her hand across her mouth she gasped:

'Leave me alone! Don't touch me! Don't ever touch me again, Robey Midwinter'

Sobbing, she flung past him, out of the house, into the street where cool air hit her like a slap to her face.

What had she done? What new madness had she let loose and what would be the outcome of it? She had wondered about Robey's arms, longed for the feel of his lips on hers, and now she knew.

They wanted each other with an intensity that was frightening and she had never, ever, to let herself be near him again. She had to close her ears to the sound of his voice and close her heart against the memory of his kisses.

Biting on her knuckles, she began to run. The cobbles were sharp beneath the soles of her dainty shoes and the pain gladdened her, reminding her that her loyalty lay no longer in the Three-streets. She was Sarah Holroyd now and she had to remember it always.

But another man's kisses still burned her lips and her heart beat madly with the remembrance of his closeness and even as she neared the gates of High Meadow her body was still a torment of unsatisfied need.

'Dear heaven,' she whispered. 'What will be the end of it?'

Eight

Sarah wandered in search of company, her footsteps echoing behind her in the emptiness of the house. She liked the warm, homely kitchen with its smell of scrubbed tabletops and she liked Cook, whose big brown teapot was always at the ready.

She smiled, recalling the delights of Señor Umberti's warehouse in Manchester, the swish and rustle of silks and satins, the velvets, soft to her touch.

She had spent the morning choosing materials for her ball-gown and cloak and to add to her enjoyment David's good humour seemed completely restored, the coldness of the previous night forgotten. And that, Sarah supposed, had been entirely due to the sense of guilt which had prompted her to behave more lovingly toward him. Indeed the shame she felt at the remembrance of Robey's kisses had made her go out of her way to make atonement for her slide from grace and to vow, yet again, to banish him from her mind.

Cook was relaxing, her feet on the fender, enjoying the peace left behind by Charlotte's departure.

'I got the victuals off, ma'am,' she remarked comfortably. 'Sent them down in the tub-cart with the stable-lad.'

'You're a good woman,' Sarah smiled. 'One day soon you shall come with me to the school and see for yourself how the children enjoy your cooking.'

'Aye, hunger's a wicked thing,' Cook sighed, 'and that's not the worst of it, if all I hear is true.'

'What did you hear?' Frowning, Sarah set down her cup.

''Twas the stable-lad told Mrs Parkes. Had it from the school lady. One of the apprentices got hurt this morning – lamed on a machine strap.'

'At Low Clough?'

'So it seems,' Cook nodded reluctantly. 'But happen someone got it wrong in the telling. No cause for you to go fretting, ma'am.'

No cause at all, Sarah thought uneasily, but people didn't make mistakes about accidents in the mill.

'I'm going to Hollinsdyke,' she whispered. 'Will you send someone to the stables, please? Tell them I want the carriage – quickly!'

She took the stairs two at a time, her heart pumping dully, and, flinging on a cape, was waiting at the front door long before the carriage arrived.

'Take me to the mill-school,' she cried, wrenching open the door, dismissing the coachman's attentions with impatience. 'And *hurry*!'

Leaning back against the cushioned interior, she closed her eyes and tried not to think. But the memory of the dreadful day from her childhood would not be pushed aside and she lived again through another accident, saw her mother's face, pale with shock, and her father's fine body, made hideous by one of Low Clough's machines.

Now it had happened again, this time to a child, and it had to stop. If Luke Holroyd would do nothing, she vowed, then David must be made to. Somehow, those great clattering looms had to be made safe.

*

The mood in the schoolroom was subdued. Small heads jerked up as Sarah entered.

'I've just heard!' she gasped. 'Is it bad? Who's hurt?'

Maggie Ormerod's eyes were red-rimmed and her lashes spiky with tears.

'Oh, Sarah. It's Billy,' she whispered.

'*No!*' The breath left Sarah's body. 'Where is he? I must take him to High Meadow. He must be properly nursed!'

Stunned, she was stumbling to the door when her arm was grasped with unaccustomed roughness.

'Sarah! Stay here! There's nothing you can do. There's nothing any of us can do. He's dead. Billy's *dead*, do you hear?'

'Dear God.' The words left Sarah's lips in a terrible moan and her eyes wandered aimlessly around the room, searching for the child, questioning the truth of Maggie's words, disbelieving, even as she stared at the empty desk. 'Please, no? Not Billy-Boy?'

A terrible coldness swept over her and her eyes narrowed into slits of wrath. There was no grief in her heart, no tears for the crying. She was gripped instead with a vicious anger, a fearful, raging hatred that made her want to lash out in fury, tear down every accursed stone that made Low Clough with her bare hands.

'Someone,' she hissed, 'will suffer for this!' and turning on her heel dismissed the carriage with a curt nod. 'Someone will pay, if it takes the rest of my life!'

Her heels banged angrily on the cobbles as she strode like a creature demented towards Low Clough.

'On my mother's soul, he shall pay!'

'I tell you, Master, it's not safe in the mill! I'd be off home, if I were you. The mood's ugly, down there.' Aaron Silk rubbed his shaking hands together, his ferret nose twitching. The feeling in the mill was such that it almost screamed aloud in its outrage. A child in arms could have sensed it. 'They're of a mind to wreck the place, sir!'

'Over my dead body they will!' Luke growled. 'And anyway 'twas an accident. The bairn slipped. Someone must have spilled oil on the floor. Find out who did it, Silk, and I'll have him fined and sacked!'

'Wouldn't do any good, Mister Holroyd. They were striking for money before, but it's a matter of principle, now. A child has been killed – one of their own . . .'

'You talk as if I'd done it,' Luke glowered.

'Well, sir, they're holding you responsible. They're not waiting till Saturday. They're coming out on strike right away.'

Luke strode over to the window. The scene outside seemed normal enough; he could still hear the crash of the looms yet the small windows looked out with a malevolent stare and the eyes of those who crossed the yard were downcast as if they guarded a secret.

'How soon is right away?' Luke demanded.

'I don't know, Master, but *they* do. It'll only take the lifting of a finger to bring everything to a stop.' He looked anxiously toward the door. 'I'll have to go. I've been away from my desk for long enough. Folks'll notice . . .'

'Aye, cut along,' Luke mumbled thoughtfully, 'and if you hear anything else tell Dinwiddie at once.'

Nasty little pest, Luke brooded as Silk sidled out. Nasty, but necessary. A mill-master must be forewarned at all times. He wished, though, that David had not taken it into his head to escort Sarah to the Manchester shops, then stay behind at the Cotton Exchange. But he'd been running Low Clough, Luke reasoned, before the lad was born. Doubtless he'd manage alone for one afternoon.

He looked down again into the mill-yard; *his* mill-yard, *his* mill, every stick and stone of it. There had been trouble before and there'd be trouble again, but he would survive! He always had!

Sarah shut her bedroom door and refused to open it. Secretly she had been glad David was still in Manchester. She needed time alone to compose herself, control the anger that blazed white-hot inside her. By some small miracle she had been able to blot Billy-Boy from her thoughts, leaving her mind open to malice and hatred, leaving room for the bitterness there to fester and multiply.

She had decided against going to the mill and confronting her father-in-law. For once in her tempestuous life, icy logic had taken a hand and she realized she had to do nothing in anger.

It was her own fault, she acknowledged. She had let the Holroyds charm her, dull her natural antagonism. How could she, a product of the Three-streets, have been so blind? No mill-owner was to be trusted, not even David's father.

There was an ache in her throat and a pain where her heart should have been. She needed to let loose the tearing sobs that threshed inside her but the time for tears had not yet come. Later she would weep for the child.

There was a tapping on the door. 'Cook's sent you a tray, madam,' a small voice called. 'She says you're to try to eat something.'

'I don't want it,' Sarah choked. 'Go away and leave me alone!'

Dry-eyed, she flung herself face-down on the bed. She was lying there in the darkness, when David came home.

Gently he stroked her tumbled hair, whispered softly to

her. She didn't move or answer him, yet he knew she was not asleep.

Best leave her alone tonight, he sighed. In the morning he would talk to her.

Sarah awoke to a feeling of shadowy dread, fighting wakefulness, remembering which day it was and what had to be done.

Amazingly she had slept, but sleep had not dimmed the heartache of yesterday nor dried up the tears she had scorned to cry, and the feeling of self-reproach still hung brooding over her.

She turned her head warily. Even in the curtained dimness she could see that David had not slept beside her. But that, she admitted as she tugged on the bell-pull, was all she could expect when she had pretended sleep at his approach.

'What time is it?' she asked the housemaid who drew back the curtains.

'Nearly eight o'clock, ma'am. The Master and Mr David have almost finished their breakfast,' she added tactfully, holding out a silver tray. 'This letter came half an hour back, by messenger.'

Sarah picked up the envelope with dismay, recognizing Maggie's hand, knowing before she tore it open exactly what would be written there.

She read it with distaste, then crumpling it into a ball, flung it into the hearth.

When the carriage had crunched down the drive, Sarah threw back the bedclothes, then, washing and dressing quickly, ran down to the kitchen.

'I don't want anything to eat,' she murmured, 'but can I sit here for a while?'

'Of course you can, ma'am,' Cook assured her, 'but

you'll do yourself no good by fretting over the child. Nothing's going to bring the poor mite back. Is it the funeral today?' she added, her plump face creased in sympathy.

'At eleven o'clock,' Sarah whispered.

'Ah. Best done quickly. I suppose the parish is seeing to it?'

Sarah nodded, tight-lipped, anger sulking inside her. She wanted to lash out, make the whole of creation suffer. She marvelled that the world should go on spinning, that people could go about their daily lives as if nothing had happened.

'Billy is dead!' she wanted to scream. 'And it is my fault! I should have taken him away from the workhouse, but I didn't. I should have found him a kindly home, but I couldn't spare the time!'

It would have been so easy. She had only to ask David and he'd have done it for her. But David slept alone last night, she brooded, then left for Low Clough without even wishing her goodbye.

'Mister Holroyd and Master David went early this morning,' Cook supplied, breaking uncannily into Sarah's thoughts. 'I took my breakfast with Mrs Parkes and she's of the opinion there'll be trouble at Low Clough before this day is out.'

'I don't doubt it,' Sarah acknowledged soberly. She didn't care for the stiff-backed housekeeper but she was forced to agree with her observations. Before the day was over, she pondered fearfully, the Lord only knew what might have happened.

'Try to take a cup of tea,' Cook fussed, lifting the brown pot from the stove-top. 'There's nothing like tea for lifting the spirits.' She spooned sugar into a cup. 'Come on, now,' she coaxed. 'Sup it up.'

Obediently Sarah took it. She didn't want it but it gave her the excuse she needed to sit in the homely kitchen and bask for a little while longer in motherly concern.

'I'm going to the funeral,' she announced defiantly, wincing as the steaming liquid burned her mouth. 'It'll anger Mister Holroyd, I shouldn't wonder, and it won't go down well in the Three-streets either, but I'm going!'

No amount of disapproval would keep her away. It would be part of her punishment.

'Oh, Cook. It's such a heartbreak,' she choked, her eyes wide with grief. 'Such a terrible heartbreak . . .'

Sarah stepped down from the carriage at the outskirts of Hollinsdyke then ordered the coachman back to High Meadow.

Can you be at the schoolroom at ten o'clock? Maggie had written.

Head bowed, Sarah walked slowly. She had dressed in a plain grey skirt and white blouse tied with black ribbon. Over her head she wore her mill-shawl, pinned beneath her chin and the rough, familiar feel of it gave her strange comfort.

The schoolroom was silent and Maggie sat at her desk, hands clasped, staring at the empty desks. She jumped eagerly to her feet as Sarah entered, gathering her into her arms.

'I'm glad you've come,' she whispered. 'I thought at first there'd only be me.'

'Nothing would have kept me away,' Sarah choked. 'I loved that child. I tried not to, but I did love him.'

'Then that makes two of us,' Maggie smiled tearfully, 'and a loving farewell is better than a fancy funeral.'

And Maggie was right, Sarah thought grimly when they reached the undertaker's shop. There was no pomp or display when an orphan child was given back to the Lord. Just a handcart and the undertaker's assistant in his second-best suit. Three shillings and sixpence the parish allowed for a charity burying and such a pittance did not allow for black crêpe, or a glass-sided hearse and mourning carriages.

Sarah touched the little coffin, reading the words roughly printed there.

William Chapel.

Pauper.

Aged about 9 years. A.D. 1870

R.I.P.

'*Rest in peace!*'

She spat the words as though they were an obscenity. How dare they do this to Billy-Boy?

She drew on her breath, biting back the curses she wanted to fling at the uncaring world as she felt the grasp of Maggie's fingers on her own.

'Hush, Sarah. Stop your sorrowing. There's nothing either of us can do.' Gravely she laid a posy of wild flowers on the tiny coffin.

I should have brought him some blossoms too, Sarah chided herself silently. The gardens at High Meadow were golden with daffodils, bright with flowering shrubs. She should have gathered an armful, scattered them over the miserable cart.

'Happen you're right,' she choked, answering the handclasp with fingers that trembled, then, straightening her shoulders, she fell into step behind the bumping cart.

Brown eyes haunted her and defenceless little hands seemed to reach out and touch her cold heart.

'William Chapel,' she spoke her thoughts aloud. 'He was always Billy-Boy to me. I never knew he had a name.'

'Nor had he,' Maggie shrugged, 'but they called him William when they found him abandoned in the chapel. They're got to have something, I suppose, to write down in the register.'

The cart jolted slowly through the back streets of Hollinsdyke. At every house the windows had been shuttered and women stood in small huddles, eyes downcast as they passed.

Nearing her old home Sarah's mouth ran dry and a sudden trembling took hold of her limbs. She swallowed hard on the anxiety that bubbled in her throat. The women of the Three-streets would be there. They would stand in silent judgement on her; they'd stare with dull, accusing eyes into her heart and read the shame that beat there.

Maggie sensed the heightening tension in her and pointed ahead. Still and silent, a knot of men and women waited at the top of Tinker's Row. Then as one their heads lifted and, led by a man with a black scarf knotted at his throat, fell into solemn step behind Sarah and Maggie.

Robey had come, brought them his support! Sarah let go her anxious breath. Suddenly she felt protected by his presence, uplifted by his strength.

'Walk on to Low Clough,' Maggie ordered the undertaker's assistant, then seeing the alarm in Sarah's eyes whispered.

'It's all right. There'll be no bother at the mill. Robey'll see to it . . .'

*

Luke Holroyd stood fretting at the window of his office, hands clasped behind his back, staring down into the mill-yard.

'Something's wrong,' he muttered. 'I know it.'

'Don't worry so, Father,' David urged. 'Just because Silk said the strike was to be brought forward –'

'Silk's not often wrong,' Luke interrupted. 'Besides, I can *feel* the trouble. It's like there's dynamite down there, ready to blow sky high any minute.'

'They were supposed to have walked out yesterday and they're still working,' David reasoned. 'If it rested with me, I'd send Silk packing. He's a trouble-maker.'

'But I'm sure he's right, for all that,' the elder man defended, 'and if you knew the moods of Low Clough like I know them you'd be bothered as I am!'

His head jerked upward as the small boy who had been leaning against the gates ran swiftly across the yard and disappeared through the weaving-shed doors. Almost simultaneously the mill hooter blared once, twice, three times.

Luke bit hard on his lip. There was no call for the hooter. It needed an hour, yet, to dinner-time. He raised his eyes skywards.

A cotton bale on the spinning-room hoist jerked to a standstill in its upward lift then swung suspended from side to side.

The hooter blared again and the weaving-shed doors slammed open.

'They're walking out!' Luke gasped. 'And something's happening in the street!'

The funeral cart came to a stop outside Low Clough gates. Over his father's shoulder David saw the pathetic coffin and Sarah standing beside it. Her head was bravely high but her eyes were closed in pain.

'Father! It's the child!' he gasped. 'It's Sarah's Billy-Boy. How could I have been so unthinking? I must go to her!'

'Nay – that you'll not!' Luke rasped. 'See, the gypsy's with them and half the Three-streets too. If you go down there now you'll be begging for trouble. Go and tell Dinwiddie to send for the constabulary, if you want to do something useful. Tell him I want them here fast, but don't go down into the street if you value your health. It's not your wife's safety you have to fear for!'

His father was right, David acknowledged, but the sight of Sarah's stricken face squeezed his heart into a spasm of pain.

'Very well,' he jerked. 'I'll not interfere, but neither will I have the police called in. I'll not have the constabulary break up a funeral procession. Let them at least bury the child with dignity!'

'Dignity!' Luke howled. 'They're not mourning! Midwinter's using the boy's death against me for his own ends, can't you see that?'

'No, I can't, sir. Tell me in all honesty. Can you swear that you and I aren't in any way to blame for that unhappy sight down there? A small boy was killed in *our* mill on one of *our* machines – machines we should have fitted with guards!'

'Now see here, David; whose side are you on?' Luke spluttered.

'I don't know, Father, but this time you're wrong about Midwinter. Maybe soon he'll use the child's death against you, but at this moment the workers need no prompting from anyone. That protest is an act of comradeship. Leave them alone! Let them mourn!'

*

They streamed from the weaving-shed and the spinning-room, the women carrying flowers, the men wearing armbands of mourning crêpe. One of their own had been killed and they rose as one to walk with him to his grave, parade their silent grief.

Luke stood unmoving, watching and remembering, recalling the long-ago years when he had worked in that same spinning-room. Downtrodden, they'd all been but in time of direst trouble there'd been the most wonderful solidness about them. They'd stood firm against the mill-masters, caring for each other, sharing the little they had without question.

But the boot was on the other foot now and Low Clough was *his*, Luke brooded. He'd schemed to get it, worked until he was ready to drop to pay back the bankers who held it in mortgage. He was a mill-master, now. From clogs to clogs in three generations his wife had mocked, but he'd show her. He'd show his ungrateful workers too! He'd risked all he had to give them work. He'd kept Low Clough running when other masters had shut down their looms; he'd paid their wages, regular as the clock, every settling-day. Now in return they turned snarling and bit the hand that fed them! They walked out as one man in silent condemnation, gratitude forgotten!

'Very well, David,' he jerked, tight-lipped. 'Let them have their funeral. We'll keep the law out of it, if that's what you want!'

'I do want it, sir. I know it'll be for the best. You can't blame them for their anger, but it will die down and then we can talk, get them back to work again.'

'Can we, by the heck? Can we just?' Luke growled, his mouth curving down like the jaws of a gin-trap. 'We'll have to see about that!'

He stood watching as his workers filed past the little boy's coffin, silently covering the cart with their flowers. Then they formed a quiet, orderly line behind it and walked with bowed heads to the graveyard behind the parish church.

William Chapel, Pauper, would be buried there, his funeral oration intoned by the pink-cheeked curate. His coffin was shoddy, his bier mean, but no one would ever be laid to his rest with greater love than the boy who was left as a babe on the steps of Daisy Street chapel.

As the last of the procession disappeared from his view, Luke Holroyd turned sharply on his heel.

'Well now,' he ground. 'We'd better see what's to be done. Have Dinwiddie come here, if you please.'

The request was curt, an order no less, and David knew better than protest, even though he failed to see what help the counting-house manager might be.

When the man minced in Luke nodded gravely and indicated a chair.

Dinwiddie sniffed, hitched up his trouser creases, then sat carefully, his eyes expectant, eager to witness a fight in which he would have no active part.

'You saw what happened, Albert?' Luke demanded gravely. 'You saw that charade down there?'

'That I did, Master, and downright disgraceful I call it.'

'Aye. It didn't please me either, so now we must see what's to be done. I want those gates shut, Albert. I want them locked and bolted and barred! I'm closing Low Clough down. Those workers of mine walked out at their own pleasure and they'll come back at mine!'

'Eeeeeh!' Dinwiddie's chin sagged.

'Father! You can't do that,' David gasped. 'What you propose to do amounts virtually to a lock-out!'

'It *is* a lock-out. Low Clough is *my* mill and, if I don't choose to work it, then it's entirely *my* business!'

'But it's wrong! I'll grant you the workers shouldn't have acted as they did, but two wrongs don't make a right!'

'Did you hear me, Albert?' Luke murmured. 'Get the counting-house staff sent home, then Silk can see to things. And if I were you, lad,' he jerked, turning on his son, 'I'd get myself back to High Meadow and read the riot act to Sarah when she comes back!'

'Father! *Please?*'

But David's pleading fell on deaf ears. Incensed beyond measure the mill-master was intent upon revenge.

'All right,' David jerked, 'but I think you are making a terrible mistake, Father. And when you've realized it, don't expect *me* to dry your tears!'

Shaking with outrage he slammed from the room and the two men heard his footsteps clattering down the stairs.

'Eh, Albert, maybe the lad's right,' Luke ventured. 'Happen it'll do no harm to sleep on it.'

'Nay, Mr Holroyd. Thy lad, if I might make so bold, knows little about the ways of a cotton-mill and nowt about mill-workers! You were t'Master of Low Clough long afore he'd cut his first tooth! A lesson's what that lot need!'

'Aye, that I was,' Luke ruminated, 'and happen you could just be right, Dinwiddie. Happen a short sharp lesson'll not come amiss, at that!'

Dinwiddie smiled, walked sedately from the room, then closing the door behind him ran as fast as he was able in search of Aaron Silk.

Wearily Sarah slipped into High Meadow by a side door. How long she had walked after leaving Billy's graveside she couldn't tell, for the tears she longed to cry still evaded her and her heart was cold with angry grief. Now she needed to lay her torment bare, talk to David about it. David would understand. He was kind and compassionate and wouldn't deny her the solace she yearned for.

The study door was open and angry words spilled out into the hall. Without shame, she stopped to listen.

'I'll do as I think fit!' It was Luke's voice. 'I'm still master here, David. *I'll* give the orders!'

'But it's insane, Father! There'll be fighting in the streets! And where are you to find enough spinners and weavers?'

'I'll find them in Manchester, lad, where spinners and weavers are begging in the streets. They'll jump at the chance of work in Low Clough. Silk'll go there on the first train tomorrow and the mill will be working again inside three days.'

'But where will they live? Had you thought of that?'

'They can be quartered in the old warehouse, that's where. It's rough, but it'll mean bread in their bellies. They'll not care, if it means working again. And the Low Clough folk who walked out this morning can go hang!'

'But they didn't walk out, sir! It was only a protest. They'd have come back, if you hadn't locked the gates!'

'Nay. My mind's made up,' Luke flung. 'They said they could get more money at Syke Mill; let them go there.'

Sarah had heard enough. Fury blazed afresh inside her. How could he do such a thing? It was mad and wicked. It was all she needed to hear. Without thought she turned and ran back the way she had come.

Luke Holroyd had gone too far this time, taken leave of his senses. Fighting in the streets, David had warned. When she told Robey what the mill-master intended, Sarah exulted, there'd be that, all right!

Jubilant, she saw no wrong in what she would do. Her father-in-law was to blame for Billy-Boy's death and now he had given her the chance to even the score. And, by God, she would make him pay!

It was late afternoon when she walked into the house in Canal Street. Her father was sitting, as he always was, in the chair by the kitchen hearth, staring fascinated into the fire.

'I'm seeking Robey,' she announced without preamble. 'He's not at Maggie's house and they don't know where he is. Do you?'

'No, lass, I don't,' Caleb retorted. 'What's your business with him?'

'Mill business,' Sarah snapped. 'If you see him, tell him Luke Holroyd's closed Low Clough down.'

'Tell me some news.' Caleb's eyes were mocking.

'All right, then! Tell him an' all that the mill's going to be working again on Friday – with cheap labour from Manchester!'

Caleb raised his head, his eyes disbelieving.

'On your honour, girl?'

'I swear it. He's sending Aaron Silk to bring in spinners and weavers. Robey's got to be told.'

'Then tell him yourself. Likely he's walking on Moor Top.'

Sarah sighed impatiently, then, shaking her head at her father's disinterest, walked wearily away.

Did no one care? Now, it seemed, there was no way left but to find Robey.

She knew her wayward heart was leading her into danger. Just to think about him set her nerves twanging and voices screaming caution in her head. But she had to warn him. Billy's death had to be paid for and only Robey could help her now.

*

She saw him, tall against the skyline, and when she waved he stood still and watched her approach.

'If it isn't Mrs Holroyd,' he called softly. 'All dressed up in her mill-shawl!'

'Please,' she whispered. 'Don't let's fight. I'm sick to death of this awful day and I've wandered the streets till I'm weary. I came to tell you,' she choked, 'that Luke Holroyd is sending Silk to Manchester for cheap labour. He's opening the mill to them, come Friday. It's true. You've got to believe me.'

'I believe you,' he murmured, eyes narrowing. 'But why are you telling me? You're a Holroyd now. Your loyalty is to your husband.'

'My loyalty is to the Three-streets, to my own people,' Sarah flared. 'I can't stand by and see them deprived of work, driven cap in hand to the workhouse.'

'And?' he prompted.

'And there's Billy-Boy,' she acknowledged reluctantly. 'If there'd been guards on the machines he'd be alive now.'

'So it's revenge you're looking for?'

'Aye,' she admitted. 'Revenge. And if you won't help me it'll make no difference. I'll not rest until –'

'Hold on now, Sarah,' Robey interrupted, taking her hand in his. 'Sit down and get your breath back. You look ready to drop. When did you last eat?'

'I don't know,' she murmured, sinking to the cool spring grass beside him. 'But hunger's nothing new to me.'

'Maybe not, but driving yourself to distraction won't help.'

'And sitting here won't help either. Luke Holroyd mustn't be allowed to bring in strike-breakers. There's little enough work in Hollinsdyke as it is. What are you going to do about it?'

'Tonight? Nothing,' he said simply. 'And all we need do tomorrow is to see that Silk doesn't get on that train. It won't be too difficult to persuade him. Silk's a poor little worm. He'll see sense. And after that,' he shrugged, 'the mill-master must be made to see reason.'

'He's a Justice of the Peace,' Sarah brooded. 'He's got the law on his side.'

'He's got the law in his pocket, more like, but he can't fight the people. So what's really troubling you, Sarah Makin? Is it Billy-Boy at the bottom of all this?'

'Aye,' she choked. 'I loved him. It's my fault he's dead and I can't forgive myself. I could have taken him out of the mill, found him a kindly home, but I didn't. I was too busy playing the grand lady.'

'We're all wise, with hindsight.'

'But he was such a defenceless scrap, a babe, and I don't think he'd known a day's real happiness in the whole of his life,' she whispered. 'He was cold and hungry and most times unloved.'

'You loved him, Sarah.'

'But not enough, it seems. He trusted me, waited for me at the mill-gates like a lost little soul. The morning he was killed I was buying satin, for a ball-gown . . .'

Her voice trembled and the long-denied tears rose again in her throat. Covering her face with hands that shook she choked:

'What will I do, Robey? His face haunts me.'

'There, lass, there.' Strong arms wrapped her round, held her tightly. 'We're all to blame. We stand by and let them work children in the pits and mills. We're *all* guilty.'

His sympathy was too much, the comfort of his arms too great. With a sob, Sarah gave way to the tears she had been unable to shed. Her grief was heart-rending and anguish arose from her throat in despairing gasps. She wept until there were no tears left to cry, until she lay spent in the cradle of his arms.

'Oh, Robey,' she gasped. 'You can't believe the remorse inside me.'

'But I can, Sarah. I turned my back on a child too.'

'*You?*'

'Aye. Emma's child. Emma was my sweetheart. We loved each other and wanted to wed. But I was proud. I wanted to give her the earth, so I left her, tramped to Liverpool and signed on a ship that was making the round-trip.'

She stirred in his arms and he laid his cheek gently on hers.

'I was away at sea for nearly two years, but when we paid off I had a hundred sovereigns in my pocket. I had enough to buy a cottage and a plot of land, but –'

For a moment he didn't speak and Sarah sensed the anguish inside him, felt the slow thudding of his heart against her own. Then, with a shrugging of his shoulders, he whispered:

'When I got back home, Emma was dead and buried. She'd taken consumption and because she couldn't work there was only the workhouse to go to. I went there and they showed me the child. Emma had died, two days after it was born.'

'And what became of it?'

'I looked at it with disgust, God forgive me, and left it there. It was another man's bairn, you see. She hadn't been able to wait, I thought in my anger, but it wasn't like that. Emma was a good girl. She'd been seduced by a mill-owner's son, then deserted.'

'And now you hate all mill-owners?'

'Aye, that's why I go from town to town, righting wrongs, making them pay. I vowed that day I'd hold every mill-owner in creation responsible. I vowed it, over Emma's grave. I swore to make trouble for the likes of them till the day I died.'

'But what brought you to Low Clough? Why Luke Holroyd's mill?'

'Nothing special. I was on my way here and I met a man. He was a cripple, with a terrible bitterness inside him. There was a score to settle, it seemed to me, so I asked him where I'd find lodgings –'

'My father?'

'Aye. His cause seemed as good as any.'

'And the babe?' Sarah brooded. 'What became of the little one? You should have fought for *her*.'

'Aye. She's the conscience inside me. I found the young buck who'd wronged Emma and thrashed him. I enjoyed doing it, Sarah, and it was worth the three months in prison it cost me. But when I was locked up I had time to think. I would take Emma's child, I decided, because that's what she'd have wanted me to do. I'd take it out of that workhouse and foster it with a good woman, pay her well for caring for it. But I was too late. When I went to claim the little thing I was shown another grave. I don't know what the bairn died of – hunger, I shouldn't wonder. Emma had called her Charity, so they told me. Now there's a name to shame a man.'

He sighed, then Sarah felt the straightening of his shoulders, the tossing back of his proud head.

'So now I live on the pennies the poor drop into my begging tin and if there's no money I go hungry, like the people I try to help go hungry. It does me no harm. A man should know the feel of fire in his belly sometimes. And mill-masters will come to fear the name of Robey Midwinter.'

'I'm so sorry,' Sarah whispered.

'Then don't be. I don't want pity, bonny lass. Pity softens a man, makes him forget what he's sworn to do. And I'm happy enough, or was, until I met you.'

'*Me?* What did I do?

'You walked into my life one night, collecting money for Liza Nuttall's man. For one moment I thought you were Emma come back and it was like a knife twisting inside me.'

'So because I looked like her you taunted me? I was alive and she was dead?'

'That's about the truth of it and, when you married young Holroyd, I tried my best to hate you.'

'And you succeeded, Robey Midwinter. Two nights ago you came to High Meadow to give notice of the strike and you looked at me as if I were beneath contempt. Why did you do such a thing?'

'Because I'd found I could neither hate you nor get you out of my mind. There was no need to come to the house. I could have gone to Low Clough, I suppose, but I'd been over-long in the ale-house and there was a black mood on me. I wanted to see you with *him*, so it would help me forget you. Why did you wed him, Sarah?'

The early evening was soft, the purple twilight gentled with gold, and because it was a time of enchantment that might never come again there seemed no place on that hill-top for lies between them.

'I wed him because of you and Maggie,' she whispered. 'You tormented me and I tried not to care for you. But I did care. I would imagine what it would be like to sleep in your arms –'

'Maggie?' he jerked. 'You thought that Maggie and me were pledged?'

'Well, aren't you? I saw you kissing one day and there was nothing genteel about it.'

'I don't deny it. Maggie's a grand lass and I'm a man – there's man's blood in my veins. Maggie is good to kiss, but there's no bond between us. How could you have been so stupid, so thoughtless?'

'Oh, I don't know.' She closed her eyes wearily. 'It's the way I am. There'll be no changing me.'

'But didn't you realize? That night we met, you and I, here on Moor Top – we talked together amiably, yet all the time you knew that next day you'd marry David Holroyd.'

'And do you remember that you picked me primroses, Robey Midwinter?' she cried, anguished. 'Did you know I took them with me to the church when I wed him, pinned to my shawl?'

'No, Sarah, I didn't. I'm as proud and headstrong as you are, bonny lass. But it's not too late.' He gathered her closely again, whispering softly, his lips close to her cheek. 'Come away with me, love.'

'No, Robey! No!' She pushed him away from her, scrambling to her feet, her eyes wide with panic. 'We can't be wed, you know it!'

'I'm not asking you to marry me. I'm asking you to be my woman. There's no room in my life for wedlock and I'd not be giving you riches. Life would be good, though. We'd be companions, lovers, friends. There's a fire in you that matches mine; we'd fight wrongs wherever we found them. With you beside me, Sarah lass, I could change the world!'

'Don't!' she cried. 'It isn't fair. I want you so much, but my duty –'

'Duty? To a man you married in a fit of pique? Will you throw away the substance for the shadow, then, wonder for the rest of your life what it might have been like, sleeping in my arms?'

Roughly his lips found hers and longing surged through her, setting each small pulse in her body throbbing with need. She tried to think of the promises she whispered before the altar: *Keep thee only unto me.* She tried, but her mind was a surge of confused delight and her body so limp with longing that she was forced to cling desperately to him.

'No!' she moaned. 'No, Robey!'

But even as her lips denied him her heart shouted with joy.

'Sarah, sweetheart.' His voice was soft in her ear, his arms strong and sure about her. 'I need you so much.'

She closed her eyes in silent submission as they slipped gently to the grass at their feet and the scent of the earth lulled her senses like wine.

Above them, dipping and drifting in the darkening sky, a curlew called softly, but they did not hear it.

The sky was indigo velvet and the first star of evening low in the sky. Fingers entwined, shoulders touching, they lay bemused and shy, reluctant to speak lest the magic be lost.

It was Robey who pulled them gently back to earth. Gathering her into his arms again he whispered:

'You can't leave me now, Sarah. When my work here is finished, say you'll come with me.'

'I don't know. I can't think, darling. David is my husband and I owe him –'

It seemed wrong, at that moment, even to speak his name and guilt flushed her cheeks.

'You owe him *nothing*, Sarah. You belong to me, now.'

'I'm married to David,' she insisted dully.

'And it's me you love!' he exulted. 'I won't let us be parted.'

'Don't, Robey. Give me time to think things out,' she pleaded. 'If you press me now I shall say yes and that wouldn't be right. I've done so many foolish things in the past, rushed head-down at life without a thought. This time there must be no mistakes. I must be sure.'

'Maybe you're right,' he conceded reluctantly, 'but it'll not stop me wanting you.'

She smiled into the darkness, then, kissing the tip of her forefinger, laid it gently to his lips.

'Hush now. Don't spoil this loveliness. We've so much to be thankful for, you and me. We're young and alive, Robey, yet down there, in that awful town, there are people who are old and sick and hungry.' She raised herself on her elbow and looked out into the dark distance, over to the hollow below them where Hollinsdyke lay. 'There's a little boy who –'

She stopped suddenly, eyes narrowed, and tugged at his arm.

'Look! Down there!'

Smoke billowed upward, illuminated in a fiece red glow, and great tongues of flame licked at the sky.

'Something's ablaze!' he gasped, struggling to his feet. 'It's big – like a mill – though which one it is I can't tell.'

But Sarah knew. To the left of the fire the spire of the parish church stood black against the glow and to the north the tall towers of the Town Hall were clear to see. There was no doubting the position of the blazing mill.

'It's Low Clough!' she gasped. 'It's burning from end to end!'

Nine

There could be no doubting it. The mill Sarah had cursed so passionately was ablaze.

'Hurry,' Robey jerked, grasping her hand. 'I must go. They'll need help.'

Picking their way, slipping and sliding on the rough path they stumbled through the darkness to the road that led to Hollinsdyke.

'How could it have happened?' Sarah panted.

'Cotton dust exploding, I shouldn't wonder,' Robey flung, over his shoulder, 'or maybe a gas-jet . . .'

He peered ahead, muttering under his breath as the gravel beneath his feet shifted, sending him skidding downward at a giddy run.

Briars reached out along their path, tearing Sarah's skirts, clawing at her ankles, but she blundered after him, refusing to cry out, knowing there was worse to come, that this was only the start of the nightmare.

There'll be trouble at Low Clough before this day is out.

The words beat inside her brain as the sombre prophesy began to turn into stark reality. But how had it happened? Mill fires were commonplace and usually put out quickly. Mill-workers were experienced fire-fighters, quick to preserve their livelihood, knowing only too well that a burned-out mill was of use to no one.

But Low Clough had been idle, its workers shut out by Luke's anger, so how, Sarah fretted, had the fire begun?

Robey left her at the end of Clough Street.

'Stay here,' he commanded. 'Yonder's no place for a woman.' He looked at her thoughtfully, then said, 'This changes nothing. I still want you.'

'I know,' she whispered. 'But give me time.'

'I'll grant you that,' he nodded soberly, 'but I'll not wait for ever for an answer.'

Trembling, she watched him go, trying to find comfort in the remembered joy of their coupling, but she was cold with shock and an indefinable fear seemed to have taken hold of her senses.

A fire-cart clattered past, bell clanging, the horses straining beneath the cracking whip, and she cowered for shelter in a doorway.

This is my doing, she thought, panic rising unchecked in her throat. I called down misfortune on Low Clough, ill-wished Luke Holroyd. I am to blame.

Drawn by morbid fascination, she walked toward the mill, eyes round with horror. Flames licked from every window like ghoulish tongues and a snapping filled the air as the roof timbers blazed frenziedly. Silhouetted against the glow, men and women toiled in a chain, passing along buckets of water, and she recognized them as Low Clough workers, the spinners and weavers Luke Holroyd had locked out.

Wide-eyed she stood, trying to gather in her thoughts but her muddled mind refused to accept reality. It was as if she had stepped from heaven into hell, as if her new-found love was a dream and she had been awakened from it roughly to stare into a nightmare.

Why did she crave vengeance? She had watched the earth receive the tiny coffin and vowed that Billy-Boy's death should not go unpunished. Why hadn't she realized that a graveside oath was the most binding of pledges?

'Heaven help me, I'm a wicked creature,' she whispered. 'I meant it, Lord. I was angry because I blamed myself for Billy's death and I wanted revenge. But not this; never this.'

'Sarah!' Hands grasped her shoulders roughly. 'Where have you been? I've been out of my mind with worry!'

David wiped a sleeve across his face, anger mingling with relief. His shirt was torn, his clothes drenched. Smoke had blackened his face and his soft pale hair, making it hard to distinguish him from the roughly dressed men around them.

'You've been gone all day. I've had people searching the streets for you!'

'You might have known where I was,' Sarah whispered dully, unwilling to meet his eyes lest he should see her betrayal there. 'I went to Billy's funeral.'

'I know,' he gasped impatiently. 'But that was hours ago.'

'Oh, leave me be,' she choked. 'I was upset. I couldn't think straight. I just walked and walked, I suppose.'

And found comfort in another man's arms, her conscience reminded.

'Dearest, I'm sorry.' Anxiety giving way to relief he gathered her to him. 'You're back safely now and that's all I care about. The carriage is standing by in Water Street. Go home. I'd feel better if you did.'

'I'm staying,' she jerked stubbornly, shrugging away his arms. 'There must be something I can do to help.'

'Then, if you must, go to my father. Try to keep him out of harm's way. He's badly shocked.'

'Yes, he would be,' she murmured, her face wooden. 'He loves that mill, doesn't he, like it was his child?'

'Oh, my dear, forgive me.' Quick to recognize the rebuke, David's voice was instantly contrite. 'I should have realized how much Billy-Boy meant to you. I should have been with you. I'm so sorry.'

'Oh, stop saying you're sorry!' she gasped. 'It's over now. Leave it. Let the child rest.'

She drew her shawl around her, unable to look into his face, and turning abruptly she left him, her back stiff with defiance. She wished she could hate him as she hated his father. She wanted Robey, and David stood between them, yet she felt only pity for him and anger against herself for being so weak as to care that she had wronged him.

Luke was standing alone by the mill-gates when Sarah found him.

'Come away, Master,' she demanded, tugging at his sleeve. 'You're much too near. If anything should fall –'

But he stood his ground as though he needed to be near his mill until the end.

'Eh, lass,' he choked. 'This is a terrible night.' He turned to face her and she was shocked to see that his cheeks were wet with tears. 'Who could have done such a thing?'

'Done?' Sarah hissed. 'You mean it wasn't an accident?'

'No, by heaven, it wasn't!' he ground. 'How could it be? The mill wasn't working. That fire broke out in four different places. 'Twas deliberate!'

He closed his eyes as if the sight was too much to bear, as though he were standing helpless, watching the dying of a beloved mistress.

Scattered over the pavement lay the mill books and ledgers and the solemn-faced clock from the wall of his office, carried out of the counting-house while there had yet been time, and beside them Dinwiddie stood trembling, his bowler hat askew, a black tin cash-box clutched in his arms.

'Deliberate?' Sarah demanded, the uneasiness inside her refusing to be ignored. 'What proof is there?'

'I can *feel* it,' Luke ground. 'That's proof enough for me. Besides, there's someone in there.' He nodded grimly toward the mill. 'He's been seen by a fireman and Silk caught sight of him too.'

'Silk'd tell you black was white,' Sarah flung, 'and you'd believe him!'

But even as she spoke her eyes followed Luke's pointing finger and she knew then why she had been so afraid.

'See?' he demanded triumphantly. 'On the top floor? Didn't I tell you?'

She had seen him, stark against the flames, his head thrown back defiantly, his twisted limbs grotesque against a backcloth of fire, and though she could not hear him she knew he was laughing.

'Father!' she cried, her voice a whimper of disbelief.

The ground beneath her feet tilted and her head spun so that she had to grasp Luke's arm to prevent herself sinking into the blackness that swirled around her. But she did not fall fainting at his feet, for through the blackness came the memory of Caleb Makin's bitterness.

'*Luke Holroyd is going to get his comeuppance and I want to live long enough to see it. I want to stand there, and laugh!*'

Words her father had used hit her like a whiplash, shocking her into instant alertness.

'*I'd give anything to see this filth about me burning.*'

She forced her eyes upward again, praying that what she had seen was unreal, a frightening apparition born of her guilt-ridden conscience.

But Caleb was no ghost. A flesh and blood man stood at a top-storey window, calling down defiance, contemptuous of the danger around him.

'It's Caleb!' Luke gasped. 'What's he up to? If he doesn't shift himself there'll be no way out!' He cupped his hands to his mouth. 'Caleb Makin! Come down, man, before it's too late!'

Sarah closed her eyes, willing her father to safety, directing him with her mind to the gantry-like bridge that connected the mill to the counting-house. The fire hadn't reached there yet. Hadn't he the sense to save himself?

But a madman knows no sense and her father was mad. He'd been mad for years, locked away in his own little hell. She had known it and chosen to ignore it.

'Caleb! I'm coming in!' Dashing across the yard, ignoring the cries of warning, Luke ran headlong into the blazing building. 'Hold on, Caleb, old friend. I'll get you out!'

'Go after him,' Sarah pleaded as he disappeared through the weaving-shed doors. 'He'll be killed! Won't someone *do* something?' Blindly she ran forward. 'Father-in-law, come back!'

Dimly above the noise she heard her husband's voice.

'*Sarah! Sarah, look out!*' and she felt herself being thrown violently off balance to fall, arms flailing to the ground.

In that instant the mill roof crashed in, sending up a cascade of sparks, setting free the pent-up fire to roar flaming into the sky.

'The wall! It's going!' a voice cried. '*Run!*'

Urged by the instinct to survive, fear pumping strength

into her limbs, Sarah flung herself forward, scrambling blindly on hands and knees away from the danger. A pain shot through her head, agonizing in its intensity, and red flashes forked before her eyes.

With a gasp, she fell insensible.

She was sitting on the pavement when she came to, with Dinwiddie bending over her anxiously rubbing her hands.

'What happened?' she mumbled, pain crashing through her head.

'Eh, how you weren't killed I'll never know!'

'Something hit me,' she whispered, wanting to close her eyes again, drift back into the cushioning blackness.

'Aye, a piece of rubble. The side wall caved in and you'd have been under it if it hadn't been for Mister David. He pushed you out of the way.'

'David?' Sarah choked, dry-mouthed. 'Where is he?'

She struggled to her feet then swayed as the ground beneath her tilted.

'*Where is he*?' she demanded.

'Over yonder,' Dinwiddie nodded grimly. 'He was hit by a lump of falling stone. The doctor's with him. It's his head, they say. Hurt bad, I reckon.'

This is a nightmare, Sarah thought wildly. A living, seeing nightmare. She felt the urge to laugh and laugh, but tears were coursing down her cheeks.

'Mrs Holroyd,' Dinwiddie urged, shaking her arm, 'let me help you to the carriage.'

'No! I must stay here.' She would be all right, really she would, if only the weeping would stop. 'Just give me a minute.' Gulping hard on her tears she choked:

'Send someone to High Meadow, Mr Dinwiddie. Tell them what has happened and ask Mrs Parkes to have a bed ready and clean strips of linen. And hot water – plenty of it!'

Then she ran to her husband's side, fearful of what she might find, her throat tight with apprehension.

David lay unmoving, his clothes wet and muddy, his face ashen beneath the grime. The man beside him nodded, then rose to his feet.

'I am Doctor Harcourt, ma'am.' He raised his hat briefly. 'I fear your husband is unconscious,' he murmured. 'How long it will be before he recovers I cannot tell. There are no visible signs of injury, a fact which disturbs me, for it may be that the contusions are internal. If that is so, there is very little we can do.'

Sarah gazed with horror at the still form. David had saved her life, perhaps at the expense of his own. He loved her and she had betrayed him.

'Let him be all right,' she prayed desperately. 'And Caleb my father, and Luke – please get them out safely.'

She looked again at the blazing mill, at the mill-yard, choked with smouldering rubble, at the man who lay still as death at her feet and realized she had just asked for a miracle. And miracles never happened, she thought dully. Especially in God-forsaken Hollinsdyke.

'Doctor Harcourt,' she breathed. 'I don't want my husband to go to the infirmary. I want him nursed at home.'

'You have chosen wisely,' the doctor nodded, 'and I will come with you, see him comfortably settled.'

'Thank you, sir,' she whispered gratefully, hugging her shawl around her trembling body, knowing that if she lived for a hundred years more she would never forget this night.

It was then she saw Robey, pushing his way toward

her. He was stripped to the waist, his body gleaming with sweat.

'Sarah! They told me you'd been hurt!'

'No. I'm all right.' She nodded toward the improvised stretcher. 'David took the brunt of it. The doctor is worried about him.'

She lifted her eyes to his, silently begging him not to make demands, and he read her thoughts as though she were a part of him.

'Don't fret, bonny lass. Go where your duty lies,' he said gently.

She nodded, unable to answer him for the guilt and love that fought within her.

'Will I have Maggie come to you?' he asked.

'No. I'll be all right.' She needed time to think, sort out her thoughts, arrange things in their proper order. Best she should be alone. 'I must go now. David is in need of me.'

She stopped, looking over his shoulder to the police constables who pointed in their direction. She knew at once that something was wrong. She could see it in the set of their faces, their slow, sure walk.

'Are you looking for me?' she demanded, fear icing through her. 'Who sent for you?'

'You'll be young Mrs Holroyd?' the elder of the three remarked, touching his hat in a brief salute. On his arm he wore the rank of sergeant and a polished wooden truncheon swung aggressively from his jutting fingertip. 'It was Mr Luke Holroyd sent for us, ma'am, and not without good cause, it would seem!' Then turning to Robey he demanded, 'Are you Robey Midwinter, and do you lodge at Dan Ormerod's house, in Albert Court?'

'Aye.'

'Then can you tell me where you were tonight between half-past seven and nine o'clock?'

'I can,' he retorted, his eyes narrowing as the men inched menacingly closer. 'But I won't!'

'Then I must warn you, Midwinter, that you are suspected of maliciously causing the fire at this mill and tell you that you are not obliged to answer my questions.' The words were spoken clearly and carefully, their implication unmistakable. 'But, if you can satisfy me that you were seen to be elsewhere at that time, then you have nothing to fear.'

'I was nowhere near the mill. I was walking,' Robey asserted. 'I was on Moor Top hill.'

'And is there someone who saw you?'

'There isn't, but I *was* there.'

'Robey!' Sarah gasped as the implication of the questioning became clear. 'That's not true! You were –'

'I was alone,' harshly he cut her short. '*Alone.*'

'But someone can prove you were there. Tell them,' she pleaded.

The sergeant shrugged. He would get nothing from Midwinter, but the woman was a different matter. Young Mrs Holroyd knew something. Her frightened eyes gave her away and the agitation in her face. She'd be the one to tell them.

'Well now, ma'am? Can you throw any light on this matter?' He spoke softly, suggestively. '*Could* someone have seen him on Moor Top hill?'

'No one saw me!' Robey spat. 'I was alone but I *was* there and it's up to you to prove different!' Then, rounding on Sarah, holding her eyes with his own, he hissed, 'Say nothing, do you hear? *Nothing.*'

'Well, Mrs Holroyd?' the sergeant pressed. 'Is there something we should know?'

'There's nothing,' Robey flung, his voice angry. 'Leave her alone, I tell you!'

'As you wish,' the policeman shrugged, 'but you leave me no choice. Robey Midwinter, I am arresting you on suspicion of wilfully causing the firing of Low Clough mill and warn you again that you have the right in law to remain silent.'

With practised alacrity the constables seized his arms, jerking them behind his back, clicking handcuffs on his wrists.

'Robey!' Sarah gasped. 'Tell them!'

The sergeant hesitated, raising a questioning eyebrow, but the man they called the gypsy threw back his head, laughing.

'Tell them what? There's nothing to tell, Mrs Holroyd. Go home. Take care of your husband and leave me to look after myself.'

With that he turned on his heel, a constable on each arm and strode defiantly away.

'Sergeant,' Sarah gasped. 'Why are you doing this? What right have you to handcuff him? What is he to be charged with?'

'It could be arson, ma'am.'

'But that's a serious offence. How can you be sure he did it?'

'I'm as sure as I can be, Mrs Holroyd. And I said it *could* be arson he's charged with. It might be worse. Much worse!'

But Robey hadn't set fire to Low Clough, she thought wildly. He couldn't have. 'Say nothing!' he'd commanded. But there could be worse to come, the sergeant had said and, if that were so, how would it be possible to remain silent?

'We are ready, ma'am.' A hand grasped her arm and the doctor's precise voice rasped into her thoughts. 'We must make haste . . .'

'I'm coming,' she whispered, her voice strange-sounding in her ears. 'I'm coming.'

She stumbled after him in a daze. The world had gone mad. Completely mad.

Mrs Parkes was waiting at the front door of High Meadow as the carriage drew to a gentle halt. Behind her, her plump face creased with anxiety, Cook nodded her sympathy.

'Everything is in order, ma'am,' the housekeeper murmured, directing the men who carried David's still body into the house. 'And I took the liberty of sending a telegraph message to Mrs Luke, in Cumberland.'

'Thank you,' Sarah breathed, hurrying upstairs behind the doctor. Oh, but it would be good to have Charlotte back, to hand over all responsibility then find a small, dark corner in which to hide herself away from the frightening world.

'Cook and I will stay close at hand.' The housekeeper's voice was firm and reassuring and Sarah wondered why she could have ever imagined her to be cold and aloof.

The clock ticked slowly, loudly, emphasizing Sarah's aloneness, sending apprehension coursing through her. She wondered what fresh misery the night could unfold and if she would be strong enough to bear it. She was still reeling from the blow the doctor had delivered, just before he left.

'I'm afraid I must leave you alone,' he had said, his fingertips measuring the pulse at David's wrist, 'but I shall call again at first light. And of course you must send for me at once, if there is any change.'

Mutely Sarah nodded.

'At no time must the patient be left. He must be watched constantly.'

'I understand,' Sarah whispered. 'How long might it be before he awakens?'

'That I cannot tell. I've known similar cases to be many days before improving.' He fingered his beard, his face grim. 'I am afraid you must accept the fact, distressing though it is, ma'am, that your husband could sink into a coma from which there will be no awakening.' For the first time that evening he looked at her kindly, his eyes softening. 'And now, will you compose yourself, my dear, for I fear I have news to impart that can only add to your burdens.'

Sarah rose to her feet, her eyes wide with panic. What more could happen? What new madness was to come? But in her heart she already knew.

'It's my father, isn't it?'

'I'm sorry. It happened when the roof collapsed. The police sergeant wanted to tell you, but I forbade it. I undertook to break the sad news myself, when you had had time to adjust to your husband's injuries.'

'And David's father?' she choked, stiff-lipped.

'Mr Holroyd is dead too. They were brought out and laid in the counting-house.'

'Dear heaven –'

'*Worse to come*,' the sergeant had said.

Sarah hid her face in her hands, closing her eyes tightly, shutting out the horror. If she wasn't so numb, she thought, she could scream and scream until she awoke from this dreadful nightmare.

Perhaps she too was going mad? Perhaps it was all in her mind? But her mud-covered clothes were real and her sodden shoes and the smell of the fire on her hands.

She opened her mouth and let out a piercing scream

and in that instant she seemed to hear Charlotte's voice, sharp with rebuke.

'*Stop it at once! Pull yourself together!*'

As if she had been slapped, her cry ended in a moan.

'I'm sorry,' she choked, her body shaking with pent-up sobs. 'Forgive me.'

'Of course, ma'am. Of course.' He patted her arm awkwardly. 'Let me ring for a sip of brandy and perhaps someone to sit with you.'

'No, sir, I thank you,' her voice was low, but firm. 'I would like to be alone to compose myself. And if I need help I have only to ring.'

'Then, if you are sure, I must leave you,' he said reluctantly. 'There are things I must see to, at the mill.'

'I am quite sure, and thank you, Doctor Harcourt, for your help. You have been very kind.'

She had nodded a goodbye, straightening her back and lifting her chin as Charlotte would have done. And until Charlotte returned, she realized, she had to shoulder all responsibility herself.

The hours passed slowly. She was living, Sarah thought, through the longest, the most terrifying hours of her life.

She looked dully at her husband's inert body. His hands in hers were cold, his breathing shallow, and he lay without even the smallest sigh escaping his lips or the briefest flickering of an eyelid.

A gentle tapping on the door caused her to spring to her feet, grateful for the nearness of another soul.

'Miss Ormerod's come, ma'am,' the wide-eyed housemaid whispered. 'Will you see her?'

'Of course,' Sarah nodded. 'But what time is it?'

'It's morning. Gone eight o'clock.'

A new day; a new beginning. Sarah longed to throw

back the curtains, let in the sunlight, but this was now a house of mourning and had to remain deeply shrouded until the dead had been laid to rest.

'Show Miss Ormerod into the small sitting-room, then ask Mrs Parkes if she will sit beside Mr David's bed,' she asked, her body limp with gratitude that Maggie had come.

The school-teacher was standing by the fireside her face warm with sympathy. She held out her arms and Sarah flew into them like a child in need of comfort.

'There, there,' Maggie soothed. 'It's all right. Nothing more can happen now.'

'But it's all so awful – a bad dream. And it's so lonely in this great house – so dark and still.'

'Things are always worse before they get better,' Maggie smiled gently. 'I've come to say how sorry I am about – well, about everything, and to let you know that if you need me . . .?'

Sarah nodded gratefully. 'Bless you,' she choked.

'And how is your husband, Sarah? It was a brave thing he did.'

'Yes. I owe him my life. But there's no change. He just lies there. Oh, I need so much to talk to someone, Maggie.'

'Aye, there's things to be said on both sides,' Maggie nodded. 'Happen this isn't the right time, but they'll have to be talked about, sooner or later. You know what I mean?'

'I think so. I think the police will come to see me before very long and I've got to have things sorted out in my mind before they do. 'But I'm so weary,' she sighed, 'I can't think properly.'

'Then let's take it gently, put first things first, shall we,

Sarah? Happen then we'll find we're both bothered about the same things.'

Not until they were settled comfortably before the fire did Sarah say:

'You want to talk about my father?'

'I do. I'm right sad he's gone, but he was a sick man, Sarah, and most times in pain. He's at peace now and it's the living we've got to care about. It wasn't Robey set fire to Low Clough. I know you are burdened with trouble, but it's got to be said. They've arrested an innocent man and I think you know it!'

'What do you mean?' Sarah gasped. 'Why should I know it? Who have you been talking to?'

'To Robey,' Maggie acknowledged quietly. 'They let me see him this morning at first light.'

'And he *told* you? He told you that –'

'He told me nothing, save that he didn't do it. But I know he didn't. It was your father, wasn't it, Sarah?'

'What makes you so sure – about my father, I mean?' Relief washed over Sarah. 'Who's been talking?'

'Only your father. He told me, you see – as near as makes no matter – that he was going to do it. Billy-Boy's death upset him badly, brought back his own injuries. He said you'd told him that Luke Holroyd was bringing in cheap labour and I think that was the last straw.'

'Yes, I told him that, I admit it, but he didn't seem much put out, at the time.'

'He was, though. Underneath he was mad with rage. He came to Albert Court, asking for Robey, muttering about Low Clough. "That cursed mill," he was saying. "One day someone's going to burn it to the ground." I was worried about him. I told him to go home then went out to try to find Robey. It wasn't any use, though. He could have been anywhere.'

'Aye, he could have been,' Sarah admitted, low-voiced, 'and you're right, Maggie. Hard though it is to admit it, I know my father was to blame. But I'd hoped Robey could convince the police he'd had nothing to do with the fire. I'd hoped to keep my father's name out of it, but it'll all have to come out, I suppose,' she shrugged.

'And you think that'll be the end of it and everything will be all right? You think the police are going to believe you?' Maggie whispered. 'Oh, no! They want it so that justice can be seen to be done. Robey has caused them a lot of bother of late and this is the chance they've been hoping for. They'll say he's trying to lay the blame on a man who can't defend himself.'

'But my father was there, in the mill.'

'They'll say he was a madman, Sarah; they'll say he just got himself trapped there . . .'

'Then what's to be done?' A small pulse of fear beat at Sarah's throat. 'How can we convince them?'

'I don't know. I asked Robey outright where he was last night, but he wouldn't say. He's hiding something, but I'll find out what it is, I swear it!'

Sarah sat unspeaking, staring into the flames. Maggie was right. The police would never accept that her father had caused the fire. They would want a living scapegoat, not a dead one. She alone could prove Robey's innocence, but, in doing so, she would condemn herself for the wanton she had become.

But would it matter? Soon she had to come to a decision. She had to choose between the man who loved her and the man who held her bewitched. Maybe, if things were brought into the open, that decision would be made for her.

But not just yet. She had taken all she could, and besides, there was David to think about. How could she hurt him so?

'I must go to my husband,' she jerked, rising abruptly to her feet. 'He could awaken at any moment and I want to be there. Can I order the carriage for you, Maggie? It's a long step back to Hollinsdyke.'

'No, I thank you. Think of the talk in the Three-streets,' Maggie smiled, pulling on her gloves. 'And the walk will do me good. I've a lot of thinking to do. Someone in Hollinsdyke knows where Robey was last night, someone who must come forward and prove he couldn't have fired the mill. She's got to be found.'

'*She?*'

'Of course. It's got to be a woman,' Maggie flung tersely. 'Why else would he be so cussed stupid, will you tell me? But I'll find her. I'll not rest, until I do! I'll leave no stone unturned –'

'Oh, why can't you leave it?' Sarah gasped. 'Don't you know that when you start turning stones all sorts of nasty things can crawl from under them? And what is it to you, Maggie? Why are you doing all this?'

'Don't you know? Hadn't you realized how much Robey means to me? I've loved him since he first set foot in Hollinsdyke. Oh, he'll never love me,' she whispered, her eyes wistful. 'No woman will ever completely own his heart. But I'd be glad to accept what he was willing to give. I'd go with him, if he asked me, to the back of beyond.' She looked up, smiling softly. 'There now, I've said it. Tell me I'm a fool, Sarah.'

'No, I'll not do that. But go easy, dear friend. Don't get hurt.'

'I'll try not, but there's nothing so foolish on the face of this earth as a woman in love,' Maggie sighed, gathering Sarah to her, kissing her goodbye. 'And I'll come again soon. Try not to worry too much.'

Sarah stood in the doorway, watching until Maggie's

small, determined figure had rounded the bend in the drive, then, sighing, she closed the heavy doors and walked reluctantly upstairs.

Maggie was right. No one would ever get inside his heart, she conceded. No woman would wholly own him. Not even Emma or the chance-child called Charity who was his conscience.

No one will ever possess Robey Midwinter, she thought, but I at least know what it is to lie in his arms. So look if you must, Maggie, for the woman who can free him. You'll not find her – not until she chooses to be found. And when that time comes the whole of Hollinsdyke will know who she is, because happen she'll walk out of town at his side!

Slowly she opened the bedroom door and, nodding to the woman who kept vigil there, took her place at the bedside again.

'He didn't move, Mrs Parkes? There's been no sign of – ?'

'No, ma'am, I'm sorry,' came the gentle reply. 'But take comfort. Mr David is very dear to us all and we are praying hard for him,' she whispered, closing the door quietly behind her.

'And he is dear to me too,' Sarah's heart sighed. 'He is a good, kind man who loves me truly and it is because of that love that he lies here now, a step away from death. If I could, I would love him as he deserves to be loved, but my stupid heart won't let me. Soon I must make a choice and it will be the most heart-breaking thing I will ever have to do . . .'

Taking the cold, still hand in her own, Sarah held it to her cheek.

'Oh, David,' she whispered, 'I have made such a mess of it all. No matter what decision I come to, someone I care for will be hurt . . .'

Ten

The afternoon slipped slowly by and still David lay unmoving in the darkened room. At his side Sarah sat thinking of her father's wasted life, remembering him as he once had been, his mind and body whole. Better she should think of him that way than the bitter, twisted man he had become; better by far she should grieve for the handsome, laughing man who died, really, the day the Low Clough machine mangled his body. And from that time on loathing had festered inside Caleb until it finally destroyed him. And yet, Sarah thought sadly, Luke Holroyd had plunged without thought into the blazing mill.

I was taught to hate him, Sarah pondered. I blamed him for Billy-Boy's death, yet he died for my father without thought for himself.

Now they lay side by side; the crippled spinner and the mill-master, equal in death. Now David lay sick, his life in Fate's inconstant hands, and Robey had been wrongfully imprisoned. And all, she admitted wearily, because I was determined to have revenge, because there is a wilful streak in me that has been my undoing.

If only she was not so tired, so numb. If only Charlotte would return, take the load from her weary shoulders. If only –

'If only I had once stopped to think,' she whispered to the impartial room, as a tear ran down her cheek.

Charlotte came home to High Meadow in the early evening, alighting from the hansom-cab with her customary aplomb. Dressed in black, widow's weeds floating behind her, she was in complete control of her every movement. Not even death, Sarah thought, peering through the bedroom curtains, could catch her mother-in-law unawares.

Relief washing over her, she ran to the banister, leaning over. Never had she thought to see the day she would be grateful for Charlotte's presence, yet here she was, weak with relief, almost smiling a welcome.

'My dear,' Charlotte sailed up the stairs. 'This is a sad homecoming.' She held Sarah at arm's length. 'Heaven preserve us, girl, you look dreadful! When did you last sleep?'

Without waiting for an answer she hurried into the sickroom.

'How long has he been like this?' she whispered, the mask slipping from her face as she looked sadly at her son.

'Since last night. The doctor is very worried.'

'Doctor Harcourt,' Charlotte jerked, 'is an old fool! My son has a robust constitution; of course he'll get well. He must,' she ended in a whisper.

Sarah reached for the older woman's hand, pressing it reassuringly. 'I'm so sorry,' she whispered, 'about everything. Mr Holroyd was a very brave man. He tried to save my father.'

'Sorry?' Charlotte smiled wryly. 'Ah, yes. We all have much to be sorry for, but it's too late now, for regrets. I spent my life hating every minute I was married to Luke. If only I'd put as much effort into trying to care for him a little more.'

Peeling off her gloves, unpinning her bonnet, she sank sighing into the chair at her son's bedside.

'How did it happen?' she demanded brusquely.

'It was my fault,' Sarah breathed. 'David pushed me out of harm's way when the wall fell and got hurt doing it. Don't be angry with me.'

'No one is going to be angry,' Charlotte replied, 'and it's plain to see you've had more than enough to contend with. Parkes shall sit with David while I interview the undertaker and you, my gel, shall be put to bed with a laudanum draught. You look as if you haven't slept for days!'

'It seems as if I haven't,' Sarah choked. 'I don't think I shall ever sleep easy again. I shall always blame myself.'

'Tut, girl, there's no putting back the clock. Just oblige me by taking yourself off to bed!'

It was good to be bullied so, Sarah thought drowsily as she lay back against the pillows. She wanted to sleep and sleep and when she awakened she wanted to see David's head on the pillow beside her, know that her greatest worry was the choosing of material for a ball-gown, that Billy-Boy would be there, waiting for his soup, and that Low Clough was as it had always been.

Yet to wish that would be to banish the loving she had shared on the twilight hill-top and that she could never do. That loving was real and because of it she was faced with an agonizing choice. David was kind and good and loved her as she didn't deserve to be loved. David had put his life at risk for her sake. And Robey promised her nothing but hardship and a heart that could never be wholly hers. But he could turn her bones to ice and her blood to fire and last night, when she lay in his arms, she had reached up and touched the stars . . .

*

Sarah awoke reluctantly, wanting to sleep longer but knowing she had not to, instinct directing her thoughts to the sickroom. Pulling on a robe she swayed unsteadily, for the laudanum still held her bemused.

'Thank heaven you've come, child!' Charlotte jumped to her feet as Sarah pushed open the door. 'He's coming round, I'm sure of it. His eyes moved.'

Sarah stood motionless, watching her husband's still face as Charlotte moistened his lips with water. His breathing was more regular, she conceded, but, that apart, she could see no change in his condition. Was her mother-in-law seeing only what she wanted to see?

'Are you sure?'

'Of course I'm sure. He *will* get well.' For a moment Charlotte gazed tenderly at her son, then taking a deep, steadying breath, said quietly:

'Sit down, Sarah. You and I must talk. I want you to know that when David brought you here I was deeply angry. But you are married now and I realize I must do all I can to help.'

'Please?' Sarah begged uneasily. 'Can't we leave it? Can't we talk later?'

'No. I am determined to have my say, so please listen. Whilst I have been sitting here, Sarah, I have had time to think and I know it will be best, when David is well, for me to leave High Meadow.'

'But, ma'am, there's no need –'

'There is every need. There cannot be two mistresses in one house no matter how big it is and besides I want to go. I came here unwillingly as a bride and I have known little happiness in this place.' She sighed, her voice unsteady with emotion. 'The fault was mine. Luke needed to be loved and I refused him. I should have tried harder, Sarah, as you must try.'

Sarah lowered her head, her agitated fingers plucking at the edge of the counterpane, her heart thudding heavily.

'I think in time you and David will find happiness together,' Charlotte urged softly, 'and when your children come there'll be noise and turmoil in this mausoleum and I shall visit from time to time and spoil them dreadfully.'

'But where will you go?' Sarah whispered.

'There are plenty of places, I suppose,' the older woman shrugged. 'Luke settled money on me when we married. I have hardly touched it. Perhaps I shall buy a small house in London. I'm not sure yet. I only know that you and David must be left alone together.'

'Please don't say any more!' Sarah pleaded, guilt surging through her. 'Don't make plans. It tempts Fate.'

'Maybe,' Charlotte smiled ruefully. 'Maybe not. I only know I shall not stay in Hollinsdyke. This is David's house now and it will be up to you, Sarah, to do what I never did. You must make it into a *home*. You will give the orders, from now on. You are the mistress of Luke's Folly now,' she whispered bitterly. 'I bequeath it to you gladly.'

'And if I don't want it?' Sarah gasped. 'If I don't want to be mistress, give orders?'

'Then you must learn. It's not only High Meadow. You have the people of Hollinsdyke to think about. You have no choice.'

But she *had* a choice, Sarah thought wildly. Robey wanted her. Soon he would come and she would have to give him her answer. She would have to choose between love and duty, poverty or riches. Her loyalty lay with David, her heart with Robey.

She closed her eyes. *Please, Lord, help me . . .*

Then her head jerked up and she drew in her breath.

'There!' Charlotte cried. 'David moved. You saw it too, didn't you? Oh, pray for him, Sarah! Pray as you've never prayed before! Make a bargain with the Almighty,' she urged desperately. 'Promise Him that if David recovers you will try to be a loving wife, that you will learn to care for your husband.'

'But I do care,' Sarah cried, sadly. 'I have never shirked my wifely duties.'

'Duties? Is love a duty, then?'

Mutely Sarah dropped her gaze, unable to look into her mother-in-law's eyes.

'I know you didn't care for my son when you married him. I could read it in your eyes,' Charlotte pressed. 'But I know he is very much in love with you. Won't you try, Sarah, as I should have tried?'

Wide-eyed, panic taking her limbs and shaking them mercilessly, Sarah looked at her husband. She felt like a small, trapped animal. Had she to make it, that bargain with God? Had she to promise, then, that in return for David's recovery she would remain his wife? Was it her destiny to stay in Hollinsdyke or should she follow Robey, help him right wrongs, fight for lost causes? Charity, they said, began at home, but was she brave enough to try to forget the wildness that flamed through her at Robey's touch? Was it really true that blazing passion flamed hot and died quickly? Did Robey love her as she loved him?

David loved her. David had been prepared to die for her, she conceded soberly. She owed him her life and now he was fighting for his own. Did she have a choice?

Hesitating no longer, she took his hands in her own and silently began to pray.

Please, Lord, help him. Let him awaken soon and be

well. He's a good man and if you'll give him back, I'll stay with him, be a good wife. I'll try to love him as he loves me. I swear it Lord, on Billy-Boy's soul . . .

Then weakly she began to cry and her tears were for a love that was over, for a moment of passion that had to fade into memory, for a woman whose heart was breaking.

'Don't weep, child,' Charlotte whispered. 'It's going to be all right. Compose yourself. David must not awaken to tears.'

Hastily Sarah dabbed her eyes, grateful that the housekeeper should choose that moment at which to enter the room.

'Excuse me, ma'am.'

Placing a tray on the bedside table she stood waiting, her hands clasped.

'What is it?' Charlotte demanded.

'There is a caller, ma'am. A gentleman.'

'But didn't you tell him we are not receiving until after the funeral?' Charlotte fretted.

'I did, but he insisted.'

'Then you shall see him, Sarah,' Charlotte shrugged. 'Explain that I will receive him later. Ask him to leave his card.'

Smoothing her hair, straightening the folds of her skirt, Sarah sped down the stairs, glad to be away from the sickroom, to have cause to forget, if only for a few moments, the decision she had made.

The front door was open and a man stood on the topmost step. He was tall as a tree, his dark hair curling about his ears and the arrogant set of his head was endearingly, heartbreakingly familiar. Through the jumble of her thoughts and the mad, glad beating of her heart, Sarah heard herself say:

'Good-evening, Mr Midwinter.'

'Good-evening, ma'am.' Robey inclined his head gravely. 'Can we talk – privately?'

'Please come in.' Her voice was little more than a whisper.

'No. I'll not do that.'

'Then a turn in the garden, perhaps?'

Oh, why were her legs so weak? Why was it so hard to breathe? She had made up her mind and there would be no going back, but did the sight of him have to torment her so? Did his nearness have to set her fingers tingling to touch him?

'They've let you go, Robey?' They'd had to, of course. The evidence they'd arrested him on was far too flimsy. Now, she thought with a shiver of relief, nothing need be told. No blame would attach itself to her father's name; no one need ever know that she and Robey had been lovers.

'Someone came forward,' he nodded. 'And don't worry. They know nothing.'

'Then how?'

She clenched her hands tightly for fear she should fling herself into his arms, willing him not to touch her lest her resolve should shatter.

'I'm leaving,' he ground, ignoring her question. 'Tomorrow. I came to tell you and say goodbye.'

'Leaving?'

'Aye, and taking Maggie with me.'

Near breathless, Sarah stopped in her tracks. Had he struck her, the pain could not have been more fierce. 'But when I saw you there, I thought –'

'You thought I'd come for you, like I said. But things have changed. I'll have to take Maggie away from Hollinsdyke.'

'But *why*?'

'Because I owe it to her,' he insisted doggedly. 'This morning she perjured herself for me. She told them at the police-station that she'd been with me on Moor Top hill. They didn't believe her, at first, so she told them we'd been making love there. When a woman as straight as Maggie Ormerod admits to something like that, they've no choice but to believe her. And I suppose,' he shrugged, 'they remembered what you'd said when they arrested me, about someone knowing where I was . . .'

'And now you think you owe her something?'

'I know I do, Sarah. What she told them isn't a thing to be admitted lightly. Maggie's a respectable girl and she'll lose her good name when it all gets around. Even in the Three-streets a woman doesn't give herself cheaply.'

'I did, Robey.'

'So you did, Mrs Holroyd,' he acknowledged, as if her giving had counted for nothing. 'Oh, and Maggie said to ask you to have a care for her folks. Her father's sick and there'll be no money coming in now.'

His eyes met Sarah's calmly, his gaze steady. 'She said you'd understand.'

'Yes. Tell her not to worry,' Sarah whispered, her lips so stiff it hurt her to speak. 'I'll see they're well looked after.'

He held out his hand, but she would not take it. To touch him would have been more than she could bear.

For a moment he looked into her eyes and she willed him with all the longing in her anguished heart to break down her resistance and take her in his arms just once more. But he did not touch her.

'Don't fret, Sarah,' he said gently. 'The police will let it drop now. There'll be no satisfaction gained by laying the blame on a dead man.'

He smiled briefly, then with a toss of his head strode quickly away across the grass. At the belt of trees he stopped abruptly and, turning to face her, raising his hand in a farewell salute, he called softly:

'Goodbye, bonny lass.'

'No!' Sarah cried. 'No!' but he was gone, disappearing from her sight in the blinking of an eye, and in the stillness around her it was as if he had never stood there, never spoken her name or looked at her with pity.

'God!' she moaned, hugging herself tightly, trying to stop the violent trembling of her body. She hadn't known how she would tell him, how she would find the strength to send him out of her life, yet he had given her no choice.

Maggie had lost her good name, but what had Sarah Holroyd lost? Now she would live with the knowledge that every time she looked at David, if God saw fit to spare him, she would remember what she had become.

Maggie had won. Gentle Maggie with the soft voice and tender blue eyes. Maggie had known she could never have Robey's love so she had made sure of the next best thing – his respect.

Sarah closed her eyes. The grass beneath her was tilting and her legs refused any longer to support her. Grief tearing at her heart she sank to her knees.

Lord, but it was almost *funny*! She had loved Robey so, been torn apart by the longing to follow him, yet he had never cared for her, not really cared. Not once, even in the spellbinding wonder of their loving, had he whispered the words she longed to hear.

Tears filled her eyes and she rocked back and forward on her knees, giving way to the tearing sobs that shook her body, cries born of despair and the searing pain of rejection. She had given all and there was nothing left, not even her self-respect. She, Sarah, was the loser.

And so Cook found her.

'Mrs David, ma'am,' she puffed. 'Oh, get up, do! Don't take on so. It's all right. He's going to get well!'

Clucking gently, she pulled Sarah to her feet, smiling into the tear-ravaged face.

'Don't grieve, ma'am. Mr David's awake. He's asking for you!'

A breeze lifted the lace curtains and the sun was warm on their faces as Sarah and David sat beside the open window of the bedroom.

It was impossible, she thought, looking out at the April garden and the hills of Moor Top green beyond it, to believe she could have lived through such torment.

The relief she felt at her husband's recovery had been overshadowed by the joyless duty of the burial of their dead.

Luke had been borne with great array to the iron-railed plot where all future Holroyds would lie, and Caleb her father had been laid to his rest beside the tiny, posy-strewn grave of the little orphan. She had found comfort in that. It seemed right they should be together.

'Goodbye, Father,' she had whispered. 'Take care of Billy-Boy for me. He's so little, so helpless . . .'

And now they were faced with a period of mourning when their dress would be sombre and decorum demanded they should withdraw from social life for many months. The duty letters had been written on black-edged notepaper, the Charity Ball and all other engagements cancelled, and until society was satisfied that their dead had been sufficiently lamented they must remain in self-imposed seclusion.

It suited Sarah very well. Such melancholy matched her mood. Now she was truly Sarah Holroyd, for all the trappings of her past were gone; her father, Billy-Boy, Maggie, Robey and the mill.

She had returned alone to Low Clough, standing among the ruins, gazing at the hollow windows that stared back at her like dead, accusing eyes. Only the counting-house remained and almost two hundred mill-workers from around the Three-streets had been made destitute.

David reached for Sarah's hand. He was paler, and thinner, but well at last and impatient to end his enforced convalescence.

'What are you thinking about?' he whispered. 'There is such sadness in your eyes, Sarah. Can't you tell me?'

But it was a sadness that could not be shared. Guilt such as hers could not be absolved, or even halved by the telling. She had to bear it alone.

'I was thinking about the mill,' she murmured. 'What will you do about it?'

'We will rebuild, of course!'

'But is there the money?'

'Enough and to spare. My father was a cautious man and believed firmly in insurance. There'll be another Low Clough and, the sooner I can be up and about, the sooner we can make a start.'

'Your mother is determined to leave,' Sarah whispered. 'I wish she would stay. There is so much I don't know about being a mill-master's wife. You'll have to be patient, David.'

'There is all the time in the world. You'll soon get used to it.'

All the time in the world, her heart echoed bleakly. A lifetime in which to learn, and to pay.

Outside, a lark soared singing into the sky, unhindered as the wind, and she followed it until her eyes were dazzled by the sunlight and its song could no longer be heard.

Sadly David watched her. It was as if she had built her grief around her like an invisible shell and defied anyone to breach it. It was as though she had withdrawn into herself, determined to share her misery with no one. Her face was pale, her eyes large and luminous. He wanted to take her in his arms, shield her from the world, but he could not. She was a stranger.

'Why are you looking at me so?' Sarah demanded, a small smile playing briefly on her lips. 'Is there a smut on my nose?'

'Your nose is perfect,' he replied with forced gaiety. 'Cannot a man look at his wife, especially when she is as lovely as you?'

'Please don't,' she whispered. 'You are so kind, so warm-hearted, and I don't deserve you.'

'Let me be the judge of that,' he returned, taking her hands in his own.

'But how can you love me, David? You know so little about me.'

'I know all I need to know,' he smiled gently. 'When I thought you were in danger, when the mill wall fell, it was as if my whole future flashed in front of my eyes and I saw it stretching empty, if you were not to be there to share it with me. And as for people saying I was brave – it wasn't any act of heroism made me fling you to safety. It was pure selfishness, because I was not prepared to live without you.'

She stared at him mutely and he looked into her eyes, stark with torment, loving her so much that it throbbed aching inside him.

'Don't grieve,' he pleaded. 'You have suffered so much, but all sorrow passes. Nothing that is hurtful ever lasts. Believe me, Sarah.'

All sorrow passes. Would that she could be sure of

that. If only she could know that the guilt would diminish and the agony fade, if she could forget the hurt of a lover's betrayal, try harder to remember the bargain she had made with God.

Give him back and I will stay with him, try to love him as he loves me . . .

The lark was descending and she could hear its song once more. It had flown high into the sun and now it had to come down to earth again.

Once, Sarah yearned, she had briefly touched the stars and now she too had to free herself of all soaring memory and take her place at her husband's side. There was work to be done, promises to be kept. The sorrow would pass; David had promised it would.

'Oh, but we must build a fine new mill,' she whispered fiercely. 'It must be light and airy, a good place to work in. We must care for the orphans and those who are sick now because of Low Clough. Let's give it another name, so we can forget.'

'No, the name shall remain,' David insisted gently, 'so we can *remember*.'

She looked at him, longing to lay bare her soul, knowing she could not, must not. There was only one way to receive absolution. She had to earn it.

'You will be well soon,' she smiled. 'When the doctor allows it, what shall we do?'

'We will get out of this room, out of this house,' he laughed. 'We will go to Moor Top hill. We shall walk and walk . . .'

She nodded, knowing how right he was. For him, it would be a happy return to where it had all begun; for her, there would be a ghost to lay, memories to banish and a promise to be renewed.

'Yes, David, we will walk the hills again,' she whispered.

He looked at her with tenderness. There was pain in her eyes, still, and secrets he could never share. He knew it only too well, but suddenly the way ahead seemed clearer and in that instant he knew beyond all doubt that she would come to care for him as he cared for her. She would love him, given time, and until then his heart held love enough for the two of them.

Taking her hand he raised it to his lips and gently kissed the upturned palm.

'I love you, my Sarah,' he whispered. 'I shall love you always.'

Always. It was a long time. It stretched into forever, but time was his. And he would wait.

All the Sweet Promises

Elizabeth Elgin

CROSS MY HEART . . .

Vi's life is shattered by the arrival of a letter telling her that her husband is missing in action. Then, when her Liverpool home is destroyed in an air raid, the WRNS becomes her only reason for carrying on. For upper-class Lucinda, who sees life mapped out along a predictable route of engagement, marriage and motherhood, joining up provides a means of escape. And for the lovely Jane, there is little choice when she gets her call-up papers. Their backgrounds couldn't be more different, yet together they will share their finest hours.

Beautifully written and wonderfully evocative, *All the Sweet Promises* is the compelling story of three young women as they enter the WRNS during the dark days of the Second World War, and of the men, both British and American, with whom they find love. Deeply moving and poignant, it captures the unique spirit of love and adventure, of promises made in the heart, and broken on the rack of war.

ISBN 0 586 20804 6

Whisper on the Wind

Elizabeth Elgin

YESTERDAY HELD SECRETS, TOMORROW HOLDS LOVE.

The Second World War. For men, an era of terrible devastation, broken lives and perhaps a glimpse of heroism. But for many women, a time of opportunity, a new-found freedom, a challenge in a changing world. For Kath Allan and Roz Fairchild it's a time for shadowy secrets and forbidden love.

Against the express wishes of her long-absent husband Barney, Kath joins up as a landgirl and moves from the bustle of Birmingham to work on Mat Ramsden's farm in the Yorkshire countryside. For the first time in her life she feels she belongs. Kath blossoms there like a flower in the sun and, free from the rigid restrictions of Barney and his family, begins to believe that she has a right to happiness on her own terms. But freedom can bring temptation. And temptation can be dangerous.

Next door the Fairchild estate has been harnessed for the war effort. Roz, exempted from call-up to work on the land, has something to hide from her grandmother – but her grandmother too has secrets of her own.

Returning to the period she evoked so well in *All the Sweet Promises*, Elizabeth Elgin captures once again the hearts of her readers with a moving story of women caught in the emotional crossfire of war.

ISBN 0 586 21198 5